Gables of Legacy

VOLUME FOUR

An ETERNAL BOND

OTHER BOOKS AND AUDIO BOOKS BY ANITA STANSFIELD:

First Love and Forever

First Love, Second Chances

Now and Forever

By Love and Grace

A Promise of Forever

When Forever Comes

For Love Alone

The Three Gifts of Christmas

Towers of Brierley

Where the Heart Leads

When Hearts Meet

Someone to Hold

Reflections: A Collection of Personal Essays

Gables of Legacy, Vol. 1: The Guardian

Gables of Legacy, Vol. 2: A Guiding Star

Gables of Legacy, Vol. 3: The Silver Linings

Gables of Legacy, Vol. 4: An Eternal Bond

Gables of Legacy, Vol. 5: The Miracle

Gables of Legacy, Vol. 6: Full Circle

Timeless Waltz

A Time to Dance

Dancing in the Light

A Dance to Remember

Barrington Family Saga, Vol. 1: In Search of Heaven

Barrington Family Saga, Vol. 2: A Quiet Promise

Barrington Family Saga, Vol. 3: At Heaven's Door

Barrington Family Saga, Vol. 4: Promise of Zion

Gables of Legacy

VOLUME FOUR

An ETERNAL BOND

a novel

ANITA STANSFIELD

Covenant Communications, Inc.

Covenant

Cover images: map © Photodisc, Inc./Getty Images; linen photography by Leon Woodward.

Published by Covenant Communications, Inc.
American Fork, Utah

Printed in the United States of America
First Printing: August 2003

13 12 11 10 09 10 9 8 7 6 5 4 3

ISBN 13: 978-1-59156-294-8
ISBN 10: 1-59156-294-5

For the Swans

The gilded world that we create will never break apart
the loved ones who are nurtured here, bound by soul and heart.
Jess Byrnehouse-Davies, 1891

Chapter One

South Queensland, Australia—The Present

Jess Hamilton sat on the side veranda with his feet up. His newborn son lay contentedly in the crook of his arm, making sweet noises as he drifted to sleep. Jess smiled toward little Michael and touched his wispy dark hair—close to the color of his own—before he was distracted by a burst of laughter from across the huge lawn. The laughter of children playing mingled with the laughter of the adults gathered in the nearby dining room, where the French doors had been left open onto the veranda. The combination blanketed Jess with a warm peace that he considered a miracle. The laughter itself seemed a miracle when every person within his range of hearing had one thing in common: they had all attended the same funeral just a few days earlier—and today they were laughing. But that's the way Michael would have wanted it.

Jess could well imagine his father looking down upon this group of friends and family gathered at his home, finding deep contentment in seeing that there was peace and joy among them in spite of the deep loss they'd all experienced. Jess was grateful that some company had remained following his father's funeral. He dreaded the silence of the house once they were all gone, and he prayed that the adjustment to his father's absence would not be too difficult.

"Hey there, little brother," Allison said, startling Jess from his thoughts. He looked up to see his half-sister taking a chair close by.

She was significantly older than he, with five children of her own, all old enough to be in school. Still, he couldn't resist saying, "Be careful who you're calling little. Younger, perhaps. But not littler."

"True," she chuckled softly and leaned back in her chair, looking across the lawn to where the children were playing. "What *are* they doing?"

"I'm trying to figure it out. I think it's a combination of wrestling and tag; something Joshua came up with, I believe."

"Of course," Allison said and focused her attention on the participants of the game in question, ranging in age from three to seventeen. Joshua O'Hara was the ringleader, as he always had been around other children. The O'Haras were unofficially a part of the family, since Joshua's father, Sean, had been a sort of foster child to Michael and Emily Hamilton at one time, and they had all remained close ever since. The O'Haras lived in Utah, in the same city as Allison and her family, and their two families had become especially close. Sean and Tara O'Hara and their four children had come from Utah for the funeral, along with every other member of the Hamilton family, and they had decided to extend their stay and make somewhat of a vacation out of the trip. Jess's other two half-sisters and their families had left this morning, and he was grateful for Allison staying on—and Sean as well. They had both proven capable of helping him through crises in the past, and he was grateful to have them nearby now.

"Did Emma get back?" Allison asked, her voice filtering through the distant laughter.

"Not yet," Jess said, glancing to the driveway where it disappeared into the trees and curved around the house. He knew that his youngest sister's drive into town was routine, and there was nothing to worry about. But he felt worried for her in general. She had been the most solemn since their father's passing, even though she had seemed to be well prepared for cancer to take Michael from them prematurely. Emma was his only full-blooded sibling left living, since their brother James had been killed in a car accident with his wife, and Emma's twin, Tyson, had died as an infant. The other three girls were from their mother's first marriage, and Jess couldn't deny a deep kinship with Emma, even though he felt immensely close to Allison in a different way. Emma was the only sibling still unmarried, and perhaps the very fact that she didn't have a spouse to lean on made her feel somehow more lonely. He could only guess where her head was since she had been unwilling to say much, but he felt instinctively concerned for her and wished he knew what to do about it.

"She'll be all right," Allison said, as if she'd read Jess's mind.

Jess turned toward her, startled. With exaggerated innocence, he asked, "Who?"

She laughed softly. "You know very well who. I'm worried about her too, but don't forget that she lives with me, and she will until she gets her degree, and I will take very good care of her."

"As you always have, I know." Jess sighed.

"I'm more worried about *you,* if you must know," Allison said.

Jess sighed again. "Well, that would make two of us."

"Four," she corrected.

Jess shot her a stern glare. "Who exactly have you been gossiping with?"

"Our mother and your wife, if you must know." Jess's thoughts momentarily strayed to Tamra. His sweet wife was one of the greatest miracles in his life, and he couldn't even imagine how he would be coping at all without her. "And we're all worried about you," Allison added.

"And why should this be any harder for me than anybody else?"

"Because you're the man in charge now; you inherited all the responsibility with the estate, the stables, the boys' home, the—"

"You can stop now," Jess said curtly, not wanting to admit how the reminder made him bristle.

"Well, you're the patriarch of the family now, so to speak, and that's no small burden." She paused and seemed to be studying his face. "So, we're worried about you."

"I'll be fine," he said, feeling as if he were lying. "Don't forget that I have good people working for me, and I have my mother living under the same roof. She'll keep me on track."

"I'm sure she will," Allison chuckled. "But we both know you hadn't intended on taking everything over for many years to come. Dad did his best to prepare you, but it's—"

"No small burden; I know. You already said that. I'll be fine."

"I'm sure you will, but . . . just remember, I may be going back to Utah, but I'm still your big sister, and you can call me anytime you need to talk or cry or just . . . talk."

Jess turned toward her and absorbed her genuine offer. "Thank you," he said warmly, then he turned to look out over the lawn and added sternly, "*Older* sister."

"I beg your pardon."

"More mature, I meant to say."

"Of course," Allison said and they laughed together.

After watching the children settle into a tight group on the lawn, with a game that seemed more quiet, Allison commented, "That Joshua is an amazing kid. He just has this gift with people—especially kids. I've had him stay with my kids a number of times. He's amazing. I'd wager he's going to do great things with his life."

"Maybe Sean would let me keep him for a while and he could do some great things with *my* life."

Allison chuckled. "You could ask, but I don't think Sean will go for it, especially since Josh isn't even out of high school yet."

"Probably not, but it's a nice thought."

"Daddy, daddy!" a little voice called and Jess turned to see Evelyn running across the lawn toward him. He chuckled as she climbed onto his knee and he held her with his free arm.

"Did you have fun with Josh?" he asked.

Evelyn nodded firmly then turned her attention to her little brother. Little Michael was in actuality Evelyn's cousin, but since her parents had been killed in her infancy, Jess and Tamra had officially adopted the four-year-old and loved her as their own. Her strawberry blonde hair reminded Jess of Allison's; her features were a sweet reminder of his brother.

A minute later Josh stepped onto the veranda and held out a hand toward Evelyn. "Should we go read storybooks now?"

Evelyn giggled and jumped down, taking Josh's hand.

"She really likes you," Jess said to Josh. "Maybe you should stay here when your family leaves and I'll put you to work."

Josh chuckled. "Sounds good to me. It would beat the heck out of school."

"Ah, you love school and you know it," Allison said. "Straight A's I hear."

Josh glanced down humbly. "Come along, Evie," he said and they went inside together. Jess and Allison exchanged a warm smile as two of Allison's children ran to catch up with them. A few minutes later Allison went into the house as well, leaving Jess alone with his sleeping son. He looked out over the view and drew a deep sigh, overcome with a familiar combination of grief and contentment. He was still sitting there when Emma returned from town. She parked the family's Toyota Land Cruiser she'd been driving and stepped onto the veranda.

"How are you?" Jess asked.

"I'm fine," she said and seemed to mean it. "How are you?"

"I'm fine," Jess said again, feeling as if he were lying. He knew she was perceptive and feared further questioning, but she just sat beside him without pressing it any further. They sat in peaceable silence while she held his hand, and that alone made him feel better. He could almost literally feel Emma's strength in her touch, and he felt certain she would be all right.

When the baby woke up Emma took him to find Tamra so that he could be fed. Jess went inside and found Josh still in the nursery, building block-castles on the floor with Evelyn and Allison's youngest child.

"You should consider a career with children," Jess said.

Josh looked up and smiled. "I'm thinking about it," he said. "I'm just not sure what."

Josh's father, Sean, appeared at Jess's side, leaning in the doorframe. "He's aspiring to be the ward nursery leader," Sean said and Jess chuckled.

"Someone's got to do it," Jess said.

More quietly, Sean asked, "You doing okay?"

Jess sighed. "As good as could be expected, I suppose." He forced a smile toward Sean. "I'm glad you're still here, but I'm not looking forward to your leaving."

"Well, the kids are having a great time—and so are we, for that matter. We all needed a vacation." He put a hand on Jess's shoulders. "We've still got a few days left."

The following morning Jess and Sean each drove a vehicle to take Allison's family, Emma, and their luggage out to the private hangar ten minutes away from the house. Isolated as they were, owning a couple of private planes had been a great blessing for the family. Today Emma, and Allison and her family would be flying to Sydney where they would catch a flight back to the States. Murphy, the stable master and a longtime friend of the family, would be the pilot. Although Jess had his pilot's license as well, he was grateful that Murphy was able to make the flight, since he preferred staying close to home for a number of reasons.

It was difficult saying good-bye, and Jess dreaded having Sean's family leave in a few days. He reminded himself to enjoy the moment and as soon as Jess and Sean returned to the house, they saddled a couple of horses and went for a long ride, going slowly and talking about the changes they both felt since losing Michael. Jess was deeply grateful for Sean's insight, since he worked as a psychologist, and he was also very spiritually minded. But he was equally grateful for Sean's love of his family—and especially Michael—which gave him strong empathy for the grief Jess was struggling with.

In the weeks preceding Michael's death, Jess had found undeniable peace with the knowledge that it was his father's time to go: and the Spirit had clearly witnessed to him that the matter was in God's hands. He had every reason to believe they would be reunited in eternity, as he lived for that blessing. But the reality of living without his father had settled in hard and fast, and he wasn't sure how he would cope. Sean reminded Jess to press forward with faith, one day at a time. Jess knew it was good advice, but at the moment he felt formlessly weary and somehow inadequate to carry the burden that had now officially been left on his shoulders.

When the time came, seeing Sean's family leave was as difficult as Jess had expected, but once the plane had lifted into the air, with Murphy at the controls, Jess turned to see Tamra standing beside him. He sighed and took her into his arms, pressing his hand over the curly red ponytail that hung down her back. He closed his eyes and inhaled deeply while he silently thanked God for bringing this good woman into his life. He concluded that no matter what happened, she would always be at his side. She had helped him come this far through many struggles. And she would be by his side no matter what life chose to dish out in the future. For that reason alone he had cause to be deeply grateful.

"I love you, Tamra Hamilton," he said, drawing back to look into her eyes.

She smiled and pressed a hand to his face. "And I love you," she muttered and kissed him.

"Then I guess we'll get by without Sean somehow," he said, watching her mouth twitch into a smile.

"Yes, I suppose we will. But you can call him once in a while anyway—just for the sake of it."

They drove the short distance to the house, where Tamra went inside to rescue Emily from the children, and Jess went to the boys' home to check with Mr. Hobbs, the administrator, and find out how behind on work they might be. The home was one of the biggest burdens left to Jess. He'd always enjoyed the work he'd done there, and he knew the business well, but in the past when a difficult matter arose, his father had been by his side. Being there without him still felt foreign, even though he'd been too ill to be a part of the business many weeks before his passing.

A few hours later Jess left the home and wandered out to the highest part of the lawn. Looking out over the vast stretch of land that had recently been bequeathed to him, he felt an overwhelming sense of dread. The view was beautiful, with the flat land eventually merging into the distant mountains. It was home and he knew it well. But he felt unequal to the tasks of caring for all that came with his inheritance. There was the boys' home, the stables, and the household, including his mother and Sadie, who had worked with the family for many years. Included in both family businesses was the responsibility he felt to those who were employed there, not to mention the troubled boys who were entrusted to their care. Jess closed his eyes and concentrated on the Australian breeze caressing his face. He uttered a silent prayer and committed himself to following Sean's advice. *Press forward with faith, one day at a time.*

* * *

Tamra lifted Evelyn up to wash her hands at the kitchen sink, then she scooted her out of the room.

"I'm certain you can get supper done a lot faster without Evelyn's help," she said to Sadie on the way out.

"Oh, she's a joy," Sadie said, her eyes smiling.

"Most of the time," Tamra said with a wink and ushered Evelyn up the stairs.

"Should we go see what Grandma is doing?" she asked Evelyn. "Maybe we can help her while little Michael is sleeping."

"We can help her," Evelyn said excitedly and Tamra chuckled, wondering if Emily would appreciate Evelyn's *help* as much as Sadie had. Tamra knew from the baby monitor clipped to the waistband of her jeans that the baby was still sleeping. With the laundry gathered and underway, she felt compelled to check on Emily, not wanting to leave her on her own for too long. Emily had given no indication that she couldn't handle the adjustment of losing her husband to cancer, but Tamra still felt concerned for her. She considered it a great blessing that they were all able to live together in this huge family home. Interacting through the ins and outs of everyday living had made it easier for all of them to get through Michael's death, and she felt confident it would help them move forward now.

With Evelyn's hand in hers, Tamra hesitated in the open doorway of Emily's bedroom, taken aback by what she saw.

"What are you doing?" Tamra asked.

Emily barely glanced toward Tamra then turned her attention back to the clothes that she was emptying out of the wardrobe. "Oh, hello," she said brightly, but she said nothing more.

"What are you doing?" Tamra repeated, stepping into the room.

"Grandma's makin' a mess," Evelyn said.

Emily laughed softly. "Yes, Grandma *is* making a mess."

"And again I ask," Tamra said, "what *are* you doing?"

"I'm moving my things to another room," she said, her attention focused on sorting her clothes. Some she removed from hangers and tossed into a pile; others she laid in a stack over the bed. "Some of this stuff I haven't worn in years. We might as well pass it along to charity. And I was hoping you'd be willing to help me go through some of Michael's things. I don't think I can do it on my own."

"I'd be happy to help, but . . . why the move?" Tamra considered the years Emily had shared this room with her husband, and the fact that Michael had actually died here. "Are the memories difficult?"

"Yes, they are. But the memories are everywhere. It's not that. I just . . . need a change, I suppose. Besides, this room should be yours now. This is the master bedroom, and it rightfully belongs to you and Jess, so—"

"That's really not necessary," Tamra insisted. "The room we have is more than adequate and—"

"I know it's not necessary." Emily stopped what she was doing and looked directly at Tamra. "But it's proper; it's the way it's always been done. Michael and I took over this room soon after we were married, and his mother stayed elsewhere. I'm taking her room now. It's a nice room and it's . . . appropriate."

Tamra felt momentarily helpless. This move that Emily was determined to make seemed to represent the huge changes that had occurred in her life since losing her husband. A part of her wanted to argue with Emily, to insist that she should stay in this room and hold onto the years she had spent here with Michael. But a part of her understood Emily's desire for a change, and she couldn't help thinking that she might well do the same thing if she were in this position. Then it occurred to her that one day she might be.

"What can I do to help?" Tamra asked, pushing up the sleeves of her sweatshirt. "The baby should sleep a while yet."

Emily smiled and asked her to start bagging up the clothes that would go to charity and move them out into the hall. Evelyn pitched in as well, actually managing to be more help than hindrance. Tamra was about to ask what she might do next when Jess appeared in the doorway and bellowed, "What are you doing?"

Emily repeated her explanation and firmly stopped the protest that was evident in Jess's eyes. "Well, I can't stop you from moving out of this room," he said, "but I'm not sure I'm ready to move into it."

"Well, it will be ready when you are," Emily said, her voice distant as she tossed some of Michael's belongings onto the bed. Jess noticed his father's old reliable hat hanging over the edge of the mirror. He took it down and ran his fingers around the flat brim. The style was nearly identical to a hat Jess often wore, but this particular hat was probably older than Jess was, and like a broken-in pair of shoes, it simply had a look of Michael Hamilton. He studied the hat with his fingers for a full minute while Tamra and his mother were apparently oblivious, then he eased it onto his head, recalling that his father had worn the same size. He contemplated his reflection in the mirror while a clear memory appeared in his mind of how his father had looked in that hat. He was startled to hear his mother gasp and turned to see her staring at him, eyes wide, a hand pressed over her mouth and the other to her heart. A deathly quiet settled over the room. Even Evelyn seemed to sense the need for silence. Jess met his mother's eyes and watched huge tears brim there before they fell down her cheeks.

"I'm sorry," he said, pulling the hat off abruptly. "I didn't mean to—"

"No, it's fine," she said, wiping her hands over her face. "It's just that . . . you look so much like him . . . the way he looked when I first came here . . . to be married. He wore his hair much the same way then . . . that you do now and . . ." Her voice broke. "You just look so much like him. It's like . . . going back in time and . . ."

She sat down on the edge of the bed and cried harder than Jess had seen her cry through the entire ordeal of Michael's illness and death. He tossed a helpless glance toward Tamra before they sat on either side of Emily and took her hands. "I'm sorry," she said with her head against Jess's shoulder. "I know beyond any doubt that this is the way it has to be. I know this is the plan our family was meant to live from the beginning. I just . . . miss him so much."

"I know," Jess said. "We all do."

They sat together in silence for a few minutes before Emily turned and hugged Jess tightly. "I'm so grateful for you, Jess; and for your sweet family." She turned and hugged Tamra. "I just don't know what I'd do without you."

"The feeling is mutual," Tamra said.

"Amen," Jess muttered, his voice cracking as he looked down and surveyed the hat in his hands. Following an awkward silence, he added, "May I keep the hat?"

"Of course," Emily said. "You should have it." She turned and glanced helplessly around the room. "I'm not sure what to do with all of your father's things. I wonder if . . ."

"You don't need to do that right now," Jess said. "There's no hurry."

"No," Emily said, "but leaving his things lying about isn't going to make me feel any closer to him than I already do. There are some things that are certainly sentimental, and there are certain things that I want to distribute among those who love him, but most of his belongings are just *stuff*."

"Hey," Tamra said, "you know those beautiful wood chests in the basement; they're each filled with keepsakes from Michael's grandparents and great-grandparents. Maybe we should get some kind of chest for the things that you want to keep."

Emily's face lit up. "What a brilliant idea."

"And you can keep it in your new room, and have it close to you," Tamra added.

Emily took a deep breath and blew it out slowly. "Yes, I really like that idea. Perhaps we could go into town tomorrow and see what they might have available."

"Let's make a day of it and have lunch out," Jess said. "I've got a couple of quick errands and I believe we need some groceries."

"That sounds wonderful," Emily said. "And we can deliver all this stuff to charity while we're at it."

At Emily's insistence, Jess helped her go through his father's things. At first he felt somewhat disconcerted to be doing such a task, but his mother's matter-of-fact example helped him enjoy the opportunity to reminisce over certain aspects of his parents' life together. While Tamra cared for the baby and helped Sadie prepare supper, Jess and his mother sorted and talked and laughed—and cried. By the time supper was ready they had made great headway, and Jess had a handful of keepsakes—including the hat—that he took to his room and set out; things that would warmly remind him of his father at any given moment.

The following morning Jess checked in at the boys' home with Mr. Hobbs, then he went back to the house to find Tamra helping his mother put his father's things into boxes.

"I want to ship these to your sisters today," Emily said. "If you want to find the packing tape, we can finish up."

Jess went to the office and returned with the packing tape and some address labels for his sisters that he'd printed off the computer.

"Oh, wonderful," Emily said when she saw them.

Jess couldn't help feeling unsettled as he taped up the boxes, thinking of how his sisters might feel when they opened them. He said to his mother, "I hope you're calling to warn them what you've got in here. Opening them might not be easy."

Emily looked a little surprised then said, "I guess that would be a good idea."

"Yeah," Jess said, his sarcasm subtle. At times his mother seemed to be handling all of this so well that he almost felt guilty for missing his father so desperately. She seemed to have a layer of peace, even a deeper connection with Michael as his wife, that the rest of the family didn't have. At least he could be grateful that she had that peace. Caring for a grieving mother who refused to be consoled could be an adventure he wouldn't want to encounter.

Once the packages were ready to go Jess loaded them into one of the Cruisers they owned, along with the bags and boxes of his father's belongings that would be donated to charity. He forced himself not to think about what they were doing as he buckled Evelyn and little Michael into their car seats and they all headed into town. Jess kept himself detached from his feelings as they deposited the donations and mailed the packages. But Emily and Tamra were equally quiet and he had to believe their thoughts were in a similar place.

The mood lightened as they shared lunch and Evelyn's antics kept them entertained. Little Michael was good until the last few minutes of their meal, then Tamra went out to the Cruiser to nurse him while Jess helped Evelyn finish up and paid the bill. They drove to a furniture store and Emily had no difficulty picking out the perfect cedar chest for Michael's belongings. It had a slightly rugged look, but fine and sturdy. "Just like your father," Emily declared. She paid for it and made arrangements for it to be delivered the following day.

Through the drive home that quiet melancholy set in again, and Jess wondered how they could all feel this way but find it so hard to talk about. He thought of how they had been able to openly discuss the situation preceding Michael's death, but since the funeral, it had become more difficult. Deciding he hated the quiet, and he was grown-up enough to admit to his feelings, he broke the silence by saying, "I miss him."

"We all do," Tamra said, reaching for his hand.

A minute later Emily added, "I find myself looking around the house for him, wanting to tell him something, and when I realize he's not there, I just stand there and feel so lost."

"I've done that," Jess admitted.

"Me too," Tamra said. Then the quiet settled in again.

Jess felt better when he walked into his room and saw his own keepsakes of his father there. He took up the hat and put it on, and fingered the odds and ends on his dresser that had belonged to Michael. They stirred warm memories and he was reminded that his father's spirit lived on, and his memories were far more precious than any tangible memento.

His thoughts were interrupted when Tamra entered the room, wearing a smile. "You'd never guess what we got in the mail," she said.

"You're right, I could never guess, so tell me."

"Look," she said and handed him a card. He smiled when he saw that the return address on the envelope was from Tamra's mother. Their relationship had been strained, to say the least. Myrna had pretty much disowned Tamra when she had chosen to serve a mission. A great deal of mending had taken place since then, but her communications were still few and far between. But here in his hands was a very nice card, congratulating them on the birth of their son. She had handwritten a few words, expressing how cute he was in the pictures they'd sent. Tamra's beaming face made it clear how much this meant to her.

"That is really cool," Jess said, and then he hugged her. They had much to be grateful for.

The following morning Jess worked in the boys' home and had lunch in the cafeteria there before he sat through a meeting with Hobbs and the instructors and resident counselor. He returned to the house to find that the cedar chest had been delivered. Tamra was sitting in the rocking chair in Emily's new room, nursing the baby, while Emily carefully put Michael's belongings into the chest. Jess noticed that she had all of his journals, and a copy of each of the novels Michael had written. He always felt a little taken aback to realize that, among all else, Michael Hamilton had been an accomplished author. During Jess's childhood, he remembered Michael writing at the computer and having deadlines. He'd seen the books and heard people talk about them, and copies had always been in the family library. Tamra had read them when she'd first come here. But he never had. He picked one of them up off the floor and thumbed through it as he stated the obvious, "I never read them."

"I know," Emily said without diverting her attention from carefully folding Michael's favorite denim shirt.

"They're very good," Tamra said.

"Do we have extra copies?" he asked. "Like . . . copies I could keep?"

Emily stopped what she was doing and looked up at him with a hint of a smile teasing her lips. "Come with me," she said and he followed her downstairs to the family office. She opened a closet and pulled a box down from a shelf and set it on the polished blackwood desktop. Inside was a complete set of the two separate trilogies that Michael had written. Jess took one of them out and pressed his fingers over the words printed on the cover, *Crazy's Day, a novel by J. Michael Hamilton.*

"Amazing," Jess said softly.

"Yes, it is actually, especially when you realize that it was his success as a writer that brought us back together."

"Really?" Jess asked. "How is that?"

"He was on a book tour, promoting a new release, and he ended up in the town where I was living; Orem, Utah to be exact. Looking back I can honestly say that I was prompted to go to the mall one evening and I found the book and learned that he would be coming. Of course, I was still married at the time, but not many months later my husband was killed, and your father came back into my life."

"Wow," Jess said and chuckled as he thumbed through the pages, then he noticed something handwritten on the first one and stopped there. It took a minute to convince himself that his eyes were not deceiving him, but sure enough it said, *To my son, Jess, the finest son a man could ask for. May your every dream come true. J. Michael Hamilton.* Jess watched his father's handwriting blur against the mist in his eyes. He heard the crack in his voice as he asked, "When did he write this?"

"Not long before he died. It just . . . came to him one day that each of the girls had a set of books, but you didn't."

"And why is that?" Jess asked, then he almost wished he hadn't when she answered gently, "You never asked."

Jess swallowed carefully and she went on, "But he knew that one day you would have a desire to read them. So he signed a personal inscription in each one and told me to put them away and give them to you when you asked. So, there you are. Your very own set, all first editions."

Jess swallowed again with more difficulty, forcing back emotion that threatened to completely consume him. He felt a tumultuous mixture of grief, regret, and gratitude. He put the book back into the box and picked up the box. "Thank you," he managed to say. "I will treasure them always." He hurried from the room and took the books upstairs to place them reverently on his personal bookshelf in the sitting room just off his bedroom. He was grateful to be alone when the emotion bubbled out of him. He sat down and cried for several minutes, then he forced himself to his senses. He went into the bathroom and washed his face before he returned to his mother's new room to find her closing the chest and pressing her hands over it with the same reverence he'd taken in handling his new books.

Tamra entered the room from putting the baby down to sleep and the three of them worked together to move the remainder of Emily's belongings from the master bedroom to the room where Jess remembered his grandmother staying for many years, until she'd become terribly ill preceding her death and she'd been moved to a room on the main floor. Evelyn followed them back and forth, then went to play in the nursery. They took a break for supper then returned to put the finishing touches on the room. Emily was obviously pleased with the results, and long after Evelyn had gone to bed, they sat in her new room visiting and reminiscing. When Emily finally declared that she needed to get some sleep, Jess and Tamra left her room and wandered slowly to their own.

"Just a minute," Jess said before they entered, and Tamra followed him to the master bedroom that had been emptied except for the huge bed and its matching furnishings. Jess flipped on the light and leaned his shoulder against the doorjamb. Tamra stood silently beside him while he absorbed the memories for several minutes, the most prominent being how his father had died in this room, with his family gathered around him. It had been an incredibly spiritual experience, and the memory of it was peaceful rather than morbid, but difficult nevertheless.

Tamra heard Jess draw in a deep, ragged breath before he stated, "I can't sleep in this room."

He turned and walked away and she flipped off the bedroom light and followed him, well aware that he was crying. She entered their bedroom, where a bedside lamp was lit, to find Jess standing at the window, looking out into the night. She pushed her arms around him from behind and held him tightly for a few minutes before she said in a soft voice, "Your mother said when you were ready, we could take the room. This room is fine. I don't care if we stay here indefinitely. As long as I'm sharing my room with you, it doesn't matter where it is."

Jess turned to look into Tamra's face. She always managed to say the right thing at the right time. He kissed her warmly and held her tighter, feeling immeasurably grateful to have her in his life. She kissed him again and pressed a hand into his hair, murmuring close to his lips, "I love you, Jess. And everything's going to be all right." She kissed him again and again, and he knew that she was right. As long as he had the strength of her love, everything would be all right.

Chapter Two

Long after Tamra fell asleep, Jess found it difficult to relax. He knew he should rest while he could, knowing that little Michael would be awake for a feeding far too soon, but sleep eluded him and he finally slipped into the sitting room where he took down the novels his father had written. He read the inscription in each one, marveling at how they each had a separate and personal sentiment. He touched his father's handwriting each time, wishing he'd had the insight to read these books long ago. Deciding it was better late than never, he put them all back on the shelf except for the first, which he opened and began to read. He was quickly amazed to realize that it was actually a very good book. As he became immersed in the story he had to stop and remind himself that his own father had written it.

When Tamra got up to feed the baby, she peeked in and asked if he was enjoying the book. He just smiled and told her he was before he continued reading and she took the baby to bed to nurse him there. He finally had to go to bed when his eyes wouldn't read another word, but over the next several days he had his father's book within arm's length, carrying it everywhere he went and reading during any snatch of time he could find. When he finished the first one he moved right into the second, marveling at his father's talent, especially when his writing had been only a brief part of his life, and something he'd been very humble about.

After breakfast one morning, Jess remained in the kitchen to help Tamra with the dishes while Sadie took Evelyn for a walk and his mother went upstairs. They talked about the novel Jess was reading, laughing over the humor so craftily integrated into the story. Jess was still laughing when the phone rang. He reached for it and couldn't keep a chuckle out of his voice as he said, "Hello."

"Hello, Jess." Sean's voice was steady, but pained.

Jess's heart raced and his throat tightened. "What's wrong?" he demanded. "What's happened?"

Tamra's eyes widened and her expression mirrored his own instinctive panic. For a split second he wondered if his reaction had been too presumptuous, then a stifled sob emitted through the phone. "What?" Jess insisted, reaching for Tamra's hand to squeeze it tightly.

"I'm sorry," Sean finally managed to say. "I told myself I could do this without . . . getting upset, but . . ." His voice broke into another sob.

"Just take a deep breath and tell me what's happened," Jess said gently while a host of possibilities marched through his mind, each one making his heart ache.

He heard Sean draw three sharp breaths before he managed to say, "There was an . . . accident."

Jess squeezed his eyes shut. That word *accident* touched far too many personal chords for him—and for his family. When Sean said nothing more, Jess forced back his own fear to gently prod him. "I'm listening."

"It's Joshua," Sean said on the wave of another sob. "He was . . . His bike . . . A car . . . A drunk driver . . ."

Jess pulled his hand from Tamra's to press it over his mouth, fearing he would scream into the phone as the image began to take hold in his mind. Sean became upset again and Jess forced his voice enough to say, "Just tell me what happened, Sean. Is Joshua . . ."

Tamra's chin quivered and her eyes turned moist as she began to perceive what Jess was hearing. Once again he heard Sean force back his grief enough to say, "He's . . . gone, and I just . . . can't believe it. I . . . thought I knew how to deal with grief . . . better than this. I just can't . . . believe it and . . ." Again he became too upset to speak.

Jess took a deep breath and told himself he could fall apart once he got off the phone. He thought of Joshua, how they'd grown to care for the boy during his recent stay here, and a tight knot gathered in the pit of his stomach. He forced his thoughts to the moment. "Okay, listen to me, Sean. We're on the next flight out of here, but it will take some time to get there. Are you going to be all right until we can—"

"Yes, yes of course," he insisted, but he didn't sound convinced. "I was hoping you'd come. I need you . . . and Emily and . . ." His voice broke again. "I need Michael."

"Well, he can get there a lot faster than we can."

Sean made a noise that sounded more like a relieved chuckle.

"Perhaps they're together, Joshua and Michael," Jess said, feeling unnaturally calm as he said it. He saw tears spill down Tamra's cheeks as she heard full evidence of what Sean had told Jess on the phone.

"Perhaps they are," Sean said, sounding more calm himself.

"Have you called Allison?" Jess asked, knowing his sister lived in the same area as Sean, and she could be there much faster than it would take them to fly halfway around the world.

"I couldn't get hold of her," he said. "I'll keep trying, but . . . will you try, too? I don't know if I can . . ."

"I understand. We'll call her. Just try to stay calm and we'll get there as soon as we can."

"Thank you," Sean said and hung up quickly as if he couldn't hold it together another second.

Jess looked at the phone scornfully and put the handset into the cradle. The moment his hand was free of it, the sorrow rushed out of him and he was grateful to feel Tamra's arms come around him, and the evidence that she was crying with him.

He finally forced himself to calm down and said, "We've got to tell Mother . . . and get some flights arranged and . . ."

"Come along," Tamra said, taking his hand and pulling him to his feet. "There's no time to waste. Sean and Tara need us."

They found Emily in her bedroom, writing in her journal. Jess knocked at the partially opened door and pushed it further open. "Oh, hello," she said brightly and stole a quick glance toward them, then her eyes shot back toward them and stared as she perceived that something was obviously wrong. "What is it?" she demanded, coming to her feet.

Jess cleared his throat carefully. "That was Sean . . . on the phone, and . . ." Emily pressed a hand over her mouth. "It's Joshua . . . he's been . . . killed."

"Good heavens," Emily muttered with steamy tears showing in her eyes. "What happened?"

Tamra looked to Jess intently and he realized that she'd not heard what little he knew before they'd come upstairs. He cleared his throat again, more loudly this time. "Uh . . . Sean was upset, so I don't know much, but . . . apparently he was on his bike . . . and was hit by a drunk driver."

Tamra and Emily both gasped. Emily sunk onto the edge of her bed and Tamra hurried to a chair. Jess decided that was a good idea and quickly sat down himself. For a few minutes they all cried, then Emily took a deep breath and said with perfect confidence, "It was his time to go. His test was finished. He's with other loved ones now."

Jess and Tamra exchanged an amazed glance before they both looked pointedly to Emily. Jess had to say, "You sound so sure."

She looked subtly surprised. "I am sure," she said and came to her feet. "We have much to do. Sean is as good as family, and he needs us. Jess, you check with Murphy and Mr. Hobbs and let them know we're leaving. I know Hobbs isn't feeling well, but Shirley can help him keep everything under control; she's done it before. I'll get the travel arranged. Tamra can start packing. Perhaps it would be best if we leave Evelyn with Sadie. You know how Sadie loves to look after her, and she'd not enjoy the long flights. We would manage if we had to, but under the circumstances, Sean's family doesn't need a toddler around the house getting into everything."

"I agree," Jess said and Tamra nodded.

"Let's get to it, then," Emily said and hurried from the room.

"Your mother is an amazing woman," Tamra said.

Jess was surprised to hear Tamra echo his own thoughts on the same subject. "Yes, she is," he admitted and reached out to touch Tamra's face. "And so are you." He shook his head slightly. "Where would I be without you? I can't even imagine."

Tamra returned the gesture by touching Jess's face, then she pressed her lips quickly to his. "There's no need to imagine. I will always be here."

Jess smiled and took a deep breath. They both hurried from the room and went their separate ways. While the baby slept, Tamra hurried to pack her own belongings and all she would need for the baby. Evelyn enjoyed helping her as Tamra explained that they would be going away and she would stay with Sadie. Evelyn seemed completely at ease with the prospect and became preoccupied with helping Tamra fold her clothes and put them into the suitcase. Tamra got out a suitcase for Jess and gathered the basics of what she knew he would need, then she read some storybooks with Evelyn before Emily found her and announced, "I've talked to the girls, so they all know what's happened. Allison is with Sean and Tara now. The flights are arranged and we'll be leaving in less than two hours in order to make our flight from Sydney."

"I'm nearly ready," Tamra said. "Do they know when to expect us?"

"I talked with Tara," Emily said. "She's relatively calm, but said she doesn't think it's fully hit her yet. She said Sean isn't doing well at all, and she's never seen him like this." Emily swallowed carefully and took a deep breath. "She thinks it hasn't hit her yet because she hasn't seen Joshua since it happened. Sean had to identify the body, and . . ."

"Oh, help," Tamra muttered, feeling sick to her stomach.

Emily's voice startled her from her thoughts as she added, "I saw Jess on his way to the stables a while ago. Why don't you find him and let him know when we're leaving. I'll hurry and pack and make some sandwiches to take with us."

Tamra took Evelyn by the hand and headed down the stairs, saying a prayer in her heart for Sean and his family. And she couldn't help wondering what marvelous work might be taking place on the other side of the veil that such amazing people were being taken home. Her gratitude deepened for the gospel and the understanding it gave her of such things. She prayed that Sean would be able to reach through his grief enough to take hold of that understanding.

* * *

Jess found Murphy in the office, adjacent to the main stables, where the horse business was overseen. Murphy had been the stable master here for many years, having taken over the job when his father had passed away. As Jess understood it, Murphy's great-great-grandfather had worked for Jess's great-great-grandfather when this estate had been young and raw in the nineteenth century. Jess and Murphy had a deep mutual respect, even though their values and lifestyles were very different. Murphy was a good man, a little shorter than Jess, with a husky build and a brusque manner. His hair was thick and dark and never looked combed. And he only shaved every three or four days, which gave him a rugged unkempt look in spite of his always being clean and as well dressed as a man could be who worked with horses all day every day. He lived in the overseer's house on the estate with his aging mother, Susan, and had cared well for her through many health problems.

Michael's death had been difficult for Murphy, and there had been a distinct soberness about him since the loss had occurred. Jess had taken every possible opportunity to appropriately share his testimony with Murphy of life after death, and his knowledge that it had been Michael's time to go. Murphy always listened politely, but he never said much and Jess suspected he was more being polite than really absorbing anything that Jess had told him. But today as Jess entered the office, Murphy looked up with a broad grin that he'd not seen since Michael's cancer had taken hold with a death grip. Jess momentarily forgot about the grievous news he'd gotten from Sean and asked, "What's up with you? You're actually smiling."

Murphy chuckled and glanced down almost shyly, which was so out of character that Jess knew immediately what had to be going on. "It must be a woman."

Murphy's eyes turned pleasantly defensive. "What makes you think so?"

"Because I've *never* seen that expression on your face before, and I've *never* seen you take more than five minutes of interest in a woman. Two plus two is four. What's up?"

Murphy chuckled. "Well, actually, it is a woman." Jess laughed and Murphy added, "I met her in town a few weeks back when I was ordering the usual supplies. We've only gone out a couple o' times, but—"

"You went on a date?" Jess laughed, exaggerating his astonishment. "Did your mother faint when you told her?"

Murphy chuckled. "You're wicked, you know that. No, she didn't faint, but she was pleased. And I was going to say that we've been emailing a lot and . . ." He shook his head and chuckled. "I really like her, and I do believe she likes me, too."

"Well, that is wonderful news. I wish you the best. Has your mother met her yet?"

"Yes, actually. They hit it off rather well. I took Mother into town yesterday and we stopped in at the salon where she works; she does hair and stuff." Jess chuckled at the obvious glow of pride in Murphy's face.

"Well, you'd best be sending her some flowers or something, I'd say. Butter her up before she finds out what you're really like," Jess teased then laughed as Murphy actually blushed.

"So, what did you come out here for?" Murphy asked, forcing a sober expression. "Was it to give me a bad time, or . . ."

Jess felt his countenance fall as he remembered the news he'd gotten earlier, and his need to leave everything in Murphy's hands while they traveled to Utah. Murphy's voice faded as his brow furrowed in concern. "What's up with you?" he asked gently, obviously picking up on Jess's grief.

"We got some bad news this morning," he announced and went on to explain the situation and that they would be leaving. Murphy's expression returned to the more recently typical confused sorrow. But he said nothing beyond assuring Jess that he would see that everything was taken care of in Jess's absence. They went over a few things and agreed to keep in touch by phone if anything came up, then Jess returned to the house to see how plans were coming along. He met Tamra and Evelyn who had been coming to find him. Evelyn ran to meet him and jumped into his arms. He squeezed his eyes shut and held her tightly, trying to comprehend how Sean must feel to lose a child. He couldn't even imagine. Then he realized that his mother had lost two of her own children, as well as a daughter-in-law. Perhaps that's why she was able to so quickly come to the peace of knowing it was Joshua's time to go; she'd gained a great deal of experience in such matters. His respect for his mother deepened, and his heart ached more deeply for Sean and Tara as Evelyn giggled and rubbed her nose against his in a typical greeting.

"You and Mama and little Michael and Grandma are going away in the plane," she announced. "And I get to stay with Sadie and we're going to bake in the kitchen and have a tea party with dollies and teddy bears."

"Well, that sounds pretty fun," Jess said, winking at Tamra. "Why don't you go on the plane with Mama and Grandma and I'll stay here and have a tea party with Sadie."

Evelyn screwed up her face. "No, I wanna have a tea party," she insisted.

"Very well," Jess said, exaggerating his disappointment, "I suppose I'll have to go with Mama and Grandma, but I'll sure miss you. When I come back we'll have a tea party of our own."

Evelyn nodded eagerly and squirmed out of his arms, having caught sight of Mrs. Murphy's big yellow cat prowling in the grass. "Here I am, Ginger," Evelyn called as if they were the best of friends. Jess watched as the old cat rolled onto its back and allowed Evelyn to scratch its belly. The cat was always eager to take any attention she could get, and Evelyn loved to make the cat purr.

"They have a deep and abiding relationship," Tamra commented, somewhat facetiously.

Jess chuckled in agreement then said more seriously, "I pray our children outlive us. I don't know that I could bear losing one of them—under any circumstances."

Tamra looked into his eyes. "The Lord promises that he won't give us more than we can bear."

Jess gave a humorless chuckle and stuffed his hands into his pockets. "Yes, but . . . I know for a fact that my opinion on what I can bear is a lot different from the Lord's."

"Still, you've gotten through; you're still standing."

"Thanks to you," he said, reaching for her hand.

"And I'm still standing thanks to you," she said. "So, you see, the Lord gave us each other so that we could bear whatever might be required of us in this life."

Jess took her into his arms and held her tightly. "I'm sure we could get through whatever we have to," he said. "Still, I pray that I don't outlive my children—or you. I need you; all of you."

"The feeling is mutual," she said and eased back. "Now, come along. I started your packing but I don't know what else you want. We must hurry."

On their way up the stairs, Tamra repeated all that Emily had told her about her arrangements and her conversation with Sean's wife. "Tara suggested we stay at the same inn where members of Sean's family would be staying. That way we can meet together more easily without crowding Sean's home, so your mother made reservations there."

"Sounds good," Jess said. "And everything else is . . ."

He was interrupted by the squeaky infant noises coming from the monitor that Tamra had clipped to the waist of her jeans. Jess chuckled. "His Majesty is awake."

"Now, just because he orders us about and we cater to his every whim doesn't make him the king around here."

"If he's not the king, who is?" Jess asked lightly.

"You are," Tamra said with a little laugh.

"No, I'm the one who caters to every whim of the tiny little king in diapers—any hour of the day or night."

"He won't be an infant forever," Tamra said.

"Then maybe there's hope that we'll get some sleep again someday."

"Perhaps," she said as the noise on the monitor turned to a healthy cry and they entered the nursery. "Now, what were you saying?" she asked as she lifted little Michael out of his bed and cuddled him against her.

"Everything's under control with Hobbs and Murphy. Now let's just hope that Sean can keep it together until we get there."

"Let's hope," Tamra said and they went to the bedroom to finish packing.

* * *

Murphy drove them out to the hangar and helped load their luggage before he returned to the station. They were quickly in the air with Jess piloting the plane. Little was said between them through the flight as they each seemed lost in thought over the reasons for their long journey. They arrived in Sydney with enough to time to get a late supper in the airport and board the flight that would take them to Los Angeles through the night. Fortunately the hum of the jet engines seemed to have a calming effect on little Michael and he hardly made a peep as he awakened for his regular nightly feedings. They all took turns holding him as he slept, and they managed to sleep as well. Although, Tamra pointed out, "Now he'll want to be held all night *every* night."

"Yeah," Jess chuckled, "and we'll have to get a tape recording of a jet engine to get him to settle down."

They had breakfast in the L.A. airport and boarded a flight to Salt Lake City, arriving late morning. After a quick lunch in that airport, they rented a car and headed south to Lehi where their hotel reservations were. The Timpanogos Inn was just off the freeway and easy to find, and its location was less than a ten-minute drive from Sean's new home in Cedar Hills. Watching rain fall from their second-story window, Jess phoned Sean to tell him they'd arrived. Fifteen minutes later he knocked at the hotel room door, just as Tamra laid a sleeping Michael down in the crib. Emily came through the door from her adjoining room just as Jess opened the door into the hallway. Sean slumped into Jess's arms, holding to him tightly. Jess returned their brotherly embrace with fervor, aware of Sean trembling as his grief rose to the surface then gained momentum. Tamra closed the door and bolted it, exchanging a concerned glance with Emily. The women both sat down as Sean continued holding on to Jess, apparently oblivious to anything but his own sorrow. He finally eased back, wiping at his face with his sleeve. "I'm sorry," he said, but he showed no embarrassment.

"It's all right," Emily said, making Sean aware of her presence. He moved abruptly toward her and she rose to accept his embrace. It too was long and tight, then he turned to embrace Tamra, as well.

Sean slumped onto the edge of the bed, saying with a hoarse voice, "I'm so glad you're here. None of my family has arrived yet, but I can't talk to them the way I can you, and . . . I know I'm making it harder for Tara and the kids. It's like . . . they're looking to me for the answers . . . as if I'm supposed to be the strong one, or something. And I . . ." His voice cracked with grief. "I just . . . can't keep it together. I've never felt this way before. I've lost loved ones before; my parents, Michael. Good heavens, losing Michael was one of the most difficult things I've ever dealt with. But I did it. I worked it through. But this . . ." He gave a bitter chuckle. "I can't sleep. I can't eat. And I'm the one that's made a living telling people how to handle their grief. Now I feel like some kind of . . . hypocrite. Now I feel like all these years I had no idea what I was talking about. I just . . ." He tossed his hands into the air then pressed them roughly into his hair. "I just . . . can't believe he's gone, and . . . it feels so wrong, and . . ." He let out a stifled sob. "And I feel so . . . lost and . . . helpless, and . . ." He hung his head and cried.

Emily sat beside him on the edge of the bed, putting her arm around his shoulders. He slumped into her embrace, crying like a child while Jess and Tamra looked on, shedding silent tears. Jess watched his mother wipe her own tears away, and he felt inexpressibly grateful for her strength and wisdom. Sean had been there for him in the face of crisis a number of times in the past, but Jess doubted he would be any good in returning the favor. He felt lost and helpless himself to guide Sean through this vale of sorrow.

As Sean's emotion quieted down, Emily pointed at the tissue dispenser and Jess took the box out and handed it to his mother, before he sat down with Tamra close beside him. Emily wiped her own tears then took out three more tissues and handed them to Sean. He sat up and blew his nose, tossing the wad accurately into the nearby wastebasket.

"Now listen to me, Sean," Emily said with a firm gentleness that was typical of her when she needed to be in charge of a sensitive situation. "You are not a hypocrite. The grief counseling you've given to others through the years has been valid and helpful."

"I can attest to that," Jess said. "You were right on in helping me get past losing James—and my father."

"You know your job and you do it well, so don't go mixing up the present situation with that. Of course the reality can be more intense than discussing it in theory, but that doesn't make your theories false. Can you agree with that?"

Sean hesitated then nodded, as if he was willing to accept what he was being told because he had faith in Emily, but he had his doubts.

"Secondly, you can't fairly compare something like this to losing your parents—or even Michael. You loved your parents, I know. And in spite of some challenges in those relationships, you were able to mend bridges and find resolution there with each of them before their deaths. They both lived long, full lives. And as much as you loved them, they had not been a part of your everyday life for many years. The same with Michael. And you had time to prepare with Michael. The grief came over a longer period of time. When the shock of his cancer came, you had the opportunity to spend time with him and resolve much of your grief before he even died. What you are dealing with now, Sean, is the shock of having someone you love, who was a part of your daily life, torn from you with no warning."

Fresh tears welled up in Sean's eyes as he listened, watching Emily, stunned and in awe. Emily took Sean's hand into hers. "I have been where you are, Sean." Her voice became shaky. "I could never tell you how it felt to be called into our mission president's office and told that James and Krista had been killed, and Jess was in a coma. I felt as if the world had stopped spinning and I would be sucked hopelessly into a pit of despair. I was so upset for so many days that I have no idea how I managed to even pack and get home. I managed to keep it together most of the time when others were around, but I spent every minute I could get away with behind closed doors, crying my eyes out. And Michael cried with me. He was every bit as shaken as I was. The funeral is like a blur in my memory, but somehow we got through it. I kept praying that the pain would be taken from me, that I could feel peace, that I could cope. I remember moments of thinking that God had surely abandoned me in this, that this horrible occurrence was all wrong and He had allowed it to happen only to punish and torment me."

Sean's eyes filled with such perfect empathy that Jess knew she had just described exactly how he was feeling. But fresh tears trickled down Emily's cheeks as she tightened her hold on Sean's hand and said with conviction, "But gradually everything changed. The peace didn't come to me suddenly. It was gradual and it took time. I only know that a day came when I was able to look inside myself and know beyond any doubt that it had been James and Krista's time to go, and I knew that God had not abandoned me at all. In truth, He had carried me through my darkest moments, but I was too caught up in my grief to recognize His hand wiping away my tears."

Heavy tears trailed down Sean's cheeks. Emily reached up to brush them away, only to have them immediately replaced by fresh ones. "You mustn't be hard on yourself for your grief, Sean. Keep trusting in the Lord and give yourself some time to work it through. He'll give you the strength you need when you need it, and with time you will come to know that it was Joshua's time to go, just as it was James and Krista's—and Michael's."

Sean swallowed hard. "Was it?" he asked with a subtle edge to his voice, like a rebellious youth questioning a parent's wisdom.

An unwavering conviction rose in Emily's eyes, but she turned the question around. "What do you think, Sean?" When he didn't answer she added, "You know the gospel is true, and you know the doctrine that helps us understand the meaning and purpose of death. As I understand it, a righteous person is only taken from the earth when it is their time to go. I believe we all come here with a predetermined life span. In Doctrine and Covenants, section 122, the Lord tells Joseph Smith that '. . . Thy days are known, and thy years shall not be numbered less; therefore, fear not what man can do, for God shall be with you forever and ever.' That scripture helped me understand that it was Michael's time to go. If we're not living foolishly and creating circumstances that separate us from the protection of the Spirit, then we will go when it's our time to go. No amount of faith or action can override God's will in this or any other matter. You know all of that."

"I thought I knew," Sean said, looking at the floor. "But this just feels so . . . wrong."

"Wrong from whose perspective?" she countered. "You're completely consumed with your human emotions right now, Sean. You have to wade through them enough to let yourself feel what the Comforter has to tell you."

Sean said nothing but the meaning in his expression was clear. Jess was just wondering if his mother would let it drop and allow him time to absorb what had been said, but Emily said firmly, "You look as though you think I'm lying to you." Silence hung tensely before she added, "Do you think I would lie to you?"

"No, of course not, but . . ."

"But?" Emily pressed.

"I just don't know how it could be right, when . . ." Sean's grief escaped in a surge of new tears. "I just keep thinking . . . if only we hadn't moved to this neighborhood, or . . . if I had given him a ride instead of . . ." He became too upset to speak and Emily waited patiently while they all shed tears on Sean's behalf.

When Sean calmed down somewhat, Emily asked gently, "Instead of what, Sean?" He didn't answer and she added, "Are you blaming yourself for this?"

He said nothing but his eyes made it clear that he was—at least to some degree.

"Talk to me, Sean. You know more than anyone that you're not going to make sense of your thoughts while you keep them all bottled up inside of you."

Sean shook his head and let out a tense chuckle. "Who has the doctorate in psychology here?" He looked directly at Emily and added in a tender voice, "Your life's experience leaves me in awe, Emily Hamilton. You deserve an honorary doctorate in psychology."

Emily glanced down. "That's nonsense. There are a good many people in this world who have been through at least as much as I have—many who have been through much worse."

"But not many who have come through it so well," Sean said. "And I've seen much evidence of that."

"You've survived a great deal yourself," Emily said to him. "Perhaps you're losing sight of your own strength and the notches in your own belt that have come from overcoming life's challenges. Maybe I should remind you that you went face first through the windshield of a car and took months to heal from more injuries and broken bones than you could count. And what about the fact that you went for a long time with very little use of your hands, and the surgeries and time it took to make them whole. Have you forgotten that you were disowned by your family when you joined the Church? And how you drove to Utah in an old beat-up truck with little more than faith to get you there?"

Tamra listened with growing amazement. She had heard bits and pieces of Sean's past, but never put quite this way before. Her heart quickened almost painfully when Emily went on to bring up something that Tamra had never heard before.

"And surely you haven't forgotten that you married a woman who was pregnant from a rape, and you stood by her while that child was put into the arms of the parents who would raise it."

Sean's eyes filled with a confused wonder in the same moment that Tamra put a hand over her mouth to keep herself from responding audibly to news that tore at her heart. She'd had no idea. Her heart overflowed with tender compassion on Sean's behalf as he said with a trembling voice, "Actually, I *had* forgotten."

"You've survived a great deal, Sean," Emily said, touching his face and hair as if he were a little boy. "Surely you will survive this, as well."

"But . . ." he protested, "nothing was ever so difficult as this."

"Perhaps," Emily said, "and perhaps it's perspective. I believe trials are relative. How much grief did you feel when you discovered that the woman you loved was a rape victim? And how much grief did you feel when you watched her give birth to that baby and then give it away? How much grief did you feel when you went to see your mother on her deathbed, and your father told you that you had no right to be there? Maybe this is harder. In my experience, there is little in life as devastating as losing a child. But the point is that you've gone through grief before and you've healed and moved on. This is new and raw and you're still in shock. You need to trust in the Lord, give it some time, and not be so hard on yourself. Give yourself permission to grieve."

Sean shook his head and let out an ironic chuckle. "How many times have I said those very words to others?"

"Where do you think I heard it?" Emily asked.

"I'll never forget when you told *me* that," Jess said.

Following some minutes of silence, Emily said, "Why don't you tell us why you're blaming yourself for this. Better that you talk it through than hold it inside. And perhaps it's too difficult to discuss with Tara just yet."

"I can hardly look her in the eye," Sean admitted.

"Why?" Emily asked, seeming more concerned than she had since Sean's arrival.

"I don't know. Perhaps because I *am* blaming myself. Perhaps I'm wondering if she's blaming me, too."

"Has she said anything to indicate that she's blaming you?" Tamra asked.

"No," Sean admitted, "but . . ."

"But what?" Emily pressed.

"Well . . . it was my idea to move to a new neighborhood. It seemed kind of impulsive, but . . . a number of things had happened with the kids at school that made me feel uncomfortable. And there was a bad situation brewing with a couple of the kids in the neighborhood that Josh had spent far too much time with. I also had a patient that was pretty unstable that had figured out where I lived and had caused some problems. Nothing that concerned me; there was certainly no potential danger, or anything. I simply thought that to move without leaving a forwarding address would solve that problem. I had an associate that was selling this house; it was a beautiful home, about the same size as the one we had, but the neighborhood and schools were better according to him. It sounded like a good idea, so we did it. But now I have to wonder, if Josh hadn't been in that place at that time; if we hadn't lived there, then . . ."

"Then what?" Emily asked. "Did you move into this house against Tara's will?"

"No."

"Did you not make the decision to buy the house and move through prayer? Did you not agree that it was best for the family?"

"Well, yes, but . . ."

"There are no buts, Sean. The move was right and you know it was right. If it was Josh's time to go, it wouldn't have made any difference where you lived."

Sean looked dubious as he said, "But maybe if I had given him a ride to the school instead of . . ." His voice broke. Emily waited patiently, as if she sensed his need to unburden himself. He finally cleared his throat and said, "He came and asked if he could take the car to the school . . . for a rehearsal and I told him I needed it for a meeting at the church. He asked if I could give him a ride and pick him up later. I told him the weather wasn't that bad and he could ride his bike. The high school was less than half a mile away. He didn't complain but I knew he wasn't very happy about it, and . . . that was the last time I saw him alive."

"Sean," Emily said gently, "it's going to take time for you to come to terms with all of this, and you're going to have to get your own answers in order to be completely at peace. But trust me when I tell you that if it wasn't his time to go, he would have been protected. People have near misses on the streets all the time. The Spirit prompts and guides and warns us to keep us safe from all kinds of potentially dangerous situations. If it hadn't happened that way, it would have happened some other way. I know it; I know it beyond any doubt."

Sean looked inquisitively at her. "How do you know it?" She glanced down and he clarified. "You're not just speaking in generalities here, are you." It wasn't a question. "Are you trying to tell me that you *know* it was Josh's time to go?"

Jess wanted to blurt out that he seconded the question, but he just squeezed Tamra's hand more tightly, sensing that she was wondering the same thing. They exchanged a quick glance then turned their focus back to Emily as she lifted her tear-filled eyes to Sean and said with conviction, "Yes, Sean, I'm telling you that I know it was his time to go. He is with many loved ones on the other side—including Michael."

Sean's chin quivered and his eyes glistened with moisture. As if in response to a silent question that he'd been unable to voice, Emily added firmly, "I feel Michael close to me; not always, but . . . often enough to know that he is still with me in caring for our family and loved ones. I can't tell you how I know, Sean. It wasn't a thunderbolt, or even a burning in the bosom. I simply . . . knew . . . that Michael was there to receive him, and . . ." Emily's voice broke and a serene conviction filled her countenance. "And . . . Michael knew he was coming before he got there."

Jess was startled when he felt a chill rush over his shoulders in a way that he recognized as the Spirit bearing witness that what he'd just heard was true. He met Tamra's eyes and saw evidence there that she had felt it, too. The Spirit suddenly became so strong in the room that Jess hardly dared breathe for fear of breaking the spell.

They all sat in silence for several minutes, with varying degrees of emotion. Then the phone rang and Jess reached for it. Tara's voice sounded mildly panicked as she said, "Jess?"

"Yeah, it's me."

"Have you seen Sean?"

"He's right here. Do you want to talk to—"

"Yes, please," she interrupted, sighing audibly.

Jess handed the phone to Sean. He looked surprised, then concerned as he took it. They all listened quietly as he said, "I'm sorry, I . . . guess I left the cell phone in the car. I didn't mean for you to worry." He was quiet for a minute then said, "Yes, actually, I think I do feel better. How about you?" Silence. "We need to talk. I'll leave here in a few minutes."

He hung up the phone and turned around, shrugging his shoulders sheepishly. "I . . . uh, guess I left pretty upset and . . . she was worried."

"Understandably so," Emily said. "*Do* you feel better now?"

"Yes, I think I do," he admitted. "I know it will take time, but . . . you've given me a lot to think about."

"What goes around comes around," Jess said.

"Excuse me?" Sean looked baffled.

"I can recall a number of times when you've given me a lot to think about."

Sean gave a sad smile then embraced Jess tightly. "Thanks for being my brother," he said.

"The feeling is mutual," Jess replied.

Sean hugged Tamra, saying, "You're the best thing that ever happened to him."

"I think it was the other way around," Tamra said, touching Sean's face tenderly.

Sean hugged Emily long and hard, whispering with emotion, "You have no idea how blessed I am to have had two mothers in my life." He drew back and looked into her eyes. "You have given me so much. When I think back over that list of struggles you mentioned, I realize that you and Michael were there to help me through most of them, in one way or another. Thanks for being here now."

"What goes around comes around," Emily said and smiled warmly.

Chapter Three

Sean left with the promise to call later and give them specific information about the viewing and funeral. Once he was gone, they decided to rest while the baby was sleeping, and before the jet lag caught up with them. Jess had been up from his nap for a few minutes when Sean called, late afternoon, to tell them that his sister's family had just arrived at the same hotel and they were going down to the indoor pool. Jess got off the phone and said, "I think I'll go swimming. Want to come?"

"Not really, why?" Tamra asked. "Did you even bring a swimming suit?"

"No, but Sean's sister and her family are probably down by the pool."

"Oh, I want to go," Emily said. "I haven't seen Maureen for years."

After Tamra had fed the baby, they all went down to the pool and found Maureen sitting with a book, wearing jeans and a sweatshirt, while her children swam. They had a good visit, mostly focused on the blessings of the gospel, since Maureen and her family had all joined the Church a few years earlier. She repeatedly expressed her gratitude for what she had learned about life after death, and wondered how she had ever coped with losing loved ones in the past.

The following morning the remainder of Jess's family arrived, although most of the children had remained home. They all had a good visit and went out to a late dinner following the viewing.

The funeral went well and turned out to be a beautiful service. Jess and his three brothers-in-law all had the privilege of being pall bearers, and the spring weather was pleasant for the graveside service. Jess noted that Sean, Tara, and their children had all had bouts of tears, but they seemed to be holding up quite well.

Emily suggested that all of her own family go back to the hotel and spend some time together there, and not bombard Sean and his family right after the funeral. While they were crowded into Jess and Tamra's hotel room visiting, Jess's cell phone rang. He stepped into his mother's adjoining room to answer it where he could hear, and Murphy's voice came through clearly.

"What's up?" Jess asked.

"Well, Sadie's not feeling so good. I took her into town to see the doctor and Shirley looked out for Evelyn in her office. Evelyn's been real good and she's doing fine. And the doc's not sure what's up with Sadie. He's ordered some tests. Now before you panic, she's really not that bad off, and we don't want you to rush home because Tonya's helping out with Evelyn and—"

"Who is Tonya?" Jess asked.

"Remember that girl I told you about?"

"The one that likes you?"

"That's right. Well, she came out to spend some time with Mum and me, and she stuck around to help with Evelyn when she realized the situation. She doesn't have to go to work for a few days, and she's visiting with Sadie and chasing the little one. So everything's all right. Just wanted you to know what's going on. Don't hurry home."

Jess sighed. "Okay, well . . . thank you. And thank Tonya for me. Or better yet, make sure she's there when I get home, and I'll thank her myself."

"I'll see what I can do."

"Thanks for keeping the important stuff under control, Murphy. I don't know what I'd do without you."

"It's my job." He chuckled. "And I'm keeping the not-so-important stuff under control, too. A bonus wouldn't hurt."

Jess laughed. "You already make more than I do."

"Only because you don't actually write yourself out a paycheck."

"Well, maybe I should."

Murphy said more soberly, "How's Sean doing?"

"As good as could be expected. We were thinking of heading back in the morning, but I have this feeling we need to stick around a few more days. So, if you say everything's okay there, I think we'll do that."

"Sounds great. I'll let you know if anything changes."

Jess ended the call and returned to the other room, sitting down beside Tamra. "Who was that?" she asked quietly so as not to interrupt the joke that Allison's husband was telling.

"It was Murphy. I'll tell you later."

When the rest of the family had gone to pay a visit to Sean's home, Jess told Tamra and Emily about the phone call. Then he told them what he'd told Murphy. "I have this feeling we shouldn't go home just yet. I was thinking how nice it was to have Sean's family stick around for a while after the funeral when we lost Dad, but . . . I think it may be more than that. I don't know. Maybe I just want to stay because I wish there was something I could do. Whatever the reasons, I'd like to stay a few more days. What do you think?"

"Sounds fine to me," Emily said.

"I had the same feeling," Tamra admitted.

"Well, it's settled then," Emily said, then to Jess, "Why don't you arrange for a flight home the first of the week."

The following morning Jess's sisters that had flown in for the funeral left to return home, along with their husbands. Jess, Tamra, Emily, and little Michael went to Sean's home to see how they were doing. They arrived to find that Allison and her husband had taken Sean's other children to a movie and to spend the night at their home in Provo. Sean was doing much better than he had been the day they'd arrived, but Tara was extremely upset. Her family had all come for the funeral and they'd been very supportive, but now they'd all gone home to different states. And now that all the formalities had been taken care of, she missed her son beyond words.

Jess and Tamra left to take a walk in the backyard with little Michael, who was being fussy, while Emily had a quiet talk with Tara, and Sean held his wife's hand. They returned to the house to hear more laughter than tears from the front room and figured it was safe to intrude and join the others. The conversation was focused on pleasant reminiscing over Joshua's life and all the joy and happiness he had brought to those who loved him. Sean and Tara both admitted that they'd each come to know for themselves that it had, indeed, been Joshua's time to go. But, oh, how they missed him!

The baby began to fuss again and Jess rose to walk the room with him while they visited. The doorbell rang and he reached for it since he was already on his feet. On the porch he saw a young man he'd never seen before, who looked very much like a missionary. He wore a dark suit, white shirt, and tie. He was clean cut and nice looking, and he had that certain glow about him. Jess was willing to bet money he'd not been home from a mission very long. The young man looked extremely nervous as he said, "Are you Dr. O'Hara?"

For a moment Jess wondered if this could be the disturbed patient that Sean had tried to hide from when he'd moved, but instinctively he knew this kid had his life well put together.

"Uh . . . no," Jess said. "Just a minute and I'll—"

"I'm Dr. O'Hara," Sean said, appearing at his side. "What can I do for you?"

"Hello," he said nervously, extending his hand, "my name is Joshua Raine." He gave Sean a firm handshake, then put his hands behind his back. "I wouldn't expect you to remember me. I mean . . . I don't remember you, really. But . . . I wondered if I should try to call first, but I prayed about it and . . . I hope it's okay to tell you that. I know from the funeral that you're active in the Church, and . . . anyway I . . ."

Jess saw Sean discreetly pass him a curious, but not concerned, glance as this young man kept talking. Jess glanced toward the women seated out of view of the door and noticed them all listening with the same curiosity as the boy continued.

"Well, I hope I'm not out of line. If I am, feel free to kick me out and tell me to never come back, but I . . ."

"It's okay, young man," Sean said gently. "I can tell you're extremely nervous. Why don't you just say what you need to say."

Jess wondered if this young man might have some connection to Sean's many years of counseling. Had he helped this boy as a young child? Or his parents, perhaps?

"Well, all right . . . the thing is, I've been looking for you since before my mission. I finally found you, or I thought I had, right after I got back, but then the letter I sent came back with no forwarding address, and I was devastated. And then I saw the obituary. And it's the weirdest thing because I never read the paper, but I opened it at a neighbor's house and there it was and I knew my prayers had been answered. I went to the funeral, but I didn't think it would be appropriate to talk with you there, but . . ." The young man actually got tears in his eyes. "It was a beautiful funeral, and I'm so sorry for the loss of your son. And I'm really sorry that my name is Joshua, too. I hope that doesn't . . . like . . . feel weird to you or anything but the thing is . . ."

Jess noticed that Sean seemed almost mesmerized by this young man, and a quick glance at Tara revealed a look of deep concentration, as if she was attempting to put something together in her head. Something akin to shock came over her face and she jumped to her feet, appearing at Sean's side, gripping his arm tightly. The young man stopped talking abruptly as their eyes met. With a cracking voice, Tara asked, "Did you say your name is . . . Raine?"

The boy nodded and said with equal emotion in his voice, "You must be . . . Mrs. O'Hara." Tara nodded and he added what Tara obviously already knew from the expression on her face. "Then you are the woman who gave birth to me."

Jess gasped and heard Sean, Tamra, and Emily do the same. Tamra and Emily rose and rushed to the doorway just as Tara opened her arms and Joshua Raine moved through the door to awkwardly embrace her. Once they had their arms around each other, they both wept. Tears rose into Sean's serene eyes as he quietly closed the door. Tara finally stepped back, laughing through her tears, wiping at her face.

"I can't believe it," she said. "There's hardly a day that goes by when I don't wonder about you, but since we lost Joshua, you've been on my mind a great deal. I didn't even admit it aloud to anybody, but . . ." She laughed. "No one but God Himself could have known how much it would mean to me to have you come back now."

She hugged Joshua again, then he turned toward Sean, who hugged him as well, saying, "It's good to see you again."

"Again?" Tamra asked.

"I saw him the day he was born, but not for long." Sean ushered everyone back to their seats and motioned Joshua to a chair. "Come, we have a great deal to catch up on." Once they were seated he made introductions then said, "So, tell us about your mission, young man. Where did you serve?"

Joshua beamed as he replied, "Ireland."

A hush fell over the room. Joshua looked around, seeming baffled and asked, "Is there . . . something wrong with . . . Ireland?"

Sean chuckled. "No, of course not. That's where I served as well. My parents were Irish; first-generation Americans."

Joshua showed a warm smile toward Sean as a deep unspoken connection seemed to draw them together. Then, as eagerly as any returned missionary, Joshua recounted some of the highlights of his mission among the Irish people. Sean told some mission stories as well and they all laughed together while Tara gazed at this young man, her expression filled with awe and the perfect joy and pride that any mother would feel in hearing her son tell of a successful mission.

When a lull came in the conversation, Emily asked, "Forgive me if I'm being nosy, but I can't help wondering how you came to find your birth mother."

"Oh, that's not nosy," he said, "but it is rather a long story."

"I don't think we're in any hurry," Jess said.

"I'm certainly not," Tara added.

"Before you tell us that," Sean said, "I have to ask you . . . Well, did you always know you were adopted?"

"Absolutely. My parents were very open about it. As far back as I can remember, they told me the story of how I came to be their son."

"How exactly would that story go?" Tara asked in a tentative voice.

Joshua offered her a warm smile and said without breaking eye contact, "They told me that in this world there are many kinds of angels. And one of the most rare and precious is the kind that came here willing to give life to people like me, who were meant to be born to people like them, who were not physically capable of having children of their own. They told me that the angel who gave me life was among the most noble and beautiful of her kind, and that she sacrificed and suffered a great deal so that we could be a family."

Joshua finally glanced down and sniffled loudly. Sean put his arm around Tara's shoulders and handed her a tissue. She wiped at her steady stream of tears as Joshua added, "Of course, when I became old enough to understand, they told me more of what exactly you had suffered and sacrificed, and that one of the reasons you were so noble and precious is that many women in your position would have aborted the baby and felt no remorse. And I personally don't think that God would have condemned you for doing so, under the circumstances. But you saw it through—for me—for us."

Silence ensued for several minutes, except for a chorus of varied sniffles. Sean finally asked, "Was it difficult for you, knowing you were adopted? You don't have to answer if you don't want to, but I have to admit that's the question I've wondered over most. I didn't want you to think we didn't love you and want you. You must know that we were married when you were born, and we were in a position to keep you. But we just knew that you weren't meant to be ours. Still, I've wondered how that decision affected you."

Joshua smiled at Sean and said, "I never felt unloved and unwanted. Of course, my parents are wonderful people; I couldn't have asked for better. But they always treated my adoption as if it was the greatest event in history since the discovery of the gold plates."

They all chuckled before Sean said, "So, tell us more about yourself."

Joshua told of his hobbies and school experiences. He was an Eagle Scout and had graduated from high school with honors. He was presently working at a retirement facility and was going to school in nursing. He was dating but hadn't found anybody special so far. He had one younger sister, who had just turned fifteen. His parents had taken her in as a foster child when she was three months old. She'd been taken from an abusive situation, and it was a long, hard road to finally gain custody of her, and to eventually adopt her and have her sealed to them.

Joshua finally left very late, and with obvious hesitancy. They exchanged phone numbers and email addresses and promised to keep in close touch. When he was gone, Sean turned to Tara and asked, "So, how are you . . . really?"

She laughed through fresh tears and exclaimed, "It's a miracle. I'm just so . . . grateful."

"Amen," Sean said and put his arms tightly around his wife.

Jess hugged Tamra with one arm and his mother with the other, grateful that they'd been blessed with the privilege to be a part of this miracle.

Over the next few days they spent quite a bit of time with Sean's family, and Joshua came for dinner the evening before they were scheduled to return to Australia. Sean and Tara's other children accepted him openly and with warmth. They too had always been made aware that another half-brother existed somewhere, and they were all glad to be able to get to know him. Again they had a good visit and it was evident that this young man had already helped heal the wounds left by Joshua O'Hara's untimely death.

That same evening, Tamra found it amusing to see Jess and Sean sitting at the dinner table long after the meal was over, reminiscing over the years of Jess's childhood when Sean had lived in their home. They talked as if they were truly brothers. When something came up about Jess's accident, Tamra feared the conversation would become somber and bring them back to the more recent death they were all struggling to deal with. But Sean pushed up his sleeves and said, "Okay, I bet you can't beat this." Tamra had forgotten that Sean too had once miraculously survived an accident until he showed Jess a scar on his arm that was ghastly.

"Oh, I've got that beat," Jess said and pulled up his pant leg to show a gruesome scar that Tamra was familiar with. For half an hour the men compared scars, laughing and joking in a way that Tamra had once believed could never be possible. She felt warmed to see this new evidence of Jess's healing and how far he'd come. There had been a time when he never could have talked of the accident he'd survived without getting upset and dooming himself to unreasonable guilt over something that had been completely beyond his control. Tamra smiled at her husband and listened with pleasure to his ongoing antics with Sean. They truly were brothers in spirit.

The flights home were long and exhausting, but they returned to find that Murphy had managed to keep everything under control—in spite of a number of challenges. They immediately met Tonya, a woman with dark hair cut short into a flattering style. She was slightly heavy with a pretty face and long, brightly painted nails. She was easy to like with a friendly manner and she was obviously not afraid to work hard as it became evident that she had been staying in their home and taking care of Evelyn, under Sadie's supervision. Tonya had taken some time off work to help with Evelyn, and had obviously won the child's approval by the amount of time she'd spent playing dollies and having tea parties. And the last couple of days Tonya had taken to running back and forth between Evelyn and Murphy's mother, while Murphy kept everything else under control. Apparently Susan Murphy wasn't feeling well at all. The doctor had assured them it was just a virus, but given the ongoing condition of her health, even a simple virus could prove to be complicated and would often lead to other problems. Murphy was understandably concerned, but Tonya had made certain that everyone was comfortable and cared for. Sadie absolutely adored the woman and raved of her fine qualities. And while Sadie refused to be coddled and fussed over, the results of her tests had come back that morning and she had a fairly severe case of diabetes. She was due to enter the hospital the following morning to get her blood sugar leveled and to learn how to test her own blood and properly administer insulin to herself. Given her age and the apparent, rapid progression of the disease, the situation didn't look good.

After getting the report on Sadie and Susan, Jess went to the boys' home to learn that Mr. Hobbs had taken a turn for the worse with his health problems and had not come in at all during most of the time Jess had been gone. Shirley had been managing to keep everything under control—barely. There were several pending fires that Jess would need to put out, as Shirley so quaintly put it. Hearing the details of those fires, the weight of all that he needed to oversee settled fully onto his shoulders. He tried not to think of the deep piles that were accumulating on his desk, and the burdens they represented. This was not how he'd imagined fully taking over the boys' home when the time came. Leaving to return home, he attempted to force the negative thoughts out of his mind, and he managed to face his family with a smile, but his heart felt heavy.

* * *

That evening Jess sat down with Tamra and his mother to discuss what should be done given the new developments. Murphy was doing well at handling the horse business, and he had told Jess that he felt confident he could keep everything there under control, and still be able to look after his mother. The obvious solution to the boys' home was that Jess would be taking over as full-time administrator, replacing Hobbs. It was what he'd always dreamt of doing, and technically he was prepared to do it. Practically speaking, he felt he could handle it, but the time it would demand felt daunting. And he didn't admit to how thoroughly unconfident he felt over the matter. Tamra was willing and eager to help him as much as it was possible, keeping Evelyn and little Michael as her first priorities. Emily and Tamra felt certain they could care for Sadie through whatever might arise, but after talking to her doctors over the next couple of days, and several phone conversations with her children, they all had to agree that the best solution would be for Sadie to take up permanent residence with one of her children. She had stayed with them for lengthy periods in the past, and they were eager to have her in their home and care for her. The situation was great for Sadie, but Jess, Tamra, and Emily all admitted that it was difficult to see her go. Her son picked her up directly from the hospital and they all said their good-byes there. Three weeks later Evelyn was still asking when Sadie was going to come back and play with her, and she simply didn't want to accept her parents' explanation that Sadie wouldn't be living with them any more.

Jess settled more deeply into his job at the boys' home, deeply appreciative of Tamra's help and support. And once in a while his mother even pitched in to help solve a problem. Little Michael became more responsive to his surroundings and smiled at anyone who would make funny noises in his direction. Evelyn loved to play with her baby brother, and Emily loved to help look after both of them. Jess had to admit that in spite of his father's absence, they were settling into a new pattern of life rather well.

A letter arrived from Sean, and Jess read it aloud over the dinner table. He especially liked the part that said, "We see Joshua regularly. He's come to dinner and has shared family activities with us many times. We have met his parents and have shared dinner with them, as well. What marvelous people they are! There is no describing what a great gift this is, that our Heavenly Father would guide this fine young man back into our lives when we so very much needed something to fill the hole that our own Joshua had left in his absence. We are doubly grateful that you were with us to share our great discovery and to see the evidence of how loving and merciful our Heavenly Father truly is."

"Amen," Tamra said after he'd read that part a second time.

"We truly are blessed," Emily said. "All of us."

"We are indeed," Jess added. Little Michael made a happy noise from his little seat and Evelyn giggled. Under the circumstances, Jess figured life was pretty good. But he sure missed his father.

* * *

Tamra came awake with the aroma of food titillating her senses. She felt sure she was dreaming until she heard Jess chuckle and opened her eyes to see him holding a bed tray.

"Breakfast in bed, my love?" he asked.

"Oh, my," she said and laughed as she sat up against the head-board and tried to force her eyes to stay open. "Wow," she said, taking in the French toast, bacon, and orange juice, in front of her, complete with a red rose laying across the tray. "To what do I owe this terribly romantic occurrence?"

Jess chuckled. "You're joking, right?" She looked up at him, completely dumbfounded and he laughed. "Are you still too asleep to think clearly, or have you honestly forgotten?"

In a straight voice she said, "I know it's not our anniversary, because we already—"

"You *have* forgotten," he said and chuckled deeply.

"Forgotten what?" she demanded.

"It's your birthday!"

Tamra laughed. "It is?" She thought about it. "So it is. Nobody ever took notice of my birthday except you, so you can't expect me to remember such things."

"Well, it's a good thing you've got me around," he said and sat on the edge of the bed, talking with her while she ate. Once she was finished, he said, "Hurry and get showered and dressed. I have a surprise for you, and since I thought of it months ago, I just can't wait any longer. The anticipation is killing me, and it's a miracle that I've managed to hold out this long. So hurry."

Tamra laughed and hurried into the bathroom to shower. Once she was dressed and ready for the day, she found everyone in the kitchen. Jess was washing dishes with Evelyn standing on a chair beside him, helping. Emily was holding the baby.

"Well, happy birthday, my dear," Emily said.

"Thank you. So far, it's marvelous."

"As it should be," Jess said, "but it's only just begun. And as soon as I finish up here, I'll show you your surprise."

"I can't wait," Tamra said and sat at the table to leaf through a magazine that had been left there.

"You know, I was thinking," Jess said, "this really is an awfully big house."

"It certainly is," Emily added. "I think I lived here for years before I actually saw every room and knew how to find my way to all of them. Some rooms are shut off and haven't been used for years."

"Really?" Tamra said intrigued. "Come to think of it, there are probably a lot of rooms I've never seen."

"Well, the house was originally built by a man who was very much trying to compete with his neighbor, who was the son of an English lord with a great deal of money. That house was burned to the ground, and the second house—this one—was built as an exact imitation."

"I recall that story from Jess Davies' journals," Jess said.

"And Alexa's," Tamra added, referring to the original Jess's wife.

"Amazing. And I bet there are rooms in this house that haven't changed much—if any—since Jess and Alexa were first living here in the 1880s."

"They're probably dustier," Tamra said and they all laughed.

Jess finished up the dishes and dried his hands, grinning as he said, "Okay, now you can see your surprise."

"I'm waiting on the edge of my seat," Tamra said.

Jess comically looked at the chair she was sitting on and said, "It doesn't look like it."

Tamra chuckled. "Just a figure of speech."

Jess took her hand and pulled her to her feet. "Okay, close your eyes."

"Oh, not that kind of surprise," Tamra said.

"Oh, you must close your eyes," Emily insisted.

"Mama close her eyes," Evelyn said to Jess.

"Okay, they're closed," Tamra said and Jess led her by the hand into the hall.

"Don't cheat," Jess said.

"I promise," Tamra laughed softly. After traversing what seemed endless hallways, she asked, "Are we there yet? Or are you taking me in circles?"

"Yes, and yes," Jess said and she could hear him opening a door that actually squeaked on its hinges.

"Which means?"

"Yes, I was taking you in circles . . . just a little bit. And yes, we are there."

Tamra heard Emily laugh and Evelyn did the same, as if she sensed the excitement.

"Okay, you can open your eyes now," Jess said. "And we did dust in here, in case you're wondering."

Tamra slowly opened them, first noting the brightness of the room with the drapes pulled back. She immediately knew she had never been in this room before, and now she understood the purpose of the conversation in the kitchen that she had believed had no connection to her *surprise.* She felt baffled until Jess turned her around and right in front of her, impossible to overlook, was a grand piano, with a large white bow and a red rose laying over the top. Tamra gasped and turned to Jess, silently questioning what this meant. He grinned like a child and said, "You told me once that you had always wanted piano lessons as a child, and you never got them. So I have arranged for a fine piano teacher to come here once a week and give you lessons."

Tamra laughed. "Really?"

"Really," Jess said and she threw her arms around him.

"And of course you needed a piano for piano lessons, so . . ."

"You didn't go out and buy this piano just because—"

"No, I didn't buy it," Jess said. "I inherited it, and now it's yours. It came with the house."

Tamra drew back from Jess, asking Emily, "Does someone in the family play? I didn't know that—"

"Well, some of the girls had lessons, but none of them were ever passionate about it. This is the piano they used, but . . . it was here long before then."

"We had it tuned and put in good order," Jess said.

Tamra felt something tingle inside of her as she pressed a hand over the piano and asked, "So, who exactly was the piano purchased for?" With her fascination for Jess's ancestors, she couldn't help hoping that perhaps his grandmother, or perhaps a great-aunt, had owned and used this piano.

"I told you," Jess said. "It came with the house."

Tamra looked at him skeptically. "But the house was built in the 1880s."

"That's right," Jess said. "And since you've read all of my ancestors' journals, you should know that this is the room where Alexandra Byrnehouse-Davies came to play the piano." Tamra put a hand over her mouth as the tingling increased. "The piano was here before she got here, but she was the first to play it, and she played it a great deal through her life." He put his hand over Tamra's where it rested on the piano. "This was *her* piano, and I have a feeling she would be pleased to know that now it is yours. It's been kept in good repair, and should last for many years yet."

Tamra pushed her arms around Jess again and wept. Jess exchanged a smile with his mother while he held her. "I can't believe it," Tamra finally said, wiping her face with her hand. "I never imagined anything so incredible." She sniffled loudly and admired the piano. "Oh, I *did* always want to play. *Always!* There have been so many times when it's just ached in me, but then I started to believe that I was just too old."

"Never," Emily said.

Tamra began her lessons the very next day, and found herself drawn to the piano every spare minute she had. She would take Evelyn and the baby to the music room, and a collection of toys and baby paraphernalia took up permanent residence in the room so that she could practice and keep the children close by. She liked her teacher, and even more she loved the sense of fulfillment that came to her just to have her hands on the keys, even though her playing was still childlike. For her, the piano was like the icing on a beautiful cake that represented the life she had found with Jess. She simply couldn't imagine being any happier than this.

Chapter Four

Tamra had her hands deep in the meatloaf she was mixing when the phone rang. Jess was at work and Emily had gone into town to do some shopping. She hurried to wipe off her hands with a paper towel but Evelyn grabbed the phone before she could get to it. Washing her hands under the tap she heard Evelyn say somewhat indignantly, "Tamra is my mama."

"Thank you, Evelyn," Tamra said, taking the phone from her. "Hello."

"Hey, Tam," a male voice said, and it took her a moment to place its familiarity. Her brother had never called her before.

"Mel?" She laughed softly. "I can't believe it. What's up?"

"Well," he said, "the news isn't good."

"What's happened?" she asked, knowing it could only be about their mother. Mel had no contact with anyone else that Tamra even knew.

"Mom had a stroke, and—"

"Good heavens," Tamra gasped. "Is it bad?"

"Yeah, it's pretty bad."

"But doesn't it take time to know how bad it really is and—"

"Well, it happened a couple of weeks ago, but—"

"And you didn't call me until now?" She couldn't help being frustrated. "Well . . . is she going to be all right? Is she in the hospital or—"

"She's still in the hospital, but they can't keep her there much longer. I guess she's going to have to go to a nursing home. I sure can't take care of her. I got the bar to run, and even if I didn't, I'm no nursemaid. Anyway, you know she doesn't have any money, so—"

"Wait a minute," Tamra interrupted, trying not to feel *really* angry. "Tell me how she is. How bad is it?"

"Well . . . she's completely lost use of one side of her body. She can't do much of anything for herself, and I can't understand what she says at all."

Tamra sighed and squeezed her eyes shut as hot tears burned into them. She'd never been close to her mother, and more often than not, she had felt little better than contempt toward her. But she was still Tamra's mother. And this was truly tragic.

Tamra listened as her brother rambled on for several minutes. It became evident that his visits to the hospital had been few, and he was content to take over the bar where he had worked with his mother for years. He seemed to take the attitude that Myrna's life was basically over, and he was ready to write her off now. He was ready to put her into whatever nursing home the government might provide. She finally got off the phone and stared at the wall for several minutes before she forced herself to finish the meatloaf and get it into the oven. The baby woke up and Tamra went upstairs to feed him, taking Evelyn along, then she took both the children with her into the boys' home, through a door that joined it to the house. She unlocked it with a key and locked it again before she moved quietly through the halls and down the stairs to the main office.

"Hello, Madge," she said to the woman seated at the desk there. "Is Jess with anyone or—"

"He's just going over some paperwork, I think," she said and stood to take the baby. "Do I get to hold this little one while you see him?" She laughed. "He looks so much like his daddy."

Little Michael smiled, making Madge laugh again. Madge then guided Evelyn to a chair where she could sit and play with some odd toys that she kept on her desk.

"Thank you," Tamra said and slipped into Jess's office.

"Oh, hi," he said, glancing up with a smile, then his countenance fell. "What's wrong?"

"It's my mother," Tamra said, her voice shaky. Jess shot to his feet and moved around the desk. "She had a stroke. It's bad. I just . . . don't know what to do."

The tears came again, but this time they were absorbed by Jess's shoulder. When she had calmed down Jess guided her to a chair, saying gently, "Now, tell me everything you know." She repeated her conversation with her brother, and the frustration she felt at his apparent indifference and desire to simply put his mother away and be free of the problem.

While Tamra was stewing over her anger toward her brother, Jess said, "Maybe we should bring her to live with us."

She sucked in her breath and looked up at him until he touched her chin to close her mouth. "Do you have any idea what you're saying?"

"I know that she's your mother. And I know that we have enough money at our disposal to do whatever is best for her—and you. She could live with us, and we could hire someone to help care for her. Or if you prefer, we could arrange to get her in a care facility close by so that you could see her as much as you like, and you would know that she was being well cared for."

Tamra watched her husband in amazement, grateful beyond words for his generosity and his willingness to open his home. She felt she had to point out, "My mother was difficult and horrible when she wasn't crippled. Would you really want her in your home?"

"Like I said, I want what's best. And if that's what's best, I'm sure we could live with it."

Tamra thought about that for a minute and had to admit, "She may be crippled but she still has a brain. Perhaps I need to see what she wants."

"That's a good point. And if she prefers to stay in her hometown, we can at least contribute to getting her in a decent place, and we can keep close touch with those who are caring for her. There's nothing better we could do with our money than care for family and friends who are in need. If she's as bad off as you say, she's not going to be spending any handouts on booze and cigarettes."

"No," Tamra said sadly, "I'm afraid her smoking and drinking days are done. Rhea's husband died of a stroke and . . . Good heavens. I bet Rhea doesn't know. Mel wouldn't have told her."

"Not likely," Jess agreed.

Rhea was Myrna's sister, who lived in Sydney. Tamra had always been closer to Rhea than her own mother, and she was the reason Tamra had come to Australia in the first place.

"Okay," Tamra stood up, "I'm going to call Rhea, and . . . if it's all right with you, I'm going to Minneapolis to see my mother and find out what she needs—and what she wants."

"Alone?" Jess asked, alarmed.

"Well, I have to take Michael with me since I'm nursing. You're too swamped with work to go, and your mother will have to watch Evelyn, so . . . I guess I'm going alone, unless I can talk Rhea into going with me."

"Well, I'd feel better about that than sending you alone with a baby."

"I'll see what I can do."

Tamra collected the children from Madge, but she had to bribe Evelyn to get her to leave Madge's desk with all of its fascinating decor. Back at the house she called Rhea and explained the situation, but her aunt was unusually quiet and offered no opinion whatsoever. Emily returned from town just as the meatloaf was coming out of the oven. Tamra shared her burden with her mother-in-law while they were waiting for Jess to come in for supper. As always, Emily's advice was sound. "The Lord knows what's best. Pray about it and the Spirit will guide you. As far as bringing your mother to live here, I certainly don't have a problem with it. We have the space, and like Jess said, we can hire someone to help care for her so that it's not a burden. But it could be a learning experience for all of us."

Tamra shook her head. "You don't know my mother. She's vulgar and crude. She's mean and obnoxious."

"And she's crippled and barely able to talk at all."

"Well, she'll still find a way to be crude and obnoxious."

"Pray about it," Emily said, putting her hand over Tamra's on the table.

That night Tamra prayed long and hard about it. She fell asleep praying and woke up doing the same. She called the hospital where her mother was staying and spoke with a nurse that had worked with her a great deal. At least she understood better what she was dealing with, but she felt even more discouraged. Bringing her to their home just didn't feel right, although she couldn't pinpoint any specific reason. Perhaps at some level she simply didn't *want* her mother living in her home. But leaving her in Minneapolis didn't feel right either. So, she kept praying and the following day she felt even more confused.

Rhea phoned late in the afternoon and immediately sounded more like herself. "I'm so sorry, honey, about the way I was on the phone the other day. As soon as you said that word 'stroke' my memories just shot back to losing Art and I just felt kind of . . . frozen. But I'm getting it together now and I've been thinking, and well . . . I think I would like to bring Myrna here to live with me, if it's all right with her, of course." Tamra refrained from gasping and simply listened. "You know I don't need to work since I've got the money Art left me. I've got plenty of space and it wouldn't take much to make the house accessible for a wheelchair. I know she can be ornery, but I know how to handle her, and well . . . the thing is, I've just been feeling for weeks now like I need some purpose and meaning to my life. What better thing could I do than take care of my sister? I'd like to do it, or at least give it a good try. If it gets to be too much, we might have to come up with another solution, but . . . the problem, honey, is that I just don't have the resources to go and get her and while I've got money enough to support myself, I'm not sure I could afford what it would cost to actually take care of her. So, I guess what I'm saying is that I'll take care of her if you'll foot the bill."

"I think that sounds wonderful," Tamra said tearfully. "It's the perfect solution, as far as I can see. I'll talk with Jess, but I'm sure he'll agree, since he already offered to pay for her care."

"Well, that sounds like the good Lord's looking out for me and my sister, in spite of our shortcomings. You're a great blessing to us, honey, and it has nothing to do with all that money you married into. Although, you certainly got yourself a good catch."

"Yes, I did," Tamra said, "and it has nothing to do with that money I married into."

They laughed together and Tamra ended the call before she hurried to the boys' home to tell Jess the good news while Emily stayed near the children. He was pleased with the solution, and equally pleased that Rhea would fly to Minneapolis with her. Emily was eager to look out for Evelyn while Jess was working, and the flight arrangements were quickly made. Jess took a day and flew Tamra and the baby to Sydney, where they met Rhea at the airport.

Tamra found it more difficult than she'd expected to say good-bye to Jess. This would be the longest they'd been separated since they'd been married. "I'll be back in less than a week," she said, but it seemed like forever. While Rhea held the baby, Jess kissed Tamra long and hard, pulling her completely into his arms.

"I'll miss you so much," he said, pressing a hand over her face. He kissed her again. "Take good care of my son."

"I will," she promised, "and you take good care of my daughter."

"Of course." He smiled. "Call me."

"I promise," she said and he kissed her once more.

"Okay, I think that's good," Rhea said. "They're going to take off without us if you two keep this up."

Tamra reluctantly boarded the plane and became distracted by trying to keep little Michael happy. "This is his second flight to the States," Tamra reminded Rhea, "and he's not even four months old."

"Well, at least he's not wanting to crawl or toddle around, then you'd really hate this."

"Yes," Tamra chuckled, "I'm sure I would."

Michael proved to be almost as good as he'd been on their first flight to America. They arrived in Minneapolis late and got a room. After a good night's sleep they had some breakfast and went straight to the hospital where Myrna had been since her stroke. Tamra and Rhea both cried when they saw her, but the amazing thing was that Myrna cried too. Tamra couldn't recall ever seeing her mother cry; she'd always been too stubborn and ornery to cry.

Until that moment Tamra had forgotten that her father's mother had been unable to communicate due to a stroke. Recalling how she had once had long one-sided conversations with her grandmother, Tamra sat beside her mother and showed her the baby and told her all about what was going on in her life. Tamra listened closely as Myrna attempted to speak, and she was able to make out, "I'm a grandma," as she pointed at the baby with her good hand.

"That's right, you are," Tamra said.

Myrna muttered, "Beautiful baby," three times before Tamra understood, then she agreed wholeheartedly.

"He looks like his father, don't you think?" Tamra said then continued talking, telling her mother how they would like to take her to Australia to live with her sister. "What do you think about that, Mother?" Tamra asked, looking closely into her eyes. "We feel it would be a whole lot better than a care facility, but we need to know what *you* want."

Myrna mumbled something that neither Tamra nor Rhea could understand and Tamra reworded the question, "Do you want to live with Rhea?"

Myrna's response was a definite yes, with a sparkle in her eye that seemed to say she was pleased and relieved by the idea. Tamra felt heartsick to think of how Myrna had likely been dreading being put away in some low-budget facility with no friends or family around to offer support. She felt deeply grateful to be in a position to help her mother, and for Rhea's willingness to open her home.

Through the next few days, Tamra had a chance to visit with her father and stepmother, who lived in the same city. They were thrilled with the opportunity to see the baby and spend some time with him, and they eagerly watched out for him while Tamra and Rhea spent a great deal of time at the hospital, learning all they would need to know to care for Myrna and safely transport her to Australia. She gradually began to understand what Myrna was saying more easily, which could be a detriment at times when her bad language came through.

The return flight was long and difficult, but the flight attendants were helpful and patient. At times Myrna was pleasant and appreciative, but at others her familiar characteristics would come through and Tamra was amazed at how belligerent she could be. She was grateful that only she and Rhea could understand much of what Myrna said—especially when her typical colorful language began to fly.

Tamra felt such exhausted relief when they met Jess in the Sydney airport. While Rhea held the baby she flew into his arms and heard Rhea say to Myrna, "They're kissing again. Sweet isn't it?"

"Sweet," Myrna muttered.

Tamra took notice of the book in Jess's hand, "Still reading, I see."

"Yeah, I'm on the fourth book now."

"And what do you think?" she asked.

"It's incredible," he said. "I only wish I had read them when he was around to talk about the stories."

"No regrets," Tamra said, pressing her hands to his chest. "He knows you're reading them now, and that's good enough."

Jess smiled at his wife, so glad to see her again. As his attention was drawn reluctantly away from her, he got down on one knee beside the wheelchair and took both Myrna's hands into his. "Hello, Mother," he said. "It's good to see you again. I hope you'll enjoy my homeland. And if this sister of yours doesn't feed you enough chocolate, you just let me know and I'll bring you to stay with me for a while."

Myrna's eyes smiled and Jess moved behind the chair to push it once he'd held his son and fussed over him for a few minutes. "I do believe he's changed," Jess commented while Tamra walked beside him.

"Yes, infants change quickly."

"Your mother seems in pretty good spirits," he said more softly.

"Don't let her fool you," Tamra whispered. "She's still got a foul temper and a foul mouth, but Rhea's pretty good at keeping her in line. We've arranged for a nurse to come and stay with them for the first few days, and then to stop by each day and make sure they're doing all right, and then, of course, Rhea will need to get out regularly so she doesn't go insane. But I think we've got it all under control."

"Great," Jess said, then he escorted them and all of their baggage and equipment to a new van he had purchased for Rhea to drive. It had a wheelchair lift on the side so that Myrna could be put in and out easily.

Rhea squealed with excitement and said, "I was wondering what we were going to do about that."

Jess, Tamra, and little Michael spent the night at Rhea's to help get a routine underway, and they didn't leave until the hired nurse arrived the next day. Tamra found it difficult to say good-bye to Rhea and her mother, but they promised to keep in close touch by phone and email.

"Now, you let us know if you need anything," Jess told Rhea, "anything at all." He knelt beside Myrna and added, "One of these days I'm going to come and get you and take you for a ride in my plane, and you can come and see where we live and stay with us for a while. Would you like that?"

She indicated that she would and they finished their good-byes. They took a cab to the airport and were soon on their way home, with Jess at the controls.

"I sure missed you, Mrs. Hamilton," he said with fervor.

"I missed you, too," she said, reaching for his hand.

Tamra was thrilled to finally arrive home. It was so good to see Evelyn and Emily, and she made a visit to Susan Murphy, since she still wasn't feeling well, and the doctors couldn't quite pinpoint what the problem was.

The following morning Tamra stayed in bed until past noon, only coming awake enough to feed the baby when he needed it. Jess got up with Michael and once he'd gone to work, Emily just brought him to Tamra when he needed to be fed. Tamra got up and ate but still felt exhausted.

"This jet lag is killing me," she said and with Emily's offer to watch the children she went back to bed. But three days later, she had to admit to Emily, "Maybe this is more than jet lag. Maybe I'm coming down with something."

"And maybe you're just exhausted," Emily said. "It hasn't been that many months since you had a baby, you've been getting up for night feedings since then, and that trip was anything but restful."

"Maybe," Tamra said and told Emily how grateful she was to have the children's grandmother in the house before she went to bed in the middle of the afternoon.

Rhea called that evening to tell them that things were actually going well and she was enjoying her new self-appointed calling in life to care for her sister. They had settled into a routine and were getting along relatively well.

The following morning, Tamra woke up feeling sick to her stomach. Certain that she *was* coming down with something, she stayed even closer to bed than she had the past couple of days. She felt a little better as the day wore on, but still exhausted. The next morning she felt sick again and the thought flitted through her brain that if she didn't know better she would think she was pregnant. Then she gasped. "Know better than what!" she spouted into the vacant room. Then she rushed down the hall to the nursery where Emily was rocking Michael.

"Oh, good morning," Emily said. "Jess went to work early. He didn't want to wake you."

Tamra blurted, "I thought a woman couldn't get pregnant while she was nursing a baby."

Emily looked more amused than surprised. She snorted a little laugh. "That's what some people say, but I know differently. That's why Amee and Alexa are fourteen months apart."

Tamra pressed a hand over her stomach, hoping to quell her increasing nausea. "Why didn't you tell me that?" Tamra demanded, but not unkindly.

Emily chuckled. "You didn't ask." Her smile deepened. "Are you trying to tell me something?"

Tamra sunk into a chair. "I'm afraid I am. I mean . . . I think I am."

"Nauseated?"

"Yes."

"I have to admit that I've wondered if that wasn't the reason you've been so tired."

"And you didn't say anything?" Tamra asked.

Emily chuckled again. "I'm just the mother-in-law," she said with a little smirk. "I don't want to be a *meddling* mother-in-law."

"You couldn't be that if you tried," Tamra said, then she hurried to the bathroom to be overtaken by dry heaves.

After Emily brought her some dry toast and herb tea, Tamra's stomach finally calmed down. And that's when she started to cry.

"You *must* be pregnant," Emily said, sitting beside her and taking her hand.

"And what if I am?" Tamra cried. "How can I feel this way while I have an infant to take care of—and a four year old—and Jess is so busy with work and he needs my help and . . ." Her words faded into tears that were out of character for Tamra in facing a crisis.

Emily put an arm around her, saying gently, "I'll tell you how you do it. One day at a time; that's how. I did it, and you can do it too. But you have something I didn't have."

"What's that?" Tamra asked, wiping at her tears.

"First of all, you have a husband who is actually sensitive to your needs and helps with the children whenever possible, and he will not begrudge the extra time he may have to put in at work because you're not able to help him. And secondly, you have a mother under your own roof. I'll do everything I can to help you and we'll get through this together."

"Oh, you're right," Tamra said, hugging Emily tightly. "I am truly blessed. Forgive me for complaining. I just . . ."

"I know. It's a shock when you haven't planned on it, but I believe babies come when they're meant to. Why don't we go into town and have lunch out, and you can get a test to be sure. Getting out might do you some good."

Tamra agreed and she had to admit that once she got some decent food in her stomach, it did feel good to get out. The test was definitely positive, and Emily spent their time at lunch trying to help Tamra deal with the shock that she would be having two babies barely more than a year apart. Tamra could only think how grateful she was to have a mother-in-law who was also her best friend.

When they returned home, Tamra had Emily drop her off at the main door to the boys' home, then she took the children to the house with her. Tamra took a deep breath and went inside, knowing that Jess needed to be told right away. She couldn't get through one more minute of feeling this way without his knowing.

"Hello, Madge," Tamra said without enthusiasm.

"Ooh, you don't look so good. You okay?"

"A little under the weather," she said. "Nothing to worry about. Is Jess—"

"Go on in. He's on the phone but he's been on that call forever. He'll likely welcome an excuse to get off."

Tamra went quietly in and closed the door behind her. Jess looked up and smiled. He held up a finger to indicate he would just be a minute. She sat down and waited, realizing she felt nauseous again. Jess said, "Yes," and "Okay," a number of times before he said, "Well, that sounds great. We'll be in touch. Something's just come up and I need to go." Then it took him another five minutes to finally get off.

"What a pleasant distraction," he said after he'd hung up the phone. Then his brow furrowed. "But you don't look so good. Maybe you should see a doctor or—"

"I already did," she said. "Your mother took me while we were in town."

"And?" he asked, his concern evident.

Tamra concluded there was no way to say it except to just say it. She felt too awful to come up with some clever way to let him know. But she couldn't hold the tears back as she simply said, "I'm pregnant."

Jess looked momentarily stunned before he said, "You're kidding."

"No, I'm not kidding, Jess."

"But . . . I thought that couldn't happen while . . ."

"Well, so did I. But maybe we should have thought to ask someone who actually knew the truth—like your mother. She said that's why Amee and Alexa are so close together."

Jess leaned back in his chair and let out a breathy chuckle. "Wow," he said. Then he laughed. And Tamra burst into audible tears.

"What's wrong?" he asked, moving to kneel beside her. "Aren't you happy about this? Don't you want another baby?"

"Of course I do. I want as many of your babies as the Lord thinks I can handle, but . . . I just hadn't expected this . . . so soon. I don't feel recovered from the last time. And I already feel so . . . exhausted and . . . sick. How can I take care of a baby and feel the way I felt last time? And how can I take care of two babies?"

"Mother and I will be there," he said. "It will be all right."

"And what will you do without my being able to help you here?" She motioned with her hand to indicate his work. "There's simply no way I can do it with the way I feel."

"I'll manage," he said. "We'll just take it one day at a time, and everything will be all right." He held her tightly and kissed her brow and she believed him. He laughed again and she looked up at him, realizing he was happy about this, and she wondered why she couldn't share his enthusiasm. A rush of nausea reminded her of the reasons.

Jess walked her back to the house and straight to bed with Emily's blessing. "I'll bring the baby when he needs to be fed," she insisted as they walked past the kitchen on their way to the stairs.

Jess tucked Tamra in and kissed her brow. "It's going to be all right," he said gently and she wanted to believe him. But over the next several days, Jess was so busy with his work that she hardly saw him except at supper. She was always too sick to share breakfast with him, and he ate lunch in the boys' home. Murphy's mother took a bad turn and Emily felt like she needed to be with her as much as she could. Tamra insisted that she could watch her own children. Emily had done it alone, and many women did. But as Tamra lay on the nursery floor watching Evelyn play, and trying to keep Michael happy, she couldn't even imagine how she would get through the length of her pregnancy. And when she thought of two more car seats, a double stroller, two cribs, and the work and worry such things represented, she couldn't hold back the tears. Of course, she knew that pregnancy made her more emotional, and she was likely blowing it all out of proportion, but she simply couldn't help how she felt.

And then Murphy called Jess in the middle of the night from the hospital. Tamra was grateful that Jess had answered, certain she couldn't take any more drama.

"It's my mum," Murphy said and Jess could clearly hear the panic in his voice.

"Slow down and tell me what's wrong, Murph," Jess said.

"She's not doing well at all. I brought her in a while ago. The doc says there's nothing more they can do; they're not even sure what's wrong." His voice broke. "I can't do this alone, Jess. I know it's the middle of the night, but . . ."

"I'll be on my way in five minutes," he said. "Don't worry about it. I'm glad you called."

Jess hung up the phone and pulled on his jeans while he repeated to Tamra what Murphy had said. "I don't know how long I'll be," he said, pulling on a T-shirt.

"Is there anything I can do?" Tamra asked, leaning up on one elbow.

"Yes, find another priesthood holder and have him meet me at the hospital. You can start with our home teachers." He pulled on his boots. "Tell him I've got the oil; just come."

"I'll do it," she said and sat up. "You be careful and let me know what's going on."

"I will," he said, pausing in his rush to give her a fervent kiss. "I love you, Mrs. Hamilton," he said and rushed from the room.

At the hospital, Jess found Susan barely clinging to life, and Murphy crumbling over the prospect of losing his mother. He felt as if death was becoming some kind of epidemic with people he cared for. Tonya sat holding Susan's hand; the patient was blatantly weak and moaning softly with a restlessness that indicated she was in pain. Trying to not draw Susan's attention, Jess struggled to get Murphy to calm down. He'd only been there about twenty minutes when Brother Burton, one of their home teachers, showed up to help give Susan a blessing. Jess explained to Murphy what they were going to do. He said nothing but seemed pleased. As Jess laid his hands on Susan's head, attempting to feel the words he needed to say, he was surprised to have them come so quickly and clearly. He was doubly surprised to hear himself repeat a concept that his mother had shared with Sean soon after Joshua's death. Susan was told that the length of her life on this earth had been predetermined, and she would not leave until that time came. Jess found himself wondering if that time would be soon, and a moment later he heard himself promising her that she would return to the home where she had raised her family and enjoy time there with her loved ones. When the blessing was complete, Jess stepped back and looked up to see Murphy staring at him, his eyes wide with astonishment. He was distracted when Susan reached for his hand, looking up at her son with hope in her weak countenance. Murphy gently kissed his mother then abruptly left the room. Jess followed him, glancing toward Brother Burton who seemed to understand as he began a quiet conversation with Tonya.

In the hall, Murphy spoke to Jess, his voice tinged with anger, "How can you possibly know something like that?"

Jess answered calmly, "I just said what I felt like I was supposed to say."

"The doctors have said there's nothing they can do. How can you give her false hope like that?"

"Her or you?" Jess asked and Murphy's expression showed defensiveness before he looked away abruptly. "And how can you be so sure that it's false? I don't know what the Lord's will is for your mother, Murph. I do know that it wouldn't hurt for us to exert a little faith on her behalf."

"Like you did for your father?" Murphy countered angrily.

Jess felt as if he'd been slapped. He took a deep breath and said firmly, "It was my father's time to go, Murphy. I know that beyond any doubt. If it's your mother's time to go, there's nothing anyone on this earth can do about it. And if it's not, she'll get better."

"You just told her she would go back home."

Jess just repeated, "I said what I felt like I was supposed to say. It's in the Lord's hands, Murph."

Murphy looked angry as he went back into his mother's room. Jess followed him in and nearly bumped into him when he stopped abruptly. For a moment it was difficult to tell if Susan was dead or asleep. He heard Murphy draw a sharp breath just before Tonya smiled at him and said softly, "She's resting better than she has since we got here." The monitors attached to her proved that she was breathing evenly.

Brother Burton visited a few minutes longer then left. Jess called home to give them a report then he stayed and sat quietly with Tonya and Murphy while Susan slept. Nothing was said between them, and he sensed that Murphy was angry, or at the very least confused and upset, but Jess hoped that his staying, even in silence, would prove his devotion to this good man who had always been a true friend.

Jess finally left before dawn at Murphy's insistence. "You need to get some sleep, and since I'm not coming to work today, somebody's got to see that the horses get fed."

"The hands will take care of it. Don't worry about it."

"Thanks for coming," Murphy said and shook his hand, but there was a definite tension between them.

Returning to the station, Jess checked in with the stable hands that were on duty and was assured that they would see that the important work was taken care of. He checked in at the boys' home where the day was just getting started, and the staff promised to cover for him while he got some rest. He went into the house and found Tamra resting with the baby sleeping at her side. Evelyn was on the floor nearby with puzzles, coloring books, and doll clothes scattered everywhere. Tamra reached for Jess's hand. He plopped his head onto the pillow and she eased closer to him.

"How are they?" she asked quietly.

"Susan was still resting when I left. Murphy's not doing well at all."

"Oh, I hope she'll be all right," Tamra said. "She's such a sweet woman. And poor Murphy; bless his heart."

Jess held Tamra as she started to cry, but when her emotion became steadily worse, he eased back putting his hands to her shoulders. "Hey, what's wrong?" he asked, pushing her hair back from her face.

"Nothing's wrong, really, but . . . everything's wrong, and . . . I just don't want to be pregnant." She heard Jess gasp and realized how that must have sounded. She hurried to clarify, "I want this baby, Jess, I do. I just don't want to go through this again. I feel so much more tired and sick than I did before, and it wasn't real great before."

"Well, you're likely still run down from having that last baby."

"Exactly. I just don't feel ready to do this again. I know I should be grateful to have your mother here to help me. And I know I should be grateful that you're a good husband and father and you help me when you're here; some women don't have that, and I *am* grateful; truly. But . . . you're so busy, and . . . the thing is . . . I want to be helping you in the boys' home. I want to take care of my own children. I want to help Murphy and Susan and anybody else around here that needs help. I don't want to be helpless and waited on. I want to take care of my own children," she repeated.

Emily's voice came from the open doorway. "Forgive me; I couldn't help overhearing." She moved toward the bed, saying gently, "The last thing I want to be is an intrusive mother-in-law. The two of you are perfectly capable of handling your struggles on your own. If my help with the children is causing a problem for you, Tamra, I want you to talk to me about it."

Tamra took a moment to think about this in relation to what she'd just said. Then she panicked. "Oh, no! That's not what I meant. I appreciate your help with the children. I'm so grateful to have you here that I almost feel guilty. I only wish that I felt good enough to be completely responsible for the children and . . ." Tears overtook her again.

Emily sat on the edge of the bed and took Tamra's hand. "May I tell you what I think?" she asked and Tamra nodded. "I consider your family being with me in this home a huge blessing. I could have never gotten through Michael's death without you and Jess and the children here. After putting so much effort into caring for Michael, I feel out of sorts. My hands feel empty and useless. I don't like to see you so miserable, Tamra, but I must admit that I'm grateful for an excuse to feel needed. Still, the last thing I want to do is step beyond my bounds and interfere with your mothering. You're a wonderful mother and wife, and it's your rightful place to say how this family should be governed. So, if it's all right with you, I will help when and where I can with the children so that you can rest and get past this difficult point in your pregnancy. When you want to be alone with your children, or I'm getting too involved, just let me know. You won't hurt my feelings."

Tamra threw her arms around Emily's neck and cried harder. She pulled back, wiping at her face. "I'm sorry I'm such a bawl baby. I don't think I've ever cried so much in my life."

"It's all right. It's really true what they say about those pregnancy hormones making you more emotional. Better that you cry it out than hold it inside." Emily drew a long breath. "And there's one more thing I'd like to say, if I may."

"Of course," Tamra said.

"Serving others is a part of the cycle of life, Tamra. You've lived a difficult life. You fought your way out of a horrific childhood, served a mission with no family support, and you made a good life for yourself. I have seen you selflessly give and serve since the day I met you. If I was looking out for your children while you were being a lazy freeloader watching soaps and eating chocolates, I would certainly have a problem with that. But if I can help you get through this difficult time, I am only too glad to help." She tightened her hold on Tamra's hand, and her voice cracked. "Helping you is a blessing to me, Tamra. I am so grateful to have you and your family in my home. You are not a burden to me."

"Or to me," Jess said, pressing a kiss to Tamra's wet cheek.

"There was a time," Emily said, "when I was down flat in bed for many weeks with a pregnancy."

"Boy, I remember that," Jess said.

"But years pass and it just doesn't seem that significant anymore," she added. "At least the illness of pregnancy has some great results. Many people are down with chronic illness that has no purpose or meaning."

"That's true," Tamra said. She sniffled loudly and Jess handed her a tissue. "Thank you. I think I feel better. I truly am grateful to have you here. Both of you." She touched Jess's face and kissed him quickly. "You raised a fine son, here," she said to Emily.

Emily smiled. "So much like his father." She stood and brushed her hands together. "I think I'll go cook some brunch. Why don't we all go down and have a decent meal, and then maybe we should all take a nap."

"Brunch sounds wonderful," Jess said.

After a quick shower, Tamra found Jess sitting at the kitchen table with Michael on his lap, and Emily helping Evelyn wash up since she'd already finished eating. They sat down and had a blessing after Evelyn had run off to play. The French toast and bacon smelled good, but Tamra felt little appetite.

"You should eat," Jess said gently, noting how she mostly pushed her food around her plate.

"I'm just afraid I'll end up losing it in half an hour," Tamra admitted

"Hey," Emily said, "didn't the doctor prescribe something for you last time that helped?"

"He did actually," Tamra said with a note of hope. "I'd actually forgotten. I remember now. I was horribly ill until after my first appointment when he gave me a prescription for the nausea, and one for the heartburn. It didn't completely go away, but it did help immensely. Oh, Emily, you're a genius."

Emily just chuckled. "I'll call the doctor as soon as we're finished eating and see if we can get something called in. Then Evelyn and I can go into town later and pick it up. If there's anything else you need—anything you're craving, for instance—just let me know before then and I can . . ."

A knock at the side door interrupted. Jess rose and went into the hall to answer it. He was startled to see Murphy standing there, and the stunned look on his face left Jess certain that he was about to hear of Susan's death in the hours since he'd left the hospital. Before Jess could find the words to ask, Murphy said with a quavering voice, "She's going to be all right. She woke up feeling fine . . . asked for something to eat. They can't find anything wrong with her. She can come home tomorrow."

Jess couldn't hold back a hearty laugh as he hugged Murphy tightly. "That's great news!" Jess said and found Murphy holding onto their embrace while tears streamed out of him. "It's okay," Jess muttered more softly.

"I thought I was going to lose her."

"I know," Jess said.

Murphy finally eased back and pulled a bandanna out of his pocket to wipe his tears. He looked into Jess's eyes and said, "The prayer you said for her . . . it was a miracle."

"It was the power of the priesthood," Jess said.

Murphy looked as if he'd like to ask a thousand questions, and Jess was eager to answer them. But he also looked like he might fall over. "Come in," Jess urged. "You could use something to eat, I'm sure."

Murphy allowed Jess to guide him into the kitchen where Jess repeated the good news and the women expressed their joy at Susan's miraculous recovery.

"Sit down," Jess said, "you must be starving."

"There's plenty," Emily insisted.

"Thank you," Murphy said, seeming dazed.

Jess put a plate in front of him with a fair helping of French toast and bacon. But he'd only taken a couple of bites when he put down his fork and looked directly at Jess. "When I thought she wasn't going to make it, I kept thinking about your dad's funeral. There was such a great feeling there. And I remembered . . . when you spoke, you talked about that life after death stuff . . . and . . ." Huge tears rose in his eyes and his chin quivered. "I know that eventually I *will* lose my mother and . . . I just have to know . . . Do you really believe that's true, Jess?"

Tamra felt Emily reach for her hand beneath the table and they both squeezed tightly. They were witnessing a potential miracle here, and they both knew it.

"Yes, Murphy," Jess put a hand on his shoulder and looked into his eyes, "I do. In fact, it's not just belief. I know. I know it's true." Jess leaned a little closer and his voice lowered. "I want to share something with you that I've told no one except my immediate family members. It was a sacred experience for me, and not something I take lightly or talk about freely, but I feel that I should tell you."

Murphy nodded eagerly with anticipation in his moist eyes.

"Even though you weren't at the church meeting where it took place, you know that we have a tradition of blessing our babies to officially give them a name." Murphy nodded again. "We blessed little Michael the Sunday after my father's funeral. All of the men in the family and some of our close friends, who all hold the priesthood, were gathered in the circle with our right hands holding the baby, and our left hands on each other's shoulders." Jess's voice quavered and lowered further. "I felt my father standing beside me, with his hand on my shoulder. I knew beyond any doubt that his spirit was with me." Murphy's eyes widened and Jess added with conviction, "I don't just suspect or believe that happened. I know it."

A marked light came into Murphy's eyes and Jess couldn't help thinking that the true miracle here was not necessarily Susan's recovery. He patted Murphy's hand where it rested on the table, certain they were on the brink of some great things happening in his life.

Chapter Five

They all stayed in the kitchen for another hour while Jess answered Murphy's questions, and Tamra ate dry toast instead of her breakfast. Emily slipped away only long enough to make that call to the doctor's office on Tamra's behalf. Murphy finally insisted that he needed to see to his work enough to keep everything afloat. Jess suspected that he needed some time to absorb everything that had been said. As Murphy headed for the door, Jess said, "Hey, Murph, after your mother gets home and things settle down a bit, I could arrange for some missionaries to come out here and teach you the whole plan and answer your every question. We can be there, too."

Murphy showed a wan smile. "I think I'd like that. Thanks."

"You're welcome," Jess said. "And don't be doing too much work, now. Nothing's going to fall apart while you take it slow for a few days. You look exhausted." Murphy nodded and left the house.

"I think I need to get some rest before I go back to work," Jess said and rose from the table. He kissed his wife and mother and hurried upstairs, falling asleep as soon as his head hit the pillow.

He woke up after three o'clock feeling better and freshened up before he checked on Tamra then went to the boys' home. He walked into the office to hear Madge say immediately, "Good, you're here. I was about to call you at the house. Harry called from downtown. They picked up a boy this morning that needs a place to go and he was hoping we'd have an opening."

"And what did you tell him?"

"Don't worry. I know the drill. I told him he had to talk to you."

"Thank you," he said. Through some difficult experiences in the past, they had taken up the policy to determine *openings* in the home depending on the situation with the boy. And Michael had taught Jess that the bottom line was gut instinct. If Jess felt good about it, then he'd take a boy on. If not, he would encourage the government to place the boy in foster care elsewhere.

"What do you know?" Jess asked as Madge followed him into his office and watched him leaf through his mail.

"He was removed from the home by the police this morning. Only child. School teacher filed an abuse report. One too many suspicious bruises. Typical story. Kid says he's clumsy and keeps falling down the stairs, but he's scared senseless when he talks about it."

"Good heavens," Jess said, tossing the mail to the desk. "I never stop being amazed at how people in this world treat their children. How old is he?"

"Six."

Jess looked at Madge sharply. They'd not had a boy that young in many years. It would require extra care and attention from the entire staff. "Get Harry on the phone."

A few minutes later Madge hollered from her office, "Pick it up; I got him."

"Harry," Jess said into the phone. They exchanged typical small talk then Harry gravely repeated what Madge had already told him. He added more perspective when he said, "The mother is technically in the home, but she's apparently so doped up on antidepressants and tranquilizers that the kid is pretty much left to his own resources when he's not in school. Teacher says he's a good student; just quiet. Father's a big-time lawyer."

"Ooh," Jess said, knowing what that meant, "then this kid comes with a potentially big-time court battle."

"Most likely. I think the mother is a victim here, as well. But she's not in any position to take care of a child—at least until she can straighten herself out—and she's obviously not protecting him from the abuse. So, what do you say? Have you got room for this one?"

Jess didn't even have to think about it. "Bring him out," he said. "I'll have a room ready."

Jess got off the phone and stuck his head out the door to where Madge and Shirley could both hear him. "Hey, is Joseph still in a room by himself?"

"Yes," Shirley answered.

"And how's he doing? Still good?"

"Great, yes," Shirley said. "Why?"

"We're getting a new kid. Put him with Joseph. He's going to need special care. I think he and Joseph will be good for each other."

"Cool," Madge said as if she'd been told she'd just won a great sum of money. "When will he be here?"

"As long as it takes for Harry to get the paperwork together and drive him out here. Shirley, will you see that everything's ready for him, and let the others know we have a new arrival coming? Madge, you help me get through whatever else is pressing so I can spend some time with him when he gets here."

"You got it," Madge said at the same time Shirley rose from her desk, saying, "I'm all over it."

While Madge was assessing the situation, Jess picked up the phone and dialed the house. Tamra answered. "Guess what?" he said. "We're getting a new boy. A six year old."

"Really?" she said in the same excited tone of voice Madge had used. "What's his name?"

"Nathan Gooding," he reported and briefly explained the situation. "I need to get back to work," he said. "Just wanted you to know, and . . . Oh, I love you, Mrs. Hamilton."

"I love you too, Jess," she said. "Thanks for being my Mr. Hamilton."

"A pleasure, my dear. I'll likely be late since I'm behind anyway."

"It's okay. You just take care of those boys. I'll see you later."

"Thank you. And tell my mother thank you, as well."

"I will," Tamra said and they both hung up.

Jess felt a nervous excitement anticipating the new arrival, while his thoughts were often drawn to Murphy and the miracles taking place. But seeing Susan come so close to death urged memories of losing Michael close to the surface until he had to force them back in order to accomplish all that he needed to do.

When Harry pulled up just outside the front doors of the boys' home, Jess was met in the main hall by Shirley, Madge, and the home's resident counselor, Ray. Jess felt something prick his heart when Harry walked through the front door holding a bag and Nathan Gooding's hand. The boy looked about the right height for a six year old, but definitely on the thin side. He had thick blond hair and big blue eyes—scared eyes. And across Nathan's right cheekbone was a nasty bruise that merged into a black eye; it was the kind of bruise Jess had seen on stable hands after they'd been engaged in fist fights. Madge seemed to have read his mind when she whispered near his side, "You don't get that kind of bruise from falling down stairs, now do you."

"No, ma'am," Jess replied quietly. Then he stepped toward Nathan and squatted in front of him. "You must be Nathan." The boy nodded timidly. "I'm Mr. Hamilton. That's Ray," he pointed, "and he likes to talk a lot and he has this great play room that you get to go see later today. That's Shirley. She can help you with anything you need. And that's Madge. Just between you and me, I think she's a bit silly." Madge tossed Jess a comical scowl. Nathan showed a hint of a smile.

"So," Jess added, "I understand you get to stay with us for a while. Are you nervous?"

"A little bit," Nathan said in a quiet voice.

"Well, that's okay. I think I'd be nervous too. But you know what? Everything's going to be okay. We have lots of other boys here, and they were all nervous when they first came, too. And now they all like it here. Well, except for Rodney. He doesn't like anything. Would you like to have a look around? And you can go see your new room and meet the other boys."

"Okay," Nathan said.

Jess stood and held out a hand. Nathan actually took it. They usually didn't. He figured that was a good sign. "Madge," he said, "you see that Harry gives you the information we need."

"Yes, sir," she said with a smirk.

"Ray, Shirley, you're with us."

They went first to the dormitories and Nathan brightened when they entered the room he would share with Joseph. Shirley pointed out the drawers and closet space for his things, and which bed was his, then Nathan ran to the window and looked out eagerly.

"Wow!" he said. "What a great window!"

Jess smiled toward Ray and Shirley. Ray said, "You like windows, Nathan?"

"Yeah, I do," he admitted.

"Why is that?" Ray asked, leaning in the window sill beside the child.

"I liked to look out my window and see what the other kids were playing next door."

"Did you ever play with the other kids?" Ray asked.

Nathan looked down. "Nah, I had to stay in."

"Why is that?"

Nathan glanced to all three adults before he looked out the window and said. "I don't know. I just had to stay in except for when I went to school."

"If you like windows, you're going to like the next place we're going," Jess said and led the way to the gabled attic.

"Wow!" Nathan said again as they entered. He ran across the clean-swept wood floor to look out each of the three gabled windows, as if the view might be different, even though they all faced the same direction. "I like this room," Nathan said. "What do we do in here?"

"All kinds of things," Shirley said. "Sometimes we just come here to talk; sometimes we play games here since there's lots of space and no furniture. And we always have our Christmas party in here."

Nathan smiled and led the way from the room, as if he was eager to see what else they might find. Jess was the last one out, taking a long moment to gaze over his shoulder into the empty room. He pondered the significance of the room, and the symbolism of the gables. His great-great-grandparents had built this home around the gabled attic, and the room had a tradition of good luck; almost magical. Jess knew the gables and their facing east had held deep significance for his forebears and their personal struggles, and their hope had been that every boy who came within these walls would leave here stronger and better prepared to face the world, in spite of the difficult circumstances that might have brought them here. Jess closed the door and followed the others down the hall, saying a silent prayer of gratitude for being able to carry on the wishes of his ancestors. And he prayed that Nathan Gooding would respond well to the magic of the gabled attic, and the refuge from the world that it represented.

Nathan loved the library, and through his innocent conversation they were able to assess that books were one of his favorite things. But his father liked football and model airplanes, and the only things his parents ever bought him were related to those things, even though he would rather have books. He picked out a stack of books that Shirley said he could take to his room and bring them back when he'd looked at them all he wanted to.

Nathan became nervous again when they went into a classroom to meet part of the boys, then they went into another room to meet the rest of them, including Joseph, who would be his roommate.

"He's a lot bigger than me," Nathan said quietly to Jess.

"Yes, most of the boys are. We don't get many here as young as you are. Just think of all the big brothers you'll have looking out for you. That's the way we do it here. We put the newer and younger ones with boys who have been here longer so that they can help with whatever you might need. Joseph is one of the nicest boys here." Jess hesitated a moment and added, "Joseph came here because his father would get drunk and hit him and lock him in the closet." Nathan's brow furrowed and his eyes darkened. "When he first came here he was mean to the other boys because he didn't know how to be any other way. Now he's learned that most people in the world are kind, and if he's kind to others, he'll be much happier."

Nathan thought about that for a minute and said, "He looks happy now."

"Yes, I believe he is," Jess said.

Following another minute of silence while Ray and Shirley pretended to be distracted elsewhere, Nathan said, "My dad didn't get drunk. He was just mad all the time."

Jess swallowed carefully. "Did your dad hurt you, Nathan, the way Joseph's dad hurt him?"

Nathan's breathing sharpened and his eyes showed unmasked fear. "Do I have to go back and live with my dad? Because if I tell on him and go back, he'll . . ."

"No, Nathan, if your dad is hurting you, you don't ever have to live with him again. I promise."

"Yeah, he hit me lots of times; real hard."

Jess swallowed the anger that always rose in him when he heard of such things. He reminded himself that his job was to help boys get beyond such hideousness, and that's what he was doing right now. He smiled at Nathan and couldn't resist touching his face. "Well, nobody is going to hurt you again, as long as you're here with me. Ray and Shirley and everybody here will take good care of you. If anything happens that hurts you or scares you, I want you to talk to one of us about it right away and we'll do everything we can to help, okay?"

Nathan nodded. "Can we go see the playroom, now?"

"Of course," Jess said and they all went to a room filled with a variety of toys where they set Nathan loose to play. What Nathan didn't know was that it had a one-way mirror and hidden video cameras and his play would be observed and analyzed. Ray had spent years of research on how the way children play gives insight into the life they've lived.

Jess left Nathan in Ray's care and went back to his office to finish up the necessities. He arrived at the supper table just as his family was finishing their meal. His mother had gotten some prescriptions for Tamra, but she confessed they were making her sleepy and it would take a while to know if they were going to help. She kissed him and went up to bed once he'd given her and Emily a report on little Nathan.

Jess went to Murphy's home at the other end of the lawn to see how he was doing, and he ended up visiting with him until it was time for bed. After returning home, he climbed carefully between the sheets, so as not to wake Tamra.

The following morning Tamra felt significantly less nauseated, but she found that the medication did make her a bit sleepy which contributed to the feelings of constant exhaustion. But she was grateful for the improvement she felt and determined that she simply couldn't expect to accomplish anything beyond the bare necessities through the next several weeks. She just hoped that it would ease up toward the middle of the pregnancy, as it had done the last time.

Murphy's mother came home from the hospital feeling weak but doing well, and in good spirits. Murphy was thrilled to have her back, but her brush with death and her subsequent miraculous recovery had left him somber, as if his mind was continually caught up in deep thought. Tonya spent a great deal of time with Susan, helping care for her whenever her work schedule permitted. The two of them got along well, and Jess grew to like and respect Tonya even more as it became evident that she was genuinely compassionate and giving.

A few days after Susan's return home, Jess drove into town to pick up the full-time elders and bring them out to the house. They would be having supper and staying the night since they were so far from town, and Jess anticipated that Murphy would have a lot to talk about; at least he hoped so.

Murphy's questions began over the supper table and merged smoothly into the first discussion. And one discussion merged into another as Murphy's eagerness spurred the elders along. Jess held Tamra's hand and watched the magic unfold as Murphy seemed to find the answers that filled holes existing inside him, and the missionaries glowed with fulfillment to see the message they shared lapped up so eagerly. When Tamra nearly fell asleep on Jess' shoulder, he helped her up to bed and returned to find Murphy agreeing to read certain passages in the Book of Mormon, and to pray about them with the desire of finding out for himself if the book was true. The real miracle came the next morning at breakfast as Murphy bounded into the kitchen with sleep-deprived eyes that glowed with unmistakable conviction.

"It's true," he said to the elders, then to Jess, "It's true! I don't know how I know. I just know. It's just like when you knew your father was with you. I just know. Do you know what I mean, Jess?"

"Yes, Murphy," Jess said, "I know exactly what you mean."

They visited a while longer before Jess had to go to work, and Murphy drove the elders back into town so that they could make it to another appointment. Through the following week Murphy met with the elders two more times and often sought out Jess to ask him questions. They all felt certain that Murphy would choose to join the Church—a prospect that gave them all great joy. But Jess hoped that Murphy would take time and be completely ready.

A week after Murphy's initial meeting with the elders, Jess met late morning with Ray to get a full report on his evaluations of Nathan Gooding. He showed every classic sign of being abused by his father and terrified of him. Even though he had suffered physical and emotional abuse, at least there was no sexual abuse, which was more difficult to treat. Nathan actually had a fairly good perspective on life in general. As a result, he quickly opened up to Jess and Ray. His mother apparently deserved credit for this. Nathan had talked of how his mother had told him that there was something wrong with his father and most fathers weren't that way. For most of his life, Nathan's mother had been an anchor for him, even though she had apparently lacked the courage or resources to get herself and the child away from the situation. But in recent months his mother had apparently gone over the edge with severe depression.

"They don't come any easier to help than this boy," Ray concluded. "He's blending well, even though he's much younger. He's eating up the education and he loves working with the horses. He occasionally says that he misses his mother, but he often follows up with the fact that she was always asleep, anyway."

"So, he was missing her long before he came here."

"That's right."

Jess was pleased with the report and for a moment he thought of how he looked forward to sharing it with his father. He felt briefly startled to remember that his father wasn't around to talk to any longer. Then he focused on the other boys that Ray had been working with. There were some behavioral challenges to deal with, but nothing they hadn't seen before and couldn't handle.

Ray had only been gone from his office a minute when Madge peered in, saying, "One of the hands just phoned from the main stable. Murphy's been hurt. He says to come quick."

"Good heavens." Jess bolted out of his chair and sprinted out the front door, around the house and across the lawn to the stables. He found Murphy on the ground near the main door, with a number of hands gathered around.

"Did somebody call for an ambulance?" Jess demanded, pushing his way through.

"That is not necessary!" Murphy snarled.

"Well, you must not be hurting too badly if you can growl at me," Jess countered. "What happened?"

"I was on my way up the ladder to fix those shingles on the roof. My foot slipped and my leg twisted as I went down backward."

"Ouch," Jess grimaced. "Do you think it's broken?" He nodded to where Murphy was holding both his hands just above his knee.

"No. I'm absolutely certain it's broken. I heard it snap."

"Ouch," Jess said more vehemently.

"Do you want me to drive him into town?" one of the hands offered.

"No, I'll take him," Jess said, "but you can call into the house and have my mother check on Susan. Let my family know where I've gone. And you," he nodded toward another hand, "bring the Cruiser around so we can help him in."

Murphy showed no obvious signs of pain until they attempted to move him into the Cruiser. Then Jess actually felt scared, wondering how bad it was. Once he was settled into the reclined seat, he was able to breathe deeply and settle down, but as Jess drove toward town, he could tell Murphy was in pain. He figured some conversation might distract him.

"I should have warned you, Murph."

"About what?"

"Bad things tend to happen to people who are investigating the gospel."

Murphy stared at Jess as if he'd turned purple. "How can there be any connection?"

"Because there are two great opposing forces in this world, Murphy, and one of them doesn't want to see anything good take place—especially when it comes to people coming into the Church." Jess went on to talk about the war in heaven, and some of his own experiences with opposition—both personally and related to things that had happened to investigators on his mission.

Murphy listened but said little; he was obviously preoccupied with the pain. Following a lull of silence, he said, "I asked Tonya to marry me."

"Really?" Jess laughed. "That's great! Especially for a guy who has hardly gone on a date in his entire life."

"Well, I never found anybody worth taking out. Besides, I was busy."

"I'm not that much of a slave driver," Jess said lightly.

"No, and neither was your father. Anyway . . . I asked her."

"And?"

"She said yes," Murphy said, his voice sad.

With concern, Jess asked, "That's good, isn't it? Is it because you're in pain that you sound so blah, or—"

"I told her about the Church thing; how I've been talking to missionaries and . . ."

"And?" Jess prodded.

Murphy's voice quavered. "She doesn't want anything to do with it."

Jess sighed loudly. "Oh, I see."

"So, if it's right for me to be baptized, does that mean it's wrong to marry Tonya? Or is it the other way around?"

"Are you wanting my honest opinion, Murph, or are you just speculating out loud?"

Murphy looked directly at him. "I want your honest opinion, or I wouldn't have asked. And if I don't remember this conversation after they do whatever they're gonna do to me, I want you to tell me again later."

"I know that you know the Church is true. And I know that you know what you need to do. Being baptized and committing your life to living the gospel is a choice that I believe should supercede all else. It may not be easy, but it's right. And in the eternal scheme of things, you have to do what's right. And if Tonya is the right woman for you, and if you know that the same way you know the gospel is true, then you need to give her your whole heart with a very clear understanding of where your convictions lie. And if she loves you as much as you love her, she'll respect that, even if she doesn't agree with it. And if she is the right one for you, she just may come around one day."

Murphy actually smiled. "That's what I was hoping you'd say."

"You already knew all that, didn't you. You were just testing me."

"Well," Murphy shifted in his seat and grimaced, "I learned something recently about getting answers from the mouth of two witnesses. In this case, that's me and you."

"So what are you going to do?"

"I'm going to join the Church, just as soon as this leg of mine will get me into the water."

Jess erupted with an emotional laugh. "That's the best news I've heard in a long time; well, maybe not so long."

"And what news equal to that have you heard recently?"

Jess smiled. "Tamra's pregnant."

Murphy chuckled. "Oh, that *is* good news. Is that why she's been looking so under the weather?"

"That's why," Jess said. "She's having a rough time, but it'll be great."

"I'm sure it will."

They arrived at the hospital and Murphy was moved from the Cruiser directly to a gurney by a couple of muscular male nurses. Jess was reminded of Joshua Raine and his desire for a career in nursing. He concluded there were many aspects of nursing that men were simply more capable of doing.

"Will you call Tonya for me?" Murphy asked as he was being wheeled into the emergency area. He told Jess her mobile number and he quickly wrote it down.

"I will. Don't worry. Everything will be fine."

Jess made the call and it took great effort to calm Tonya down and assure her that Murphy was going to be fine. He called home as well and told Tamra he was going to stay until Murphy got out of surgery and was settled. He called the boys' home and took care of some business over the phone.

Tonya arrived at the hospital just after Jess had been told that they were taking Murphy into surgery to set the bone. While she was sitting beside him, nervously flicking her burgundy fingernails, Jess couldn't resist saying, "So, I hear Murph popped the question."

She looked surprised, then she smiled and glanced down. "Yeah, he did."

"And did you give him the right answer?"

"If yes is the right answer, then I certainly did."

"Well, congratulations," Jess said. "He's a good man. I've known him since I was a kid. Well," he chuckled, "we were both born and raised right there where we live now, for the most part, and I've never seen him do or say anything that's lessened my respect for him."

"Amazing," she said. "I keep trying to find something wrong with him, but I just can't seem to do it. I mean, he's a little rough around the edges, but I think that's the way a man ought to be. That's what makes a man a man, if you know what I mean."

"Not really," Jess chuckled, "but I'll take your word for it."

They talked of trivial things to keep their minds off what was happening in the operating room. Occasionally Tonya couldn't restrain herself and she jumped up and paced the room. Jess wanted to bring up religion, but he felt it was better to keep his thoughts to himself. As soon as word came that the surgery had been successful and Murphy would be fine, Jess put him in Tonya's care and left the hospital, first calling home to let Tamra know he was on his way. She told him she was about to go to bed, but she'd be waiting for a goodnight kiss.

Jess was surprised to find it raining—and hard—when he left the hospital. He was fairly wet by the time he got to the Cruiser, but it was a warm rain and he didn't feel chilled. Once he got off the paved roads, he realized the visibility was horrible due to the continual wall of water pouring over the windshield. The wipers just couldn't go fast enough to keep up with it. He was grateful for his familiarity with this road that led to his home and nowhere else, but his head began to ache from the intensity with which he had to focus on the headlight beams in order to stay on course. With no warning something appeared in front of him. He couldn't tell if it was a rock or an animal, alive or unmoving, but it was big. He swerved to miss it and the next few seconds became eternal.

An unfathomable fear seized him as he watched the beam of the headlights spin and then flip. He had the sensation of being on an amusement park ride as what was up became down, and down became up. Memories of the accident that had killed Evelyn's parents and his best friend rushed through his mind, clashing with images of the people he loved. He heard himself scream that he wasn't ready to die, then he just screamed. Glass broke and metal creaked then everything became still except for the continuing downpour. Once Jess accepted the reality that he was conscious and breathing, he realized he was hanging upside down in the seatbelt. He wiggled his fingers and then his toes, then he audibly thanked God that he had survived and was uncrippled.

It then occurred to Jess that he definitely needed help. It was pitch black and pouring. The window on the passenger side had broken and rain was pouring in, but the window next to him had remained intact and wouldn't open since the controls were electric. He resisted unfastening the seatbelt for fear of falling on his head and injuring what wasn't already injured.

"Phone, the phone, where's my phone?" He realized how shaken he was by the fact that he was not only talking to himself, his voice was hoarse and quivery. "Oh, God help me! Where's my phone?" he almost shouted, frantically feeling around himself for where it might have fallen. The phone beeped to warn of a dying battery and he almost laughed as he reached for it on the ceiling below his head. The bad news was that he likely only had power to make one call. He debated only a moment on whether he should call home or triple zero for emergency help. His fingers efficiently dialed home while he prayed that one of the women he loved would answer the phone quickly.

"Hello?" Tamra said in a half-asleep, panicked tone.

"It's me," he said, his voice still shaky. "Oh, Tamra I love you."

"I love you too, Jess. What's happened?" She sounded fully awake now.

"Now don't panic," he insisted. "My phone might die here and . . . I've been in a little accident. I'm all right, but I need help."

"What happened?" she insisted. "Where are you?" Her breathing became sharp.

"I'm okay, Tam." The battery warning beeped again. "Breathe deep and listen to me. Call for help. I'm not more than ten or fifteen minutes from home, and I don't think I'm too far off the road, but the rain was so bad that I'm not sure. Tell them to get a helicopter out here and get me out of this thing, and then you stay right there until I call you again. Do you hear me?"

"Okay, I'll call them." Again a beep. "Are you sure you're okay?"

"I'm fine. My phone's dying. I've got to go. Please don't panic or—"

"Jess!" Tamra screamed into the phone as it went dead. She realized she was shaking as she frantically pushed the button and listened for a new dial tone before she dialed triple zero, walking toward Emily's room as she did. She knocked then walked in and found Emily sitting in bed, reading. Her expression of surprise turned to acute concern as Tamra said into the phone, "My husband just called me from his mobile. He's been in an accident and I think he's stuck in the vehicle." Emily sat up straight and reached for Tamra's hand as she sat on the edge of the bed. She answered their questions and gave them directions to where she believed he was. With assurance that they would find him, Tamra was once again left with a dead phone in her hand.

"What did he say?" Emily demanded. Tamra did her best to repeat it while she paced the room.

Ten minutes later she rushed out of the room, saying, "Listen for the children. I'm going to find him."

"He told you to stay put," Emily said, following after her. "I think you should. It's pouring out there and you're pregnant. They can help him. You can't."

"But . . ." Tamra realized she was sobbing as she pulled jeans on beneath her nightgown then quickly exchanged it for a sweatshirt. "What if it's worse than he said? What if he was only okay long enough to call me and . . . he's stranded . . . and what if I never see him again and . . ."

"Okay, calm down," Emily said, taking Tamra by the shoulders. "Take a deep breath before you hyperventilate. He's going to be just fine. Just calm down."

"How do you know he'll be fine?" Tamra shouted.

Emily shouted back, "Because I refuse to outlive any more of my loved ones!"

Tamra was stunned into silence. She'd never heard Emily use that tone of voice before. Emily stepped back, apparently surprised by her own reaction. "I'm sorry," she said, obviously more upset than she'd let on. Tears trickled down her face as she said in a whisper, "Go find him. Be careful. If it were Michael I would do the same. I'll look after the children."

Tamra hugged her quickly and hurried down the stairs, amazed at the energy she felt that had not been with her for weeks. She pulled on her rubber boots that always waited near the door for these occasional downpours and the inevitable mud that followed. Then she put on Jess's oiled drover coat, knowing it would keep the rain off better than anything she owned. And she opted for his flat-brimmed hat for the same reason. When she stepped outside, the hat kept the rain off so well that she determined it was designed with that shape for a reason. And she had always thought it simply made Jess look especially dashing.

Tamra drove slowly and carefully, grateful to note that the rain was letting up a bit, but still definitely heavy. She began to wonder if he'd been further away from home than he'd said, or perhaps he'd gone off the road further than he'd thought and she'd missed him. Then the headlights glanced off something that made her gasp. She stomped on the brake and reminded herself to breathe as she realized what she was looking at.

"Heaven help us," she muttered and reminded herself of Emily's advice. *Take a deep breath before you hyperventilate.* There before her was the vehicle Jess had been driving—upside down. She left the Cruiser running with the lights pointed that direction, and stumbled through the mud toward the other vehicle, terrified of what she might find.

Chapter Six

Jess saw the beam of lights and sighed with relief. He was beginning to think that help would never come. He heard tapping on the glass beside him, but he couldn't see anything through the mud-splattered window. Then he heard footsteps in the mud near the broken window opposite him. He looked that way as a body dropped down and reached through the open window. He expected to see the face of a rescue worker, but it was Tamra's voice calling his name that he heard just before she wriggled her shoulders through the broken window and took his hand into hers.

"Jess, you're still alive," she said as if she truly hadn't expected him to be.

"Yes, I am," he said, "but what in the name of heaven are you doing here?"

"I had to be with you," she said and started to cry. She touched his face and kissed his hand. "Are you okay, really?"

"I can feel my legs and wiggle my toes. But my head feels horrible. I was thinking about a news story I heard once; how a roller coaster got stuck and these people were upside down for hours until rescuers could get them all out. I guess it could be worse."

"Oh, it could," she said, crying harder. "I love you, Jess."

"I love you too," he said, crying himself. "You really shouldn't have come out here. But I'm glad you did."

"So am I," she said. "If you . . ." She hesitated. "Did you hear that?"

"I did," he said as the definite hum of a helicopter came closer.

Once the helicopter had landed, Tamra reluctantly eased back and hovered nervously in the rain at a safe distance while they carefully pulled Jess from the wreckage. The rain had stopped by the time they had him aboard the helicopter, and she felt comforted by the rescuer's words as he closed the door on Jess and turned to tell her, "I think he's just bruised and scraped up, but we want to have him checked out to be sure."

Once the helicopter was in the air, Tamra sat in the Cruiser and sobbed for ten minutes, then she forced herself to calm down enough to call Emily on her cell phone to give her a report. She could hear Emily's relief through the phone, and she promised to see that all was well with the little ones so that Tamra could be with Jess at the hospital. She drove carefully, grateful the rain had stopped. And she had to admit that she was grateful she no longer needed to be there to nurse little Michael. She'd been disappointed when the doctor suggested she stop nursing for the sake of maintaining her health through the pregnancy. It made sense, but it had still saddened her. At this moment, however, she was grateful that Emily could give Michael what he needed and she could be with her husband.

Tamra felt an eery sense of déjà vu as she approached the hospital. She'd been too focused on her panic to think of it until now, but how could she forget the night, when she'd barely known Jess, and she had found him after he'd taken an overdose of sleeping pills? She had called for emergency assistance and had waited frantically for the helicopter to arrive. And then she had driven to the hospital, almost expecting to find Jess already dead. Tamra cried an endless stream of tears as she drove, contemplating her gratitude that Jess had survived then—both the physical and emotional trauma he had suffered. At the time she hadn't known that he would end up her husband and the father of her children, but now she couldn't imagine her life without him. And she was equally grateful that he had been spared any serious injury this time. Jess was alive and well, and it was a miracle.

Tamra knew she looked horrible when she walked into the hospital, still wearing Jess's long coat. She'd opted to leave his hat in the car. She was guided to his bedside by a kind nurse, and once they were alone, she pressed her face into the pillow beside his head and wept uncontrollably.

"I'm sorry," she finally said. "I cry more than any woman on the face of the earth."

"Well, I've had a few tears of my own," Jess admitted, then he lifted his hands to show her how they were trembling. "I can't stop shaking." He chuckled without humor. Tamra held up her own shaking hands and he chuckled again. "I really thought I was dead, Tamra. I just couldn't imagine how I would survive an accident *twice* in my lifetime. But here I am."

Tamra saw tears leak from the corners of his eyes into his hair. She wiped them away then pressed her brow to his. "I'm so grateful," she muttered, then she shared her earlier thoughts about the night he'd attempted suicide, and they both cried a little more.

A few minutes later they took Jess away to do a CT scan and make certain he didn't have any internal injuries. Tamra waited nervously outside of radiology until he was finished, then she waited with him for the results. She was nearly asleep in a recliner near his bed when the doctor finally appeared with the news that Jess was a walking miracle. No internal injuries. Not even a hairline crack in any of his bones. But he suggested they both get some rest before they headed home. Tamra called Emily from the phone in the room to give her the news, then she handed the phone to Jess.

"Hello, Mom," he said and heard her crying.

"You really are okay."

"I really am," he said, "well . . . beyond this inability I have to stop shaking."

"That would be something we have in common," she said.

Jess hung up the phone and turned to look at Tamra. He reached a trembling hand toward her in the same moment that hot tears rose in her eyes. She leaned over him to embrace him tightly then she pressed her lips to his.

"I'm so grateful," she muttered and hugged him again.

"So am I," he said, pressing a hand through the length of her hair. "I thought I was dead; I really did."

"I thank God that you're not," she said through a stream of ongoing tears. "There are so many people who love you, Jess . . . who need you, and depend on you. But no one loves you or needs you more than I do."

They talked a few more minutes then Jess encouraged her to relax in the recliner near the bed and get some rest. Her exhaustion was visible and he prayed she wouldn't end up ill from this little adventure. Tamra's even breathing let him know that she'd fallen asleep quickly, but he knew that pregnancy made her so tired that she could sleep practically anytime, anywhere. Staring at the ceiling, he wished that he could do the same. As images of the accident plunged over and over through his mind, he finally called the nurse and asked for something to help him sleep. He was grateful that their communication hadn't disturbed Tamra, and equally so to find himself relaxing quickly from the medication he'd been given. He woke to find the room still dark. He had the sensation that he'd emerged from a bad dream, but he couldn't recall its content. He was grateful to find himself safe and comfortable, in spite of a growing ache in his muscles. Recalling his reasons for being where he was, he marveled at the miracle that he was alive and well. He turned to see Tamra sleeping in the recliner nearby and again was struck by how blessed he was.

Jess slipped back to sleep, mostly aided by the medication that was still in his system. He woke to daylight and met Tamra's eyes as she reached for his hand. "It's nice to see you alive," she said.

"It's nice to be alive," he said.

Once Jess was officially released, they phoned his mother to let her know what was going on, then they checked on Murphy to find that he was doing well, beyond the pain he was in; he would be ready to go home the next day.

"Hey, is that a bruise on your face?" Murphy asked.

Jess touched his face as if he might find a smudge of dirt there, but it hurt to the touch and he felt an unpleasant shudder go through him as he was reminded of last night's incident.

"Yeah, well . . . I had a little encounter with a rainstorm on the way home last night, and I never made it home."

"We spent the night here, actually," Tamra said and went on to explain when Jess didn't seem to want to.

Murphy sat with his mouth open, listening. He finally said, "What is it you were telling me yesterday about opposition?"

Jess chuckled. "Yes, well . . . I'm living proof that the protection of angels is more powerful than any opposition we could come up against."

Murphy smiled and exchanged a firm handshake with Jess. "Get some rest," Jess said. "I'll come and get you in the morning."

In the parking lot, Jess said to Tamra, "I would prefer that you drive home."

Tamra looked stunned. "You can't start that again," she insisted, recalling Jess's aversion to driving following his last accident. And it had taken him years to get over it.

"I'm not going to start that again," Jess said. "I'm just a little . . . shaky still, and . . . I would really appreciate it if you'd drive home."

Tamra got into the driver's seat and Jess closed her door before he walked around and got in the other side. They said little through the drive, and arrived home to find Emily running out the side door and across the lawn. She threw herself into Jess's arms, crying.

"Oh," she said as she drew back and took hold of his shoulders, "you really are all right."

"I really am," he said.

She took his face into her hands and gave him a tearful smile before she turned to embrace Tamra then she took her by the shoulders. "I'm sorry, my dear, for what I said last night. I was frightened and upset, but—"

"What *did* you say?" Jess asked.

Emily looked down, seeming embarrassed, before she admitted, "I just . . . said that I refused to outlive any more of my loved ones."

"I should hope so," Jess said.

"Yes, well . . ." Emily's voice softened with emotion, "I was upset, and . . . the truth is that the span of our lives is in God's hands. I have known beyond any doubt with each death we've been close to that it was their time to go, and nothing I could do would change that. So, I apologize for my outburst, and I know that God will see all of us protected for as long as we are intended to be on this earth." She smiled in an obvious attempt to ease a tense moment, then she took both their hands and moved toward the house. "I've got some enchiladas in the oven for lunch. Michael is napping, and Evelyn is feeding raisins to her dollies. I'm sure she'll be glad to see you."

Jess was, indeed, glad to see Evelyn—and the baby when he woke up. Just being with them and doing something as simple as sharing lunch with his family seemed like a miracle.

"By the way," Emily said in the middle of their meal, "when are the two of you going to move into the master bedroom?"

"The room we have is just fine," Jess insisted.

"Yes, I know it's fine," Emily protested, "but you should be—"

"It's fine, Mother," he said, hoping she would drop it. He could never put into words his reluctance to take this step that seemed a tangible symbol of taking over the full responsibility that had been left to him. He didn't feel ready or worthy for such drastic measures. Just the term *master* bedroom made him uneasy for reasons he couldn't explain. He didn't feel like the master of anything; he rather felt inadequate and mostly scared. And he preferred to stay in the room where he and Tamra were comfortable.

He was relieved when the subject was dropped, and Emily said, "I spoke with your sisters this morning and told them what happened."

"Oh, that's just what they need," Jess said, "another family crisis to worry about."

"There's nothing to worry about," Emily said. "It's over and we're all grateful that you're okay."

"And how are my sisters doing?" Jess asked, hoping to divert attention away from himself.

"They're doing well, as far as I can gather," Emily said. "They're all keeping busy."

"That's good then," Jess said with a sudden longing to be with his sisters—some in particular. He truly missed them.

When lunch was finished, Tamra went upstairs to lie down. The exhaustion of her pregnancy, combined with the drama of Jess's accident, had done her in. Jess went to the boys' home, where rumor of his accident had spread, and everyone was ridiculously happy to see him. He was grateful to find that Shirley had everything under control, for the most part, and he saw to the absolute necessities in a couple of hours. He went out to the stables to find one of the assistant stable masters ready to report that all was in order, and that he had been in contact with Murphy by phone and several employees would each be taking a few extra hours to help cover for Murphy until he could get around enough to get back to his work.

Jess returned to the house, late in the afternoon, exhausted. But he heard the piano and felt inclined to go to the music room, rather than straight up to bed. He found Tamra there, practicing without much enthusiasm, but at least she was there. Evelyn sat on the floor feeding a dolly with a plastic baby bottle, and little Michael was in his battery-operated swing, making googly noises and sucking on his fist.

"Before long they're going to have you playing for the ward choir," Jess said from the doorway. Tamra stopped playing and smiled at him. Evelyn ran into his arms.

"That's a long ways off—if ever," Tamra said.

"It's good to hear you at it," Jess said, knowing her practicing had waned a great deal since she'd become ill with her pregnancy, and just last week she had finally let her teacher know that she would have to postpone lessons until she felt better—which meant after she'd recovered from giving birth.

"I enjoy it," she said, picking out some notes. "I just feel too tired to sit here for long."

"It's only temporary," Jess said and pressed a kiss to her brow before he sat on the little sofa with Evelyn on his lap.

"How are you feeling?" Tamra asked.

"Every muscle in my body is sore," he said, "and I think I have a few bruises. Other than that, I'm fine. I still get shaky when I think about it, though."

"Yes, so do I," Tamra said and moved to sit beside him, putting her head on his shoulder.

"My two favorite girls," Jess said, hugging Evelyn with one arm and Tamra with the other.

"What about Grandma?" Evelyn asked indignantly.

Jess chuckled. "Well, I love Grandma, too. I guess that means I have three favorite girls."

Evelyn demonstrated three with her fingers just as little Michael let out a squeal that seemed to express his perfect joy. They all laughed and Jess hugged Tamra again, pressing a kiss into her hair. He was so grateful to be alive.

* * *

The next day Jess picked Murphy up at the hospital and got him settled into his house with all that he needed, including his cordless phone so that he could call him or one of the stable hands for help. Susan was getting around some, but she wasn't up to waiting on

Murphy more than a little here and there. Jess returned to the boys' home to get to work, and through the course of the day all of his sisters called him at different times to see how he was doing. He didn't get a lot of work done, but it was good to visit with each of them, and it helped ease the yearning he'd had to be with them. He found that he especially enjoyed his visit with Emma. She seemed to be doing well with her college courses and her job as a medical receptionist. She was keeping busy and staying healthy. But when the topic of their father's death came up, she cried audibly through the phone, prompting Jess to shed tears of his own. He wanted desperately to just hug her, long and tight, and he couldn't help thinking how nice it would be if she ended up settling nearby one day, so that they could be closer. But it was as their father had once said: she spent far too much time in the States to ever end up settling down in Australia.

On the third night after the accident, Jess woke in a cold sweat, breathing heavily. And this time he *did* recall the content of his dream. He had dreamt of the accident happening again, just as he'd remembered it. Except that in the dream, his hanging upside down in the seatbelt, surrounded by darkness and rain, created an anxiety so intense that it had startled him awake, his heart pounding. He prayed himself into calmness, knowing from past experience that trusting in the Lord was the only way to spiral himself out of his fears, as opposed to spiraling deeper into them. But he never did go back to sleep, and he finally got out of bed feeling spent already, with a big day ahead of him.

Late afternoon, Jess felt the strain of his missed sleep, combined with the impact of his recent accident. He'd been sore and achy to a point that had not deterred him in doing what he needed to do, but it was beginning to tell on him. He called it quits at work and went home to tell his wife and mother that he was going to bed. He slept immediately and woke in the dark to hear Tamra's voice gently saying, "Jess, honey, I've brought you some supper. Are you awake?"

"Yes, thank you," he said and she turned on the bedside lamp.

"I didn't want to wake you, but you need to eat, and—"

"It's okay," he said. "I'm starving. It smells good." He leaned against the headboard and she moved a tray from the side of the bed to his lap. After he'd eaten several bites, he said, "And what?"

"What?" she asked, disoriented.

"You said, 'and' before I interrupted you. Given that and the fact that I can tell you're concerned about something, I want to know what's going on."

Tamra sighed. "When you're finished eating, Murphy wants to talk to you. He's pretty upset, but he wouldn't tell me why. He didn't want me to wake you, but I got the feeling if he didn't talk to you tonight he'd get no sleep at all."

"Well then," Jess said, "it's a good thing I got a nap."

"Do you think it's about Tonya?" she asked.

Jess had filled her in on what Murphy had told him previously, and he said with confidence, "I'd bet money on it."

Once Jess had eaten and freshened up, he spent a few minutes with each of his children and his mother before he kissed Tamra goodnight, knowing he wouldn't return until she had far surpassed her evening limits of exhaustion and she would likely be sound asleep when he returned. He walked across the lawn to the little house on the estate where Murphy lived and knocked at the screen door before he pushed open the heavy door behind it. Murphy was seated on the sofa with his broken leg propped up on a pillow on the coffee table. His anguish was visibly evident in his face.

"Thanks for coming," Murphy said as they sat across from each other in the little front room. "Mother's asleep in the other room."

"It's not a problem. How's the leg?"

"Oh, it still hurts, and I'm making good use of those pain pills, but it is getting a little better. I can get around without wanting to scream."

"That's good then," Jess said, then Murphy gave him a brief report of the work he had been overseeing by phone and by having his assistants come to the house. When he finally stopped talking business, Jess asked, "What happened?"

"I told the elders I was ready to be baptized and we set a date," he said.

"That's great," Jess said with all the enthusiasm he felt over such a prospect, but the reason for Murphy's grief came rushing out quickly behind the joyous announcement.

"Tonya told me it was either her or the Church."

"She actually said that?" Jess countered.

"She did."

Jess was thoughtful a minute while Murphy pressed his fingers together nervously and Jess could almost see him trembling. Jess prayed silently for guidance and allowed his thoughts to settle before he said gently, "So, what are you going to do about it?"

"I . . . just don't know what to do. I . . . really feel like I'm supposed to be with her, but how can I be if she's going to hold such attitudes? I just . . ." He became so upset that he couldn't go on.

Jess asked softly, "Would you like me to give you a blessing?"

Murphy's eyes lightened, but he asked, "I thought that took two men, and there isn't another Mormon within an hour of here."

"It takes two for the healing of the sick, but it would be perfectly appropriate for me to give you a blessing that might help give you some comfort and guidance . . . if that's what you want."

"Oh, I do," Murphy said.

Jess asked Murphy if he would first offer a prayer, and Jess marveled at his humility and his desire to do what was right. He felt tears gather behind his closed eyelids as he recalled the countless times Michael had approached Murphy about reading the Book of Mormon or visiting with the missionaries, but he had stubbornly resisted. Had Michael's death been the first step to Murphy gaining the humility he needed to be ready? Had his mother's brush with death so soon afterward continued the groundwork that had been laid? Whatever the reasons, Jess knew that his father's influence had greatly contributed to Murphy's being ready to accept the gospel now. And he was grateful.

When the prayer was finished, Jess laid his hands on Murphy's head and allowed the words to flow through him. He was freshly amazed at the power of the priesthood, and how he could feel himself become a conduit for the words of the Lord, given to him through the Spirit. Murphy was promised with great conviction that as he drew the courage to take this step, he would be blessed to receive the desires of his heart, that he would grow old surrounded by his children and grandchildren, and a loving wife. Jess noted that the way the words came gave no indication as to whether or not his wife would be Tonya.

When the blessing was finished, Jess sat down across from Murphy and gave him a few minutes to absorb all that had been said. When the silence grew too long, Jess said gently, "Look at me, Murphy." He leaned his forearms on this thighs in order to face Murphy more closely. Murphy looked him in the eye. "This is a decision that you have to face your Father in Heaven with. What are you going to do?"

Murphy swallowed carefully and cleared his throat. "I'm going to become a member of the Church, no matter the cost. And I know that all will be well."

Jess smiled and took Murphy's hand. "You are golden, my man," he said. "Such conviction doesn't come along often."

"But . . ." Murphy added, his expression darkening, "I just don't know if I can bear losing Tonya."

"If your relationship with Tonya is meant to be, then it will work out. If it's not, then it will be better for you in the long run, even if it might be more difficult now."

Murphy nodded stoutly and Jess could see him visibly gathering courage to move forward. "Hey," Jess said, acting on a thought that wouldn't leave him, "do you think Tonya would agree to come to dinner at our house tomorrow . . . with you, of course?"

"Probably, why?"

"Okay. Do you think she'd get upset if I just come right out and tell her that I'd like to talk to her about the Church and answer her questions?"

Murphy took a deep breath and looked thoughtful. "Coming from you, I think she could handle that. She's not the fly off and get angry kind of woman. She just says what she thinks and expects others to do the same, so . . . why not? What have we got to lose?"

"Okay. Do you want to invite her or should I?"

"I'll let you, since you offered. But don't you think you should be consulting your wife and mother before you invite guests to dinner? I doubt you'll have time to cook it, and getting a pizza delivered out here costs a fortune."

Jess chuckled. "So it does, and you're probably right." He picked up Murphy's cordless phone on the coffee table and dialed his house. "Hello, Mother," he said.

"What are you up to?"

"Chatting with Murphy."

"Oh, that's nice. Is everything okay?"

"It will be. Hey, I'd like to invite Murph and Tonya over for dinner tomorrow evening, but as Murphy pointed out, I don't get a lot of time for cooking. I know Tamra doesn't have plans, but she's also not up to doing much, so is it all right with you if—"

"That sounds wonderful," Emily said. "We'll look forward to getting to know her better."

"Great. Thank you, Mother. You're the best."

"Nah, I'm just your favorite mother."

"Yes, that too," Jess chuckled and got off the phone.

"Okay," Jess said to Murphy, "what's Tonya's number?"

Murphy repeated it as Jess dialed and she answered right away. "Hey Tonya," he said, "this is Jess Hamilton."

"Hello," she said, sounding pleased. "What can I do for you?"

"Well, we'd like to have you and Murphy and Susan over for dinner tomorrow evening."

"That sounds nice," she said, sounding slightly skeptical. "Is there a special reason?"

"Well, I'm glad you asked, because there are several reasons, actually. First of all, since Murph has practically been a member of the family for as long as I can remember, we thought it would be nice to get to know the woman who has stolen his heart." She laughed softly and he continued. "Secondly, we need to celebrate the forthcoming event, and maybe we can even help with the wedding; we could talk about that."

"This is sounding better," Tonya said.

"Good. I'm hoping to butter you up for this last one. I don't want you to be offended, but I wanted to tell you straight up front that we'd like to talk with you about Murphy's interest in the Church. He's told me that it's something you're having trouble with, and we were hoping that we might be able to just talk about it and answer any questions you might have. We're not trying to convert you, or anything. We'd just like to have an open and honest conversation."

It was silent for a long minute until Jess began to wonder if she'd hung up on him. "Hello?" he finally said while Murphy chewed on his knuckles.

"Hello," she said. "I appreciate your being honest with me, as opposed to just bringing it up over dessert."

"Okay," Jess drawled.

"Sure, I'd love to come to dinner. Tell my sweetie I'll talk to him in the morning."

"I'll tell him," Jess said and got off the phone. He turned to Murphy and said in a high-pitched, simpering voice, "Tell my sweetie I'll talk to him in the morning."

Murphy chuckled, then sobered as he demanded, "Well?"

"She's coming. She said she appreciated my honesty."

"Yes!" Murphy cheered then playfully slapped Jess on the shoulder.

"And how about we fast together until dinner, for her heart to be softened. Couldn't hurt."

"Sounds like a great idea."

"And you know what, Murph?" Jess said as he moved toward the door. "I sense that she really is a good woman with a good heart. I really think it will be okay. I saw worse dilemmas than this on my mission."

"Did they work out?"

"Some of them. I can tell you one thing for certain. When you make those covenants and stick to them, you *will* be blessed. In spite of any opposition that can be dished out, you will feel the changes in your life. I can promise that."

Murphy smiled. "Thanks, Jess. You're the best friend a guy could ever ask for."

Jess smiled in return, wondering why he felt suddenly sad. "Is there anything I can get you before I go?"

"Nope, I'll be fine. Thank you."

Jess walked slowly back to the house, pondering the stars above him and feeling his thoughts drift to his father. He thought of Murphy's reference to friendship and realized that was one thing he'd truly missed in his father's absence. The friendship they'd shared had gone far beyond their relationship as father and son. Jess could talk to his father about anything, and he knew that Michael had felt the same way. He missed that.

The following morning at the breakfast table, he was still considering the friendship he'd lost with his father. He didn't eat due to his fast, but he sat at the table to spend some time with his family before work. Observing his mother interacting with Tamra as they discussed plans for the day, he envied the friendship they shared that was comparable to the relationship he'd once shared with his father.

When Emily went in the other room, Tamra reached for his hand and kissed him quickly. "What are you thinking about?" she asked. He marveled at how well she could read him, and he reminded himself that he had Tamra's friendship, a trust and understanding that went deeper than any relationship he'd ever known. He was grateful for that, especially when he considered that his mother had lost an equivalent relationship at her husband's death.

Jess smiled at Tamra and kissed her back. "I was just thinking how blessed I am," he said and hurried to the boys' home to get his work under control.

The day went relatively well, and just before dinnertime Jess called Murphy and asked, "Anything I can help you with? Do you need me to carry you to the house, or anything?"

Murphy chuckled. "No, thanks. I can hobble on these crutches just fine. Tonya's already here. We'll be over shortly."

"Does your mother need help with—"

"She's resting, actually," Murphy said. "Your mother brought her over some dinner already when she said she wasn't up to going out. She's eaten and gone to sleep. She's got the phone to call if she needs anything."

"Okay," Jess said. "We'll see you in a few minutes."

Dinner went well. Jess was pleased to see the way Tonya interacted with Emily and Tamra so easily. It wasn't difficult to imagine what good neighbors they could be, and he believed that Murphy truly had found a good woman. He prayed for the hundredth time that day that her heart would be softened.

After the table had been cleared and dessert brought out, Tonya said, "Well, we've gotten to dessert and nobody's brought up this religion thing. I kept hoping someone else would do it, but if you're not going to, I guess I'd better."

"Okay, you've brought it up," Jess said. "Why don't you tell us what you think."

"Well," she drawled and tossed a concerned glance toward Murphy, "I'm very much in love with a good man, and I want him to do what will make him happy. But . . . quite frankly, I don't want anything to do with religion. *Any* religion. And I really don't want my husband to, either."

"May I ask why?" Jess said. Tonya looked at him contemplatively but said nothing. "That's a pretty strong opinion; certainly not indifferent. There must be a reason."

"Yes, I believe there is," Tonya said, "but it's not my favorite topic of conversation."

Jess met Murphy's eyes and saw his astonishment. He obviously had no idea what she was talking about. Murphy then turned to look at Tonya. Her eyes met his, filled with concern before she looked down. "I guess it's good to get all of this out in the open before we get any closer to the wedding. The thing is . . . I grew up in a very religious home, although I would call it more . . . pious. My father was strict beyond belief. He preached the fear of God to us at the top of his lungs, and he would beat us if we didn't adhere to his interpretation to the letter. My mother stood by him implicitly. She was oppressed and downtrodden. Quite frankly, having religion in my home was what I would describe as fire and brimstone."

Following a long moment of silence, Emily said gently, "Under such circumstances, one doesn't have to wonder why any form of religion would be difficult for you."

Tonya's eyes responded to Emily's empathy before she said in a ragged voice, "I believe in God. I really do, but I cannot fathom Him being the fearsome, angry creature that religion dictates. I hold to the belief that He exists and He expects us to be good and serve others. But I think religion is something that men have concocted to control and frighten others into submission in the name of God, and I simply cannot have that in my home."

"So," Jess said, "are you saying that you believe religion is religion and they would all be the same straight across the board? And that any person who practices any religion would behave just as your parents did?"

Tonya looked taken aback. "Well, when you put it that way, it does sound awfully prejudiced, doesn't it."

Jess just smiled at her and said, "Would you give us the opportunity to tell you a little bit more about the gospel and how we apply it to our lives? And I swear to you if Murphy ever uses religion against you, I will personally belt him in the jaw."

Tonya chuckled and tossed an affectionate glance toward Murphy. She leaned back in her chair and said, "Okay, tell me. All things considered, I'm willing to keep an open mind."

"Well," Jess said, "first of all, one of our main focuses is family. The scriptures teach that a man should love his wife as Christ loves His Church. In fact, Christ's example of unconditional love, tender teaching, and gently leading His sheep are the very principles we are taught to follow in dealing with our fellow men, and most especially our families. People are imperfect, and I'm certain we have people who belong to this Church who treat their families badly. But the gospel is centered in Christ, who is perfect, and we as individuals try to emulate Him in all things. We consider religion a means to structure our lives and follow established guidelines that will give us peace in a difficult world, and happiness at the very core of our lives. The plan that we follow is all about returning to live with our Heavenly Father, who loves us and wants us to be happy. Your father's behavior would not be approved or endorsed by our leaders. That kind of attitude is what we refer to as unrighteous dominion, and it would be considered completely inappropriate. You are welcome to ask any question you like of any member of the Church, and you can start right here with these wonderful women." He motioned toward Tamra and Emily. "My mother was raised in the Church. Tamra joined as a young adult. Ask them how they feel about living in a home where religion is dominant. Come to church with us. Watch the families. Look at the women and see if they look oppressed and downtrodden. A few might. But I believe that is due to dysfunction in the family, not the Church they belong to."

Hope rose into Tonya's eyes, along with a distinct glisten of moisture. She didn't commit to going to church, but she did ask, "Do you think it's possible to have a good marriage with such a difference between us?"

"It's certainly not ideal," Jess said. "Our Church members are strongly encouraged to marry within their religion, for obvious reasons. And I can certainly understand why. However, I have known of more than one success story that occurred otherwise."

Tamra interjected. "I think the bottom line with every big decision is that you go to the Lord with it and do it because you know it's right. If two people get the right answers and stay committed to living with trust, commitment, and mutual respect, great things can happen."

Emily added, "When I accepted Michael's proposal, I believed we would be doing just that."

"What?" Jess asked.

"I was a member. I believed he wasn't."

"You believed?" Murphy asked.

"Well, he had actually joined the Church, but I didn't know about it until after he'd proposed. It's a long story that I'll have to share with you some other time. The point is that I felt completely confident that we could have a good marriage and raise a happy family. It's not an ideal situation, and I believe such differences can bring challenges. But if you're both in the marriage for the right reason, and you're committed to seeing the challenges through, I believe it's possible. There can be worse things to live with in a marriage," she added with a tone of voice that Jess recognized. She'd lived through an extremely difficult marriage prior to marrying his father. "I would simply advise that you make a very clear agreement straight up front on what role Murphy's beliefs will play in your home. There are things that will be important to him, and things that will be important to you. If you make an agreement and both stick to it, there will be no room for contention over religion. If either of you ever feels the need to adjust that agreement, you simply have to discuss it openly and make those adjustments mutually. Of course, that would apply to every issue in marriage, not just religion."

Emily leaned her arms on the table and looked directly at Tonya. "You're obviously a good woman, Tonya. And Murphy's a good man. Do you think it's possible that you could respect his beliefs, and allow him to respect yours?"

Tonya looked toward Murphy and tears spilled down her cheeks. Jess could see visible fear in Murphy's face, as if he was expecting Tonya to simply tell him that she couldn't live with it. Jess was proud of him when he leaned forward as well, saying earnestly, "There's something I'd like to say."

"I'm listening," Tonya said tearfully, and her emotion increased as Murphy bore a strong testimony of his knowledge that the gospel was true, and of his need to embrace it. He told her what a wonderful family the Hamiltons were, and of the good example they had always been to him. He told Tonya of his love for her, and his belief that they were meant to be together. He expressed how his deepest wish beyond joining the Church would be to spend the rest of his life with her, and that perhaps one day she would understand his faith enough to embrace it as well, and they could be together forever. But he made it clear he would not nag her or coerce her to join the Church, and that it would not be an issue between them. He finished by telling her once again that he loved her, but his heart dictated that he must be baptized, with or without her blessing.

Following a stark minute of silence, Murphy added firmly, "And if you could be there when it happens, I think I'd be the happiest man alive."

Tonya sniffled and wiped her face with her napkin. "I must admit," she said, "I was afraid that religion would turn you into my father, but when I look at the big picture, I know that's not true. I love you too," she said, "and I will support you in whatever you feel you must do, so long as it doesn't end up hurting me."

Murphy laughed with tears in his eyes. "I swear it," he said. "I could never hurt you."

Jess lifted his brows and exchanged a subtle smile with Tamra, then his mother. It seemed this story was going to have a happy ending. And with any luck, Tonya's heart would be softened further with time, and their ending would be the happiest.

Chapter Seven

Tonya left a short while later, without anything more being said specifically about religion or marriage. Jess helped Murphy get home after she'd gone, and they walked slowly across the yard, the speed dictated by Murphy's crutches.

"I learned a lot tonight that I didn't know," Murphy said.

"About the gospel?"

"That too."

"Then what?" Jess asked.

"I learned a lot about communicating effectively; something Tonya and I obviously weren't doing." He looked at Jess earnestly. "I'm grateful, Jess . . . more than I could ever tell you. I have no doubt you were inspired in the things you said to her. With all of that in the open, I think we're going to be just fine."

"It looks that way," Jess said.

When Murphy was settled with everything he needed, and certain that his mother was all right, Jess walked slowly back toward the house until his eye caught the wrought-iron fence nearby. It surrounded the little family cemetery where many of his ancestors were buried—along with his father. By the light of a partial moon, he walked a familiar path through the gate and to his father's grave. He knelt beside it and reverently touched the stone where his father's name was engraved. The stone looked startlingly new among the others, even in the moonlight. He found himself talking aloud to his father, as he did on occasion, and it felt good to tell him about what was happening with Murphy, even though he knew that Michael was likely well aware of the situation already.

Jess returned to the house, feeling warm inside, as if he truly had just shared a conversation with his father. How grateful he was for the knowledge of eternity that helped him understand how it was possible to feel close to his father. Miracles truly had not ceased.

* * *

Two days later Jess went to check on Murphy. He first sat with Susan and visited for a short while. She was feeling better every day and in good spirits. He asked how she felt about Murphy joining the Church and getting married. She was pleased about both prospects, and dearly loved Tonya. Jess then went in the other room, where Murphy was sitting with a good book—and grinning.

"What's up?" Jess asked, impulsively straightening the room where Murphy had endured his confinement with his leg propped up.

"I set a date."

"For what? To get married or be baptized?"

"Both," Murphy said and laughed.

Jess sat beside him and they embraced tightly. "That's great," Jess said. "So, what can we do to help?"

"Well, I'll have this cast off in a few days and they can replace it with a removable brace. I figured a white plastic bag over it ought to work."

"Sounds good," Jess chuckled.

"There is one thing you could do for me . . . if you wouldn't mind."

"Anything," Jess said.

"Would you do the honor?"

Jess felt confused. "The honor?"

"Would you be the one to baptize me?"

A thousand thoughts raced through Jess's mind in a single moment. Did Murphy have any idea that Jess had never performed a baptism, even though he'd served a mission? Did Murphy know that it was something he'd always longed to do? He'd observed how close Murphy had become to the elders who had been teaching him, and he had simply assumed that one of them would perform the baptism. For a second he nearly protested, feeling almost unworthy of such a privilege. But the light in Murphy's eyes lured him to say, "It would be an honor."

Jess looked forward to the baptism with great anticipation. When he sat down next to the baptismal font, dressed in white, with Murphy beside him, dressed the same, it was easy to imagine his father nearby, smiling over this glorious occasion. Jess looked over his shoulder to see his family seated close by, and Susan with them. He smiled and winked, then turned his attention to the half sheet of paper in his hand that constituted the printed program. He was startled by the name and couldn't resist teasing Murphy. He whispered in his ear, "Donald Eugene Murphy? And I thought your name was just 'Murphy.'"

"When you work with a bunch of stable hands, you get called by your surname."

"But I knew you when you were a kid."

"Well, your dad used to call me the same thing he called my dad. So, I guess it's his fault."

"Well, I prefer Murph," Jess said.

"Fine, but when you baptize me, get the name right. I want the record straight."

"Not to worry, my friend. It will be."

Murphy glanced around anxiously before he said, "She's not here yet. She said she'd be here."

"Then we'll wait," Jess said. The meeting began without her and Murphy's anxiety increased visibly. But after the first talk had been given by one of the elders, Tonya appeared in the door, wearing a nice pantsuit. She smiled at Murphy and moved quietly to sit beside Tamra. Jess glanced back once to see Tonya holding little Michael against her shoulder.

The baptism went smoothly, and the Spirit was strong. Once Jess and Murphy had changed into dry clothes, Jess also confirmed him a member of the Church. When the blessing was finished Murphy rose and embraced Jess tightly. They turned to see the women with tears in their eyes—even Tonya.

When the meeting was over, Jess took the family, the elders, and Murphy and Tonya and Susan out to dinner. They had a marvelous visit, but the day proved to be long and difficult for Tamra. By the time they left the restaurant she was feeling ill and more exhausted than usual—which was pretty bad. She typically slept long nights and took a couple of naps through the day just in order to feel presentable for meals and minimal outings. She had been determined to enjoy the baptism—and she had. But now that it was over, she admitted to feeling horrible. She slept on the way home and Jess helped her up to bed, kissing her brow as he tucked her in.

"I love you, Tamra," he said.

She smiled and touched his face. "Have I ever told you how handsome you look in white?"

"Not recently," he said.

"Well, you do," she said and pushed her arms around his neck. "Thanks for being the kind of man who wears white—for the right reasons."

Jess kissed her again and left her to get some sleep.

* * *

Three weeks after Murphy's baptism, he married Tonya in the upstairs hall of the Hamilton house. It was Emily's idea to hold the wedding there, since that's where she and Michael had been married—and generations of ancestors before them. Michael had been a new member of the Church at the time and unable to be married in the temple.

The wedding was quiet and simple and everything went well, in spite of Murphy still wearing a leg brace. While Murphy and Tonya were on their honeymoon, his work in the stables was managed rather smoothly without him. The hands had gained some practice through Murphy's absence due to his broken leg. Jess was only called in a couple of times to handle a minor crisis.

Work at the boys' home progressed as well. Jess felt himself settling more comfortably into his routine, although there always seemed to be far too much work to accomplish in a day. Beyond that, his only real concern was with Tamra. The time she spent in bed due to her pregnancy didn't improve at all as the weeks passed, but the doctor had given her a clean bill of health and all Jess could do was remain supportive and remember that it wouldn't last forever. Occasionally he found Tamra at the piano, which always pleased him. He knew how she loved it, and was grateful that it filled her as it did. But he knew she was frustrated by her lack of strength to fully enjoy it.

As always, Jess was grateful for his mother's presence in the home, and the help and support she gave to his family. And while she repeatedly insisted that helping care for his children was a blessing to her, he had to thank God for putting them into such a win/win situation. Beyond Emily asking once every week or so when Jess and Tamra were going to move into the master bedroom, he couldn't complain about his mother's place in the family.

Jess enjoyed the time he was able to spend with his children, however minimal. He often helped bathe them and put them to bed in the evenings. And a bedtime story with Evelyn was mandatory. Little Michael just seemed to get cuter every day, and as he began to crawl, Jess pulled the baby gates out of the attic and put them into the brackets that had been left from times past when babies had ruled the house.

In spite of his busy schedule, Jess made a point of talking regularly with each of his sisters, appreciating the relationships he shared with them, even with the miles between them. They all shared a common bond in missing their father. It was something they were all managing to deal with, but Jess was amazed at how spurts of grief could still come out of nowhere and assault him. But once he had a good cry he could usually move on and hope that he was living up to his father's expectations to some degree. At times he felt he was doing all right—all things considered. But at others, he felt certain that his forebears on the other side of the veil were wondering what kind of child they'd left in charge of their legacy. All he could do was keep going and pray that God would make up the difference for all that he was incapable of doing.

* * *

As usual Tamra awoke feeling ill. She ate some crackers she'd left on the bedside table to ease her nausea and forced herself to get up and shower. She knew from experience that if she gave in to the temptation to stay in bed in her pajamas all day, she would only feel worse emotionally. And the discouragement was as difficult to deal with as the illness.

While she was getting dressed, Tamra tried on three outfits before she found a long jumper that fit. She took a good, hard look at her reflection in the long mirror in her bedroom, and when she turned to look at her profile, she gasped. Instinctively concerned, she went in search of Emily.

"How are you this morning?" Emily asked as Tamra entered the kitchen.

"I'm fat," she snarled.

"You're pregnant," Emily chuckled.

"Well, I'm getting a *lot* bigger a *lot* faster this time. Look at me." She pressed her dress tightly over her belly. "If I didn't know better, I'd think I was having twins."

Tamra expected a chuckle from Emily. What she got was a hard stare. "Know better than what?" Emily asked while Tamra's heart quickened. "Or had you forgotten that I gave birth to twins while married to your husband's father?" Now she chuckled. "I don't know much about genetics, but I'd bet you have a higher chance at having twins than the average woman."

"Oh, help," Tamra said and staggered to the nearest chair, feeling suddenly light-headed. "What if it *is* twins?" she demanded.

"What if it is?" Emily countered. "Then you'll have two babies instead of one."

Tamra couldn't hold back the tears any longer. "But isn't it twice as difficult to have twins? You've told me yourself what a horrible pregnancy that was."

Emily sat beside Tamra and took her hand. "Yes it was difficult, but I had also been in a serious accident. I was still in the hospital from that accident when I realized I was pregnant. The requirement to stay in bed the last several weeks may or may not have had anything to do with that accident. I don't know. I *do* know that you're much younger than I was then, and in much better health. And I also know that God does not give us more than we can handle."

Tamra chuckled through her tears. "Well, sometimes I think that my opinion on that differs from the Lord's opinion."

Emily laughed softly. "Yes, I know what you mean, but I can testify that He really does mean it, and He holds to His promises. I've had some pretty rough times in my life, but somehow I always made it through."

"Oh, I'm sorry," Tamra said. "Listen to me complaining all the time. You *have* had some rough times, and I—"

"I was only trying to make a point," Emily said. "I've lived a good life and I've been very blessed. And you've had some rough times, too. Unlike you, I grew up with the gospel in my home, with a loving family. You're a strong woman with much to give and you are going to get through this—whatever it entails—just fine."

"Oh," Tamra cried and threw her arms around Emily's neck, "I'm so grateful for you. What do women do who don't have a mother-in-law who is also their best friend?"

Emily actually laughed. "Well, you've got me on that one. Michael's mother was always good to me and we got along well. She helped me through some tough things. But my first husband's mother was more hindrance than help, to say the least."

Tamra became lost in the conversation as Emily recounted some experiences from her past that she'd never heard before. When something came up about the twins she'd given birth to, Tamra was reminded of her present concern and something inside of her twisted into knots. *Twins?* Could it be possible? As exhausted as she felt, the very idea seemed insurmountable. Evelyn interrupted the conversation, needing help with her dollies, and Emily eagerly volunteered to remedy the problem. Alone with her thoughts, Tamra quickly realized that she would likely cope much better if she knew exactly what she was dealing with. She made a couple of phone calls and discovered that she was far enough along in her pregnancy to do an ultrasound that would determine exactly what was going on inside of her. The nurse she spoke with at her regular clinic suggested that perhaps she had gestational diabetes, which could cause the baby to grow very large, and it might not be twins at all. She told Tamra that a test could be done to eliminate that as a possibility, if she was interested. Tamra made an appointment for an ultrasound, figuring if that didn't give her any satisfactory answers, she would move on to other possibilities. At the moment, she almost hoped it was the diabetes, and guilt came right along with such a wish. As difficult as it would be to deal with such an illness and its complications, the thought of carrying, giving birth to, and raising two babies simply seemed more than she could bear.

As soon as the appointment was made, Tamra phoned Jess's office. He was on another line and Madge said she'd have him call back. The phone rang less than ten minutes later, while Emily was still busy helping Evelyn, and Tamra was putting a load of laundry into the washer.

"What's up?" Jess asked.

Tamra didn't want to tell him her suspicions until she had more to go on. And she certainly didn't want to tell him over the phone. She simply said, "I have a doctor appointment this afternoon. I was wondering if you could get away and come with me."

He sighed loudly. "I'm sorry, honey. I've got a meeting that can't be postponed." He paused and added, "I thought you didn't have another appointment until next week."

"I just scheduled this one."

His voice picked up an edge of panic. "Are you all right? Are you not feeling well?"

"I just . . . feel like something's . . ." She hesitated, not wanting to alarm him, but at the same time not wanting to talk about it now.

"What?" he demanded.

"It just feels . . . different. I'm sure it's nothing to worry about. I just feel like I should be checked. We can talk when I get back."

The regret in his voice was evident as he said, "I really wish I could go with you. I just . . . really need to be at that meeting."

"I understand, Jess, I really do. I'll be fine. I'll come find you as soon as I get back."

"I'll be looking forward to it." He sighed and added, "I really hope everything's all right."

"I'm sure it is, Jess. Please don't worry."

Tamra hurried to get off the phone and went to find Emily. "Would you be willing to go into town with me? You didn't have any plans today, did you?"

"Nothing special," Emily said. "I'd be happy to. What are we doing?"

"I made an appointment for an ultrasound."

Emily's surprise was evident. "Are you far enough along to be able to—"

"They said I was. I just . . . need to know. If it's not twins, then I fear something might not be right; diabetes or something. I'll feel better when I know for sure. Jess has a meeting, but I really don't want to go alone. I called Sister Harvey and she said we could bring the kids by while we go to the appointment."

"Well, that sounds great," Emily said. "Why don't we leave soon and I'll treat you to lunch at that Chinese place you love?"

"Sounds good," Tamra said and hurried to get ready.

Through the drive into town, Tamra tried to talk herself out of the dread she was feeling. She enjoyed her outing with Emily, and was grateful for her support. But the news she was given settled into her with many mixed emotions, and she cried silently all the way home while Emily drove and held her hand.

At Emily's suggestion, Tamra rested for a while before she went to the boys' home to talk to Jess. When she finally walked into his office, he started a conversation that immediately distracted her from her own purpose.

"Rhea called me," Jess said.

By the gravity in his voice, Tamra demanded, "What's wrong?"

"Well, nothing's wrong; nothing serious, anyway. She's got a bad cold that she just can't seem to get rid of, and it's turned into a bronchial thing. She just called to tell me that she was having someone come in a few hours more every day than they were to help with your mother, and she hoped the extra expense wasn't a problem. Of course, I told her it wasn't. But I wonder if Rhea's overwhelmed even with that, although I doubt she'd admit it. I was thinking that maybe we ought to bring your mother here for a month or so and give Rhea a break. I mentioned it to her and she . . ." He stopped when huge tears showed in Tamra's eyes.

Jess felt fear seize him as he recalled that Tamra had gone to a doctor appointment because she'd felt that something was . . . What had she said? Different? He sprang to his feet and took hold of her shoulders. "What's wrong, Tamra? What did the doctor say?"

"Nothing's wrong." She looked down. "Nothing's medically wrong, anyway."

"Then why are you crying?"

"I want to be able to help with my mother . . . I do. I'd love to have her come and stay. It's just that, I'm already a burden to you and your mother and to add more burdens upon the household just—"

"Now, wait a minute. You are anything but a burden to me *or* my mother. You know that. And as far as your mother coming, well . . .

we already decided that if she did we would hire a nurse to be with her. It won't be a burden on anybody."

"But someone's still got to . . . be aware of her and . . . spend time with her, and if I can't do that, then . . . someone else has to, and . . ."

Tamra fell apart in tears and Jess felt something uneasy prickle at the back of his neck as one too many concerns registered in his brain. He urged Tamra to a chair and sat close beside her, taking her hand. In a gentle voice that defied his growing anxiety, he asked, "Tamra, what did the doctor say?" Her eyes responded with evidence that she did, indeed, have something to tell him, but she said nothing. Jess's heart quickened and his stomach tightened, but he forced a steady voice as he pressed, "Tamra, why do you believe you wouldn't be of any help if your mother were here?"

She looked at the floor as she answered. "I'm already pretty much useless. The nausea's gotten a little better, but it still nags at me almost constantly. And I'm just so exhausted. I've never felt so constantly tired in my life, and . . ." Tamra stood abruptly and moved away, growling quietly, "Listen to the way I complain. I don't know what's become of me. I know I should be happy about this, and . . . I am. Deep inside, I really am. I just feel so . . . useless. And it's going to get a lot worse before it gets better."

"Why is that?" Jess asked, watching her expression carefully.

She tossed him a quick glance then looked out the window. "That's typical with pregnancy, is it not?"

"I don't know. Last time you did pretty well until the last month—once you got over the nausea at the beginning." He gave her a minute to volunteer what she had to tell him, but she didn't. "Tamra," he pressed, "what did the doctor say?" Still she didn't speak. "You told me this morning that something felt . . . different, but you haven't told me what."

Tamra turned to the side and he became momentarily distracted by the silhouette of her face against the window. She was so beautiful. She always had been. She looked down and pressed her dress over her rounded belly. "Look at me," she said.

"Yes," he chuckled, "you look pregnant."

"Well, last time when I was this far along, we were on vacation with your family and no one could even tell I was pregnant."

Jess couldn't deny feeling uneasy with the comparison. He simply hadn't kept track of such things. His growing anxiety threatened to pound his heart right out of his chest as he forced an even voice. "So, what's wrong, Tamra? Just tell me and get it over with." He was wishing he had canceled that stupid meeting and gone with her to the appointment. Still she hesitated and he demanded, "Just tell me what's wrong!"

"Nothing's wrong, Jess," she said as contradictory tears trailed down her face. "Everything is completely normal . . . as far as having twins goes."

Jess was glad to be sitting down. "Twins?" The word erupted on the crest of a shock wave that catapulted through his body, leaving his knees weak and his heart beating quickly. "That's incredible!" he added, the joy he felt evident in his voice. But a long glance at his wife made it evident that she didn't agree. She squeezed her eyes closed and looked away just as new tears crept between her lashes. Jess rose and stood behind her, putting his hands to her shoulders. "Is it not incredible?" She only sniffled. "Talk to me, Tamra. Tell me what's troubling you. I do believe that I'm the father of these babies, and we need to work together to do whatever we have to in order to get them here, healthy and strong, and to keep you the same way. But I can't help you if you won't talk to me."

"There's nothing I can say that doesn't sound like the complaining I've been doing for weeks now."

"Say it anyway," he said, pulling her into his arms.

Tamra cried against his shoulder, unburdening her every concern of how difficult this could be, and how useless and inadequate she felt. Jess assured her that he would always be there for her, that this experience would not last forever, and they would get through it together. She managed to stop crying while she listened, but she didn't seem convinced.

"Listen to me," Jess said, guiding her to a chair. "Life has thrown us a curve ball; no doubt about that. But we are going to get through it. We just need to reevaluate a few things. Obviously it's not a good time for your mother to come here. I'll call Rhea and just have her hire someone to cover more hours and—"

"No," Tamra said so abruptly that it startled Jess. "If you told Rhea that we would bring my mother here, then we will do it. I will not have my mother thinking that . . ."

Tamra stopped when she saw the astonishment in Jess's eyes. While she was trying to think of a way to justify her reaction, Jess asked quietly, "You won't have your mother thinking what?" She didn't answer and he asked, "What has this got to do with your mother?"

"Nothing!" she snapped, then she cleared her throat and said gently, "I'm sorry; I'm just tired. I think I need to just . . . lie down."

Jess watched her for a full minute, knowing there were deeper issues here than she was admitting to. He wanted to demand that she spill her every thought to him so they could sort it out. But there was no mistaking the stubborn set of her jaw, nor the blatant exhaustion in her eyes. "That's probably a good idea," he said, coming to his feet. "I'll walk you back to the house."

Nothing was said as Jess walked with his arm around Tamra, but she started crying again as if her world were about to end. He just held her tighter as they walked to their room, where he took off her shoes and tucked her into bed.

"You get some rest," he said, "and we can talk later this evening." She nodded, barely able to keep her eyes open. "I love you, Tamra," he said and pressed a lingering kiss to her brow.

"I love you too, Jess," she said, touching his face. "Forgive me . . . for . . ."

Her words faded into tears and Jess kissed her again. "It's all right. Just get some rest and we'll talk later." She nodded and Jess left the room. He returned to the boys' home, vacillating between exuberant joy at the thought of having twins, and deep concern on Tamra's behalf. But he'd barely walked into his office before he was confronted with several things that needed his attention. He had Madge call the house and let them know he'd be late for supper and not to wait for him. By the time he returned home, the house was quiet and the kitchen clean. He found a plate in the fridge that he stuck into the microwave to heat while he poured himself a glass of grape juice on ice. He was taking a long swallow when his mother appeared.

"I wondered when you'd make it home," she said. "Tough day?"

"Yes, actually, but nothing serious—at least at the boys' home." He glanced around. "Where is everybody?"

"The little ones are down for the night." She chuckled. "Well, I'm sure Michael will be wanting that bottle in about three hours.

And Tamra didn't even feel well enough to make it down to supper. I took some up to her. She ate and took a hot bath and went back to bed."

Jess sighed loudly and sat down at the table, pushing his hands through his hair. "I told her we'd talk when I got home. Guess I blew that one."

"I think she was too worn out to talk any more," Emily said.

"I'm worried about her," he admitted and stood to retrieve his plate as the microwave beeped.

"Well, this is tough for her—and understandably so. But she'll get through." Emily smiled and added, "Are you interested in some motherly advice on how you can help her get through?"

He smiled in return then took a minute to bless the food before he said, "I'll take all the advice I can get. I feel . . . helpless."

"Well, I've been where she is. Even though a woman logically knows that pregnancy and caring for infants won't last forever, when you're worn out, it feels like it will. And her hormones are probably on a roller coaster. So you and I are going to do everything we can to help her without taking away her opportunities to do all that she feels well enough to do. And I think you can help her most by just making sure you spend some time with her every day. Listen to her complain, tell her that you love her, and just hold her."

"Is that what my father did for you when you were pregnant with twins?"

Emily's smile was sad, her eyes nostalgic. "Yes, actually," her voice broke, "that's exactly what he did. And through other pregnancies as well. We had our challenges, and some times were tougher than others, but even when he was very busy, if he took some time to devote just to me each day, I never had to wonder if he was mindful of me. It made a huge difference, as opposed to my first husband who . . ." She laughed softly. "We don't want to go there."

Jess worked on eating his supper while his mother was obviously absorbed in tender memories. Jess couldn't think too hard about his father's absence, so he focused his thoughts on the revelation he'd received earlier today. A chuckle escaped him, drawing his mother's attention.

"What's funny?" she asked.

"Twins. I can't believe it."

Emily laughed softly. "It can be quite a shock." She reached for his hand across the table. "But you're obviously pleased."

"I am," he said. "I know it will be tough, but . . . the very idea just feels like . . . a miracle. Then I think of the way Tamra feels and I wonder if I should feel guilty for being happy about it." He looked down. "She's obviously not."

"No, I don't think that's the case," Emily said. "The two of you have hardly had a chance to talk, and it's not my place to tell you her thoughts and feelings, but from a mother's perspective I believe she is simply too overwhelmed with the reality of the challenges to fully appreciate the wonder. But she will. I think you should just come right out and ask her how she feels." She smiled again.

"I think I'll do that, first chance I get." A few minutes later, he added, "Thank you, Mother."

"For what?"

"Just for being you . . . and, well . . . I'm just grateful to have you be a part of our lives."

"The feeling is mutual, Jess. I would be lost without you and your family here with me. I can't even imagine how I would have coped. And I must admit that it's nice to feel needed. I got so used to your father needing me for so many little things . . . especially at the end. I'm glad to have your sweet wife and children needing me now."

Jess smiled at her, but his voice was blocked behind the knot gathering in his throat. There were moments when he missed his father so badly that it hurt. And this was one of those moments.

"You look tired," Emily said as he took his plate to the sink and rinsed it off. She rose and kissed his cheek. "I'll see you in the morning."

"Goodnight, Mother," he said and walked slowly up the stairs. He did his best to be quiet as he prepared for bed and slipped beneath the covers, not wanting to disturb Tamra, but she immediately rolled toward him and pushed her arms around him.

"I didn't want to wake you," he whispered and kissed her.

"You didn't wake me," she replied and kissed him. "I've just been laying here thinking."

"What about?" he asked as she settled her head on his shoulder.

She sighed loudly. "Wondering how we'll survive having three babies. Michael will be barely a year when the twins arrive."

"We'll survive one day at a time," he said. "And while it will bring obvious challenges, I believe it will bring equivalent joy." Jess paused a moment then asked tentatively, "Are you happy about this, Tamra? I mean . . . I know it's difficult, especially for you, but . . . are you—"

"I want these babies, Jess. I love them already. I'm sorry if I gave you the impression otherwise. It is hard. But they are already a part of our family and I wouldn't want it any other way." She leaned up on one elbow and looked down at him through the darkness, while she pressed his hand to her belly. "One of them is a boy," she said.

"Really?" he chuckled. "And the other?"

"They couldn't tell from the way it was positioned, but they won't be identical."

"How do you know?" he asked.

"Separate placentas," she said.

"Wow," Jess chuckled. "It's amazing."

"Yes, it is," she said.

"So, does that mean it's hereditary?" he asked. "My parents had twins, and my dad's grandmother was a twin."

"Yes, I know," she said, "but actually, there's no connection; it's coincidence. Well, I guess you can't say the way people are born into this world is a coincidence, since it's all in God's hands. But the twins in your family are not genetic. When they're not identical, it comes through the mother. So that means that your mother and I just both happened to have twins."

"And my great-great-grandmother," he added then he chuckled and repeated. "It's amazing."

"Yes, it is," she said again, and it was quiet for several minutes before she whispered close to his face, "I love you, Jess Hamilton."

"And I love you," he replied and drifted to sleep, holding her in his arms. His next awareness was Michael crying from his crib across the room. "I'll get him," he said to Tamra when she stirred.

"Thank you," she muttered as he put his feet on the floor. He lumbered into the bathroom where everything was left ready to mix the bottle of formula. He shook the bottle on his way to the crib, and he resisted the urge to coo and talk to his little son. They'd been told not to give the baby any attention or stimulation at night, which would teach him more quickly that it was time to sleep. Once the diaper was changed, Jess sat in the rocker with only a tiny beam of light coming from the bathroom to guide him as he fed little Michael and burped him. With the baby drifting back to sleep against his shoulder, he was surprised to hear Tamra say quietly, "The first time I laid eyes on you, I would have liked to see into the future to this moment."

Jess chuckled softly and whispered, "It would have scared me away forever. I don't think I was ready to consider myself a father."

"And now you're the father of four," she said.

He laughed again. "One adopted," he clarified. "We didn't have to go through the really hard stuff with Evelyn."

"She's not a teenager yet."

Jess put little Michael back into his crib and watched him sleeping a moment before he flipped off the bathroom light and climbed back into bed. Holding Tamra close once more, he whispered, "Thanks for sticking it out with me, even when I was being a jerk."

"I had no choice," she said.

"Why is that?"

"My spirit knew it could never be complete unless it was linked with yours."

"Is that how it works?"

"That's how it felt to me; still does, in fact."

"Well, the feeling is mutual, Mrs. Hamilton. But I think you'd better get some sleep."

"Yes, I probably should," she said, "but I would prefer that you kiss me."

Jess chuckled and pressed his mouth to hers, holding her as close as he possibly could with two babies between them. As he kissed her over and over, he marveled at the joy he found in being married to her, and he silently thanked God for blessing his life so completely.

Chapter Eight

Jess lay for a long while, staring into the darkness above him. Tamra slept peacefully beside him and he kept his hand on her arm, grateful just to have her near his side. He had trouble admitting—even to himself—that the dark, silent hours were becoming increasingly difficult to face. As long as he kept busy, or interacting with other people, he didn't give the issue a single thought. But alone in the darkness, uneasy thoughts and feelings crowded into his mind as he tried to convince himself that he wasn't afraid to fall asleep.

Exhaustion finally won and lured him into oblivion until the same dream began. He was driving. It was night. But it wasn't the same dream. Even in his unconscious state he seemed to perceive that he was dreaming and he knew it was different than the repeated dreams that had plagued him since he'd rolled the Cruiser in the rain. He was driving. It was night. But he wasn't alone. With his hands on the wheel Jess turned to see Byron sitting in the passenger seat. *Byron.* His best friend. It had been so long since he'd seen him. He looked well. He was laughing. Jess laughed too. He heard laughter from behind and glanced over his shoulder to see James and Krista in the backseat. *James.* His brother. Oh, how Jess had missed him! They had always been so different, but since Jess had returned from his mission to find James married and a father, they had enjoyed some great bonding time, and he'd grown to appreciate the brotherhood they shared. And there was Krista beside him. She'd grown up not far from Brisbane, a wonderful girl, the kind of girl Jess wanted to marry himself.

Jess listened to the sound of their voices as he focused on the road ahead, enjoying their teasing banter, and the simple pleasure of being with friend and family, where the lines between the two dovetailed. Jess's heart quickened unexpectedly as he noticed the headlights in his lane. He adjusted his focus, wondering if it was his imagination, then Byron said, "Aren't those headlights coming straight at us?" The following seconds were a combination of tires squealing, Krista screaming, and Jess frantically turning the wheel. Metal crunching. Glass breaking. And then he was no longer in the car. He was hovering above it, looking at himself, unconscious against the wheel. And the others. The others looked so horrible. James and Krista were holding tightly to each other. But the blood. There was so much blood. And then Jess could only see blackness. He heard voices, many voices, familiar ones and some he'd never heard before. They were crying, speculating over whether he would live or die. The blackness seemed to go on forever, until he finally found the ability to open his eyes and look around. There were more things attached to him than he could count. His loved ones were nearby, but they were crying, always crying. They tried to hide the tears and be brave, but he knew they were crying. And when they told him the truth, he understood why. He was the only survivor. And from that moment on, he wished more with each breath that he had been privileged enough to die with them. The painful steps of an anguished recovery filed through his mind like a troop of invading soldiers. And all he wanted was to die. He just wanted to die . . .

Jess came awake with a gasp and felt Tamra's hands on his shoulders. "Are you all right?" she asked close to his face, and he realized that she had awakened him. He couldn't find his voice so he just took hold of her tightly, breathing in the reality of her presence. "You were dreaming," she said gently, pushing his hair back from his face.

"Yes . . . I was."

"Do you want to tell me about it?"

"It was . . . nothing," he insisted. "Just a dream. I'm fine." He eased away and went into the bathroom where he splashed cold water on his face. He went back to bed and forced a bright voice. "I'm fine, really. Go back to sleep."

Tamra did just that, but an hour later Jess was still staring at the ceiling with memories of his dream hurtling through his mind; sequences made more horrible by the fact that they were, in truth, memories. It had really happened. And after all this time, it had come back to haunt him.

Jess finally went into the bathroom, searching for something to help him sleep. He knew that Tamra took half a sleeping pill along with some particular vitamin, as a recommendation from her doctor, to help her nausea. He quickly found the box and figured half a pill should be all he'd need. He didn't want to be drugged the next day while he was trying to get his work done. But as he popped the little pill out of the blister pack that held it, a different memory assaulted him with such force that he staggered to sit on the closed toilet seat. He lost track of the minutes passing as he stared at the little blue pill in his hand, remembering the time he'd held twenty-five of them at once. He remembered staring at them, rearranging them in the palm of his hand several times, and then swallowing them—one at a time. Jess became so filled with a tangible anxiety that he had to force himself to close his eyes and pray. Through his prayer he reminded himself—and God—that Tamra had saved his life that night, and she had guided him through many steps of healing since. He had felt the power of the Atonement in his life as the wounds of that accident that had plagued his heart had finally healed. He reminded himself that he was only taking one half of one sleeping pill. He was emotionally stable and he was not depressed. He'd simply had a bad dream that had stirred up difficult memories, and he needed to get some sleep. In spite of certain losses and challenges, his life was good and he was happy. And even if it wasn't, he knew in the deepest parts of his heart and soul that he could never take his own life. He'd already run that gauntlet. The wounds were healed, the scars were deep, it was in the past.

Jess finally forced himself to just take the half pill and go back to bed. He prayed it would work quickly as memories of the dream rushed through his mind again. He wondered if the pill he'd taken would help him sleep deeply enough to not be plagued with more nightmares. And his next awareness was the alarm clock startling him awake.

At breakfast Tamra asked him, "Are you okay?"

Jess forced a smile, hoping it wouldn't look that way. "I'm fine."

"What's wrong?" Emily asked, dishing up hot cereal.

"Nothing's wrong," Jess chuckled. "I'm fine. It's you we should be worried about." He touched Tamra's nose with his finger. "How are you feeling this morning?"

"The same," she said. "I'll probably be back in bed in an hour, but I feel better in here," she touched her heart, "if I have breakfast with you."

"Well, that makes two of us," Jess said and reached across the table to kiss her.

Evelyn dropped her spoon and asked for a clean one. Tamra rose to get it and got lightheaded. She sat back down quickly and gripped the edge of the table.

"Here, I've got it," Emily said. "You need to be careful."

"I'm tired of being careful," Tamra growled.

"Now listen," Emily said, sitting beside her and putting a hand over hers, "there's something I need to say. I know this is difficult for you, Tamra. I know you want to be able to do everything that you've always been able to do. But what you are doing right now is far more valuable than anything that I can do to help you." Tamra looked baffled. Emily smiled and touched Tamra's face as she added, "You are creating life, Tamra. It's growing inside of you. You are the incubator for two human beings. That's hard on a body, and no one can do it but you. It's important for everyone to accept that we can't be on top of everything our whole lives. We all have down times. If no one had down times, the rest of the world would have no opportunity to serve. You've given great amounts of service in your life, Tamra, and until those babies get safely here and you recover, you're just going to have to accept that your primary purpose is giving them life and allowing them to grow. Okay?"

Tamra nodded tearfully then hugged Emily. "What would I ever do without you?"

"Well, we have each other and for that we are all truly blessed."

"Amen," Jess and Tamra both said at the same time.

As they all began to eat in silence, Jess's mind wandered to his dream. He was disconcerted to realize that its memory was clinging to his daytime thoughts.

"What's wrong?" Tamra asked, startling him. "And don't tell me you're fine. If you could see your face right now, you wouldn't even attempt lying to me."

Jess turned from Tamra's stern face to his mother's, wearing exactly the same expression. There were moments when sharing a home with his wife *and* his mother simply produced a double challenge. Thankfully, those moments were rare.

"It's that dream, isn't it," Tamra said.

"What dream?" Emily demanded.

"I had a . . . bad dream. It shook me up a little. But it was just a dream. I'm fine." He laughed. "Okay, I'm fine."

"It was just a dream, Daddy," Evelyn said like a parent and he chuckled, hearing her repeat to him what he had said to her when she'd had a bad dream.

"That's right, Evie," he said. "It was just a dream."

Tamra watched her husband closely. His efforts to smile and laugh and cover his concern were evident—even admirable. But she knew him better than that. After he left for work, she wasn't surprised to hear Emily say, "He's not fine, is he."

"You noticed that, too."

"Has he said anything to you?"

"No, but . . ."

"But?" Emily pressed.

"His dream woke me up, and I had to wake him because he was scaring me." She made sure Evelyn was distracted before she added softly, "He was saying over and over, 'I want to die. I want to die.'"

"Good heavens," Emily said. They remained in thoughtful silence until she added, "We must keep an eye on him."

Though nothing more was said about it, Tamra knew Emily's thoughts were similar to her own. Jess's suicide attempt, and his subsequent emotional recovery, had been a nightmare for all of them. And his declaration—even in sleep—that he wanted to die, couldn't help but make them wonder if some measure of emotional residue was coming to the surface.

* * *

In spite of Jess's busy morning, he managed to make some phone calls to arrange for Tamra's mother to come and stay with them. Between that and his work he kept busy enough that he could almost push away the memory of his dream. Or was it the memories that had been triggered by his dream? One and the same perhaps. Whatever it was, the accident that had caused so much grief for him and his family had been exhumed in his mind, and he wasn't very happy about it.

Shortly after sharing lunch in the cafeteria with the boys, Jess phoned the house, glad that Tamra answered.

"How are you feeling?" he asked.

"Oh, the same," she said without enthusiasm. "I'll leave it at that since I'm trying not to complain."

"Well, you can complain to me as much as you like," he said gently. "After all, it's my fault you feel this way."

"It certainly is," she said with a little chuckle. Then more seriously, "And how are you?"

"I'm fine," he said as if he had no idea why she'd even ask, while at the same time memories of his dream put knots into his stomach.

"Are you sure?" she asked tenderly.

"Yes, I'm sure," he said lightly.

Her silence implied that she was hesitant to accept it, but she changed the subject, "So what's up?"

"I just wanted to let you know that I talked to Rhea, and I've made arrangements to bring your mother here for a while."

Tamra hesitated before saying simply, "Okay."

Jess sensed that she wasn't happy about it, but for reasons he didn't understand, she was determined to see it through. He attempted to console her by saying, "I've discussed it with Mother. She thinks it's a great idea, and after all, it's only temporary, and . . . Well, the really good news is that not only was I able to hire a full-time nurse, but it's June. She just finished up a job and is available. Isn't that amazing! Do you remember June?"

It took Tamra a moment to connect the name with the woman who had stayed here when Michael had been in the final stages of his cancer. She had been kind and compassionate, and had fit comfortably in with the family. "Yes, I remember," she said, wishing she could feel some enthusiasm.

"Tamra, honey," Jess said, and she felt it coming. "If there's a reason you're not comfortable with this, then you need to say so." She said nothing and he added, "When this came up before, you said you wanted your mother to come. I've got everything arranged but that doesn't mean we have to do it. There are other options."

"No, I think we should do it," she said, trying to sound more optimistic than she felt. "If June is here full time, then there shouldn't be a problem." She was thoughtful a moment then asked, "June can't possibly be here all the time. Will she —"

"June said she's worked in many situations where she's learned to maneuver her own activities around the habits of her patient, and there are a couple of nurses that can cover for her so she can have the time off she needs. It'll be fine. June will be flying to Sydney with me tomorrow to get your mother and—"

"Tomorrow?" Tamra said, trying not to sound as dismayed as she felt. As it was, she didn't see Jess nearly as much as she would like. To have him fly to Sydney and back would take an entire day—and it would take him days at the boys' home to catch up on the missed work, filling in extra hours whenever he could.

"Is there a problem?" he asked gently, as if he would be nothing but honored to grant her every wish. And she knew he probably would. He would do anything in his power to make her happy. If she asked him to make other arrangements for her mother, he would. If she asked him to hire more help at the home and spend more time with her, he would. But those boys needed him, and what he was willing to do for her mother was wonderful. So, why did she feel so grumpy about it? Perhaps because she felt just plain grumpy.

Knowing the bulk of the problem was her overactive hormones, fueled by ongoing nausea and exhaustion, Tamra simply said, "No, there's not a problem. You're very sweet to help with my mother this way. Thank you."

"I love you, Tamra," he said, his sincerity evident.

"I love you too," she said and hung up the phone, sighing.

"I couldn't help overhearing," Emily said, leaning against the nearby counter where she had been putting together a vegetable soup.

"Since you were three feet away when I answered the phone," Tamra said, "I wouldn't have expected you not to overhear. I certainly wasn't trying to hide anything; I have nothing to hide from you."

"So, I assume that was Jess."

"Did you think I would be saying 'I love you' to anybody else?"

"Your father perhaps." Emily smiled. "But I could tell it was Jess." She sat down across the table from Tamra. "May I ask what he told you that has made you look so depressed?"

Tamra felt momentarily alarmed, then she reminded herself that, just as she'd said a moment ago, she had nothing to hide. Emily was the closest thing she had to a friend.

"He's flying to Sydney tomorrow to get my mother. He said he'd talked with you about it."

"Yes, he did.

"And you really don't have a problem with it?" Tamra asked.

"Why would I have a problem?"

"Well . . . having your home invaded that way with—"

"It's your home every bit as much as it is mine," Emily said. "And it's far too big of a home to feel too invaded. June will be here to help your mother with everything she needs. And if we couldn't afford a nurse we'd manage somehow. I'm certain the Relief Society would be willing to help. I've certainly helped with similar situations in the past."

"You have?"

"Oh, yes. We had a sister in the ward who had a stroke with similar results, and the family didn't have the resources to care for her all the time, so many of us sisters took shifts helping care for her."

"I bet that sister didn't have a foul mouth and—"

"Tamra," Emily put a hand over hers on the table, "there's nothing your mother is going to say that will offend me. Besides, I heard she's not terribly easy to understand." Emily laughed softly. "That could be a blessing."

"I suppose."

A silent minute later, Emily said, "If I'm butting in, say so, but I get the feeling you're not pleased at all to have your mother coming. Is there a problem?"

Tamra wanted to scream at Emily and tell her that she was sounding just like her son. But she reminded herself that Emily was being perfectly polite and appropriate, and if Tamra said she didn't want to talk about it, Emily would respect her wishes and not be offended. But who else was Tamra going to talk to about it? She couldn't deny her appreciation for Emily's help and concern, so she did her best to swallow her pride, along with her bad mood, and just tell her how she felt.

"To be honest," Tamra said, "I'm not sure why it's bothering me. I guess I just don't want my mother to think I'm incapable of taking care of her myself and . . ." Emotion overtook Tamra with surprising intensity. Emily held her hand and let her cry until she was able to say, "I'm not sure where that came from, but obviously my feelings toward my mother haven't healed as much as I thought they had." She became teary again as she added, "I thought I'd forgiven her. I thought that . . ."

"Now, listen," Emily said in her typical wise and tender way, "having some emotional residue over the past experiences with your mother does not necessarily mean you haven't forgiven her. Forgiveness does not equal trust. You've never been able to trust her to be kind and appropriate, and your feelings about such things are simply a consequence of the years of having to deal with your mother and her difficult behavior. Your mother's gone through a drastic change in her life, and from what you've told me she has moments of being humble and appreciative, and other moments of being angry and belligerent. We will just deal with those moments the best that we can."

Tamra nodded and wiped her eyes with a tissue. "I just don't want her to bring more burden to you and Jess. You both already do so much to take care of me and the children, and I'm just . . ."

"You and the children are not a burden, Tamra, and neither will your mother be. There is a longstanding tradition in this family that you are well aware of. It's been there since Jess and Alexa first opened the boys' home in the 1880s. We take—"

"We take in lost souls; I know. I'm one of them."

"And so am I," Emily said. "Our family has been blessed with great abundance, and the scriptures teach us that with abundance comes a responsibility to help those in need. And that's what we do. That's what Jess is doing every hour he is working at that boys' home. With the financial resources we have available, caring for your mother will be made especially easy. And as I said before, if we couldn't afford to hire someone like June, we would manage somehow. I think, however, that this will work out well. Your mother will probably be more comfortable having a professional help her with personal things, and you and I can just visit with her when she needs company. And as far as whether or not your mother thinks you are incapable of caring for her yourself, it really doesn't matter what she thinks, does it? You know you're doing the best you can do, and surely your mother would understand the strain your body is under, being pregnant with twins so soon after your last pregnancy."

"My mother's not known for being compassionate," Tamra said, feeling more tears threatening to burst out of her. Fearing that she was only beginning to uncover some brand new layers of grief from her past, she forced the tears back, unable to handle anything else right now.

"Well, as I said, it really doesn't matter what she thinks. You do the best you can and stop worrying so much. When will I convince you that it's not a burden to help you and your family?"

Tamra forced a smile then hugged Emily, echoing the question in her mind. When *would* she be convinced that she was not a burden? If she knew the answer to that question, she probably wouldn't feel so completely discouraged.

* * *

The following morning after Jess left in the plane to go to Sydney, Tamra found herself decidedly nervous—although she couldn't pinpoint exactly why. She spent the morning attempting to come up with an answer. She truly felt that she'd forgiven her mother for the issues of the past. She wasn't actually entertaining negative feelings toward her mother. No, that wasn't it. Emily was right when she'd said that surely Myrna would understand Tamra's situation in being pregnant with twins, and there would likely be no expectations there that Tamra needed to meet. And Tamra had already spent time with her mother since the stroke; she didn't feel nervous about actually being able to handle the disability. So, what was it that made this situation so difficult?

Following lunch, a long nap, and more pondering, Tamra came to the conclusion that she simply wasn't comfortable with the crossing of two worlds. The life she'd shared with her mother, prior to her mission, had been filled with abuse and ugliness. Her life since coming to Australia had been riddled with challenges, but it was a good life, filled with warm memories and bright hope. Was she simply troubled by bringing the past too close to the present? Whatever it was, Jess would be arriving in a few hours with her mother and June, whether she liked it or not. She would do well to like it—or at least pretend to. Otherwise, she'd have Jess trying to analyze what the problem might be, and she honestly couldn't tell him.

It was late evening before they finally heard the plane. Tamra felt exhausted, in spite of a couple of naps, but she didn't want her mother to arrive and find her sleeping. She drove out to the hangar to meet them while Emily stayed with the children, who were already asleep. When Jess stepped out of the plane she was waiting to greet him, and they exchanged an embrace that implied he'd been gone for days.

"How are you?" he asked, looking into her eyes.

"I'm fine," she insisted with a smile. "How are you?"

"Tired, but well," he said.

"Everything went all right?"

"It did," he said, moving to help June get Myrna ready to be moved from the plane to the Cruiser.

Tamra greeted her mother with an embrace and was pleased to see positive recognition in her eyes, although she said nothing beyond a mumbled, "Hello."

While Tamra spoke with June and helped her transport all that her mother would need, she felt touched to see how Jess tenderly and patiently helped Myrna. She was truly blessed to have such a good man in her life—especially considering the models of men she'd grown up with; men who were saddled with every possible dysfunction.

When they arrived at the house, Tamra wasn't at all surprised to see how warmly Emily greeted her mother. She stuck close to Myrna, chatting comfortably in a mostly one-sided conversation while they got her settled into her room. Emily explained that the room had been used by Michael's mother for quite some time when she'd become ill and had needed to be where the family could be closer to her during the days. The location was ideal, since it was on the main floor and didn't require the use of any stairs to get to the important rooms in the home.

Tamra fought off her weariness and helped Emily warm up some supper for Jess, Myrna, and June. With Myrna's wheelchair pulled close to the table, June comfortably helped Myrna in between taking bites of her own meal. Tamra was amazed by June's finesse as a nurse. They seemed so comfortable together that one would think she'd been working with Myrna for months—not just today.

When Myrna was back in her room for the night, Tamra said goodnight and pressed a kiss to her forehead, promising to bring the children to see her in the morning. She left June to get Myrna ready for bed, while Jess went out to put the Cruiser into the carriage house and make certain all was well. Tamra was relieved to finally be able to go to bed, but it took every ounce of strength just to get up the stairs. She slept immediately and woke in the night to find Jess beside her. She went back to sleep and woke in the morning to find him gone. She vaguely recalled him kissing her good-bye, but she'd barely come awake at the time and drifted quickly back to sleep, leaving her to wonder if it had only been a dream.

Following the usual morning bout of dry heaves, Tamra fed little Michael and dressed him. When Evelyn wasn't in her room, Tamra knew she had risen earlier and was with Emily. She found them in the kitchen and, after eating some dry toast and herb tea, she left the baby with Emily so she could take a shower. Once she felt presentable, Tamra took the baby and Evelyn to her mother's room, preparing herself to be cheerful and positive. Just outside the partially open door, Tamra hesitated, hearing her mother talking very unkindly to June. Myrna's speech was slow and slurred, but the tone was all too familiar, and the occasional curse came through quite clearly. Tamra was pleased with the way June politely countered Myrna's behavior. Without being disrespectful, June made it clear that she wouldn't be treated that way. It was evident that June had worked with difficult patients before.

Still, Tamra decided this was not a good time to visit her mother. Perhaps later she would be in a better mood, she reasoned, scooting Evelyn upstairs to play while she explained, "I think Grandma Myrna is busy right now. You can meet her later."

Tamra had taken time to carefully explain to Evelyn the situation with her new grandmother who was going to stay with them. She felt that Evelyn understood, as much as it was possible for a four year old, what to expect. They had talked about the stroke that had severely disabled Myrna, and also about how Myrna sometimes said bad words and wasn't very nice, but that Evelyn just needed to be kind in return and not let it bother her. Tamra wished she could take her own advice and be able to do just that without having the experience dredge up all kinds of unpleasant memories.

After an hour in the nursery, reading storybooks and dressing dollies, Tamra resigned herself to getting this over with and returned to her mother's room. She was sitting in her wheelchair near the window while June stood behind her, combing her hair. Tamra pasted on a smile and greeted her mother warmly. Myrna smiled and said with difficulty, "Pretty view." She motioned vaguely toward the window with the hand that she could use minimally.

"Yes, it is," Tamra said. She showed her mother the baby. Myrna beamed and commented on how he'd grown. Then Tamra introduced Myrna to Evelyn. The child said nothing. She simply stared with curious eyes at Myrna and the wheelchair she sat in that was equipped with electronic controls and many accessories that a standard wheelchair didn't have.

Myrna and Evelyn sized each other up carefully, but neither of them said anything. June broke the tension with some pleasant conversation, and Tamra was grateful for her being there to buffer the situation—if not Tamra's feelings.

Within a few days Evelyn warmed up to Myrna somewhat. She often wanted to go and show her 'other grandma' certain things, and she quickly got used to Myrna's minimal—and difficult to understand—responses. Tamra appreciated Emily's help in visiting with Myrna and keeping track of Evelyn. While her fatigue and nausea showed no improvement whatsoever, she couldn't even imagine what she would have done without Emily living in the same home.

Tamra made a point to go to her mother's room a couple of times a day and sit with her while she fed the baby and burped him. It was something that had to be done anyway, and it allowed her to sit with her mother and not feel that she had to make clever conversation, as Myrna seemed to enjoy just watching little Michael drink his bottle. All in all, Tamra had to admit that the situation wasn't nearly as difficult or uncomfortable as she'd imagined it to be—but still she felt uneasy, and she wasn't certain why.

Along with Tamra's hovering uneasiness came a growing discouragement as she tried to look ahead through the months of pregnancy she had left, and then the ominous task of caring for twins. While she genuinely tried to put her focus elsewhere and be positive, she felt as if a dark cloud hung over her that she didn't understand and couldn't get rid of. And coupled with her own dark cloud, was the one she sensed hovering around her husband. He smiled and remained sweet and attentive in between his long, busy hours at work. But she knew something wasn't as it should be. She was well aware that he continued to have bad dreams, but he didn't want to talk about them so she stopped asking. She was afraid if she pressed him too hard to talk about what was troubling him, he would likely do the same to her. And she simply didn't want to talk about her ongoing uneasiness when she couldn't pinpoint any problem beyond just being pregnant and miserable. She simply resigned herself to press forward one day at a time, certain that when this pregnancy was over, everything would be better.

* * *

Jess caught himself staring at nothing while his mind wandered through memories of his recurring dream—memories of that accident. He startled himself back to the present and had to admit that his tendency to become distracted by such thoughts was becoming more and more frequent. That only made him more uneasy. He couldn't help recalling how his depression had made him frequently zone out mentally—a condition that had eventually led him to an attempted suicide. Recalling the paths his life had taken, he began to wonder what a man like him was doing in charge of so many people's lives: his family, these boys in his care. And these family businesses that sustained and supported so many were completely under his direction. He thought of Tamra's present state of health, and having her mother under their roof as well, and he couldn't deny feeling an increasingly heavy burden on his shoulders.

Jess was feeling like he couldn't possibly handle one more problem laid at his feet, when Madge came into his office and announced, "Dina just quit."

"Why?" he demanded.

"Personal reasons; that's all she said."

"No notice?"

"Nope. She just left."

"Well, that's just great," Jess snarled.

"I'll get an ad in the paper," Madge said on her way out the door, unaffected by Jess's foul mood.

Jess sighed. He knew how it usually went. Replacing an employee with someone suitable could sometimes take weeks, and in the meantime the absence of one could put a strain on many. Suddenly feeling unable to move, or even think, Jess leaned back in his chair and closed his eyes. He found himself longing for his father. He thought of how unruffled and calm Michael Hamilton could be in dealing with any problem that might arise. He was amazed at how a clear image of his father came to his mind, and he could easily imagine him sitting in the chair across the desk, his ankle crossed over his knee, laughing and talking over the business at hand. While Jess was pleasantly focused on memories of his father, the words came into his mind, *Just pray, son, and you will find the answers you need.*

Jess's eyes came abruptly open, and he felt startled to realize that he was alone in the room. Still, he felt as if his father had just given him sound, but simple, advice. And he felt better.

Jess bowed his head where he sat and silently prayed for strength and guidance. Not a heartbeat beyond the 'amen' he picked up the phone and dialed the bishop's home. His wife said he would be coming in from the farm for lunch in a few minutes and she'd have him call back.

"Hello," Jess said when the call was returned.

"What can I do for you?" the bishop asked.

"Well, I've got a problem that needs solving, and I must admit that I felt like I should call you, even though this is not my usual route for filling a position."

"I'm listening," the bishop said with a little chuckle.

"Well, I'm just wondering if you're aware of anyone in the ward in need of employment. I just had a woman quit without notice."

The bishop made a noise of interest and asked, "What does the job entail?"

"Well, it's mostly light cleaning around the boys' home, and some help in the cafeteria. We have a cleaning company come in regularly and take care of the major cleaning. This is just keeping the place tidy and helping around the place wherever there's a need. It could work for a man or woman, and it could be temporary until they find something better. Or it could be permanent if it works out."

"Well, there is someone who might be interested," the bishop said.

Jess chuckled. In spite of the prompting, he'd nearly expected to be told that he was barking up the wrong tree.

"Have you met Sister Poll?" he asked.

"I don't believe so," Jess said.

"She just moved in a couple of weeks ago, into one of the apartments not far west of the church building." Jess knew what that meant. The apartments in that area were extremely low income and not well kept. He listened as the bishop went on. "She's divorced with three children that are grown and don't live anywhere nearby, so she's on her own. The move was necessitated by hassle from her ex-husband, and she's used up what little savings she had. She's looking for work. I've only spoken with her a couple of times, but she seems like a fine woman. If you'd like I'll give her your number and you could set up an interview."

"That sounds great," Jess said.

They chatted for a few minutes before the bishop said, "So how are you?"

"Oh, we're doing fine," Jess said, feeling as if he was lying.

"I'm sure you are," the bishop said. "But fine can be relative. It's got to be tough to lose your father that way, and with twins on the way and everything, I could well imagine there's some strain in your family."

Jess vacillated between wanting to yell at the bishop for being so nosy, and wanting to cry on his shoulder because he'd hit the nail right on the head. He just swallowed carefully and said, "Yes, it's been tough, Bishop. But we have much to be grateful for, and I'm certain we'll be fine."

"Well, you let me know if there's anything we can do."

"I'll do that," Jess said and hurried to get off the phone. He distracted himself from the bishop's words by immediately dialing the number he'd been given. With any luck this would quickly solve *one* of his problems. And everything else just had to be faced one day at a time.

Chapter Nine

Sister Poll sounded eager and pleased with the job offer on the phone. Jess let her know that he would have to do a standard background check and drug testing, which she also agreed to, so they set up an appointment for an interview the following afternoon.

That evening at supper Jess discussed the situation with Tamra and Emily.

"Oh, I believe I've met her," Emily said. "I think she was introduced in Relief Society last Sunday."

"I wouldn't know because I wasn't there," Tamra said, since the previous Sunday she had been feeling worse than usual.

"I do hope it works out," Emily said. "It's nice when two people can get their problems solved by helping each other."

"Yes, it is," Jess agreed. "She'll be coming for an interview tomorrow afternoon, and she'll be going in to have the drug testing done in the morning, so they can call me with results before she even gets here. Not that I'm worried, but you just never know."

"As we've seen evidence of in the past," Emily said.

"We should have her over for supper," Tamra said. "If she's new in the ward and alone, and she'll be out here anyway, then . . ."

"That's a marvelous idea," Emily said.

"Of course," Tamra added, "perhaps I shouldn't be volunteering when I do practically nothing to help in the kitchen whatsoever these days."

Emily lifted a finger and gave Tamra a lightly scolding expression. "You're making two babies at the same time, and that's a lot of work. I have lots of practice in the kitchen, and a fair amount of energy for a woman my age."

"A woman your age?" Jess laughed. "What are you? Thirty-nine?"

Emily laughed as well. "Just keep up that attitude, Jess. And we won't tell how many anniversaries of my thirty-ninth birthday we've actually had."

After supper Jess insisted on washing the dishes with Evelyn's help, while Tamra sat in the kitchen and fed the baby. Emily went for a walk to get some exercise and give them some time alone. Tamra enjoyed her time with Jess, almost as much as she enjoyed watching his interaction with Evelyn. They were just so sweet together. In the midst of their laughter, she said, "I love you, Jess Hamilton."

He looked at her over his shoulder while his hands were still deep in the sink, washing a pan. He smiled in a way that made her momentarily forget the current challenges of life. "I love you too, Tamra Hamilton. I think you're the most amazing woman in the world and I'm the luckiest man alive to have you."

Given her emotional state, Tamra wasn't surprised at the tears that came to her eyes, nor was she surprised at the way Jess hurriedly wiped his hands so that he could wipe her tears. But she was surprised at the way she felt so undeserving of such praise from her husband. She forced her negative feelings back and returned his smile, reminding herself to count her blessings.

* * *

Jess was grateful to have his work under control before Sister Poll arrived. It was his preference to conduct job interviews—just as his father had done—by giving the potential employee a tour of the boys' home as they conversed. Michael had told Jess that he could sense a person's interest and comfort—or lack of—in the surroundings where they might be employed, and he could better gauge whether or not they were right for the job. Since, as Michael had also said, the bottom line of whether or not to hire someone came from listening to the Spirit—or gut instinct. However he put it, he prayed and attempted to block out all that was weighing on his mind as he prepared to meet Sister Poll. Her job was a simple one, but he considered every employee here important and needed, and their positions not to be taken lightly.

Madge brought the woman into his office when she arrived, and Jess rose from behind his desk. "Beulah Poll," she said, extending her hand eagerly.

"A pleasure to meet you," Jess said, surveying her quickly. She was black and slightly thick, with her hair pulled back into a bun. She didn't look old enough to have grown children. Her smile was kind, her eyes sincere. "I'm Jess Hamilton."

"And you own this place, eh?" she said, glancing around herself.

Jess gave an answer that he'd often heard his father give. "It's a family establishment. I just keep an eye on it." He motioned her toward the door. "Would you like a tour?"

"Oh that would be fine," she said eagerly, clutching her purse to her middle with both hands as she followed Jess out into the large main hall. While Jess showed her through the home he explained its history, pointing out the portraits of his great-great-grandparents who were its founders.

"And you're named after him, I see," she said, pointing at the nameplate that said, 'Jess Davies.'

"Yes, I am," Jess said proudly.

"So, what brings a boy here?" she asked, peeking through the one-way glass into one of the classrooms that was in session.

"Well, in most cases we are equivalent to a foster home that's more like a boarding school. We work with the government regarding boys that have been taken from abusive or neglectful situations."

"You must get some pretty difficult behavior with boys like that," she commented.

"We do occasionally, but we have a great staff who are well trained. The boundaries and rules are very clear, along with the consequences. But we always try to enforce that they're good boys with great potential. It's not fail proof, but we have a lot of success stories on file."

"I'll bet you do," she said almost dreamily. A few minutes later, she asked, "So, if you're like a foster family, do the boys have contact with their parents?"

"Depending on their individual circumstances, they do. Many are from such horrible situations that there are court orders to keep their parents at bay. But some have regular visitation, which is often supervised by one of our staff members."

As the tour continued, Jess casually asked her the standard questions that helped him know if she would be a good employee. Traversing a long hall they passed a security guard in uniform.

"Hello, Max," Jess said.

"How's it going?" Max smiled.

"Well, and you?"

"Couldn't be better."

Max moved on and Beulah asked, "Is that standard?"

"What?"

"Security?" She glanced over her shoulder to watch him walk away as if his presence caused her concern.

"We have a security guard on duty twenty-four-seven. It's handled by a local security company, so we have different officers, but there are a few—like Max—that we see regularly."

"Is that to . . . what?" She still sounded concerned. "To protect the boys from each other?"

Jess chuckled. "That certainly comes up once in a while, although the boys know that fighting will bring serious repercussions. The security is more to protect the boys from the outside world."

Her eyes filled with enlightenment. "You mean their parents."

"That's what I mean," Jess said.

"And do such situations arise often?"

"Not often, but enough that we're glad for men like Max, and we have a pretty sound security system with cameras and such, which is based in the main office."

"I see," she said, and they continued their tour, ending with the gabled attic. Beulah seemed fascinated with the room and Jess enjoyed telling her about it.

When Jess could think of nothing more to ask her, she filled in the lull by asking him questions, "So, you grew up here?"

"I did," he said. "The family home is actually attached to the boys' home, although you can't see it from here because of the way the drive turns, and the trees are so thick. But that reminds me . . . We'd like to have you join us for supper, if you're interested. My wife and mother would like to get to know you better, since you are the newest member of the ward."

Beulah's pleasure was evident. "I'd like that very much, thank you."

They walked back toward the main hall where Jess intended to walk Beulah the long way down the drive to the house, and turn her over to his mother so that he could get a little more work done before supper.

"How long have you been married?" she asked.

"A year last January," he said, feeling warmed just to think of his sweet wife.

They arrived in the main hall to see through the large window into Madge's office, where Emily was chatting with her. Jess introduced Beulah to his mother and the two women left together. Jess knew she would be in good hands, and she'd probably enjoy Emily's company more than his own.

He returned to the house to find the women visiting in the kitchen while Beulah helped Emily at the stove. He greeted Tamra with a kiss where she sat at the table, looking typically tired but in good spirits. The meal was pleasant and Jess felt especially good about hiring Beulah— especially seeing how well she intermixed with the family. Jess told her over dessert that she had the job if she wanted it, and she was so blatantly thrilled that he couldn't help feeling pleased.

When supper was over and the kitchen cleaned up, they all went out to the veranda to visit. While Evelyn was out running on the lawn, Beulah commented, "Forgive me if I'm being too nosy, but I noticed little Evelyn calls the two of you Mom and Dad, and you told me earlier you'd only been married since a year ago January. Does she come from a previous marriage, then?"

"Yes," Jess said, "but not one of ours. She's actually my brother's daughter, and—"

Jess was interrupted when Murphy and Tonya approached from across the lawn. They'd been out for a walk and saw them on the veranda and stopped to say hello. Emily introduced them to Beulah and they all sat and visited for a while before Tonya and Murphy moved on with their walk. Following a long moment of silence, while Beulah looked around herself with a certain awe in her expression, she commented, "You people sure live in a gilded world here."

Jess honestly couldn't say if he'd heard a subtle bite in her voice or not. But he couldn't deny that he felt offended, even though he didn't stop to analyze why before he retorted curtly, "Excuse me?"

Beulah seemed oblivious to his change of mood—although Emily and Tamra certainly weren't. Beulah went on to say, "It's just so beautiful here; almost perfect. It's like you live in this little bubble, separated and protected from the harshness of the world."

Jess was amazed at the anger inside of him in response to her statement. He forced himself to swallow hard and count to ten. He reminded himself that he'd just hired this woman to work for him. Still, he couldn't keep himself from saying, "Sister Poll, while we have a beautiful place to live here, and we are very blessed in many ways, I can assure you that we are anything but protected from the harshness of the world." He remained calm, but there was no hiding the sarcasm in his voice as he added, "When you've got some time, ask my mother about the gilded world she's lived in and how it's protected her from grief and sorrow." He came to his feet and added firmly, "If you will excuse me, I need to bathe Evelyn and put her to bed. Good night."

Tamra exchanged a troubled glance with Emily while remaining silent until after Jess had gathered Evelyn into his arms and hurried into the house.

"And I should feed the baby," Tamra said, standing as well. She attempted to smooth over Jess's terse behavior by smiling kindly at Beulah and saying, "It was so nice meeting you. I'll look forward to getting to know you better."

"And you," Beulah said, seeming more confused than upset. Tamra quickly made her escape, knowing that Emily, with her sensitive social skills, would be able to polish over any damage Jess might have done. Tamra felt far more concerned about Jess. It just wasn't like him to behave that way. In truth, his behavior reminded her a little too much of the Jess she had known before their marriage when he had been eating himself alive with unnecessary pain and guilt. Given what little she knew, she had to wonder if his bad dreams were getting the better of him. Was the stress in his life causing the nightmares? Or were the nightmares causing the stress? Perhaps it was a little of both and a vicious cycle was in play here.

Tamra fed the baby and put him down before she found Jess reading a storybook to Evelyn. When the child was tucked in for the night, Jess and Tamra returned to their room. Jess sat on the edge of the bed to pull off his boots. Tamra gently cleared her throat and said, "I can't help wondering why you got so upset with Beulah."

Jess looked at her sharply. "Because her comment was presumptuous and judgmental."

"But obviously not spoken with malice," Tamra said, remaining calm. "You and I both know that we certainly don't live in any gilded world, and we've faced many challenges. But Beulah was right when she said that it's beautiful here. We're very blessed to live and work in such a place. What she said may have been a bit presumptuous, but—"

"A bit?" Jess retorted, then forced himself to take a deep breath when he heard the tone of his own voice.

"Hear me out. In spite of any prejudiced attitude on her part, we must remember that we have no idea what kind of life she might have led, and what experiences might cause her to feel the way she does. Judging her will certainly not benefit anyone."

"So what are you saying?" Jess asked, his voice more calm in spite of the way he hated this conversation.

"I'm simply saying that it would be best if we just forget about it and move forward; let it go. She's going to be working with you, and around here a great deal. We don't want to start out with contention between us and—"

"By 'us' and 'we' you actually mean *me.* I'm the only one having trouble with this, apparently."

Tamra said nothing. She smiled and sat beside him, taking his hand. "You look tired," she said. "Let's get some sleep."

"I could go for that," he said, grateful to have the subject dropped.

The following morning Jess went to work determined to do as Tamra had suggested, and put his ill feelings aside. Beulah reported for work early and Madge was left to show her the specifics of her responsibilities. Within a few days Beulah was doing her chores efficiently, and even going the extra mile. Jess was hearing good reports about her from every member of the staff, which helped soften the single incident that had upset him so badly. Stopping to analyze the incident, he had to admit that his response had been defensive, at best. But given the present level of stress in his life, to even imply that he lived in *a gilded world* certainly hit a sore spot.

Weeks passing proved Beulah's competence and kindness more fully, and Jess forgot about the incident altogether. About once a week Emily invited Beulah to stay for supper, and she proved to be good company. Tamra especially seemed to enjoy Beulah's companionship since her health showed no improvement with the passing of time. She only became increasingly uncomfortable as the babies grew quickly inside of her. She seemed to be doing somewhat better emotionally; at least she wasn't crying and visibly discouraged most of the time as she had been earlier in the pregnancy. But a definite dark cloud hung over her, and Jess simply didn't know how to dispel it. Given his own dark cloud that was regularly reinforced by ongoing nightmares, he just had to take life one day at a time and do his best to hold everything together.

On the positive side, Murphy and Tonya were doing well and seemed happy. Tonya had even gone to church a couple of times, but beyond that just Murphy rode along with the family while Tonya remained at home with Susan. Tonya had given up her job in a hair salon, since Murphy's salary was more than adequate, and she preferred to spend her time keeping house, looking after her mother-in-law, and even helping here and there with her husband's work. She had set up a bit of a salon in her kitchen and was offering a good deal on haircuts to the hired hands, and she had trimmed Tamra's long hair once with good results. She had also taken to coming into the house every few days to wash and style Myrna's hair, refusing to take any pay. Myrna came to look forward to Tonya's visits and her animated conversation as she gently pampered Myrna and made her look beautiful.

The family had grown used to Myrna's presence in the house and she seemd to have settled in comfortably. Occasionally Myrna and June came to the table and shared a meal with the family, but more often she seemed more comfortable staying in her room. There were times when Jess almost forgot she was there, although he made a point of spending some time with her every few days. For the most part she was respectful and seemed appreciative of the help she was given, but occasionally he saw evidence of a bad mood that brought out the Myrna that Tamra had always told him she remembered from her childhood. If nothing else, seeing the evidence enlarged Jess's compassion for all that Tamra had risen above.

On a morning heavy with rain, Madge poked her head into Jess's office, saying, " Mrs. Gooding is here."

"Remind me," Jess said without looking up from the paperwork on his desk.

"Little Nathan's mother. Apparently she finally got ironed out of all those anti-depressants and tranquilizers she was on; just got out of the hospital and they said she could have some minor visitation."

"Supervised?" He tossed his pen to the desk and leaned back in his chair.

"Yes. I've got the paperwork. You said you wanted to see her first. Do you want me to attend the visit or—"

"No, I'll do it."

Madge smiled.

"What?" Jess asked.

"You've got a soft spot for Nathan; I can tell."

Jess smiled. "Yes, I suppose I do. He's a great kid."

"Yes, he is. I'll send in his mother."

Linda Gooding surprised Jess when she walked into his office. He wasn't certain what he'd expected, but this woman was very pretty with long, blonde hair, dressed in a simple black suit. Her eyes showed evidence of the harshness of life she'd endured, but they had a kind and humble quality that many of the parents who visited here did not have. Most were angry and defensive over their children having been taken away, due to abuse or neglect. And few had any desire to change their ways. But Mrs. Gooding was different.

"Mr. Hamilton," she said, extending her hand as he rose from behind his desk. She had trouble making eye contact with him, but her smile was genuine.

"Mrs. Gooding," he said, motioning her to a chair. "It's nice to finally meet you."

She nodded and wrung her hands nervously. "I understand you've been caring for my son."

"Not personally, but my staff does a very good job with that sort of thing."

"How is he doing?" she asked with yearning in her eyes and a tremor in her voice.

"He's doing well," Jess said.

"Oh, I've missed him so much. Can I see him now and—"

"In a few minutes," Jess said. "First of all, I need to give you fair warning. I don't think he's going to be as anxious to see you as you are to see him."

"What do you mean?" she asked, a hint of moisture brimming in her eyes.

"We've done extensive counseling with Nathan, and he's responded well. In spite of his father's abuse, he has a fairly healthy perspective of what a normal family life should be like. I think you've helped a great deal over the years to keep that perspective intact. However, I must be frank, through your more recent months of depression, he felt completely cut off from you. He's told us many times that he misses you, but he's quickly followed up with saying that you were never awake or with him anyway."

Mrs. Gooding looked down and grabbed for a tissue from the box on the corner of the desk. "Now, let me clarify that all of us here have dealt with many people like your husband, and your depression is perfectly understandable. You're apparently doing much better now, and we're all very glad about that. But the consequences for Nathan are something that have to be acknowledged and addressed. Our goal in this is to eventually make it possible for you and your son to be together and be safe. But that's going to take time. I'm just asking you to be patient—with Nathan as well as yourself. You can see him as frequently as the court order will allow. We just ask that you not go into this with high expectations from your son. It will take time for him to heal, and to trust you to protect him. Am I making any sense?"

"Perfect sense," she said tearfully, without looking up.

"Forgive me for being so brash, but—"

"No, you're very kind, actually. I know what you say is true. It's just so . . . pathetic. I keep telling myself I should have been stronger—for him. But I reached a point where I just couldn't hold it together any longer. I should have had the courage to get some help, to get out of there, to . . ."

"We all know that's much easier said than done, Mrs. Gooding," Jess said. He handed her another tissue and gave her a few minutes to compose herself.

"Would you like to see him now?" Jess asked.

"Oh, I would!" she said, taking a compact out of her purse to check her appearance and touch some powder onto her cheeks and nose. "All right. I'm ready."

Jess led the woman upstairs and motioned her to the one-way mirror on a classroom door where she could see her son working on an art project with his classmates. She let out an emotional sigh, then said, "Oh, he looks well! Even happy."

"Yes, I believe he does," Jess said. "Let me go and get him and you can have a brief visit."

Jess first took Mrs. Gooding to a room further down the hall, then he went back to get Nathan from his class. When they were alone in the hall, he said, "You've got a visitor."

He scowled and said, "It's not my dad, is it."

"No, we're not going to let your dad come and visit."

With some pleasure in his voice he asked, "Is it my mom?"

"It is, and she's very anxious to see you."

He looked slightly more positive than indifferent as Jess opened the door and ushered Nathan into the room. Jess watched their reunion from a discreet distance. Nathan still looked mostly indifferent, but their visit went relatively well.

After Nathan hugged his mother good-bye and was taken back to class, Jess walked Mrs. Gooding back to the main doors. "I think it went well," he said.

"Yes, I believe so," she said, sounding more positive than negative. "It was good to see him. I can come again next week, right?"

"That's right. And if all goes well we can put visits closer together. As he regularly sees that you're doing better and you're more like yourself, he'll gradually become more anxious to be with you, I believe."

"Oh, I hope so."

"We simply want to be careful. He's already been tragically uprooted once. We want to be sure he's completely ready and the circumstances are ideal before we uproot him again."

"I understand. And I appreciate all you're doing. You obviously have a fine place here."

Jess just smiled and escorted her to the door. Not long after Mrs. Gooding left, Jess received a phone call. A short while later he walked into the house to find Tamra visiting with her mother.

"Hello," Myrna said in her barely discernable way.

"Hello," Jess said, sitting beside her and taking her hand. "How are you feeling today?"

"Pretty good," Myrna said.

"Well, I've got some good news. Your sister is coming for a visit."

Myrna's eyes showed pleasure. Tamra smiled and said, "Really?"

"Yeah. She called my office because she didn't get an answer here."

"Oh, I was too slow to get to the phone," Tamra said, "and your mother's gone into town."

"Well," Jess went on, "she's finally reached a point where she feels like she's completely recovered from that nasty infection. The cough is completely gone."

"Is she going to take me home?" Myrna asked slowly and with difficulty. There was no denying the disappointment in her voice. As if to clarify she added, "I like her house, but it's nice here too. It's nice to see the children."

"Yes, it is, isn't it," Jess agreed. "Actually, she'll take you home with her eventually, but she's going to stay here for a few weeks in order to make her trip worthwhile."

"Oh, that'll be nice," Tamra said, genuinely pleased. Jess was glad to see her smile.

"Yes, that'll be nice," Myrna echoed.

A few days later, Murphy flew the private plane to Sydney to pick up Rhea, and Tonya went along with him. Rhea's arrival late in the evening provoked hugs and laughter from everyone. It was evident that Tamra especially was pleased to see her aunt, and the relationship they had shared through the years seemed to deepen over the next few weeks as Rhea became a part of the household. They lessened the hours that a nurse was on hand to care for Myrna, since Rhea was perfectly adept at caring for her sister, and even seemed to enjoy it. Rhea kept Myrna more involved with the family, and they all shared meals more regularly. And the evenings that Beulah Poll shared supper with them were especially entertaining.

Rhea also helped keep Tamra's spirits up, visiting with her and keeping her distracted from her misery. While the group around the supper table had become larger, and certainly diverse, Jess found he liked this family arrangement. There was a certain coziness in seeing both his and Tamra's mothers under his own roof, and Tamra's Aunt Rhea, who had in essence been more of a mother to Tamra than her own mother had been.

On a particularly gray evening at supper, Jess asked Rhea, "So, now that you've lived with us for a few weeks, do you still like us?"

"Oh, I do," Rhea said with exaggerated intensity, then she laughed. "I really do. Especially little Evie." She winked at Evelyn, who giggled.

"Well, you're welcome to stay as long as you like," Emily said, then she tossed an uneasy glance toward Jess and he wondered why—until she added, "I guess I should ask Jess and Tamra before I start offering their home."

Jess gave her a subtle scowl. "It's every bit as much your home as ours," he said.

"Yes, but . . . you're the master of the house now, and—"

"I really hate that term," Jess said a little too seriously. "I'm not the *master* of anything."

"Well, you would be if you'd move into the master bedroom," Emily said lightly, but Jess didn't think it was funny.

"The room we have is just fine," Jess said. Then to Rhea, "And yes, you're welcome to stay as long as you like. Move in for all I care."

With that Jess got a subtly uneasy glance from Tamra and he wondered what he might have said wrong. Before he could question it Rhea said, "You really think you could tolerate so many women on a long-term basis?"

Jess glanced around the table, realizing—not for the first time—that he and the baby were the only males in the house. But he couldn't deny his love for each of these women and he said easily, "Yes, I think I could tolerate it. Of course, I spend my days in a boys' home; that keeps everything in balance. If I—"

A crack of thunder interrupted him and they all turned their attention to the windows across the room.

"Good heavens," Emily said. "That storm sure moved in quickly."

The sky had blackened considerably, and when they were all quiet enough to listen, they could hear rain pelting madly against the roof, and the wind howling viciously.

"I think I liked listening to conversation better," Tamra said.

"I second that motion," Rhea added. Jess silently added his vote. He'd lost some of his fondness for rain since it had been the instigator of his most recent accident. He held little Michael on his lap while the women chatted about everyday things, and he couldn't deny feeling a certain appreciation for the moment, especially when Tamra reached for his hand.

The conversation was interrupted by a loud banging at the side door.

"Good heavens," Emily said, standing to answer it. "Who would be out in this kind of weather?"

Jess handed the baby to Tamra and moved into the hall when he heard Tonya at the door, apparently so out of breath she could hardly speak. When he came face to face with her, he realized she was more upset than out of breath. Their eyes met and something knotted up inside of him.

"What's happened?" he demanded as she leaned back against the closed door.

"He . . . he . . ."

"Take a deep breath, honey," Emily said, "and tell us what's wrong."

Tonya breathed deeply while Emily held her hand. "He . . . took one of the racers out . . . said it needed some pushing . . . that was nearly two hours ago . . . and the storm . . ."

"Good heavens," Emily said again.

Tonya continued, fear becoming more evident in her voice. "A couple of hands went out, but . . . they came back . . . couldn't see anything. The wind's too strong and . . . Oh! If something's happened to him, I will die. I'll just die."

"Now, calm down," Jess said gently, taking her shoulders into his hands. "Murphy's smart. He knows what to do. There's a good chance he's huddled under some rocks somewhere, just waiting out the storm."

Tonya looked more calm at this. Emily helped her out of her drenched coat and urged her into the kitchen. "You come and warm up, and we'll do everything we can to find him as soon as the weather lets up a bit."

"Should we call for help?" Tamra asked Jess as Tonya sat beside her and Tamra took her hand.

"We can," Jess said, "but we've had such things come up before, and they won't take a helicopter off the ground in this kind of weather. In fact, it has to be pretty calm before they'll go into those mountains. I'll call and notify them, and when the storm lets up I'm sure they'll start searching."

"Thank you," Tonya said as Jess left the room.

Rhea made Tonya a cup of hot cocoa and the women gave her empathy and concern. Even Myrna said, "He'll be all right."

The moment the storm had lessened to a medium rain, Jess set out on horseback with three of the stable hands. Tamra stood on the veranda and watched them ride away, their hats and long drover coats shielding them from the rain. She pulled the blanket she'd wrapped herself in more tightly around her shoulders to ward off a sudden chill, and she prayed silently that they would all return safe and well. She recalled a similar incident that Michael had once shared with her, how he'd gone out into a storm to find his sister. It turned out that she'd fallen and had a broken leg. Michael found her and brought her home. She prayed that this story ended at least that well.

Chapter Ten

Jess was cold and exhausted, and his eyes were hurting from trying to see anything out of the ordinary with the use of the powerful battery-operated search lamps they were carrying. The rain had lessened to a miserable drizzle more than an hour earlier, but the wind had a nasty bite to it, and they had been at this for more than three hours. He kept praying that he would be guided to the right spot to find Murphy—and that he would be found safe and well. He was grateful for the two-way radios that kept him connected with the other men, and the base radio at home that would keep the women aware that they were all right.

It was nearly midnight when Jess spotted the horse, but he knew before they got to it that it was dead. The other three men gathered close beside him as they scanned the area with lights and attempted to put the clues together. One of them said, "That horse is laying in the path of a flash flood. The water's receded now, but . . ."

"So," Jess said, "Murphy is either further upstream on the same path, or downstream."

"Makes sense to me," another voice said.

"Let's just pray he's in better condition than the horse," Jess said and they split up into pairs, moving different directions.

Jess found Murphy face down over a boulder just a ways upstream from where the horse had been found. As he dismounted and moved toward him, heart pounding, he prayed with all his heart and soul that he would not be faced with the worst. He barely touched Murphy's shoulder before he groaned and attempted to lift his head. Jess laughed through a profound sigh and shifted him carefully off the rock. His partner alerted the others that Murphy had been found, and Emily radioed back to say that a helicopter was finally on its way since the wind had receded enough to take off, but they were doubtful they could move into the mountains.

Between the four men they surmised that Murphy was bruised up some but he didn't have any obvious pain. What worried Jess was the pallor of his skin and the way it felt ice-cold to the touch. He was lethargic and barely responsive, which likely meant hypothermia. With the help of the other men, Jess wrapped Murphy in a couple of dry blankets that had been packed in the saddlebags. Then they put Murphy on the horse in front of Jess, who held one arm around him to keep him from falling off. The ride back seemed forever, even though Jess knew they weren't terribly far from home and they were making good time. He prayed continually that Murphy would be all right, and he kept searching the skies for any sign of a helicopter that might intervene and get Murphy to a hospital. But they arrived at the house with no sign of help. Tonya and Emily came running out just as two of the men were helping ease Murphy down from the horse. Tonya sobbed audibly when she saw the condition he was in, and her tears increased when Murphy showed her a weak smile and said, "My sweetie."

While three men carried him carefully toward the big house, Tonya walked alongside, holding Murphy's hand and crying. "Don't you die on me," she said through her tears.

"I want . . . forever," Murphy said before she had to let go so they could get him through the door.

Once inside Jess felt Tamra's arms come around him and he breathed in her presence with gratitude.

"You shouldn't be up," he said, looking into her worried eyes.

"I couldn't sleep," she said, "not until I knew you were safe. I've been lying down." She touched his face and his wet hair. "Oh, you're all right. I'm so grateful."

"So am I," he said, kissing her quickly. "Let's just hope Murphy will be all right." Then he kissed her again, betraying the passion he felt for her. Oh, how he loved her!

They followed the men carrying him down the hall and watched as Tonya resumed her place at his side as they laid him on the floor in front of the fireplace in the library. She continued to cry, and he looked half dead. A few minutes later they heard a helicopter overhead, the same moment that Murphy began shivering violently.

"I think that's a good sign," Emily said.

The emergency team took over efficiently, and they stretched the rules to allow Tonya to ride with them to the hospital. Jess promised they would be there to check on them first thing in the morning, and he made her promise to call and keep them informed. Once the helicopter had taken off, Jess thanked the men for their help and sent them off to care for the horses and get some sleep in the bunkhouse. One of the hands, who was a good friend of Murphy's, offered to stay in the house with Susan and be sure that she was looked after. The family shared hugs and went to bed, attempting to get some sleep, as well. But Jess was wide awake when Tonya called a little before three to tell them that Murphy's body temperature was almost back to normal, and he was going to be fine. They were going to do some tests the following day just to be certain he didn't have any internal injuries, and they would likely be keeping him for a day or two. She cried on the phone, then admitted that she needed some rest and she'd see them tomorrow. "There's no need to hurry here in the morning," she said. "In fact, call before you come. I might need some things."

"We'll do that," Jess said.

Tonya's tears increased again before she said, "Thank you, Jess. You saved his life."

"It wasn't just me," he said.

"Well, thank you anyway."

"I'm glad it worked out all right," Jess said.

After Jess got off the phone and reported the news to his mother and Tamra, he was finally able to sleep. But he woke just after dawn, startled from a bad dream that left him sweating. The dream was familiar as the accident that had nearly killed him played over in his mind. But as he had turned to where his best friend had been sitting, the image turned to Murphy and Murphy was dead. In his now-conscious state, Jess reminded himself that Murphy was very much alive and he was going to be fine, but he found himself feeling guilty somehow, as if this accident that could have killed Murphy was somehow his fault. It had taken him years to finally come to terms with the accident that had killed his loved ones, and to accept that it had *not* been his fault. So, why would such feelings present themselves now in this situation? He couldn't have prevented the rain, the flash flood. He couldn't have stopped Murphy from going out, and likely wouldn't have when at the time of his leaving there had been no indication of a storm. For Jess to feel guilt was ludicrous and he knew it. So why did he?

Jess dragged himself to the shower, hoping to change his train of thought. He went to the boys' home before breakfast and greeted his staff with the news of what had happened last night and that he would be taking most of the day off to visit Murphy and get some rest. He saw to the work that was absolutely necessary, and peeked in on the boys before he returned home to eat a late breakfast, then they went into town to see Murphy and Tonya.

"Are you sure you're up to this?" Jess asked Tamra.

"I'm fine," she insisted. "I can rest in the car. Rhea's staying with the children. I want to go."

"It will do her good to get out," Emily said gently as Tamra climbed into the Cruiser.

"Oh," Jess said, "we were supposed to call Tonya in case she needed some of her things or—"

"Tamra already talked to her and we got everything she needs."

"Oh," Jess said and got behind the wheel.

Through the drive into town, Jess had to tell himself over and over that there was no reason he should be nervous at the wheel, and there was no reason to believe that the lives of his wife and mother were in jeopardy by being in the vehicle with him. But the thought wouldn't leave him. He finally said to Tamra, "Do you remember what you said to me when I was nervous about driving . . . the first time . . . after the accident?"

Tamra looked mildly alarmed but he put his eyes back to the road and kept them there.

"Are you nervous now?" she asked.

"Maybe," he admitted.

"Why? Because of that last accident?"

"Probably," he said.

"Is that what has been causing your nightmares?" Tamra asked and Jess sighed loudly. He should have kept his mouth shut.

He put in a second vote on that when his mother added, "Are you still having nightmares?"

"Listen," he said, "I don't need to discuss my dreams or my emotional state. I just want to know if you remember what you said when I was nervous about driving . . . something about your patriarchal blessing."

"I remember," Tamra said.

"Well, say it again and leave it at that, okay?"

He was aware of his wife and mother exchanging a concerned glance, but he didn't care. He was just relieved when Tamra said, "My patriarchal blessing says I'm going to live a full life with many children and grandchildren. If I feel inspired to not get in a car with you, I'll let you know."

Jess sighed. "And you haven't felt inspired to not get in a car with me, have you?"

"No," Tamra said, reaching for his hand. "Honey, are you okay?"

"I will be," he said, forcing a smile.

But he knew she could see through it, even before she said, "Maybe you should talk to Sean."

"I talk to Sean every week or so," he said, with a slightly terse edge to his voice.

"You know what I mean."

"Yes, I know what you mean." His voice picked up sarcasm, "I'm sure Sean would love to hear all about my silly bad dreams. He's got far more difficult traumas to deal with in his own life."

Again Tamra and Emily exchanged a glance, as if they had some silent way of communicating. More than anything, the idea made him miss his father so much that a sudden ache filled his chest. He pressed a hand there in an attempt to alleviate it, but it wouldn't relent.

"Are you okay?" Tamra said.

Jess had to admit, "No, I don't think I am." He didn't realize he was crying until he heard the evidence in his own voice. He abruptly pulled over and stopped the vehicle. He held tightly to the steering wheel until his knuckles turned white. Tamra touched his shoulder, then put her arms around him, and he crumbled against her, sobbing like a child with a skinned knee.

"What is it, Jess?" Tamra asked gently, pressing her fingers through his hair. She glanced over the seat at Emily to see her crying silent tears with a hand pressed over her mouth.

"I just miss him so much," Jess sobbed. "I try not to let it get to me, but . . . once in a while it just . . . hits me like a brick and . . . Oh, help. It hurts." He cried harder, his head in Tamra's lap, and Tamra and Emily cried with him.

Long after Jess's sobs trickled into silence, the three remained as they were, content to quietly be together, no motivation to continue their journey, or even to speak. The silence was finally broken when Jess said, "I just can't do it."

"Do what, honey?" Emily asked gently.

"I can't be everything that he was . . . everything that I have to be in his absence. I can't do it."

"I thought you were handling everything quite marvelously," Emily said. "But if you're trying to have the wisdom and insight of a man who was twice your age, then no, you probably can't do that."

"I don't know what I'm trying to do," he said, sitting up at last. "I just know that it feels like the world is coming at me from all sides, and without him here, I just can't do it all."

Tamra and Emily exchanged a glance and Jess said, "There you go again."

"What?" Tamra countered.

"The two of you are always . . . looking at each other like that . . . as if you can read each other's minds or something. And it always happens when we're talking about my problems."

"We're just concerned for you, Jess," his mother said. "We both love you . . ."

". . . More than anyone else," Tamra added.

"Now you're finishing each other's sentences," Jess growled.

"Is there something wrong with that?" Tamra asked.

"No, I just . . ." Tears started to come again and he pressed a hand over his eyes. "I just . . . want my father here . . . to finish my sentences."

Tamra hugged Jess again and Emily put a hand on his shoulder. He shook his head and muttered, "I just cannot believe everything that's been happening. You would think that someone is out to get us."

"Life does seem that way sometimes," Emily said gently. "I believe everyone has times in their life when it feels that way. But it will pass."

Jess shook his head, feeling in that moment as if this string of trials would never pass. Last night's incident with Murphy had occurred on top of an ongoing pressure that had just accumulated too deeply. Reminding himself that he had no choice but to get a grip and keep going, Jess dried his tears and drove on toward town. He felt some relief in the outlet of emotion he'd had, but that dark cloud had not relented.

They found Murphy asleep, but he was stable and doing well. Tonya was tired and obviously pleased to see them. Not wanting to disturb Murphy's sleep, they walked to a vacant waiting area and sat down to visit. They'd only been seated a moment when Tonya began to visibly shake.

"Are you okay?" Tamra asked, reaching for her hand.

"No, I don't think I am." She forced a chuckle that turned into a sob. "I was so scared; so afraid that I'd lost him. And I just couldn't live with that. I couldn't!" She turned to Emily and asked through her tears, "How do you cope with having lost your husband? You seem so . . . happy. You handle it with such . . . grace and dignity. But I know the two of you loved each other so much. How do you do it?"

Emily took hold of Tonya's other hand and looked into her eyes. "I miss him very much, Tonya, and it's not always easy. But I have peace in my heart, because I understand that this life is not the end of what we shared."

"You really believe that," Tonya said.

"I know it, Tonya. I know I will be with him again as I live for those blessings."

Tonya seemed to be digesting Emily's words within herself. She turned to look at Jess and said, "He told me that he wants forever."

"Yes, I heard that," Jess said.

"And this morning, when he was awake, he said it again. He said that you and Tamra have forever."

Jess exchanged a glance with Tamra, more grateful than he could express to know that what Tonya had said was true. He turned back to her and asked, "Hasn't he told you how that's possible?"

"We agreed not to talk about religion."

"Okay, but surely . . . if you have legitimate questions, he would be willing to answer them and—"

"Maybe . . . one day, we could be ready for that, but . . . right now I prefer to ask you. You're not emotionally involved. I'm realizing more and more that my perceptions of religion from my childhood are greatly distorted, but . . . I don't know where to start to change those perceptions."

Jess silently prayed for guidance and tried to follow his feelings as he repeated the basic principles behind eternal marriage. She asked many questions and between him, Tamra, and his mother, they managed to answer them. When it seemed that she had heard all she could absorb in one sitting, Jess said, "Why don't you let that settle in, and you know where we are if you have more questions."

Tonya nodded and thanked them before they all returned to Murphy's room and found that he'd just awakened. He was obviously in pain from being bruised up pretty badly, but he was glad to see them and thanked Jess profusely for coming to find him.

"You'd have done the same for me," Jess said, shaking his hand firmly.

While the nurse was with Murphy, they made sure that Tonya had all she needed, since she intended to stay with him as long as he needed her. They left the hospital and went out to lunch, but they were unusually short on conversation.

On the way back, Tamra fell asleep and woke up about twenty minutes before they would arrive home.

"Are you feeling all right?" Jess asked once she'd fully opened her eyes.

"Beyond some heartburn and the usual fatigue, I'm okay for the moment," she said.

A few minutes later, Emily interrupted the silence by saying, "Tamra, how would you feel about asking your aunt and mother to stay with us indefinitely?"

Jess said with a smile, "I think it's a great idea. I've really grown to enjoy having them there, and—"

"I know how you feel about it, Jess," Emily said kindly. "I think we should hear what Tamra has to say."

Jess was startled by the implication and quickly said, "I'm sorry. What do *you* think, Tamra?"

After a long, silent minute, Tamra finally said, "I don't know if I'm comfortable with it or not."

"Okay," Emily said. "Do you want to talk about it? Or would you prefer that your mother-in-law just mind her business?"

"No, I don't want you to mind your business," Tamra said. "You've never once made me feel like you were meddling in my life, and I promise if you do I will tell you. I'm just not so sure that Rhea would never meddle. She hasn't been here long enough to have gotten past her best behavior. I mean . . . she's always been kind and I don't think she would really be bothersome in a way I couldn't handle but . . ."

"But?" Jess said.

Tamra was thoughtful, then sighed loudly. "I don't know. I'm just . . . not comfortable with it. I don't know why. Maybe it's just me. Or maybe it's this hormonal, psychotic person who has taken my place temporarily."

"I don't think it's as bad as all that," Jess said with a chuckle.

Tamra turned a sober, tear-streaked face toward him. "Well, I sure don't feel like myself most of the time, so it's difficult for me to know if what I'm basing my decisions on has any bearing or not. So, maybe you'd better just decide what to do and do it."

Jess felt helpless to know what to say. He was relieved when Emily finally spoke from the back seat. "Well, why don't we address all the obvious, logical issues, and if you have any opinions, speak up."

"Okay," Tamra agreed.

"Jess," Emily said, "why don't you tell us why you want Rhea and Myrna to stay?"

"Well," he drawled, "on the logical side, it would just be easier. If anything happens to either of them, I don't have to fly to Sydney to deal with it. We don't have to worry about getting them back and forth if Rhea gets sick or your mother's condition worsens. I also think it's good for them to be around the influence of the gospel that we can give them in our home. Evelyn's grown to love them, and the other way around." He took Tamra's hand. "I know there was a time when it was difficult for you to live in Rhea's home because of her smoking and drinking, and the things she'd watch on television."

"And her language," Tamra added.

"Yes," Jess agreed, "but I've hardly heard a bad word come out of her mouth since she got here. And your mother's doing better with that, too."

"Yes," Emily said, "June wouldn't put up with it."

"Bless June's heart," Jess said. "Anyway, since they've both quit smoking and drinking and—"

"Yes, Rhea by choice, my mother by force."

"For whatever reason, it's not an issue any more. And what Rhea chooses to watch on television in the privacy of her own room is up to her. I think we can be far more of a good influence on her than she could be a bad one on us."

"I agree," Emily said. "And well . . . personally, I just feel like it's the right thing to do. Simple as that."

"Yes, I think I feel the same way," Jess said. "I just feel . . . better somehow to know that they're here where we can take care of them. It just feels . . . right." He waited a minute and said to Tamra, "So, what do you think? How do you feel about it?"

"I don't feel anything at all," Tamra said. "I've gotten used to my mother being with us, and it's really not as bad as I thought it would be. I love Rhea and I certainly have nothing against them being here. I guess I feel almost . . . indifferent."

"Almost?" Emily asked.

Tamra sighed loudly. "Well, if I'm completely honest—which I assume you want me to be . . . "

"Of course," Emily said.

"Then I have to admit that there's something that just feels . . . weird about it. It's almost like . . ." Tamra thought about it a minute. "Well, it's like . . . my life before I came here had so little good in it, and since I came here it's been wonderful—in spite of obvious challenges. And it's just hard for me to think of . . . crossing those worlds, I guess."

"I can understand that," Jess said. "But hasn't it already happened? I mean . . . they're here and we've gotten comfortable with it. Your mother and Rhea have both come to a point in their lives where it works, don't you think?"

"I suppose it does," Tamra said. "Like I told you, I think the biggest problem is that I just don't really feel like me. Or maybe I'm just so sick and tired all the time, that I don't have any brain left at all."

"I felt that way when I was pregnant," Emily said. "It's like all your blood supply is going to the babies and there's not enough in your head to make it work properly."

"Really?" Jess said.

"It sure felt that way," Emily said.

"Yes, it does," Tamra added.

"But I can't vouch for any scientific evidence," Emily said.

"I suppose it makes sense," Jess said.

That evening at supper, Jess was wondering if he should bring up the possibility of Rhea and Myrna staying indefinitely. He almost brought it up, but decided against it for reasons he couldn't pinpoint. The following morning at breakfast, Rhea seemed a bit somber. When Tamra questioned if something was wrong, she simply said, "I was just thinking that we should probably be getting back to Sydney. My plants are probably dead by now and, well . . . time is passing."

Jess caught an unmistakable go-ahead from Tamra's eyes and quickly said, "So you're sick of us already, eh? Gotta get back to the big city."

"Oh, it's not that." Rhea looked decidedly alarmed.

"Well, what is it then?" Jess asked.

"Well," she drawled, "we don't want to wear out our welcome and . . ."

"And?" Jess pressed when she didn't continue.

"Well, Sydney is home, and . . ." Again she stammered.

"What if your home were here?" Jess asked. "What if your welcome didn't wear out?"

Rhea looked at Jess as if he had turned green, but what made Jess laugh was seeing the exact expression on Myrna's face, in spite of it being half paralyzed.

"Yes, I'm serious," Jess said. "We've discussed it, and we all want you to stay—indefinitely—if that's what you want. I understand that Sydney is where your home is, and you wouldn't have to give that up permanently if you don't want to. Or if you want to, that's fine as well. There's plenty of room. We've proven that we can get along well enough to exist under the same roof, so . . . there you have it. Consider it an official invitation."

"Well . . . I . . ." Rhea looked at Tamra, who nodded firmly, then Emily did the same. She turned to her sister and said, "I suppose we'd better think about it and . . . talk about it."

Myrna said rather intelligibly, "I don't have to think about it, so I guess it's up to you."

Jess couldn't tell if Rhea was going to laugh or cry. When the silence became awkward he said, "You know we're going to need a lot of help when we get two more babies in the house."

Rhea laughed *and* cried as she said, "Nothing could make me happier. If you're sure it's all right, I'd love to stay."

"It's settled then," Jess said, and they went on to discuss their plans.

A few days later June came to stay with Myrna while Jess flew Rhea to Sydney. He saw her safely home then returned, leaving her there to go through her things and get the house ready to sell. Then she intended to drive back in the van that was equipped to haul Myrna around more easily. She would rent a trailer for her belongings that were important to her and be on her way in a couple of weeks.

During Rhea's absence, Murphy came home from the hospital and was doing well. Tonya hadn't asked any more gospel questions, but the night before Rhea was expected to return, Tonya and Murphy came for supper. In the middle of the meal, Tonya said to Jess, "Would it be too much trouble to arrange a meeting with the missionaries?"

Murphy looked so completely astonished that Jess was afraid he'd stopped breathing. Jess broke the silence by saying, "I think the two of you need to rework that 'talking about religion' agreement."

"Yes, we probably should," Tonya said.

"And no, it wouldn't be any trouble at all. If it's all right with you, we'll arrange for the first meeting here at the house and we'll join you. I'll see to it right away."

"Thank you," Tonya said.

"In the meantime," Jess pointed at Murphy with his fork, "I bet he could answer some questions."

Tonya and Murphy exchanged a warm smile and the meal progressed while Jess exchanged subtle smirks with Tamra and Emily. It seemed this story could end up with a happily ever after—the forever kind.

* * *

Tamra was greatly relieved to know that Rhea would soon be returning. She began to question their decision to have her mother stay on when Myrna developed a terribly sour mood. Her cynicism and belligerence triggered far too many bad memories for Tamra, and she did her best to stay away from Myrna's room and let June handle her.

When Rhea arrived with the van and trailer, Tamra mustered the energy to go outside and meet her. She needed some fresh air. Tamra hugged Rhea tightly before she said, "I'm glad you're back."

"She's been on one?" Rhea asked.

"Yes, she certainly has."

Tamra almost asked Rhea the question that had haunted her most of her life: How could two sisters grow up in the same home and be so opposite in disposition? What had made Myrna so mean and difficult? But something held Tamra back now, just as many times in the past. Perhaps there was no explanation beyond simple personality differences. And perhaps she didn't want to know.

Myrna showed some improvement with Rhea around, and Tamra wondered why. But again, she didn't bother to ask. She was simply grateful that Rhea was so willing—even eager—to care for her sister.

Two nights after Rhea's return home, Jess went into town to pick up the elders and bring them out to the house. They all shared supper together, then they went to the lounge room and turned the time over to the elders to answer Tonya's questions and give the first discussion. What made the experience especially interesting was that Myrna and Rhea were both in attendance. They had declined previous offers to join them for family home evenings, but perhaps now that they considered themselves permanent residents of the house, they were more apt to become involved. Whatever it was, they both listened attentively to what the elders had to say, even though neither of them made any comment.

Tonya seemed especially fascinated with the concept of personal revelation. She was deeply intrigued with the idea that she didn't have to rely on what Murphy or the elders or even the prophet told her to believe. She could know for herself if the gospel was true, and that the Holy Ghost would testify the truth to her of every principle she was asked to live, if she sought for those answers and lived worthy of getting them.

Listening to Tonya's eager questions, and her willingness to read the Book of Mormon, Jess felt a bright hope that she would, indeed, embrace the gospel. And Murphy's happiness over the prospect didn't need to be voiced. He practically glowed as he watched his wife beginning to understand the principles that had healed his own troubled heart. Jess paused to consider the blessings of the gospel in his own life, something that he'd grown so accustomed to that he felt certain he often took it for granted. But he truly was grateful and he hoped his Heavenly Father knew the thoughts of his heart.

* * *

The following day Jess came across Beulah in the hall of the boys' home, washing some spots off the wall.

"How's it going?" he asked.

"Great, and you?"

"We're coming along," he said without much enthusiasm.

"Hey," she said as he walked past, "could I ask you something?"

"Sure," Jess said, turning back to talk with her.

He expected a question to do with the boys' home, or some concern over one of the boys. But what she said took him off guard. "You told me once that I should ask your mother about the grief and sorrow in her life, and one day I might do that. But seeing how agitated you were when you told me to do that, I thought it might be better if I asked you so we can clear the air on whatever it was I said to upset you."

Jess sighed and looked guiltily at the floor. He'd actually forgotten about the episode, and recalling how defensive he had been at the time, he felt more embarrassed than anything.

"It really doesn't matter, Beulah," he said. "I was in a bad mood that day, and—"

"Okay, but I'd still like you to tell me a bit about your mother's life . . . and yours."

Jess sighed again and motioned to the nearby stairs. They sat side by side on the steps while Jess gave a succinct summary of the struggles in his mother's life, and those that had affected Jess directly were the most difficult to repeat. When he told her about the accident that had taken his brother and sister-in-law's lives, Beulah said with compassion, "And that is how you came to be caring for little Evelyn."

"That's right," Jess said, then he went on to tell her about his father getting cancer and passing away not so many months ago. He felt so close to tears as he said it, that he had to distract himself by saying, "Now it's your turn."

With some insistence from Jess, Beulah told of her difficult upbringing, always poor and struggling to survive, and a difficult marriage to an alcoholic that had finally ended with a very ugly divorce. She told of her grown children who all had been too greatly affected by their father, and she had chosen to separate herself from them rather than become repeatedly taken advantage of by them and their difficult behavior. She finished by apologizing again for anything she might have said that was insensitive.

"It was nothing," Jess said. "I appreciate you, Beulah, and all that you do. We're glad to have you here."

Beulah smiled and thanked him for sharing her break with her, then she went back to work. Jess sighed and tried to remember where he'd been headed, forcing the conversation out of his head and the difficult memories it had dredged up.

* * *

Through the process of Tonya taking the missionary discussions, Evelyn turned five, and Tamra's physical condition worsened considerably. Due to a condition that Jess didn't understand, Tamra was in a great deal of pain if she was on her feet for more than a few minutes here and there. Consequently, the doctor told her she needed to stay down beyond trips to the bathroom and a daily shower. Tamra's discouragement deepened, knowing she had months yet to go before the babies would be born. But Jess did his best to spend as much time with her as he could—which was never enough, in his opinion. The family kept her well supplied with books and videos, and Rhea and Emily took turns seeing that she had what she needed and that the children were kept close by so that she could enjoy them without having to care for them beyond feeding Michael his bottles and burping him. Tamra's visiting teachers increased their visits, often bringing books or videos from the library along with their company and uplifting gospel messages. Tamra enjoyed and appreciated their visits, but the time still dragged incessantly.

In spite of knowing how difficult this was for Tamra, Jess left work past supper time again, feeling guilty for the time away from his wife but not knowing what to do about it. He entered the kitchen to find Beulah there, coloring pictures with Evelyn.

"Well, it's about time," Beulah said as he opened the fridge to find his plate of supper, waiting to be heated in the microwave.

"Yeah, it sure is," he said, then asked, "Where is everybody?"

"Tamra's in bed."

"Of course."

"Rhea's looking out for her sister; they're watching a movie or something. Little one just went down to bed. Your mother went to a Relief Society meeting; that meeting formerly known as homemaking."

"Aren't you supposed to be at that too?"

"I'll go next time. Your mother had something she was supposed to do, and I'd rather be with Evelyn." Beulah and the child exchanged bright smiles.

"Pardon my asking," Beulah said as Jess put his plate in the microwave and pushed the buttons, "but why exactly do you spend so much time at that boys' home?"

"It's my job," he said. "There's a lot that needs to be done."

"And you're the only one who can do it, I suppose," Beulah said.

Jess scowled at her while he waited for his supper to heat. "Have I ever told you how your straightforwardness annoys me?"

Beulah laughed deeply. "Only when you know that what I say is true."

"So, what exactly are you trying to say, Beulah? I have to work. There's nothing I can do about it."

"Well, did you ask the good Lord what to do about it?"

Jess thought about it and had to admit, "No, I guess I haven't asked him that specifically."

"Well, in my opinion, just telling him, 'please bless me' isn't going to cut it. You've got to get to the point and say, 'I need to be with my family more.'"

Jess felt stunned and couldn't find any retort. How had she managed to make the problem sound so simple?

"And it's just my opinion," Beulah went on, "but I figure you already got the answer in front of your face."

"And what's that?" he asked, scowling again.

"With all that money you've got, I would think you could hire somebody else to share all that work with. There's a lot of good people who could help take care of those boys, but only you can take care of your family. Then you could be here with these beautiful children. Your wife could use your company more too, I'd wager."

Jess wondered why he felt so stupid, and why she was so right. She seemed to have that effect on him. What was it that had made him think he had to handle so much on his own? Was he so afraid of failing that he couldn't let his responsibilities go to anyone else? Or had he just fallen into a pattern that he hadn't really taken the time to think about after Hobbs had retired and Tamra became too ill to help him? Whatever had happened, he couldn't recall his father ever working this many hours.

The microwave beeped and startled him. Beulah stood from the table and said, "It was just a thought."

He watched her leave with Evelyn to get her ready for bed before he sat down at the table to eat his meal—alone. As he prayed to bless the food, he also asked that he might be able to humbly absorb Beulah's sound advice and do something about it. Of course, it wasn't necessarily an easy solution. Simple perhaps, but not easy. Finding someone he could trust to actually help with his work wouldn't be an easy feat. But perhaps that's where he needed to exert a little faith.

Jess was still sitting there at the table when Emily came in from her meeting. He noticed that she seemed mildly upset and he hurried to ask, "Is something wrong?"

"Actually yes. I'm getting tired of people telling me they've got this male friend, or that male friend, they'd like me to meet. I'm tired of being treated like a single person."

Jess hesitated a moment then said, "I hate to point out the obvious, Mother, but you *are* a single person. People mean well. They want you to be happy."

"Well, I am happy. I'm as happy as I can possibly be under the circumstances, and I still consider myself very much married."

Jess was momentarily taken aback by her conviction. He said, "I'm not questioning you, Mother. In fact, I far prefer that you not date other men. It just seems so . . . I don't know. But it's not something I'm ready for."

"Well, neither am I. If a time ever comes when that's the proper course to take, your father will let me know. Until then, I still consider myself very much married." Jess noticed then that she still wore her wedding ring. He'd never consciously thought about it before. She went on to say, "I feel your father close to me, Jess. He is aware of his family and helping me to guide and care for them. We are on parallel paths of progression and eventually we will be reunited." She headed out the door and finished with a smile, "Good night, Jess."

"Good night," he said, stunned for the second time since he'd come home this evening.

Jess couldn't sleep that night as Beulah's words kept running through his mind, intermixed with his mother's declaration. He marveled at the faith and conviction of these women, and told himself he needed to have a little more of both himself.

The following morning after visiting with Tamra before breakfast, Jess approached his mother in the kitchen and asked, "Could you help me with a little project?"

"I probably could. What's up?"

"Well, remember how we had bedroom picnics when Dad was sick?"

Emily smiled. "I remember."

"Well, I was thinking it might be a good thing to take up again. It doesn't matter what we eat, really. I would just like to share a quiet meal with my wife, so if you can come up with something, I'll be here at six o'clock. And having you watch the kids would be great, too."

"It would be a pleasure," Emily said.

"And maybe in a couple of days, we can all have a picnic together and start making a habit of it."

"It's a wonderful idea," Emily said and Jess went to work with a prayer in his heart that he would be able to find the right person to ease his burdens at work and allow him more time with his family. And when he got a chance, he needed to thank Beulah for having the right words to say, and the courage to say them.

Chapter Eleven

Jess arrived in the kitchen a few minutes before six to see his mother just putting napkins and paper plates into a picnic hamper.

"Oh, Mother, you're priceless," Jess said.

"Anything to help keep some romance alive in this house," she said with a grin and handed him the basket. "The children are with Rhea; between us we'll keep everything under control. Just relax and enjoy your evening."

"Thank you," he said, pressing a kiss to her cheek, "for everything."

She just smiled and shooed him out of the room, handing him a thermos full of lemonade on his way.

Jess peeked into the bedroom to find Tamra leaning against a stack of pillows, staring idly toward the window. Her discouragement tangibly filled the room.

"Hello, my love," he said peering around the open door.

"Oh, hello," she said, obviously pleased to see him. She glanced at the clock. "What brings you home at this unearthly hour?"

"You," he said. "I thought it was high time you and I had a date."

"Oh, that is past due, isn't it," she said.

"I didn't figure dancing would be a good idea."

"No, probably not."

"And taking you into town for a play or a movie or something probably wouldn't go over well."

"No, not likely," Tamra said, her eyes beginning to sparkle.

"So, I thought a picnic."

"A picnic?" she asked just before he moved into the room, displaying the hamper and thermos with a great deal of aplomb. Tamra laughed out loud and her countenance brightened so completely that he kicked himself inwardly for not thinking of this sooner.

"Oh, a picnic's a marvelous idea," she said with moist eyes.

Jess knelt on the bed and leaned over to kiss her. "I love you, Tamra," he said, "and I want you to know how grateful I am for the sacrifices you make to bring our children into the world."

She became too moved to speak, but Jess just spread a checkered tablecloth over the bedspread and unloaded the hamper. They talked and laughed as they shared their meal, then Jess cleaned everything up and pulled off his boots. He leaned against the headboard beside her and put his arm around her. They talked while the room took on a rosy evening glow then gradually became dark and Tamra finally slept in his arms. Jess just held her and silently thanked God for finding ways to get through his own thick head and help him see what was important.

The next day being Saturday, Jess went to the boys' home for a short while then took the rest of the day off. There was plenty he could do there, but nothing that justified putting in more hours when he needed some time for himself and his family. While Tamra and the baby slept, and Emily was working on some project in the kitchen, Rhea took Evelyn with her to push Myrna's wheelchair on a walk outside. Jess went to the library to read in one of his father's novels, realizing that was another thing he'd not had time to do for quite a while with his long hours at work.

Jess became quickly absorbed and was surprised to hear the front doorbell. The front door was rarely used, since anyone who knew the family well always parked on the side and came to the side door near the kitchen. Jess answered the door and saw a woman who lived in their ward, although he couldn't recall her name. She was holding a dozen red roses.

"Hello," he said brightly, wondering why she looked so nervous.

"Hello," she said. "Uh . . . is your mother at home?"

"Yes, she is. Come in and I'll get her."

She stepped into the house, looking even more nervous as she glanced around. He motioned toward the front parlor and said, "Have a seat. I'll find her."

"Thank you. I'm fine," she said in a tone that indicated she hoped he would hurry.

Jess walked back to the kitchen and said to Emily, "Mother, there's someone at the front door for you."

"Really?" she asked, lifting her brows. "Who?"

"A sister in the ward; I'm afraid I don't recall her name."

Jess couldn't suppress his curiosity enough to keep from following his mother back to the front hall where the woman was waiting, but seeing her nervous face he decided it would be more appropriate for him to leave them alone. He moved back toward the library, saying, "I'll just . . ." But Emily took hold of his arm, as if she wanted him close by.

"Hello, Jean," Emily said with a bright smile. Jess could tell that his mother was acquainted with this woman, but they didn't know each other very well. "What can I do for you?" Emily asked just as Jean pushed the roses gently toward Emily, without uttering a sound. "Good heavens," Emily laughed softly, "what are these for?"

"I'm not sure," Jean said. "I just . . . felt like I should bring them to you."

Emily laughed again. "Well, that's very sweet, but . . . I don't understand why you would go to so much trouble to . . ."

Emily hesitated when moisture gathered in Jean's eyes. "They're not from me, Emily." Her voice broke. She smiled serenely. "They're from Michael; he wanted you to have them, and it had to be today."

Jess sucked in his breath and held it as he watched tears gather in his mother's eyes then fall. "Thank you," she barely managed to say.

Jean smiled and hurried toward the door. "I must go. Have a good day."

Emily said nothing being overcome by emotion; she simply nodded and Jean smiled again. With her hand on the doorknob, Jean turned back and said, "I don't know if you were aware that while your husband served as bishop, he helped me through a serious crisis. I made some bad choices and he guided me back to the right path; he helped me put my life in order, and I will forever be grateful for his kindness and compassion, and the way he exemplified the Savior's love. I don't know why he chose me to make a delivery he couldn't make, but I do know that . . ." Her emotion deepened and it took her a long moment to gather her composure. "I do know that my testimony has grown immensely this day of the reality of ministering angels, and their connection to us in this world. While I have been about this errand, I have felt reminded of how far I have come, and how much I have to be grateful for." She looked down and cleared her throat as she opened the door. "I'll see you in church on Sunday," she said and hurried out.

"Thank you," Jess said and closed the door. He watched in silent awe as his mother moved to the sofa and cradled the roses against her, inhaling their fragrance with her eyes closed. Her emotion deepened and she sobbed softly. Jess sat beside her and put his arm around her. He let her cry against his shoulder while she held the flowers tightly, as if she were holding to Michael. Jess attempted to comprehend the reality of what had just taken place, but he couldn't. He simply found it impossible to grasp the full breadth of life on both sides of the veil, and how thin that veil could be. Tears came to his own eyes as he imagined his father close by, observing Emily's tender emotion.

"Tell me," Jess urged gently once her tears had quieted. "Why did it have to be today?"

Emily sighed and looked up at him. "When I woke up this morning and realized what day it was, I felt more lonely for him than I have in weeks. I prayed that I could feel his love for me, and that he could feel mine for him."

She became emotional again and he asked, "Why today?" He knew that his father had given his mother flowers often for many occasions, and sometimes for no occasion at all. When she didn't answer he asked, "Does this day have significance?"

Emily nodded and fought for her composure. "He always gave me flowers on this day of the year. It was the anniversary of the day that he came back into my life after my first husband died. He said it was the day he'd been given a second chance at life, and he never wanted to forget how much that meant to him."

Jess swallowed carefully. "I didn't know that."

Emily smiled through a fresh surge of tears. "That's just it, Jess, *nobody* knew that. It was one of those things that we just kept between the two of us; no particular reason. It just never seemed right to tell anybody, so it gradually became a little secret between us."

"That's incredible," Jess said breathlessly.

"Yes, it is," Emily laughed through her tears.

Jess kissed his mother's forehead and wiped her face, silently thanking God for evidence that miracles, indeed, had not ceased.

On Sunday, they had a family picnic in Jess and Tamra's room. Jess even carried Myrna up the stairs to join them. He figured it would have been easier to take Tamra down the stairs, but Myrna said she'd never seen the house up there, and he decided they could picnic downstairs next time.

When their picnic was over and cleaned up, Emily suggested that they watch some home videos from last year's family vacation. "I think," Emily added, "that Tamra's seen just about everything else there is on video in this house."

"Wait," Jess said as she stood to retrieve the tape, "do you mean . . . last year, as in . . . my father is on the video?" Memories crowded into Jess's mind of all the times they'd had a video camera rolling during the final year of Michael's life. And after his death he'd completely forgotten about it.

"That's what I mean," Emily said. "Are you not ready for that?"

Jess had to think about it, but still he said, "I . . . don't know. Have you watched the videos?"

"I have, actually."

"And how did it make you feel?" Jess asked.

"I've certainly cried over them, but I like to watch the videos. It makes the memories more real."

Jess took a deep breath. "Okay, let's go for it." But he held tightly to Tamra's hand as Emily put the video in. When Michael first appeared on the television screen, talking and laughing, surrounded by his grandchildren, Jess couldn't keep an emotional noise from erupting out of his mouth. Evelyn turned her attention to the television and excitedly said, "That's Grandpa!"

"Yes, it is," Emily said, pulling Evelyn onto her lap.

"He went to live with Heavenly Father," Evelyn added matter-of-factly.

"Yes, he did." Emily smiled at Evelyn.

For the remainder of the evening, Jess sat mesmerized by his father's image on the screen. He had to agree with his mother: he certainly was crying over them, but they made the memories more clear. There before him was evidence that they had picnicked and vacationed and celebrated holidays. They had ridden horses together and they had flown his father's plane over the house. They had talked and laughed and they had been together. And oh, how Jess missed him! Still, this tangible reminder of his existence was comforting, somehow. And Jess felt grateful.

* * *

Monday proved to be a difficult day at the boys' home. Jess quickly realized why he didn't take hours off when he found his work and the needs of the boys mounting up. He never had a minute to talk with his staff about the decision to hire another administrative assistant in order to lessen his workload. And to make matters worse, notice arrived that he would need to attend a court hearing on Nathan Gooding's behalf. His father was claiming that mother and child were lying to conspire against him, and that his wife's depression had been the entire root of the problems in their household.

Jess determined that he couldn't worry over it. He knew Nathan well enough to know where the real source of the problem lay. He could only pray that the judge would be able to see through a man like Bill Gooding. And while little Nathan was completely unaware of the pending court issues with his parents, the day didn't go well for him, either. Jess was called to one of the classrooms just after lunch to deal with a dispute. Apparently one of the more difficult boys, a nine year old named Edgel, had started picking on Nathan for no apparent reason. But the teacher reported that Nathan had reached a point of frustration and he'd belted Edgel in the nose, making it bleed. And since the rule was plainly 'no hitting or fighting' Nathan had consequences to face, as well as Edgel. The boys were each required to write a paragraph about peacemaking and turn it in to the teacher before they could leave for recess, and after school time when the other boys would be playing, they would each be required to do an hour's cleaning. Jess took a few minutes with each of the boys to discuss their behavior and how it could be prevented in the future, then he left them in the teacher's care and returned to his office.

Jess left the boys' home long after supper time, and chose to walk the long way around to the house, rather than going through the connecting hallway. He simply felt the need for some fresh air to clear the day's work out of his head. He was surprised when he stepped outside to see Beulah's car still there. It only took him a moment to recall that she should have been on her way home before six. Unable to let go of a feeling that he should find her, he turned around and went back inside. The offices were locked up tightly, and the cafeteria was the same, with supper long over and cleaned away. The classrooms and library were closed for the night, and most of the boys were in the dorm game room. In fact, the only one obviously missing was Nathan Gooding. Jess questioned the supervisor on shift who told him that Nathan had said he was going to bed early.

Jess felt something tug at his heart as he left the noisy game room behind and traversed the long hall to Nathan's room. A kid that young needed a mother, not a *staff member* who would simply be there to make certain he was safe and well. Jess hesitated at the partially open door when he heard a woman's voice, then he remembered that his initial reason for coming up here was to locate Beulah. He peered carefully around the door to see both objects of his quest. Nathan was curled up on Beulah's lap, sniffling and wiping at his face while she told him a dramatic version of the story, *The Prince and the Pauper.* Jess remained, discreetly observing as she finished her story then told Nathan that the important thing about any boy, no matter what situation he might be in, was what he held in his heart. "If you hold hate or anger or sadness in your heart, then you'll be a hateful or angry or sad person. If you hold peace and love and faith in your heart, then that's the kind of person you'll be. You just have to choose which wolf you'll feed."

"Wolf?" he questioned, his tears dried up.

"Well, it's like all those things I just said are like a pack of wolves inside each one of us. There's a hate wolf, and a love wolf. There's one for peace and one for anger. And so on and so forth. The wolf that you feed is the one that will watch over and protect your heart, and the others will turn and go away because they don't get fed."

"I like wolfs," Nathan said, a strong emphasis on the 'f.'

"I do too," Beulah said. "They're beautiful animals."

"Which wolf do you feed?" Nathan asked.

"Well, I'm not always perfect at it, but I try to feed the love wolf. I think if we hold love in our heart, we'll be able to deal with life a lot easier. I think love brings peace."

"I think so too," Nathan said.

"And I think you'd better get some sleep now. Tomorrow's a brand new day, and I have a feeling it will be a good one."

"Better than today," Nathan said.

"Yes, I'm sure of it," Beulah smiled and pressed a kiss to his little forehead.

Jess slipped discreetly back into the hall before Beulah came out of the room. When she had the door closed he said, "I didn't realize that was part of your job description."

Flustered and embarrassed, she said, "I'm sorry if I . . . did something wrong. I just . . . knew he was . . . upset and—"

"You did nothing wrong," Jess said. "In fact, I think you're just what Nathan needed tonight. I think all of these boys could use a little more mothering."

"Oh, I think they could," she said with passion.

"Have you had supper yet?" he asked.

"No, I haven't," she said, "but I can just run on home and—"

"I haven't had supper either," he said. "I think we could dig something up."

They found Emily in the kitchen, reading and obviously waiting for Jess to come in. She visited with them as they ate, then Jess said he would walk Beulah to her car, but when they discovered that it was now raining significantly, Jess said, "I've got a better idea."

With an umbrella he took Beulah to the back side of the boys' home where there were four apartments. "Only two of them are occupied right now," he said. "A couple of staff members live here who don't have family, and they can be on hand in case of a crisis. The rest of the staff commutes, of course, except for the ones who actually stay in the dorms with the boys. We keep these empty apartments stocked for just such times when an employee has to stay on hand for some particular reason, or weather gets bad." He opened the door with a key then put the key into her hand. "You should find everything you need—a new toothbrush and stuff like that. I'd far rather have you stay than have you drive home in the rain. I have an aversion to driving in the rain."

"Thank you," she said.

"No, thank *you,*" he replied and she went inside.

Before she could close the door, Jess added, "Hey, it's up to you, but you're welcome to rent this place if you like. It's probably less money than where you're at, and it would save your having to drive back and forth every day." He smiled and added, "And you could ride to church with us on Sundays."

Beulah offered a tender smile. "Thank you. I'll think about that."

The following morning Madge came in to Jess's office with a number of new challenges for him, but one of the first things she said was, "We're finally getting some calls on that ad I put in the paper for Beulah's job."

Jess chuckled and they went on to their business, but after Madge left his office, the thought sunk in more fully. He went to Madge's desk and said, "On that job . . . I think we could really use some more help around here, so let's hire somebody anyway."

"To do what?" Madge asked.

"Beulah's job, of course."

"What's she going to do?"

"Help me, of course," he said, marveling at how the answer to his prayers had been right in front of him all along—just as Beulah herself had said it was.

Jess waited to tell Beulah until he'd hired someone to replace her, then he called her into his office and asked her to sit down. "If this is about that apartment,"she said, "I'd like to take it. That place where I live now is a dump."

"Well . . . I didn't want to say anything . . ." Jess chuckled. "That's great. I'll have Madge work out the details with you. But no, this isn't about the apartment, although that will make things easier for you."

"With what?" She sounded alarmed.

"With your new job," he said. "Unless you don't want it, of course. You can keep doing what you're doing if you'd like, but . . ."

"Just tell me about this new job," she said.

"Well, it involves paperwork, phone calls, good people skills, and especially helping the boys solve problems that come up. It's technically called an administrative assistant and it would be for the purpose of lightening *my* workload. Oh, and there's a raise involved. So, what do you think?"

Jess was surprised when Beulah became so emotional that she couldn't speak for a number of minutes. When she finally got control of her tears, she said, "Forgive me. It's just that . . . I don't think you have any idea what a blessing this is for me . . . in so many ways. I've made some bad choices in my life, some worse than others, and my involvement with the Church has been half-hearted sometimes. Before I moved here, things were so bad that . . . well, you don't need to know all that, but . . . the bishop there, he gave me a blessing and he promised me that if I committed myself fully to the Lord, that He would bring great blessings into my life, and I knew that meant I had to move away from my ex-husband and kids because they only caused grief for me. But I especially remember the blessing saying that . . ." Tears overtook her again and Jess waited patiently. "It said that . . . I would have the opportunity to care for children in the absence of my own children. Of course," she chuckled, "I've got my primary class, but . . . when you said what you did the other night about these boys needing some mothering, I just felt like it was me they needed, but I didn't want to overstep my job here and . . . well, I shouldn't ramble, but . . . the other thing that blessing promised was that I would have financial security for the first time in my life. And you're giving me that as well. I just . . . don't know what to say."

"Just . . . keep doing a great job," he said. "I can say something to you that I can't say to most of my employees, because they don't understand the gospel and how it works. But I want to tell you to just listen to the Spirit and it will tell you when and where you are needed. That's the best way you can help lift my workload."

Beulah grinned and thanked him again. She left his office beaming and Jess went home in time for supper with good news for his family. He prompted a picnic in the bedroom with Tamra, his mother, and the children, while Rhea and Myrna actually went into town for a movie. When the meal was winding down and Evelyn was busy with some puzzles on the floor, Jess said, "I have a confession to make."

"Okay," Tamra said.

"Well," Jess took a deep breath, "when I took over the boys' home completely, I hadn't taken into consideration that some changes had been made there that made my job more demanding than it had been for Hobbs. I've been working too many hours—plain and simple. And for that I owe both of you an apology."

Tamra reached for his hand. "I understand that you have to be there for the boys to—"

"Let me finish," Jess said, putting up his other hand. "The boys are important, but there's a lot I do that doesn't have to be done by me personally. But I came to a realization recently that . . . well, I think I've been believing I had to work every minute I could to somehow prove that I was worthy to follow in my father's footsteps—not to mention the other great men who went before him. But I realized that all of those men knew how to keep balance in their life, and even though I've tried not to neglect my family, I know I could spend more time here, and less time there, and we would all be better off. So . . . I hired someone to do a great deal of my work. It will mean less time for me with the boys, but I can't do everything. Well, actually, I gave one of our employees a promotion and hired somebody to take her job."

"Who?" Tamra asked.

He smiled. "Beulah, of course."

In response to their pleased expressions Jess went on to tell them the details of what had transpired, and how good he felt about where he had come in regard to his job. It turned out to be an extremely pleasant evening, but he went to work the following morning to be confronted with preparations for the hearing on the Gooding case. Jess felt sick to his stomach as their resident counselor, Ray, repeated his findings from many hours of working with Nathan. The ongoing abuse and the impact from it were readily evident. The good news was that Nathan happened to be one of those especially resilient children with good instincts, and he would likely do well now that he'd been taken away from the abuse. The trick was to make certain that such atrocities never happened in his life again.

The morning of the hearing Jess drove more than two hours with Ray, where they met with their solicitor for a short while before arriving at the courthouse twenty minutes early. Then they waited for over an hour, since the judge was behind schedule. When the hearing finally got underway, Jess's nerves were on edge. And when he realized that Bill Gooding was an average looking businessman with brown hair, clean cut and meticulous, he could hardly believe this was the man responsible for Nathan's abuse and his mother's abuse and depression. He just prayed the judge wouldn't be thinking the same thing. That sickness inside of Jess returned as he listened to the statements regarding the abuse of Linda and Nathan Gooding. But the sickness doubled as he listened to

Bill Gooding express a heartfelt plea to have his family put back together and to get the help needed for his wife to get beyond her depression and borderline psychotic behavior, which he claimed were the reasons she had manipulated their son into speaking against him. The judge set a date for the battle to continue and they all left the courtroom. Jess hurried in order to avoid being anywhere near Bill Gooding. Otherwise, he'd feel hard pressed not to physically hurt the man.

On the drive home, Jess asked Ray, "Do you think it's possible he's telling the truth?"

"Who?"

"Bill Gooding."

"No!" Ray laughed at the absurdity. "You have to remember that much of my observation of Nathan was done when he didn't know he was being watched. In his play he clearly shows the father figure as being angry and hurtful, and the mother and children being victimized. That's only one piece of the evidence. You know the rest."

"Yes, I do," Jess said. "It's just that . . . he's so convincing. What if he convinces the judge that—"

"I think you need more faith than that," Ray said.

"You are telling me to have faith?" Jess almost laughed. "I thought you didn't even go to church."

"You don't have to go to church to have faith," Ray said.

"Yeah," Jess said with a smirk, "but you have to have faith to go to church."

Ray just chuckled and changed the subject.

Through the following weeks the court battle over Nathan Gooding's future became heated and ugly. And Jess was right in the middle of it. He was immeasurably grateful that he'd been guided to put Beulah in the position to help him, otherwise he would have gone insane. As it was he did manage to spend more time with his family than he had been, and he got some reading in on their trips back and forth to appointments and legal meetings with Ray. But beyond his snatches of reading Jess found no time for himself whatsoever, and that's when he realized that his nightmares had been lessening—only because they suddenly became more frequent again.

The afternoon before another big day in court with the Goodings, Jess began feeling not quite himself. By early evening he knew he was coming down with something and he hurried home. He found his mother in the kitchen and leaned breathlessly against the doorframe.

"Hello," she said, glancing toward him, then she did a double take. "Are you all right? You look . . . flushed. You're out of breath."

"I think I've got the flu or something equally horrible," he said.

Emily crossed the room and put a motherly hand to his brow. "Good heavens. You certainly have a fever."

"Yes, I know. And I hurt everywhere. I don't want Tamra to get sick, so I'm going to go sleep it off in a guest room."

"Is there anything you need first? Are you hungry?"

"No, I'm fine," he said and lumbered up the stairs, pausing every three or four steps to catch his breath. He went into his own bedroom long enough to grab a few of his things and say to Tamra, "I'm not going to get close to you because I'm sick."

"No!" she protested, as if she could make the germs go away.

"I'm afraid so. I'm going to a guest room so I won't give it to you." He waved at her from the door, noting her concerned expression. "I love you," he said.

"I love you too. I wish I had the energy to take care of you." Tears rose in her eyes.

"It's okay," he said. "Knowing you wish it is good enough."

Emily checked on Jess twice before she went to bed, but there was nothing she could do beyond getting him a fresh dose of something for the pain and fever. He spent the night vacillating between sweating and chills—and not sleeping at all—with body aches that threatened to devour him. He phoned the boys' home as soon as he knew Madge would be at her desk. He told her to let Ray know he wouldn't be going with him for their appointment in court. "Send Shirley for moral support," he said. "And Beulah can cover the important stuff for me."

"It's really bad, isn't it," Madge said.

"Yes, I'm afraid it is. That's why I'm going to stay here and not spread it around. I have no idea how long I'll be down, so . . ."

"We'll just take it one day at a time," Madge said. "Don't you worry; we'll keep everything under control. And tell your mother if she needs any help, I'm not far away."

"I'll tell her," Jess said, then he got off the phone and resisted the urge to curse aloud. Instead he just growled with sarcasm, "This is just what I need."

His foul mood deepened when Ray and Shirley returned to announce that the day had been a waste of time and the court date had been postponed.

Jess spent the next few days so consumed with fever and aches that he didn't know which way was up. He spent a week after that so physically drained that he was still bound to the bed beyond an occasional trip to the bathroom. He felt frustrated and helpless as he considered all he could and should be doing, then he reminded himself that it was simply beyond his power and nothing to be suffering guilt over. Once the aches receded to a moderate level, he distracted himself by finishing the novel he'd been reading—the fifth one his father had written. Then he finished the sixth and last one, feeling almost sad that there was nothing more of his stories to read. With nothing to read that appealed to him, Jess felt drawn to watching the videos of his father again. When he'd watched everything three times, he was relieved to have Emily bring him some photo albums that he enjoyed perusing. That too got old after several hours, and Jess could only sleep so much in spite of his ongoing exhaustion. If nothing else he found he was gaining some serious empathy for Tamra's plight of being stuck in bed. It was a wonder she hadn't gone insane, and he resolved to spend even more time with her when he finally got past this and could feel reasonably certain that he wouldn't be spreading germs.

Emily initiated some phone calls from Jess's sisters, and he enjoyed visiting with each of them more than he had in a long while. They had kept in touch through email and an occasional brief call, but it was nice to have a lengthy visit with each of them. He found they were all struggling in varying degrees with missing their father—which gave them something in common.

When Jess became completely bored with television and videos, and he just didn't feel in the mood to read anything available, he wondered what Tamra managed to do with all of her hours in bed. He thought about the many times he'd found Emily, Rhea, or Tonya visiting with her, and he wished he had his father to talk to now.

Pondering memories of his father, he felt a sudden urge to read the journals of their forebears—journals that Michael had meticulously typed into a computer so that copies could be preserved and distributed to family members. When Emily came to his room to check on him, he asked if she would get the typed copies of some of the family journals—specifically, the men who had gone before him who had all worked at the same jobs he was doing now. He knew that Tamra had read all of the family journals and she had shared many stories with him, but it was something he'd never done personally—except for his great-great-grandfather's, Jess Davies, which he had read at a time of crisis, and he'd gained much from it. Now he started with Michael's father, Jesse Hamilton, who had been a young man during World War II, then he read about Michael Hamilton the first, who had come to be administrator of the boys' home in the early twentieth century, after having grown up there in his youth. Jess marveled at what great men he had come from. And while he felt inadequate to fill their shoes, he felt a certain strength come into him from their written words, and the evidence that they too had risen above many struggles.

Jess had just started into rereading his great-great-grandfather's journals when he felt suddenly improved and was able to get up and almost feel like a human being again. Encouraged by his mother, he caught up some time with his family for a couple of days while he continued to take it easy in order to avoid overdoing it. In spite of his feeling much better, he didn't feel up to attending another legal meeting for Nathan. He sent Ray and Shirley with a prayer in his heart that all would go well. But they returned with news that was anything but good. While there were still some minor issues pending, it looked as if the Goodings would be divorcing, but the abuse charges had been all but thrown out, and Bill was likely to get custody of Nathan. The very thought made Jess feel almost as sick as the flu had made him feel. He couldn't even imagine letting something like that happen. But he wasn't sure what he could do about it.

Chapter Twelve

Jess was sitting in his office feeling as if a two-ton weight were on his shoulders when Ray knocked at the open door and entered. From the expression on Ray's face, Jess knew what was coming even before he said, "We're going to have to put Nathan on the stand to testify. I'm afraid that's his only chance of being free of his father."

Jess sighed loudly. It wasn't the first time something like this had happened. But it was the first time that Jess had been this emotionally involved with the child in question. And he knew that having the child testify would likely dredge up many of the difficulties in his past that they'd been working so hard to heal.

"Have you talked to him about it?" Jess asked.

"I have, and I think he'll do fine. He's just . . . scared."

"Scared of what?" Jess demanded.

"His father, of course."

"But he must understand that his testimony will put his father away."

"He understands that his testimony will *likely* put his father away. And he understands that even so, such prison sentences don't last forever. It's a difficult position for a child to be in."

"Yes, it is," Jess growled, "and I have a difficult time tolerating people who put children in such positions."

"That's why we're in this business, Jess," Ray said and Jess took a deep breath to calm his anger.

Later that day Jess had a quiet visit with Nathan in the gabled attic. He had to admit that Nathan actually had a fairly good perspective of what was happening, and he seemed prepared. But that didn't make it easy. When he returned to his office he called several temples and put Nathan Gooding's name on the prayer rolls. And his mother's as well. Then, on impulse, he put his father's as well. Perhaps with prayer Bill Gooding's heart would be softened. But then, free agency was a big part of the picture.

On the appointed day, Emily gave Jess a little sack that held some snacks and treats for Nathan to help him get through the day. "Thank you," Jess said and kissed her cheek. He spent a few minutes with Tamra and the children before he met Ray and Nathan and they were on their way. Through the long drive, Nathan kept his hand in Jess's much of the time. They talked openly about what to expect, even though it had all been rehearsed before. They met the solicitor at the courthouse, and he too spoke with Nathan about what to expect. Jess promised Nathan they would go out for a hamburger and ice cream when this was over, then they marched into the courtroom and sat down. When Nathan saw his father he visibly cowered and clung to Jess—a gesture that Jess wished the judge had been in the room to see.

As the proceedings got underway, Jess was freshly appalled to see how perfectly smooth Bill Gooding could be—too smooth. But could the judge see through it?

When Nathan was called to the stand, Jess became consumed with nerves. Knots tightened in his stomach and his palms sweat. But his nerves lessened as he observed how well Nathan answered the questions. He was feeling much better once Nathan got down from the stand, until Jess turned to see Bill Gooding staring directly at him. The glare in his eyes was evil—plain and simple. A chill rushed over Jess's shoulders and he knew this wasn't over yet.

Jess was hoping to hear a verdict and have this over and done with, but Bill Gooding's solicitor asked for a recess until the following morning for some complicated reason that made no sense to Jess. The judge granted the request, although he specified that it would have to be in two days because something else was on his schedule the following day. Jess just wanted to have it over with, and he wasn't thrilled about having to make the drive again in two days.

Jess and Ray hurried Nathan from the courtroom, and just as promised, they took Nathan out for a hamburger and ice cream. The boy ate voraciously and seemed in good spirits, and he slept most of the way home. Ray agreed with Jess, that Nathan had done very well, and they were both relieved to have this behind them. They prayed that the outcome would be favorable.

As soon as Nathan was settled with the staff, Jess went home and rested on the bed beside Tamra, telling her the details of his day, and holding her hand. He read stories with Evelyn while sitting in the same spot, and he played with little Michael who was crawling around the room attempting to get into trouble, but thwarted by the baby-proof latches that had been securely installed on the drawers. One drawer had been left accessible and was filled with toys. Michael got excited when he was able to open it, then he took the toys out one at a time and tossed them everywhere before he climbed into the drawer and sat there, looking quite proud of himself.

"He is so cute," Jess said and Tamra laughed softly.

"Yes, he looks like you."

Michael grinned and showed budding teeth. Jess laughed and said, "I don't see the resemblance."

When Michael got tired of the drawer, Evelyn picked all of the toys up and put them back. "You are such a good helper for Mom," Jess said.

Evelyn agreed and Jess took her and Michael to give them a bath and put them to bed.

The following morning Jess had only been at work a couple of hours when Ray came into his office, wearing a grin. "We've had a miracle."

"Really?" Jess said, leaning back in his chair. "So faith works after all? Is that what you're telling me?"

Ray just laughed and leaned over his desk, saying earnestly, "Apparently Bill Gooding has an ex-wife, who got wind of the case and has testified of his abusive behavior in her marriage to him. In fact, the records from their divorce several years ago include her statement regarding his abuse of her, which is almost identical to the current Mrs. Gooding's statement. Also included in that divorce decree is a doctor's statement that Bill Gooding suffers from a mental illness that is known for irrational, violent outbursts, and more than one time in his life he has been under court order to take medication for the condition; a condition which he has been hospitalized for three times. The ex-Mrs. Gooding will be testifying tomorrow, the old divorce decree will be brought forward as evidence, and Bill Gooding is going to prison. He might be able to claim that *one* wife is simply depressed and psychotic, but not two. It's in the bag."

"Yes!" Jess laughed and they shared a high-five across the desk. "Let's just hope Bill Gooding doesn't get wind of it and do something desperate—especially with one of those 'irrational violent outburtsts.' I've seen a few desperate ones in here before, and it gets ugly."

"It will all be over tomorrow," Ray said with a positive lilt and hurried to get to work.

An hour later Jess wondered if his own words had been a bad omen when Shirley slipped into his office, looking upset.

"What's wrong?" Jess asked.

"He's here. I just saw him come in the front door, and he doesn't look very happy."

"Who?"

"Nathan's father," she whispered loudly and he recalled that she had attended some court proceedings in Jess's absence.

"Call security," Jess said quietly, grateful that Shirley had known who it was and had put him on alert.

"I already did," Shirley said nervously. "Be careful."

Jess said a quick prayer, took a deep breath, and stepped into the main hall where Bill Gooding was just approaching the offices.

"So, we meet again," Bill said snidely.

"There is a court order that forbids you to be here," Jess said firmly. "I advise you to leave immediately."

"I'll leave when I've had my say," he muttered, then with no warning Bill belted Jess in the jaw and pushed him up against the wall. He growled profanities and shouted a number of violent threats while Jess tried to imagine little Nathan and his mother subjected to this. He breathed an audible sigh when he saw Max from the corner of his eye, his pistol pointed securely at Bill.

"Just raise your hands and back off," Max ordered.

What happened next happened so fast that Jess felt sure his blinking had made him miss half of it. Bill swung around and pulled a pistol from inside his jacket, firing it twice before Max could have possibly even considered whether or not to pull the trigger on his own weapon. It only took a split second for Jess to get beyond the shock that this was actually happening in *his* boys' home, as he watched Max fall. A quick glance told him the wound was in his leg and likely not fatal. Jess lunged for the gun and knocked it from Bill's hand before he sent one fist into his jaw, and another to his middle—twice. Then Jess became distracted as a large group of boys came running down the stairs, obviously drawn by the gunfire, against their instructor's wishes.

"Get them out of there!" Jess shouted just before Bill struck his jaw, tender from the last blow. Then he hit him again—and again.

Jess was oblivious to anything but the intensifying pain until Nathan ran from among the boys, barreling into his father as he shouted, "You get out of here and leave us alone! I hate you! I hate you!"

Jess got his equilibrium back quickly as Bill struck the child across the face so hard that he reeled back against the wall and slid to the floor, howling. Anger fed Jess's protective instincts and he hit Bill so hard that it had a similar effect. Jess pulled him to his feet by his shirt collar and slammed him into the wall. Bill threw a fist into Jess's belly, but Jess held him fast and slammed him again before he hit him once more then turned him to face the wall, holding him there with the weight of his body.

"You filthy scum," Jess muttered behind his ear. "You will never—*ever*—hurt that child again."

Murphy came running through the front doors and Jess realized that Madge must have called his mobile phone. Jess heard Max say in a pained voice, "The handcuffs."

Murphy took the cuffs from Max and snapped them onto Bill's wrists while Jess held him against the wall. Bill groaned and strained against the restriction. Profanities flew from his mouth again until Jess shoved him against the wall and told him to shut up. Murphy took Jess's place in keeping Bill unable to move. He smirked and said quietly to Jess, "You look terrible."

"I'm glad you came when you did or I probably would have looked a lot worse."

Jess quickly assessed the situation, noting that Madge had made Max comfortable and was holding a towel tightly over the wound. He was conscious and seemed to be doing well, considering he had a bullet hole in his leg. Shirley was sitting on the floor, holding Nathan, and the teachers were ushering the other boys back up the stairs. Many of them glanced toward Jess with obvious concern.

"I'm fine," he said with a smile. "Everything's okay now."

Jess glanced again toward the women. "Did you—"

"Help is on its way," Madge assured him. Jess nodded and felt his head start to swim from the repeated blows. Now that his adrenalin had stopped pumping, he felt the pain of the encounter beginning to sink in fully.

"You'd better sit down," Shirley said, nodding toward a chair without relinquishing her hold on Nathan as he cried in her arms.

"I think I will," Jess said, fearing he'd pass out and embarrass himself.

The police and ambulance finally arrived, and within minutes Bill and Max were on their way back to town, one headed for the hospital, the other for jail. Jess went to the men's room and washed the dried blood off his face. He groaned at his reflection when he saw that the bruising and swelling was far worse than he'd expected. He went upstairs and had a long talk with Nathan before he left him in Shirley's care and returned to the house. He was putting ice into a plastic bag when his mother came into the kitchen. With the freezer door open she didn't see his face before he said, "I take it you ladies didn't hear anything unusual earlier."

"No, actually," she said. "Tamra and I were watching a movie; I think Rhea and Myrna were doing the same down here. Why?"

"Just wondering," Jess said, closing the freezer.

Emily gasped then briefly turned to stone, staring at him with her mouth open. "What happened?" she demanded in an emotional whisper, her hand going to her heart.

Jess slumped into a chair beside the table and gingerly put the bag of ice to his face. "Bill Gooding wanted to have a little chat—with his fists and a loaded pistol."

"Merciful heaven," Emily muttered and sank into a chair, herself. "Was anyone else hurt?"

"I'm afraid so," he said and Emily put a hand over her mouth while she waited for the news.

"Max was on duty; he took a bullet in the leg, but he's going to be okay. I'm afraid Nathan got himself into the middle of it, and his father hit him pretty hard."

"Oh," Emily moaned and tears filled her eyes.

"He's going to be okay, too. Shirley is with him. He's upset but very relieved to see his father taken away in handcuffs."

"Why would he be so foolish?" Emily asked.

"I'm guessing it has something to do with new evidence that would have inevitably sent him to prison. He was prone to irrational behavior anyway, so once he knew he was sunk, he stopped pretending. That's my theory, anyway."

"It certainly makes sense," she said. "Was anyone else hurt?"

"Yeah," Jess chuckled without humor, "I got that despicable creep at least as good as he got me." He opened and closed his fist that was tender from the blows it had delivered. "And God forgive me, but it felt awfully good."

Emily reached for his hand across the table. "I'm just grateful that you're all right; that everyone is all right."

"Yes, so am I. We were truly blessed."

"You'd better go tell your wife what happened. She needs to hear it from you."

"Yes, I'd better do that," he said and went upstairs.

He pulled the ice away from his face as he entered the bedroom and hesitated in the doorway. She set down her book and turned to look at him. He knew that's all it would take to provoke a question, and she didn't disappoint him when she demanded, "What happened to your face?"

"Bill Gooding and I had a little chat. He started talking first—with his fists."

"Are you all right?" she asked, reaching a hand out toward him.

"I am, actually. And at least it's over now." He sat on the edge of the bed and told her all the details while he realized he was shaking. That evening when it came time for family prayer he offered it himself and tears accompanied his expression of gratitude that he was safe and well enough to care for his family and his responsibilities, and that no one else was too seriously injured or killed. When the prayer was finished he saw tears in the eyes of his wife and mother.

The following morning Jess went to the hospital to see Max. The surgery to remove the bullet had gone well, and he would be up in a matter of days.

"I want to say thank you, Max," Jess said. "But it sounds so trite. There are no words to express how much it means to have someone take a bullet for you—or more importantly, for one of those boys."

"They're good boys," he said with a little smile, then he glanced down humbly. "I was just doing my job."

"You did it well, and I'm grateful," Jess said.

Following a lengthy visit with Max, Jess went on some errands and returned home to find Tamra feeling especially down. He took the rest of the day off and watched a movie with her, then they read together from the latest *Ensign* and the Book of Mormon, stopping to have a bedroom picnic with the family at supper time.

A few days later word came that the judge had granted custody of Nathan Gooding to the Byrnehouse-Davies Home for Boys until the time when a judge determined that Mrs. Gooding was stable enough to care for her son. She would be given visitation on an increasing scale in the meantime. Bill Gooding would be serving some serious prison time. Jess was pleased with the outcome, and went personally to give Nathan the good news. Beulah was with him in one of the classrooms, admiring his latest art project, and the three of them sat down together and talked quietly of the outcome. Jess felt deeply gratified by Nathan's relief, and the prospect that this child was evidence of one more chain of abuse being broken. Sharing lunch with Nathan and the other boys, a deep fulfillment overcame him in regard to the work he was doing here. He was truly grateful for the opportunity to commit his life's work to such a great cause, and pleased to have that particular challenge behind them. Observing Beulah with the boys, his gratitude deepened. She was a great blessing to him, and to them. He considered the obvious hand of the Lord in every aspect of his life, and he found it impossible to count all of his blessings before he had to return to work.

* * *

During what had become the usual evening picnic in the bedroom, Tamra noticed that Jess's face had finally healed and there wasn't even a trace of bruising left there. Watching him keep little Michael from crawling through the food spread over the bed, she couldn't deny her gratitude for being blessed with such a good man. She would be grateful when she could have this pregnancy behind her and once again be the wife and mother that she wanted to be.

When the picnic had been cleared away, a familiar loneliness crept over Tamra. She lay staring at the ceiling, aware from the angle of the light that the sun was going down. She knew that Jess was bathing Michael down the hall, and Emily was somewhere in the house with Evelyn—probably visiting with her mother and Rhea. Oh, how Tamra longed to just walk through this beautiful home, to sit in the kitchen with the family for a meal, to lounge on the veranda and watch the sun go down. She didn't know how she could possibly make it through the remaining weeks of this pregnancy without going insane. It already seemed that she'd been pregnant forever, and while she constantly tried to talk herself out of being discouraged—and she'd gotten better at keeping her spirits up—there were moments when she felt as if she'd drown in the prospect of what the forthcoming weeks would bring. She had taken to praying that as soon as these babies could possibly live on their own, she wanted to be free of the pain and illness they were causing as they grew inside of her.

Tamra sighed loudly when she realized she couldn't wait any longer to use the bathroom. Getting back and forth was the most difficult task of her days, and she had to talk herself into it, knowing that waiting any longer would only increase her pain. She moved her legs carefully over the edge of the bed and set her swollen feet on the floor. Looking down at herself, she marveled at how huge her belly had become. It was no wonder that she felt as if she would literally pop if she grew another inch. Tamra finally got to her feet, unable to keep from groaning in response to the pain and pressure. She moved slowly and carefully to the bathroom, and a few minutes later she began the process again in order to get back to the bed. "If this goes on much longer," she said to herself, "I'm going to need a commode—or worse, a bedpan."

Tamra sighed with exaggerated relief when she finally made it back to the bed and had her feet up again. She closed her eyes and attempted to breathe deeply, except that her lungs simply didn't have the room to pull in enough air for a deep breath. She heard Jess talking in funny voices to Michael in the next room as he dressed him for bed. She closed her eyes and concentrated on the evidence of his love for her and their son. She was just beginning to feel as relaxed as was possible when she was struck with a strange sensation. She gasped and her eyes flew open. She shifted her weight to determine if the moisture was simply her imagination. Then she gasped again.

"What's wrong?" Jess asked, appearing in the doorway with a freshly bathed and pajama-clad Michael in his arms.

Tamra was almost afraid to say it out loud. "I just . . . got up . . . to go to the bathroom and . . ."

"Why didn't you let me help you? I worry about you, when—"

"You were bathing the baby, and it's okay. I managed, but . . ."

"But?"

"I think my water just broke."

Jess gasped. "You think?"

"Okay, my water just broke!" she said, feeling a contraction tighten her middle.

"But it's too soon," Jess said.

"Whether it's too soon or not, I think you'd better get me to the hospital."

Jess stared at her a long moment then hurried from the room. "I'll be right back."

Tamra had another contraction in the time it took him to return with Emily—and without the baby. Emily rushed to Tamra's side, "Rhea's got the children for the moment. Let me help you get what you need while—"

"I'll go pull the Cruiser around," Jess said.

Emily stopped in her efforts to put some of Tamra's things into an overnight bag. "Wait," she said and Jess hesitated. When she said nothing more, he exchanged a concerned glance with Tamra.

"What?" he finally said.

"No, you should call triple O for a helicopter. Your father doesn't want you to drive; it takes too long. It's too risky."

"My father?" Jess retorted but Emily just gave him a hard stare.

Jess snapped himself back to the moment, making a mental note to question her on that later. He dialed triple zero and spoke in a voice that sounded more panicked than he'd realized he felt. "My wife is in labor with twins and I believe it's moving quickly. We're more than an hour's drive and I don't think—"

He was interrupted by questions about his location and a quick assurance that help was on the way. But Jess knew from experience that it would still be a while before they arrived. While Emily packed a few of Tamra's things that she might need, Jess made certain he was ready to go in between sitting with Tamra through her pains. Their growing intensity and frequency had him decidedly nervous. She hadn't had a long labor the first time. He was grateful to know that a helicopter was on its way, and not to be driving her into town.

Certain that help would be here soon, Jess scooped Tamra into his arms and carried her down the stairs. "Oh, it hurts!" she groaned as he reached the bottom of the stairs.

He quickly set her on the carpeted floor in the hall and muttered, "Tell me what to do."

"Just . . . get me to the hospital," she said.

"We're doing that, sweetie; we are."

Emily spread a clean blanket out beside her and Jess moved her over, wrapping it around her tightly. Then they heard the chopper blades overhead and Jess scooped her into his arms again. He groaned and chuckled, saying, "You've gained weight, my love."

"You think?" she growled, then she cried out with fresh pain. Emily held the door open for Jess to carry her outside, then she followed with the little suitcase. The emergency crew met him halfway across the lawn with a stretcher where he carefully laid Tamra, then took the bag from his mother and followed, staying close as they loaded her into the helicopter and secured her. One of the crew turned to Jess and shouted to be heard above the engine. "Are you the father?"

"I am," he said.

"Get in. Let's go."

Jess waved to his mother and got in beside Tamra, pushing away his memories of his experiences with emergency helicopters in the past. Seeing evidence of Tamra's increasing pain, Jess's anxiety rose dramatically, but it was softened somewhat by the efficient and compassionate way the emergency crew attended to her.

"I think we'd better not wait to check her," one of them said, and a moment later he added, "Whoa, we've got a baby coming here."

"Now?" Tamra shouted.

"It's all right," she was told by a gentle feminine voice. "My name is Laura, and we're going to make certain everything's fine."

"I can't do this," Tamra said to Jess, gripping his arms tightly. "I can't. I can't."

"You can," he said gently, putting his face between hers and the people who were helping her. "Breathe," he said, recalling well how they had done this the last time, less than a year ago. "Just look at me and breathe," he said.

"Okay, bear down," a voice from behind him said. "A couple of good pushes and this baby will be here."

"Oh," Tamra groaned then Jess coached her through taking a deep breath and bearing down. She groaned and pushed only three times before a baby's cry broke the air.

"It's a boy," Laura said with a little laugh.

"Is he all right?" Tamra demanded breathlessly, fearing he might be too premature to make it on his own.

"He's breathing on his own and he looks good. We'll be at the hospital in a few minutes and they can check him more thoroughly."

"Oh, my little Tyson," Tamra cried through a burst of laughter as he was set into Jess's arms. Then she groaned suddenly with the reminder that this wasn't over yet. Joshua was born a few minutes later.

Jess became mostly distracted by his two beautiful sons until the second placenta was delivered and Tamra started bleeding far too much. He panicked and momentarily tried to imagine what he would have done if he'd been attempting to drive her to the hospital. They got the bleeding under control in just a few minutes, but Jess doubted that he would have been able to do anything about it had he been alone with her. He silently thanked God that all was well and a moment later the helicopter landed.

Jess stayed with Tamra until she was settled and comfortable in a room, then he went with the babies while they were being checked. He kept laughing spontaneously as the joy just seemed to overflow.

"Which one is yours?" another new father asked him.

"That one," Jess said, pointing. "And that one," he added with a little laugh.

Tyson and Joshua were declared healthy and strong, in spite of being small. "Although, for twins and coming earlier than normal," the doctor told them, "they are actually pretty good sized, with their total weight at more than eleven pounds."

Tamra groaned with the evidence of why she'd been so miserable for so long.

"If they'd been born much later, they would have really been big," the doctor added. He went on to tell them that they would be keeping the babies at the hospital for a few days for observation, but then Tamra needed almost that long before she could be released.

While Tamra slept Jess phoned his mother.

"How is she?" Emily asked abruptly.

"She's fine," he said. "Everything's fine."

"Is she still in labor or—"

"Uh, no. They were born on the way."

"Good heavens!"

"Yeah, you can say that again. Tyson weighs six pounds three ounces, and Joshua is five pounds two ounces."

Emily made a joyful noise. "And everything's all right?"

"It is. They're all resting now, and that's what I'm going to do. I don't think I can come home the way I got here, so maybe you could come and get me in the morning and see the babies. We probably shouldn't bring Evelyn in just yet, and we'll make arrangements for Rhea and Myrna to see them soon."

"I'll give them the good news," she said.

"Mother, before you go . . ."

"Yes?"

"Well . . . I think when you were pregnant with twins I was kind of a brat. I just wanted to say I'm sorry for that."

Emily laughed. "It's okay, Jess. You really weren't a brat. You were just a typical boy who needed his mother."

"Well, I still need my mother, and . . . I just want to say how grateful I am that you're a part of our lives. We never could have gotten through this without you."

Emily's voice was teary as she responded, "It's a joy to help your family, Jess, and to be a part of it. Now get some sleep. It's going to become your most precious commodity."

"Yes, Mother," he said and got off the phone. He then phoned Minneapolis with no thought of the time to tell Tamra's father and stepmother the good news. They had been informed weekly of Tamra's progress, and they kept in close touch through phone, letters, and email. And they were thrilled to have the babies here and know that all was well. They planned to come to Australia to see their new grandsons sometime in the coming weeks.

Jess slept in a recliner in Tamra's room, and subsequently woke each time she did. She was obviously in a great deal of pain, but she admitted that the lack of pressure inside of her already made her feel much better. After breakfast the babies were brought to Tamra's room, and she cried when she saw them. There were obvious differences in their size and features, and they were both relieved that they wouldn't have to deal with trying to keep track of which one was which, as they would have to with identical twins.

Emily arrived after Tamra had just finished nursing each of them for the first time. She fussed and swooned over the babies, then she fussed over Tamra and gave her some much-needed compassion after her ordeal—an ordeal that Emily understood well. While the babies slept in the nursery, Jess and Emily left Tamra to get some rest. Jess kissed his wife and told her he'd return late that afternoon.

Jess and Emily went to lunch before heading home. Over the table Jess said, "Mother, I have to ask . . . How did you know that my father didn't want me to drive to the hospital?"

"I just . . . knew."

"But you clearly said that *he* didn't want me to do it."

"That's right," she said as if she couldn't understand why he was confused.

"So, you're saying that he . . . what? Communicates with you?"

"Yes, occasionally."

"This is sounding like a ghost story, Mother."

"Not ghosts, Jess, angels. And there is nothing freaky or weird about it. The Book of Mormon explains everything."

"It does?" He chuckled. "I mean . . . I've always believed it had all the answers to the important things, but . . ."

Emily reached into her purse and pulled out the small Book of Mormon she always carried with her. She handed it to Jess and said, "Moroni, chapter seven."

"Okay," he said when he had it.

"Verses twenty-nine and thirty. Read it out loud."

Jess cleared his throat and began to read, "'And because he hath done this, my beloved brethren, have miracles ceased? Behold I say unto you, Nay; neither have angels ceased to minister unto the children of men. For behold, they are subject unto him, to—"

"Him, meaning the Savior," Emily interrupted. "Go on."

"'. . . They are subject unto him, to minister according to the word of his command, showing themselves unto them of strong faith . . .'" Jess read the verses silently again. "Wow," he said breathlessly, "so what you're saying then, is that . . ." He couldn't quite put it into words.

"Under the jurisdiction of the Savior, angels minister unto those who have faith. There are simply times when your father is allowed or . . . perhaps assigned . . . to minister to his loved ones. It's something that happens according to our needs, and according to the Lord's will. I don't believe it's a blessing that would be granted to those seeking signs from loved ones, or for those who need growth in different ways. It's a sacred thing and not to be spoken of lightly. But for me, I know that it's real. That's how I feel him close at times. That's how I know certain things that he wants me to know. It doesn't necessarily happen often, but it's happened enough that I know beyond any doubt he is still working with me to care for our family."

"As you have said before. But now it makes so much . . . sense."

"Yes, it does."

"And it also makes sense that you feel that closeness to him because you are his wife, and you were closer to him than anyone else for so many years."

"Yes, that makes sense as well. But I suspect that there have been times when he has ministered to you as well."

"Me?"

"You're his son, Jess; his namesake. He's your father, your mentor. Everything that was precious to him has been left in your hands. Do you not think that he would be there to guide and strengthen you when you need that guidance? I would bet that at least once you've had a thought come to you that felt as if your father were talking to you."

As soon as she said it, Jess felt something warm burn inside of him. Instantly he recalled a handful of moments when that very thing had happened. And he'd simply not recognized the experience for what it was. He took his mother's hand and looked into her eyes, wanting to say so much but unable to come up with a single coherent word. But she smiled and touched his face, and he knew that she understood.

Chapter Thirteen

The holidays were busy and filled with excitement as members of the family traveled home to be there for Christmas, and for the blessing of the twins. And Tamra's parents came as well. The joy of the season was mingled with an ongoing sadness created by Michael's absence. But long talks among the family helped keep his memory alive and they were able to validate each other's sorrow in missing Michael, as well as the peace they all felt in knowing that he was indeed in a better place, and it had been his time to go.

The house became more quiet after the holiday company departed for home—as quiet as it could be with infant twins in residence. The anniversary of Michael's death was difficult, but Emily pointed out in her usual positive way that they were one year closer to being reunited. Jess decided he preferred looking at it that way, which would make the years of separation become less, rather than more.

Jess was pleased to see Tamra gradually feeling more like herself physically, in spite of ongoing fatigue. But it was reasonable that she wouldn't get much sleep with nursing two babies and caring for them. He and his mother helped as much as they could, but there were some things only a mother could do. Still, her joy in having these beautiful babies was evident, and Jess felt a deepening of the bond they shared as their family grew and their hearts seemed to grow in proportion.

In February Tonya was finally able to make the commitment to be baptized. And then a whole string of problems broke loose with the stable business. Jess had to fire two employees for being drunk on the job, and then the process of doing without them and hiring replacements went underway. Then a loyal hired hand was injured on the job, and a bad storm caused some damages that needed extensive repairs. But somehow Jess and Murphy managed to get through it, and Jess found his joy on Murphy's behalf indescribable as he watched him baptize his wife. In spite of some challenges, Murphy had truly been blessed for embracing the gospel.

With the passing of months, Tamra's body gradually returned to normal, but she continued to struggle with the postpartum hormone imbalance that had given her so much grief through this unexpected pregnancy. When the twins were six months old and scooting around on the floor, causing havoc and chaos, Tamra reached a new low realizing that she couldn't remember what it felt like to be without this dark cloud that hovered over her. She felt inadequate and completely incapable of handling all that was required of her. But what bothered her most was the fact that her feelings seemed to tie into her mother's presence in the home, although she couldn't figure out exactly why.

On a dark rainy day, Tamra felt as if she could do nothing right and get nothing accomplished. The children were constantly getting into things they shouldn't unless they were in the nursery, and that particular room had become old for all of them. She was relieved when the twins actually both went down for their naps at the same time. With the idea that giving of herself might turn her thoughts around, Tamra went to visit with her mother, hoping for a distraction from her foul mood. But she found her mother ill tempered and especially belligerent. As always, such moments with Myrna catapulted Tamra back to her youth, and old negative feelings began resurfacing inside of her. She hurried back to the nursery but was unable to rid herself of uneasy feelings and memories. She attempted to pray them away, but they wouldn't subside. She wondered if she was simply holding onto feelings in an unhealthy way and that was causing this turmoil inside of her. If that was the case, she wondered what the key might be to letting go of those feelings. She truly felt that she'd forgiven her mother, but the uneasiness lingered on.

Tamra was still stewing over her dilemma when Rhea came to the nursery. "I was hoping to hold one of those babies, but it's so quiet; they must be asleep."

"Yes, amazing isn't it. They don't both sleep at the same time very often."

"How are you doing, dear?" Rhea asked, sitting down across from Tamra.

"Oh, I'm all right," she said.

"And when did you take up being dishonest? I thought that was against your religion."

Tamra looked down guiltily. "I really am all right," she said. "I just . . ."

"Just what?" Rhea pressed. "I know this pregnancy has been difficult for you, and I understand how those female hormones can get out of whack. But I know you well enough to know that there's something more. Something's eating at you, and I think it's been eating at you for a long time. Maybe all those sensitive hormones just have a way of bringing those things to the surface that we might otherwise be able to push away."

Tamra let that idea sink in. "I never thought of it that way."

"So what's eating at you?"

"I just . . . wonder why I let my mother's bad moods affect me."

"Well, we both love her but we both know she wasn't a very good mother. It's not so difficult to understand why her bad moods would make you think of unpleasant memories."

"But . . . I thought I had forgiven her for all of that, and . . . I really feel as if I have forgiven her, but when she's around I just feel so . . . inadequate somehow."

Rhea was thoughtful a moment before she said, "You know, I was just thinking of something my sweet Art told me about." Tamra noted the warm nostalgia that came into her eyes as she spoke of her late husband. "He said that his father had been a difficult man, and Art had always tried very hard to please him but never could. He said his father was an old man before he finally said something that made Art feel that his father really loved and respected him. I'm no shrink, dear, but is it possible that somewhere inside of you there's just something aching to know that your mother thinks you have value?"

Tamra was surprised at the hot tears burning into her eyes, as if to verify that there was some truth in what Rhea was saying. Could it really be that simple? Was it possible that Tamra simply took her mother's bad moods personally and felt that she was being seen as inadequate in her mother's eyes?

"Let me tell you something," Rhea said tenderly. "I know she's never said it to your face, but I know she thinks the world of you. She admires you and all that you've done with your life. I think she just wonders why you would open your home and give her so much. Perhaps what the two of you need is a little more communication."

Tamra sniffled and wiped her eyes. "Sometimes I feel as if I was simply born to the wrong woman." She laughed softly. "I should have been your daughter."

Rhea gave a scoffing laugh. "That wouldn't have put you much better off."

"But you've always been so kind and loving, and my mother is so . . ."

"Difficult? Yes, I know. She was difficult long before you were born, and her difficulties have nothing to do with you, Tamra."

Tamra felt a familiar nagging feeling rise up in her. She'd often wondered over the reasons her mother and aunt were so different, but she'd always felt hesitant to ask. Suddenly the question was on her tongue, forcing its way out, as if it knew of its own accord that this was the time to be confronted. "Why is that?" Tamra asked.

"Why what?"

"Why is my mother so difficult? The two of you were raised by the same parents, in the same environment."

"An environment that wasn't necessarily good," Rhea said.

"Yes, I know, but . . . you turned out so much differently than her. You always had love and acceptance for me, and it was as if she was just so . . . wrapped up in herself, in her drinking and men that . . . she had no concern over being a mother."

Rhea looked at the floor and sighed deeply. Her expression alone made Tamra nervous. She lifted her eyes and said in a quiet voice, "You're old enough to know now, dear, and maybe it will help you understand, although it's hard to talk about. There's one big difference between me and your mother. I'm not the one who was raped at the age of fourteen."

Tamra gasped and felt her stomach tighten. Rhea sighed and went on. "She was never the same after it happened. She became promiscuous, as if such things didn't matter anymore. And she started drinking at a very young age, to block out the pain, I believe. Your father was the best thing that ever happened to her. When they were dating, she was almost like herself, but after they got married she gradually slipped into her old ways and he left her. You know that story. I think the bulk of your mother's life is filled with regret. And in spite of her present physical condition, I believe she is happier now than she ever has been—thanks to you and your sweet family," she finished with a smile.

"No," Tamra said tearfully, "I think you have at least as much to do with it. And, well, the stroke forced her to stop smoking and drinking. That alone has probably got her mind more clear than it has been since . . . her childhood." With no warning a surge of emotion jumped out of Tamra's chest and she hung her head and sobbed. Rhea knelt on the floor beside her and put her arms around her while Tamra cried long and hard. She cried for her mother's tragic life, and for the tragedy that had been perpetuated into her own life, and that of her brother and father—all from one act of violence.

Later that evening, before climbing into bed, Tamra discussed what she had learned with Jess. They talked extensively of the different perspective they felt toward Myrna and the life she had lived, knowing that something horrible had happened to her in her youth, but she'd not had the strength and guidance of the gospel that might have helped her heal and rise above it. This revelation about Myrna certainly didn't dispel the fact that she had been a difficult mother and had caused a great deal of grief in Tamra's life. Tamra had suffered much and nothing made that right. But that had been forgiven a long time ago, and now a new level of understanding opened up for Tamra.

Tamra couldn't help thinking of the abuse in her youth, and the empathy it gave her for what her mother had suffered. She couldn't help wondering why her mother hadn't had more empathy for what Tamra had suffered as a victim of the men that came in and out of Myrna's life. But discussing it with Jess helped her remember that her mother had been drunk a great deal of the time, and she had lived her life in a frame of mind that was focused on denial and oblivion to anything but her own pain. At least Tamra now understood the source of that pain.

Tamra also discussed with Jess what Rhea had mentioned about the need for validation and acceptance from her mother. "Do you think it's possible that much of my uneasiness has come down to simply feeling inadequate in my mother's eyes?" she asked. "I always felt inadequate growing up. It seemed that no matter how hard I tried, what I did was never good enough. I know that was her problem not mine, but . . ."

"But the way a parent perceives us is something that leaves a long-lasting impression."

"Yes, it certainly does. And now I have to wonder if that isn't the root of much of my depression. I know the hormones had a lot to do with it, but . . . Rhea said that maybe the hormones bring things to the surface that we might otherwise push away."

"That makes sense," Jess said, taking her hand. "And now that you understand all of this, maybe you can help me understand why *I* feel so inadequate."

"You do?" She was genuinely surprised. "I thought you'd been handling everything rather marvelously."

"Really?" He chuckled humorlessly. "It doesn't feel that way. I just . . . feel much of the time as if my father could have done it so much better, if only he were here."

"Your father had many more years of experience than you, but all things considered, I think you've done a great deal of good for a great many people."

Jess listened in awe as Tamra recounted that Murphy and Tonya had both joined the Church, and the part he had played in that. She reminded him that he had saved Murphy's life in that storm, and he had escorted Nathan Gooding and his mother into a normal life, and they were now living happily together. He had kept the family businesses running and doing well. He had helped Beulah find great joy and fulfillment in her life. He had served well in his church calling and as a home teacher, and he had been a good husband and father.

"I didn't do all of that alone," he scoffed.

"No, but you had a great hand in all of it. You're a good man, Jess, and I believe your father and those gone before him would be proud."

Jess managed a smile, but he found it difficult to believe her, even though he couldn't quite pinpoint why.

The phone rang and Jess reached for it on the bedside table.

"Hello, Sean," he said. "How are you?"

"Doing okay. How are you?"

"Well, we're coming along. You must have been inspired. We were just talking about deep emotional issues." He said it dramatically and Sean chuckled.

"Oh, I *must* have been inspired. Did you learn anything?"

"I think so, but your opinion wouldn't hurt." Jess repeated briefly what was going on with Tamra and her feelings toward her mother, while Tamra stayed close by and held his hand. Sean agreed with the conclusions they'd come to. He added one point when he said, "Tamra doesn't need validation from her mother to overcome such feelings. The only validation she needs is from her Father in Heaven. You tell her I said that."

"I will," Jess said. "And does that mean I don't need validation from my father?"

Jess went on to explain how he'd been feeling, and Sean offered the same conclusion he'd given in regard to Tamra.

"Thanks for listening," Jess said. "But why exactly did you call? Just to shoot the breeze, or is there something we can do for you? Perhaps you have some form of bribery in mind that might begin to repay you for all the free counseling you've given us through the years."

"Counseling is always free to my family," Sean said. "But actually, I do need a favor—a big one."

"Really?" Jess said, actually feeling pleased. Sean had done so much to help them, but it seemed the opportunity to help Sean didn't come up very often. "What can we do for you?"

"Well, it's a big one," Sean said. "I'm wondering if it would be possible for Tara to come and stay with you for a couple of weeks. You've always said that we were welcome any time. I can't get away to come with her, but she's really struggling with losing Joshua, in spite of many blessings in our lives. She has peace with it; no problem there. She just misses him so much. I think she's been trying to stay too busy to think about it, and she's wearing herself out. It's not horrible; she's not falling apart or anything. She just needs to get away—really away and have some time to let life catch up to her, and when I suggested her going there, we both felt really good about it. What do you think?"

"We would love to have her come," Jess said. "I can even pick her up in Sydney."

"I was hoping you'd say that," Sean said, his relief evident.

The following day Sean called back with Tara's travel arrangements, and a few days later Jess flew to Sydney to pick her up. They arrived back at the house late in the evening, and once hugs had been shared all around, Tamra took Tara to introduce her to Myrna while Emily was heating up some supper. She had met Rhea previously when Tara's family had come for Michael's funeral. Tara fussed over the twins and held one of them until Emily brought Tara some supper to eat in Myrna's room so the women could continue to visit. Jess told them all good night and went upstairs to put Evelyn to bed and then go to bed himself, since he needed to be at work early in the morning. While the women visited, Tamra watched in amazement as Tara and Rhea hit it off, conversing in a way that they'd not done on their previous meeting when there had been so much going on and so many people around. Tamra was also amazed with the way Tara spoke freely and easily to Myrna. Long after Tara had finished eating, the women sat and visited. Tara opened up and told Rhea and Myrna the experience of her son's death, and Tamra commented, "We named Joshua after her son who passed away."

"Oh, I didn't know that," Myrna said.

Tara went on to tell Rhea and Myrna about the miracle of having the son she'd placed for adoption return to her after the funeral, and the joy he'd brought into their lives in the time since. Rhea and Myrna listened as if they were hearing a fairy tale for the first time, and a few tears were shed by everyone in the room as they passed the twins around and tried to keep them content. They finally slept and were taken upstairs and put to bed before the women quickly returned to their visiting. Midnight came and went and Tamra knew she should be exhausted, but the spirit in the room was strong and warm, and she felt prone to stay there, not wanting to separate herself from it. Discreetly watching her mother, partially paralyzed and disabled from the stroke, Tamra felt recent realizations sink in a little further. Since her conversation with Jess, she'd said nothing about her feelings to anyone. But given a few days to let it settle in, Tamra had to admit that what Sean had told Jess about the situation was true—

the only person Tamra needed validation from was her Father in Heaven. And she'd felt such validation many times in her life. She simply had to take hold of the knowledge in her heart that her Heavenly Father loved her, and continue to work on putting her feelings toward her mother in their proper perspective. Seeing Myrna now, Tamra's heart filled with nothing but compassion. She could feel tangible evidence of the wounds that had healed, and the power of the Atonement that had truly lifted the burdens of abuse and animosity between her and her mother.

And just when Tamra felt that she could hold no more peace and joy, she heard her mother say, "That happened to me too."

Tara obviously didn't understand what she said, even though Myrna was evidently directing the comment to her. Rhea, who was more accustomed to Myrna's speech, repeated the comment to Tara, who then asked Myrna, "What happened to you?" Tara reached out to take Myrna's good hand as she said it, and Myrna's eyes showed a tenderness that Tamra would have never believed possible in her mother. Was she too feeling the sweet spirit in the room?

"The way you had that baby," Myrna said, "and how you gave it away." Rhea repeated the words to Tara, whose brow furrowed. Tamra and Emily exchanged a concerned glance. Rhea held her sister's other hand and observed her with warm compassion in her expression. "That happened to me, too," she said again. "Only my baby was a girl."

Tamra understood what her mother said, but it wasn't until Rhea repeated it to Tara that it began to fully sink in. She felt her chest become tight with a rush of emotion that soon found its way to her throat and eyes. Rhea had told her about Myrna being violated at a young age, but she'd said nothing about a baby! Did this mean that somewhere she had a half-sister? The very idea was incredible! She thought of the joy that Joshua had brought to Tara at their reunion, and she felt a sudden, urgent need to find the answers to a long string of questions running through her mind.

While Tamra was still contemplating those questions, Tara said, "Then you and I have a great deal in common, and much more to talk about. But I think we're all very tired."

"I am tired," Myrna said. "Could we talk tomorrow?"

"I'll look forward to it," Tara said.

Hearing the word 'tired' seemed to trigger the exhaustion that Tamra hadn't felt through their visit, and she too felt the need to get to bed. She hugged Rhea and her mother tightly, and looked into her mother's eyes, saying, "I love you, Mother. I'll see you in the morning."

Rhea smiled with her eyes and Tamra went upstairs to check on the babies while Emily went with Tara to her room to make certain she had everything she needed. Tamra wondered if she would be able to sleep with this new train of thought running through her mind, but she fell asleep quickly, and had no trouble falling back to sleep after nighttime feedings. Just before dawn she and Jess ended up both feeding a baby, sitting side by side in bed.

"Are you awake enough to converse?" she asked.

"I think so," he said through a yawn. "What's up?"

Tamra repeated what her mother had said to Tara and Jess's mouth literally fell open. "Do you realize what this could mean?" she asked and began speculating aloud on the thoughts that had come to her with such force that she had to believe she was being prompted and guided. She discussed a tentative plan with Jess before he went to work, and after breakfast Tamra pulled Rhea aside and shared the plan with her —mostly because she would need her help. While Tara visited with Myrna and Emily, Tamra and Rhea made some phone calls and got on the Internet, and within a few days—with every spare minute spent on the phone and the Internet—they had concrete plans for a little party for Myrna's upcoming birthday. Tamra's brother, Mel, would be coming to Australia from Minneapolis to surprise their mother. He had been amazingly agreeable about the prospect, but then he was getting a free trip to Australia out of the deal. For whatever reason he was willing to come, Tamra was pleased about the opportunity for Myrna to see her son again. And through a string of miracles that Tamra could hardly believe, the half-sister that Myrna had placed for adoption when she was fifteen would be coming as well. Tamra knew beyond any doubt that the Spirit had guided and prompted her to this discovery—and even the desire to pursue it. And for days after the phone call she'd shared with her half-sister, Tamra would still think about it and tingle from head to toe.

"Is this Sue Parfit?" Tamra had asked when the woman answered the phone.

"It is."

"You don't know me, but . . . Would you by chance be adopted? Born on February fourth in Minneapolis?"

"That's right," the woman said, a combination of skepticism and excitement coming through clearly in those two words.

"Well, I've been on a rather amazing search the past few days to find you, and apparently you wanted to be found."

"I have been looking for my birth mother for many years, if that's what you mean."

"That's what I mean," Tamra said. "Well, I think I've found her for you, and I'm her daughter, so that means . . ."

"We're sisters?" Sue Parfit said with emotion, and they talked for another two hours, comparing pieces of evidence that made them both agree heartily that this was, indeed, a miracle. But the most amazing thing of all to Tamra, the thing that sparked her emotions more deeply and keenly than any other aspect of the situation, was when Sue said, "May I ask your religion? I get the feeling that you're religious by the way you talk, and . . . I was just wondering."

"I get the same feeling from you," Tamra said. "I'll tell you mine if you'll tell me yours," she said lightly and they both laughed.

Then Sue said with conviction, "I belong to the Church of Jesus Christ of Latter-day Saints."

Once Tamra could find her voice through all the tears of joy, she managed to say, "So do I."

Later, Jess and Emily both cried as well when Tamra shared the news with them.

"It's a miracle," Emily said, and Tamra knew she was right.

Through the following days Tamra felt a new zest for life as she found a new friendship with Tara, and carefully planned and manipulated the surprise party for her mother. Tamra admired Tara more and more, especially considering some of the struggles she'd had in her life. She spoke openly of losing her son and it was evident that she had found peace with his death, but she missed him terribly and she had been in need of a break from the stress and strain of everyday life. Tamra was glad that Tara had chosen to take her break there and then. She had been the instrument that had brought about this wonderful discovery in Tamra's life, and she was grateful.

Tara became involved in the plans for the party, and the two of them never ran out of things to talk about as they cared for the babies, helped with household duties, and prepared for the party. Those attending would be few, but it would be a very select group. Tamra became preoccupied with imagining how it would be to meet the half-sister that she'd never known existed, and when she thought of Sue and her mother being reunited, she could hardly contain her excitement. Therefore, she was naturally deflated when Tara said one afternoon while they both fed a baby, "I've had a thought come to me that I can't seem to get rid of, so I think I'd better just say it."

"What?" Tamra asked, feeling an instinctive dread.

"Well . . ." Tara said, "I just have to wonder if . . . well . . . What if your mother *isn't* happy about meeting Sue? Maybe she isn't emotionally strong enough to handle such a reminder of the past. What happened to her obviously affected her entire life, because there's evidence of it in her attitude and her longtime drinking habit. I don't want to burst your bubble, but . . . maybe we should reconsider."

Tamra *did* feel as if her bubble had burst. She felt deflated and could only find the words, "I don't know what to say."

"Well, do you think I'm wrong? Do you think that—"

"I think you might be right; that's the problem, I guess. Maybe I was just so excited that I wasn't looking at it realistically." A long minute later Tamra looked to her new friend and asked, "So what do we do? I can't call Sue and tell her not to come. She was so excited."

"Oh, no. I think Sue should still come. The two of you need to meet and get to know each other, and . . . well, maybe she can still meet your mother, but perhaps she should be aware that your mother doesn't know, or . . . depending on how you feel, maybe you could tell your mother and prepare her, but then if she's upset, she may be more likely to be angry when Sue is around."

Tamra sighed loudly. "Okay. That certainly gives me something to think about."

Tamra thought about it so much that she hardly slept that night. She prayed for guidance and came to the decision that it would be better if Myrna didn't know about Sue . . . at least for the time being. She phoned Sue and talked with her about it, and in spite of some disappointment, she agreed that she would meet her mother without letting on to their relationship—initially at least. They also agreed that they would follow the Spirit beyond that. Tamra also phoned Mel and warned him that the news she'd shared with him about their long, lost half-sister needed to remain confidential, as far as their mother was concerned—unless Sue reached a point where she felt differently. He actually agreed with her concerns and sounded more compassionate over the situation than she had expected.

The day that Murphy flew to Sydney to get Sue and her brother, Tamra was filled with nervous excitement. However this might turn out for her mother, Tamra felt a deep thrill to think of meeting a sister that she had never known she had. She'd found sisterhood with Jess's sisters to some extent, but this was different. This woman actually shared the same blood, and Tamra couldn't deny what that meant to her. And to know that they shared the gospel was doubly thrilling.

When Tamra heard the plane overhead, she almost started to hyperventilate. She and Tara drove out to the hangar to meet them. She wrung her hands nervously as they waited for the plane to come to a complete stop. Mel stepped out first and waved at Tamra before he turned to help a woman step down. From the distance Tamra could only see short brown hair and a slender figure. Tara commented, "From here, she reminds me a bit of you."

"Really?"

"Really," Tara said with a chuckle.

"Hello," Tamra and Sue both said at the same time, then they laughed and embraced, and to Tamra it felt electric, as if their spirits had connected. Easing back from the embrace, Tamra saw tears in Sue's eyes and knew that she had felt it too.

"Oh, it's so incredible to meet you," Tamra said.

"It is, indeed," Sue replied and they laughed again.

Tamra then turned to greet her brother with a hug, realizing that she was actually happy to see him—and he was evidently happy to be there for reasons beyond the free vacation.

"Do I get one too?" Murphy asked, carrying luggage to the Cruiser.

"Of course," Tamra said and hugged Murphy as well.

Within minutes they were on their way to the house, with Murphy driving. Sue and Mel asked many questions and Tamra gave a five-minute explanation of the family history and businesses, promising more details later if they were interested.

The minute they got back to the house, Sue wanted to meet Myrna. Mel said that he preferred to freshen up first and surprise his mother later on. Jess was waiting to meet them and promised to take good care of Mel. When Tamra and Sue came to the doorway of Myrna's room, they found her sleeping, and Rhea was sitting near the window, lost in a book. She looked up when they entered, and smiled as she came to her feet, setting the book aside.

"You must be Sue," Rhea said brightly, in a whisper.

"And you must be Aunt Rhea," Sue said as they embraced tightly.

"Oh, what a beautiful girl you are!" Rhea said, taking Sue's face into her hands.

Tears streaked Sue's face as she turned to look at Myrna, saying, "And this must be my mother."

"It is," Rhea said as Sue sat carefully on the edge of the bed and wept while she held Myrna's hand.

The three women talked quietly while Myrna slept, and Tamra felt it was a blessing that Sue was able to become initially acquainted with her mother this way. When Myrna began to stir, Sue moved away and sat in the chair where Rhea had been sitting.

"Hey there, Sis," Rhea said to Myrna when she came awake. "Tamra's brought a friend to meet you."

"A friend?" Myrna repeated with the usual slur to her voice. As Rhea helped Myrna to her wheelchair, Tamra saw Sue become tearful at the evidence of their mother's disability. But she wiped her eyes and greeted Myrna eagerly and with a smile.

They chatted for a few minutes about trivial things until Tamra said, "I think it's getting close to supper time. Why don't you get freshened up while Sue and I go and help in the kitchen, and we'll see you there." Tamra bent to kiss her mother's cheek they way she typically did and added, "We're having a special supper tonight, Mother. We've got some special company, and we're eating your favorite."

"Lasagna?" Myrna said.

"That's right," Tamra answered.

"Oh, I love lasagna too," Sue said and squeezed Myrna's hand. "It was lovely meeting you. We'll see you in a while."

Myrna just gave a lopsided smile. Tamra and Sue left the room, but several paces down the hall Sue took hold of Tamra's arm to stop her as she leaned against the wall and was overcome with tears.

"Are you all right?" Tamra asked.

"I am," she said. "That's just it. It's something I've longed for for so long, and now it's happened. I know who my birth mother is, and even though she doesn't know who I am, I just feel so . . . grateful." She took both of Tamra's hands into hers. "And just to know you is such a wonderful blessing that I believe will continue to bless both our lives for many years to come."

"I'm sure it will," Tamra said, embracing Sue tightly.

They finally moved on down the hall. Tamra helped Sue get settled in her room so she could freshen up, then she promised to meet her in the kitchen shortly.

An hour later the table was beautifully set, with helium balloons and paper streamers decorating the dining room—all in blue, Myrna's favorite color. Tonya and Murphy arrived, bringing Susan along. She was wearing a nice dress and looking healthy and happy to be there. Murphy hit it off with Mel immediately. They'd obviously enjoyed their flight home and the conversation they'd shared. Tamra, Emily, and Tara were busy in the kitchen when Tonya joined them there, and a few minutes later, Sue arrived. The group was joined by Beulah as she came in from the boys' home. They were working together to put the meal on the table when Rhea entered the dining room, pushing Myrna's chair.

"Oh, Mother," Tamra said, approaching her quickly before she could see who was in the room, "I've got a surprise for you. I ordered it to be delivered all the way from Minneapolis."

"That's where I used to live," Myrna said, as if nobody else knew.

"Yes, we know," Tamra said.

"Pretty balloons," Myrna said, pointing at one cluster with her good hand.

"Your favorite color," Rhea said.

"Here's your surprise," Tamra said, taking Mel by the hand as she led him toward their mother.

"Hi, Mom," he said and Myrna laughed. She reached her hand out for Mel. He took it then hugged her quickly. He pulled a chair beside her and talked to her a for a few minutes, with Rhea and Tamra helping him understand what she was saying, then Emily announced that it was time to eat.

The meal progressed pleasantly, and Myrna seemed to be enjoying herself. Evelyn proved to be a delight, Michael made a glorious mess of his food, and everybody passed the twins around, feeding them little bites of food. Sue's expression made it evident that she was thoroughly enjoying this experience of being with her newly discovered relatives, even if Myrna and her two children were far from a conventional family. She clearly enjoyed Tamra's children, and brought out pictures of her own children, who were in college and high school. Tamra and Mel admired the pictures while they speculated on a time when their families could all get together. The subtle implications of being related were apparently lost on Myrna.

When the meal was over, Tara and Emily insisted on clearing the table and putting the food away, while Tonya and Beulah washed up the dishes, so the others could visit. When that was done, Emily came in with the birthday cake and set it on the table, where Jess started lighting the candles. Tamra had felt it would be better to wait as long as possible to spill the surprise that this gathering was for Myrna's birthday. She didn't know how her mother would react, and prayed that she would receive the gesture as it was intended—with love. When Jess said to Myrna, "I hear that today is your birthday," she looked at first astonished, then she glanced around at the decor, the people, the candles on the cake—then her eyes turned defensive and angry. The mood of the celebration came crashing down as Myrna uttered a colorful protest to having her birthday paraded in front of strangers that way, and how she hated birthdays. Her profanity came through in spite of her difficulty speaking. Emily and Sue each reached for Tamra, as if they clearly expected her to collapse, while Murphy deftly steered Myrna's chair out of the room, saying lightly, "Now we can't have that kind of talk at a party."

Rhea followed him out, saying quietly over her shoulder, "Carry on; don't worry about it. I'll calm her down."

Tamra sank into a chair, trying not to hyperventilate. "I should have expected that," she said. "I don't understand why she's that way, but a part of me knew she would be angry."

"I don't know why she's that way either," Mel said, "but it's sure like her, isn't it?"

"Still, it was a wonderful dinner," Emily said gently. "A wonderful gathering."

"I think it was good for you to organize this," Jess said, "if only so you know that you did."

Tamra looked up at her husband and couldn't hold back the tears. Sue sat close beside Tamra and put an arm around her, saying, "If it's all right with you, I think I'd like to blow these candles out. It's kind of of like my birthday today, don't you think?" Her voice was cheery and bright. "After all, I met my mother today."

"Yes, you did," Emily said, "and that's a wonderful idea. But you'd better do it before they melt into the cake."

"Make a wish now," Tamra said, wiping at her tears, grateful to be surrounded by such good family and friends.

Chapter Fourteen

The evening proved to be enjoyable, even though Myrna never returned to the party—or perhaps because she didn't. Long after the babies were down for the night, the adults visited while Tamra discovered more each minute that she really liked her sister.

When they all finally went to bed, Tamra found it difficult to sleep and was unable to do so until she came up with a firm resolve. She only hoped that Sue would agree it was the right course. She talked to her about it before breakfast, and as soon as they were finished eating, Sue and Tamra carried the unopened gifts to Myrna's room.

"What's this?" she asked angrily when they entered. "I don't want any presents. I—"

"If you swear at me, Mother," Tamra said, "I will leave this room and never come back." The packages were set on the foot of the bed while Myrna looked stunned, and Rhea looked from where she sat close by. "Everybody who was at that party last night cares for you, in spite of your nasty attitude, and they brought gifts because they care. So, we're going to open them and I think you should be gracious about it."

While Myrna was still staring, Sue brightly took up a gift and sat on the edge of the bed. "Should we see what this one is?" She carefully opened it, commenting on the lovely bow and wrapping paper, and telling her that the little gift card said it was from Tonya and Murphy and Susan. Sue talked about how she'd enjoyed getting to know them, and what good people they were. "Oh, look it's a pretty blouse for you to wear," Sue said. "And it's blue. I think you like blue, don't you?"

Before Myrna could answer, Tamra followed Sue's example and began opening another gift. Myrna said nothing, but she did begin to show an interest in the gifts and a softening of her expression. When they were finished, Tamra said, "Now that wasn't so bad, was it? Believe it or not, you are worth a birthday party, and I planned one for you because I love you." Tamra stood up to leave the room and finished firmly, "That's all I have to say. Try to have a good day."

Tamra knew that Sue stayed and visited for a long while, and that was fine. While she did, Tamra spent some time with the children and did some laundry. She had lunch in the kitchen with Tara and Emily, and Rhea came to the kitchen to get lunch for herself and Sue and Myrna. She said nothing beyond, "I think they're hitting it off."

Tamra was still in the kitchen when a knock came at the side door. "I wonder who that could be," Emily said, going to answer it.

"Oh, my gosh," Tamra said. "I forgot, but . . . I think that will be my visiting teachers. They called a few days ago to make an appointment."

Tamra was right, and Emily offered to watch the children while Tamra went to the lounge room to visit with Sisters Warren and Currant, who had consistently visited her throughout her pregnancy, and had showed much support following the birth of the babies. Tamra appreciated being able to tell them all that had happened recently with the discovery of her sister, ending with the dramatics of the previous evening. They listened with compassion, offered reassurance, then shared a gospel message that they managed to tie into the conversation they'd just shared. As they were preparing to leave, Sister Warren said, "Oh, do you take the *New Era*? I wondered if you might not, since you don't have teenagers in the home."

"Actually, we don't," she said.

"Well," Sister Warren handed her a large, flat envelope, "I came across this and just felt like you were supposed to have it. You can open it later."

"Thank you," Tamra said and escorted them to the door, where they each left her with a hug.

When they were gone, Tamra went into the kitchen and opened the envelope. Inside was a page torn from the magazine, with the torn edge neatly trimmed. It was one of those pages that she knew were called "Mormonads" and they eventually ended up on cards and posters that people hung in their homes. This particular one was the ugly duckling standing before a mirror, with a beautiful swan in the reflection. At the top was a play on words with the question in bold type: "Down on yourself?" And at the bottom it read: "Reflect on this: You are a child of God. With His help, you can reach your great potential."

Tamra smiled and hung the picture on the fridge, and she hardly gave it another thought through the next few days as Sue and Mel continued their visit. They had purposely arranged their return flight to be the same time as Tara's so that they would only have to make one flight to Sydney. It was difficult to say good-bye to all of them, but Tamra felt that she had found great friendships with Sue and Tara, and they promised to keep in close touch through letters and email. And she even felt closer to Mel than she ever had, although she doubted he would make much effort to keep in touch. Still, it had been a good visit, and a good opportunity to get to know each other better as adults.

With their company gone, Tamra's thoughts were drawn more easily to the uneasiness she felt in her relationship with her mother, and she wandered the house feeling down, wishing that Jess wasn't en route to Sydney so that she could talk with him about her feelings. Tamra knew that she loved her mother, and much healing had taken place between them. But it was as if she simply felt out of place and uncomfortable with her mother, and she didn't understand why.

Late in the afternoon, Evelyn asked Tamra if she would read some storybooks with her. Tamra gladly agreed since the babies were playing together well, and it would prove a worthy distraction from her uneasy thoughts. Tamra's heart quickened when Evelyn placed into her hands a beautiful book that she'd never seen before, entitled simply, *The Ugly Duckling.* A quick glance told her the artwork was fine and the book expensive.

"Where did you get this?" Tamra asked.

"It was in Grandma's library," Evelyn said. "She said I could read it with you."

Tamra read the story to Evelyn while her mind kept darting back to the picture hanging on her fridge, and the message it bore. But what struck her more deeply was the fact that she was holding such a book in her hands, while a corresponding picture had appeared with the explanation, *I just felt like you were supposed to have it.*

Tamra certainly knew the story of the ugly duckling, but in this particular version, there was more detail about how the egg had rolled away from its mother's nest into a duck's nest, and the struggles the little bird had endured before it finally found its place among the swans. It was somewhere on the last page that a deep, personal meaning leapt from the story into Tamra's heart with a warmth that coursed through her veins, moving her to immediate tears. And how could she possibly deny that the message she had just been given had come from the Lord? It was too coincidental, too powerful, too *incredible* to have any other explanation. And she couldn't explain exactly how she knew and understood what the Spirit was trying to tell her, but she knew it with all her heart and soul. She understood now that some people were simply born into circumstances that felt completely wrong and out of place, but it was necessary for their growth to come into such circumstances, and to follow their instincts and feelings to find something better. And Tamra *had* found something better. In the breadth of a moment she examined the life she was living, surrounded by a wonderful husband and children, and the association of family and friends that he had brought into her life. And even her newly found sister, Sue. These people were all swans, and she had found her place among them. Tamra loved her mother; she truly did. But for whatever reasons Myrna found it impossible to overcome her dysfunction and negativity, the Lord had led Tamra to opportunities and blessings as a result of her own righteous choices. And best of all, He had given her the privilege of having her mother and aunt under her roof in a situation where she could have them as a part of her life, without allowing her mother's disparaging attitude to drag her down—as long as she chose to let it roll off. And now that she had gained a new level of understanding, and had felt tangible evidence of her Heavenly Father's love, she felt that she could actually do that.

Tamra felt more excited to meet Jess at the hangar than she had not so many days ago to meet her sister. She jumped into his arms and they laughed together before she told him of her new discovery and the peace she had come to feel. And through the following days, Tamra felt herself coming back to life. She felt clouds lifting that had been with her ever since her mother had first had her stroke, and then she had discovered her second pregnancy and what had been difficult became worse. But now those struggles were behind her. She had learned much, and gained even more. She had a houseful of beautiful children, a wonderful husband and a sweet mother-in-law who gave endless love and help and support. And she had a wonderful aunt who had always been there for her. And she even had her mother here, and in spite of the challenges, Tamra was grateful for her presence. She went to Myrna's room more often to visit with her, and every day Tamra made a point to tell Myrna that she loved her. Myrna never responded, but it made Tamra feel better.

Once a week Sue called to talk with Myrna, and Tamra or Rhea would help her hold the phone for a brief conversation. Tamra told Sue once that she felt maybe it was time they told Myrna the truth about Sue's identity, but Sue said that for now it was all right this way, and a time would come when Myrna would know and be happy about it. Three days later Myrna passed away in her sleep. When Tamra called to tell Sue what had happened, they both knew somehow that Myrna was now well aware of the relationship she shared with Sue, and that she was indeed very happy about it. And they shared a new joy in the prospect of being able to do their mother's temple work once the waiting period was over.

For Tamra, losing her mother was more difficult than she'd expected, but she found a deep peace in the realizations she'd been blessed with prior to her death. And there was joy in knowing that Myrna was no longer inhibited by her crippled body, or the restrictions of the veil that would hold her back from progressing beyond her dysfunctional life.

A week after the funeral, Rhea said at the dinner table that perhaps she should consider moving on now that Myrna didn't need her. Jess, Tamra, and Emily all simultaneously glared at her in astonishment before Jess said, "I don't think so. If you believe for one minute that we can raise those three boys without your help, you are sorely mistaken."

Rhea laughed, then she cried and expressed her gratitude for being taken so fully into Tamra's family. "You've just got a little bit of swan in you," Tamra said, then she laughed as well before she added, "I'll tell you later."

* * *

On a cool Sunday afternoon, Jess suggested they have a picnic out on the lawn. Watching his children playing in the grass, he felt a deep contentment coupled with an uneasiness that caught him off guard and didn't make sense. He looked at his wife and mother, talking and laughing together. And he was grateful. Having Emily a part of their lives was a blessing too large to measure, and there couldn't possibly be any wife in the world more incredible than Tamra. With the birth of the twins many months behind her, she had become very much the woman that Jess had grown to love. She was bright and cheerful and full of confidence. And oh, how he loved her! His life was good, and he couldn't deny it. But this new uneasiness inside of him led him to believe that something wasn't as it should be. As days passed he felt as if the Spirit was trying to teach him something, that he was being taken up another rung on the ladder of spiritual progression in this life. But he couldn't pinpoint exactly what stepping up that rung entailed.

Instinctively needing the answers, Jess put more effort into his morning and evening prayers, and put more time into studying the scriptures. He finally felt drawn to read his patriarchal blessing, and was startled by a phrase that jumped out at him—a phrase he'd read many times before, but only now did it seem to hold great meaning. He quickly went to find Tamra.

"Listen to this," he said and read aloud to her while she bathed the babies. "'You will find great strength in the wisdom of those gone before you as you take hold of the spirit of Elijah.'"

Tamra stopped abruptly with the washcloth dripping in her hand. Their eyes met with strength and he said quietly, "Tell me what you think that means."

"The Spirit of Elijah is obvious. The hearts of the children are turned to their fathers and the hearts of the fathers to their children." Tears brimmed in her eyes.

"Exactly!" Jess said, pointing at her. "But for me, I think this means that it will happen when I turn to the wisdom of those gone before." Emotion tinged his voice. "I always thought it meant reading the scriptures, or learning more about church history, but it means . . ." His voice cracked so deeply he could barely say, "Their journals."

"Which you have already read."

"Yes, but . . . maybe I need to read them again. And listen to this. This is the important part." He cleared his throat and read on, "'You will be richly blessed as you keep a record for your own posterity that will enable that spirit to bless future generations.'"

Tamra gasped. "By 'that spirit' I assume it means the spirit of Elijah . . . to bless future generations."

"I believe so."

"And what are you going to do about it?" she asked.

Jess took her hand. "I'm going to keep a journal, the way my ancestors kept journals. I kept one here and there, but I need to be more serious about it. And I'm going to back up and record the important events of my life that have led up to this point."

Tamra smiled and kissed him. "I think that's a marvelous idea."

"I wish I could say I came up with it. I think I just finally listened enough to get what the Lord's been trying to tell me."

Through the following days, Jess began spending every spare minute at the computer writing his personal history. Tamra was only too glad to allow him the time, knowing it was important and that the project would go much more smoothly while he was enthused about it. With Rhea and Emily to help with the children, they just left Jess to do his work and write his story.

While Jess found fulfillment in seeing the pages of his history accumulating on the computer, he found himself facing some difficult memories with the emotional evidence that he'd not dealt with them nearly as much as he would have liked. In the midst of contemplating the accident he'd barely survived and that had killed three of his loved ones, Jess became preoccupied with memories that were far from pleasant. And then he had a repeat of the nightmare that had briefly plagued him following that last accident. He prayed repeatedly to be free of uneasy memories and be able to simply record the event and move on, but he had the dream again in more detail and woke up in a cold sweat. He found himself in Tamra's arms as she spoke soothing words to him in the dark, but one phrase in particular stuck with him far into his work day at the boys' home. She'd simply said, "Maybe you're supposed to learn something from the dream, and you'll keep having it until you do."

As that thought settled into him, Jess almost wished for the dream to happen again so that he could analyze it more deeply. But it didn't. However, after many days he realized that his memory of it was so vivid that it didn't need to. So, he sat down at the computer and simply wrote the dream down in as much detail as he could remember. And when he reread what he'd written, he was stunned to realize that he *had* learned something. Not only had he been able to effectively record the incident as a significant part of his life, but he realized now that the dream had shown him certain aspects that his conscious mind had not been able to remember.

Tamra and Emily both cried when he sat them down late that evening and read aloud what he had written. When he was finished, he turned to them and asked, "So what do you think?"

Emily sniffled and said, "I think you have inherited your father's talent for writing."

Jess snorted a laugh. "I doubt that. I don't think novels are my forte. But . . . didn't you catch anything significant there?"

"You mean like the way you could hear people talking while you were in a coma, which is something you never remembered."

"Exactly!" Jess said. "But even more amazing are a couple of other points that I had forgotten."

Emily gasped then said, "You died."

Jess nodded serenely and leaned back. "Yes, I think I did. In the dream I clearly saw the scene of the accident from above, which included seeing myself in the car. I know now that in a way I was given a choice whether to stay or go, but I knew that I needed to stay, that my purpose wasn't over. But the really important thing is that I . . . well, I had always been disturbed by what exactly happened, because I couldn't remember what I was doing when the accident occurred, and I'd always wondered if I could have done something to prevent it. I've wondered if I might have been distracted or goofing off, but I wasn't. In fact, the way the dream felt was more like . . . I was intently focused on the road, and something inside of me knew that it was going to happen, that it had to happen, and it was out of my hands."

Again Tamra and Emily cried as he talked of the peace he had found in being shown aspects of this troubling part of his past. He marveled at the guidance of the Spirit and the miracle of its communication to man.

With recording the accident behind him, Jess felt certain the remainder of his writing would be easy, but recording his attempted suicide brought back memories even more difficult, in some ways, than the accident. This brush with death had been his choice, and it *had* been in his hands. He simply tried to be grateful that he'd survived and come beyond the depression associated with the incident, but the memory stayed with him. And while it hovered there, he encountered many layers of difficult memories. As Jess continued the incredible journey of reviewing his life through his writing, he was confronted with reliving his father's death, and the many challenges he had dealt with since. Long after they were recorded and he had taken his life up to the present, Jess felt preoccupied with a hovering uneasiness that wouldn't relent. The feelings of inadequacy and incompetence crept deeply into him, bringing back the familiar taunting that he simply was not capable of living up to all that was expected of him.

The discouragement became so thick that Jess forced himself to a long fast that he ended with arduous study throughout one particular evening, wanting to be free of this inner torment once and for all. He went to bed late, but still found it impossible to sleep as a mixture of emotions and memories hurtled through him.

While the sleepless hours rolled on, Jess felt a deep, volatile emotion growing inside. He finally got out of bed and pulled on some jeans and a T-shirt, fearing his emotion would erupt and disturb Tamra. He felt his way down the stairs and out the side door. He caught his breath when he stepped outside. The sky was incomprehensibly black, making every star stand out brilliantly; they looked close enough to reach out and touch.

Jess drew a deep breath as if he could pull the scene into himself as he walked down to the side lawn. He relished the feel of the cool grass on his bare feet and recognized that it was a comforting habit he had to walk barefoot in the grass—yet he couldn't recall the last time he'd done it. He'd always considered wearing shoes a necessary evil, but he'd not gone without them beyond sleeping for what seemed months. Perhaps that was somehow indicative of the problem. Perhaps he needed to simply take more time for himself, to feel life, to ponder and meditate, and keep hold of his senses.

Jess found himself at the highest part of the lawn, where he stuffed his hands deep into his pockets and sighed again. The night was completely still around him. Not even the sound of a breeze touched his ears. Jess closed his eyes and sighed deeply, attempting to dispel the deep emotion festering inside him, wishing, if nothing else, that he could identify exactly what it was that troubled him.

Suddenly weak, Jess dropped to his knees and pressed his hands over his chest. A torrent of emotions churned and pressed forward, creating tangible pain that escaped into the night air as a distinct howl. Once the tears got started, Jess lost all sense of time as they continued on and on. Memories of many hardships assaulted him, as if he'd not fully allowed himself to feel the emotional strain he'd carried since his father's death, but it had hovered inside him subconsciously.

Trying to focus on all that he had to be grateful for, Jess's thoughts strayed to Tamra. He would be lost without her, but his heart ached for the sacrifices she had endured to bring these children into the world. He realized then how difficult it had been for him to stand back and see her suffer; he had felt helpless and responsible at the same time.

Jess couldn't comprehend how grateful he was for his mother, for her strength and example, for all she did to help his family, but he could hardly look at her without thinking that she was now a widow. Jess thought of Evelyn and how dearly he loved her, but thinking deeply on her existence always brought to mind the tragedy of her parents' deaths.

He thought of little Michael, and what a joy his son was to him and to everyone who knew him, but Jess couldn't even think the child's name without being reminded of his namesake. He thought of what his father had said when they had made the discovery of Tamra's pregnancy. Michael had wanted to see the child born, to see him grow and experience life. Well, Michael had lived long enough to hold his little grandson in his arms, but before the child had officially been given his grandfather's name, Michael had died.

And that was the root of Jess's heartache. He'd long ago found peace over his father's death. He knew it had been Michael's time to go, and he had felt the Comforter in his life, easing the sting of the loss. But oh, how Jess missed him! His every hour of work in the boys' home, overseeing the stables from a distance, and caring for his home and family, were all branded with memories of Michael Hamilton. And Jess simply couldn't rid himself of the feeling that he was not worthy or capable of filling his father's shoes.

He thought of the great men who had preceded Michael in this calling. Jess had read their journals, savoring their words of wisdom and insight, admiring their strength and virtue. But all Jess could see in himself was a man who had made nearly every possible bad choice in his youth, going so far as to nearly take his own life. At moments like this, he found it impossible to see the good he'd gained through the processes of turning his life around. All he could see were his inadequacies through a magnifying glass.

As a nearly tangible darkness surrounded Jess, he squeezed his eyes closed and forced his mind to prayer. His knees and back ached as minutes ticked by, consumed by a heartfelt plea to be free of this ongoing doubt and fear, and to be able to see in himself the strength he needed in order to keep going.

Jess wasn't certain at what point in his prayer the feeling began to change, but a flicker of something different—something light and hopeful—began to grow inside. He pressed on with his pleas to God, wanting only for that flicker to take hold and fill his soul as he knew it was capable of being filled. Again minutes ticked by as he continued to pray.

With no warning, a warm rush of wind passed over him, taking his breath away. Jess opened his eyes and looked around. There was no evidence of wind in the trees or shrubberies, no sound at all. And then it struck him. The flicker burst through him, from the inside out, and the wind rushed over him again, circling around him until it became still, and warm, and he felt full. Every dark crevice of his doubts and discouragement became immediately replaced by heat and the light of hope. And he knew . . . He *knew* that he was witnessing a miracle. While no tangible evidence touched his ears or eyes, he knew beyond any doubt that there beside him, sitting on the highest point of the lawn, were four other men. For a moment he felt each of them connect to him individually. Jess Davies, his great-great-grandfather, the man who had fought with his life to save this land from destruction and destitution, the man who had established the boys' home and had begun traditions of charity and goodness in his life. And Michael Hamilton the first, taken off the streets and away from a horrific childhood to be raised in the boys' home, and eventually to become its administrator, and the husband of Emma Byrnehouse-Davies. And there was Jesse Hamilton, Jess's grandfather, who had passed away as a young father and had never known his posterity. But Jess knew he had passed on the heritage he'd been given with dignity and honor, working hard to uphold the values and the principles that were the foundation of a strong family and a family business that changed lives for the better. And there was Jess Michael Hamilton the third, Jess's father, his friend, his mentor, his guiding star. In a single moment Jess felt their presence, the strength of their spirits, their love and approval. And then he was alone, drained of strength and left in awe of being granted such an incredible miracle. For a little window of time, God in His heaven had seen fit to allow these four great men to transcend the veil between two worlds to let Jess know that he was doing all right, and everything was going to be okay. *It was a miracle!*

Jess lay back on the lawn and watched the sun come up, more amazed every moment as he contemplated what he had experienced, feeling no doubt whatsoever that it had been real. Taking in his surroundings, he felt freshly amazed at the evidence of God's hand in the beauty and peace encircling him. He was so blessed!

Suddenly filled with new strength, Jess jumped to his feet and ran into the house. He entered the bedroom just in time to see Tamra swinging her legs over the edge of the bed to get up.

"Where have you been so early on a Saturday?" she asked.

Jess went to his knees beside her and kissed her softly. "To heaven and back," he said and laughed. She looked pleasantly baffled and he laughed again. He sat on the edge of the bed beside her and quietly told her of his experience. Tears came to his eyes, as if to verify once again that it had, indeed, happened. And Tamra cried with him. When there seemed no more to say, Jess stood up and opened the closet. He grabbed a handful of his clothes and headed toward the door.

"What are you doing?" she demanded, following him into the hall.

"We're moving into the master bedroom," he said. Then he laughed.

* * *

With his own history written and a new commitment to keep a current journal, Jess took out the journals of his forebears and read them again, finding new insights and wisdom. With the remarkable experience he'd had, feeling tangibly close to these men, he found new meaning and strength in their written words that seemed in many ways to be written directly to him.

After Jess had reread his great-great-grandfather's journals, he came across a book of carefully preserved handwritten pages in sheet protectors, and quickly realized that it was a collection of poetry, also written by Jess Davies. He quickly became fascinated by the obvious gift this man had, even though Jess didn't consider himself adept at understanding poetry. But the concepts and feelings of the poems touched Jess deeply, especially knowing that his forebear had written them. But one stanza in particular jumped out and grabbed Jess, and he read it over and over.

The gilded world that we create will never break apart
the loved ones who are nurtured here, bound by soul and heart.

It took Jess several minutes to recall that he'd heard those first few words before, and recalling the circumstances left him feeling a bit unsettled, yet comforted at the same time. He quickly took up the book and found Tamra in the nursery, playing on the floor with the children. After taking a moment to absorb the beauty and serenity of such a scene, he sat beside her and showed her the phrase of poetry.

"Do you remember," he asked, "when Beulah made a comment about our living in a gilded world?"

"And how angry you got?" She chuckled. "I remember."

"Well, it seems that perhaps we live in a gilded world, after all." He kissed her quickly and added, "It's not so much that we are immune from struggles, but it's what we do with them, and how we care for each other that creates the world in which we exist."

"Well put," she said with a smile. "Perhaps you have a bit of a poet in you, as well."

Jess gave a scoffing laugh and kissed her again.

* * *

It took several days and a great deal of work to move all of Jess and Tamra's things into the master bedroom and to make the room feel comfortable. The first night they slept in that room, Jess felt deeply struck by the reality of those who had used this room in generations past. He felt close to them as he drifted to sleep, and he awoke with the memory of a dream so clear and real that he was moved to tears. Just past six, while Tamra still slept, Jess crept to his mother's room and knocked lightly at the door.

"Come in," she called and he peered in the door to see her sitting up in bed with a book.

"I was hoping I wouldn't wake you," he said.

"No, I'm wide awake. Come in. What can I do for you?" She patted the edge of the bed beside her and he sat there, taking her hand into his.

"I had a dream," he said.

"Not the accident again?"

"No, this was different, so much different."

He wondered if his mother sensed the serenity he felt by the way her eyes intensified on him. "Tell me," she said softly.

Jess couldn't hold back a stream of warm, silent tears as he repeated what he had seen and felt. "I was kneeling at a temple altar, and across the altar, with her hand in mine, was Allison. I looked into her eyes, then we both turned at the same time to see you and Father standing beside the altar, holding hands. And then the two of you kissed and smiled at each other with perfect peace and happiness in your faces."

Emily laughed through her own tears as she obviously grasped the implication of the dream. Michael had asked Jess before he died to be certain that he and Allison made certain, following Emily's death, that the two of them were sealed, since it couldn't have been done any other way. And now he had been given yet one more miracle in his life—a glimpse of what that day would be like. Jess hugged his mother tightly and thanked God for blessing his life so completely.

Later that day Jess found Tamra in the music room, playing the piano—and he actually recognized the song as one from the Primary songbook.

"Very good," he said when she was finished, then he moved to the bench and sat beside her. "I love to hear you play; it's nice to have you back at it."

"Yes, it feels good," she said. "And I'm enjoying my lessons."

Jess put his arm around her and they sat in comfortable silence until he stood and urged her to do the same. She laughed as he led her into a waltz around the center of the room.

"We have no music," she said. "I can't play and dance at the same time."

"We don't need music," he said, looking deeply into her eyes with an intensity in his expression that warmed Tamra with his love.

"Oh," she laughed, "it feels good to actually be on my feet, and to have the energy to dance."

"And to not have two babies creating a lump in between us," Jess added.

They laughed together and continued to dance until Jess guided her to a gradual halt, and then he kissed her. And kissed her and kissed her, certain that life didn't get any better than this.

* * *

Jess was pleased to hear that Emma would be coming home in August, having made the decision to take some time off from school and live at home for a while. Emma was often on his mind, and he'd been concerned about her since their father's death in a way that he couldn't quite put a finger on. Having her under their roof would be a good thing, and he looked forward to her arrival.

Two days before he was scheduled to fly to Sydney to pick her up, he came into the kitchen after work to find Rhea putting groceries away.

"Been to town, eh?" he said.

"Yes, and now I'm going to cook that chicken stuff you like."

"Ooh," he said, "I can't wait."

"Oh, and I brought the mail in," she said, nodding toward the little desk where she'd set it.

Jess leafed through the mail and stopped cold as he noticed the large white envelope that had appeared. It wasn't addressed to him, so he certainly couldn't open it, but his heart took an unexpected leap as he realized what he was looking at. He carefully set the mail back down and walked upstairs where he found his mother and wife in the nursery. Evelyn and Michael were playing on the floor. Emily and Tamra were each rocking a baby.

"What a beautiful sight," Jess said, entering the room. "It's almost perfect."

"Almost?" Emily asked.

"If I had my way, I'd prefer that my father were here."

"True," Emily said.

Jess sat on the floor to play with the children. A few minutes later he casually said, "If you saw a large white envelope with the return address from Church headquarters in Salt Lake, what would you think it was?"

The women both laughed, then Emily stated the obvious, "It would most likely be a mission call."

"That's what I thought too."

"And the point would be?" Tamra asked.

"There's an envelope like that with the mail—addressed to Emma."

Following a moment of stunned silence, with mouths hanging open, Emily said, "You're joking, surely."

"Quite serious."

Emily let out a one-syllable laugh. "Is it possible? Would she really go through that process without saying a word?"

"It's possible," Jess said.

"Then why would she have it sent here instead of her home in—"

"She wanted to surprise us?" Jess guessed. "Maybe she expected to get here before it did."

They all laughed together again, and couldn't help speculating over where Emma's head might be. And if, indeed, she had received a mission call, where might she be going?

Jess felt an excited anticipation to see his sister as he flew the private plane to Sydney to meet her flight. When he saw her in the airport, his heart leapt inside of him. She took a flying leap into his arms in their customary greeting and they both laughed.

"It is so good to see you," he said, trying to count the months since Christmas when he had seen her last.

"It's good to see you too, big brother," she said and took his hand as they went to retrieve her luggage.

About an hour into their flight, Jess said, "So, I can't help wondering why my baby sister got a big white envelope from church headquarters." She turned toward him looking both astonished and guilty. Her expression made him laugh.

"That . . . that . . ." She stammered and he laughed again. "I didn't think it would get there until next week."

"Well, they must be terribly efficient downtown these days."

Emma looked the other direction and laughed softly. "So, it's there. Wow. I take it then that Mom and Tamra know it's there."

"Well, yeah."

"I really thought I would have the chance to tell all of you . . . before it came."

"It's great, Emma. We're all very happy about it. We were just . . . surprised. We had no idea you were even going through the process. You didn't say anything to any of us."

"Yes well, I didn't say anything to anybody, actually."

"Not even Allison?" he asked. Knowing that she'd been living with Allison, he couldn't imagine her keeping such a secret.

"Not even Allison," she stated. "I just . . . wasn't completely certain it was the right thing for me to do. I kept thinking that I'd just go through the paperwork and at some point I would get the feeling that I should let it go, and it wouldn't really happen."

Jess sensed something dark in her voice as she spoke, but he didn't feel it was the right time to question her. She had chosen a mission and the call had come. It was a glorious thing.

"I'm sorry I didn't tell you," she said. "I just didn't want everybody speculating and then wondering what had happened if I didn't end up going through with it."

"It's okay," he said. "I understand." He reached for her hand. "I'm really happy for you."

"Yeah, me too."

Emma slept through much of the remainder of the flight, and once she arrived home it took a while just to reacquaint herself with the children and get settled in. Late that evening after the children were in bed, she finally took a deep breath and opened the envelope with Jess, Tamra, Emily and Rhea all watching.

Emma squeezed her eyes shut for a long moment then pulled the pages out of the envelope. They watched as she scanned the first page, then her eyes went directly to Jess, focusing on him with an intensity that he didn't understand.

"What?" he finally asked.

"I'm going to Salt Lake City."

Jess saw tears appear in her eyes just before his own misted over. How could it be a coincidence that she would serve in the same area that he had?

She gained her composure and looked again at the letter. "Oh, wait. I just saw the Salt Lake City, but it's actually . . ." She laughed. "Oh, my gosh! The Utah, Salt Lake City, Temple Square Mission." She laughed again before she read the entire letter aloud, then she hugged everyone in the room and couldn't stop laughing. Jess shared her happiness, and couldn't describe how deeply it touched him to see her so happy, and to know that her mission would further deepen the bonds they shared as brother and sister.

A while later when everyone else had gone to bed, Jess stood at the window of his bedroom, looking out into the star-scattered sky, contemplating how thoroughly blessed he was. He hadn't quite gotten used to the view from this window as opposed to the room where he'd spent most of his life. But he liked the view, and he liked the feel of the room. He felt comfortable here. And that's what struck him. He felt comfortable. He'd successfully survived the transition of taking over all that his father had left to him. In a few short years he had gone from being depressed and suicidal and on his own, to being a husband, a father of four, and overseeing the family businesses and estate. And he was comfortable. More importantly, he was happy. He counted his blessings as he counted the stars, and the happiness deepened inside of him. And just when he thought he could hold no more, Tamra pushed her arms around him from behind and whispered near his ear, "I love you, Jess Michael Hamilton, the fourth."

"Then that explains it," he said.

"What?" she asked as he turned to face her.

"That must explain why I live in a gilded world. As long as you love me, the world I live in will always be close to perfect."

Tamra just smiled and kissed him.

PHOTO BY "PICTURE THIS . . . BY SARA STAKER"

About the Author

Anita Stansfield, the LDS market's number-one best-selling romance novelist, is a prolific and imaginative writer. Her novels have captivated and moved hundreds of thousands of readers, and she is a popular speaker for women's groups and in literary circles. She and her husband, Vince, are the parents of five children and grandparents of one and live in Alpine, Utah.

Excerpt From Timeless Moments

Vietnam
July 1972

The smell of fuel, jungle, and death surrounded the seven soldiers as they walked across the mist-covered tarmac and climbed aboard the Huey helicopter.

Their orders were exact, their mission top secret.

Low-hanging fog cloaked the landing zone as the helicopter lifted off, but a few moments later the craft broke into the clear. Vietnam, even in war, was scenic with its green jungle, thickly forested mountains, and slashes of silver rivers crisscrossing the terrain.

About four miles from X-ray, their assault landing zone, the pilot, Bryan Randall, gave the signal, and the helicopter dropped down to treetop level to fly nap-of-the-earth on the final approach. It wasn't even daylight and already, 105mm artillery pounded the area below them. Startled birds took flight as the Huey roared along at 110 miles per hour.

Dalton "Mac" McNamara's stomach tensed. The cornflakes he'd had for breakfast roiled and rumbled inside of him. He always felt this way before a mission, but today it was worse. Wondering if he would be fortunate enough to defy death yet one more day, he drew in several slow, calming breaths. Still, the question nagged at the back of his mind.

Mac sensed that the most critical part of the operation was coming—the drop. The timing had to be perfect. Not close. Not almost. Perfect. The choppers had to get in, get out, and get gone—otherwise they were an easy target. If everything didn't go precisely as planned, the enemy would be waiting when the Hueys came in. That wasn't the greeting any of them wanted. Not today. Not ever.

Still two minutes out. Below, smoke and dust flew from artillery fire where broad, low-rolling plains were dotted with trees thirty to fifty feet tall and interspersed with a few old Montagnard farm clearings and dry streambeds. There were no villages. No people. Just the enemy, shells, and hatred.

With the precision of months of training and the experience of battle, the operation continued, on time and on target. The small, tightly knit band of men was a reconnaissance group, part of the Fifth Special Forces Group out of Nha Trang, South Vietnam. At great risk, these men managed to bring in critical information that saved the lives of many American soldiers—yet often at the expense of their own. The area they were to enter was crawling with Viet Cong. The trick was to find them, close in, track their position, strengths, capabilities, and hopefully their intentions, then get out.

Mac and his men prepared themselves for the drop into battle. They had seconds, not minutes, to get out so the Huey could get back in the air. No one spoke, but the look in everyone's eyes told Lt. McNamara that they were brothers; they were a team. They would fight together, and if necessary, die together.

Randall gave the signal as they touched down, and in a split second, following Mac's lead, the men jumped out of the Huey and ran for cover. No one moved and no one breathed as the *whump whump whump* of the chopper roared away from them, then drifted further away. Tense, the men waited, a collective prayer in their hearts for Randall and his crew not to be shot down as they flew out.

Straining, they listened as an eerie stillness settled in. In the distance, several explosions shattered the silence. Smoke and gunpowder hung in the moist, tropical air.

Clinging to the last moments of peace, Mac glanced at each of his men before giving the signal. He knew it was impossible for them to land without notice, but hopefully the Viet Cong weren't aware of their exact location. The quicker they moved out and evaded the enemy, the safer they would be.

Staying low, hidden by elephant grass, the seven men crept toward an island of trees a hundred yards away. Mac paused a brief moment to listen, wishing for the sound of gunfire. The artillery would indicate the position of the enemy. But the silence remained.

Creeping stealthily, they arrived at the cluster of trees. Again, Mac and his men watched and waited, their movements unnoticed and nearly invisible.

After waiting for what seemed like an eternity, Mac nodded his head, and they walked toward the mountains. The early morning sun, hot and blazing, turned the moist jungle terrain into a steaming sauna. Sweat trickled down Mac's forehead and cheeks, trailing a path down his neck and between his shoulder blades. Brush and vines grew so thick that at several points, every step had to be carved out with a machete. Progress was slow and arduous, but progress just the same. They hoped to reach the appointed spot before nightfall.

Mac knew their route like the back of his hand. He'd studied the map, memorizing every hill, stream, and boulder. Yet knowing what they were headed for didn't bring him any comfort. The tree line ended up ahead, where they would cross several hundred yards of open field before they could disappear into the dense mountain foliage. If they made it across that field, the rest would be easy.

Sinking low in the brush, they inched their way to the edge of the clearing and looked out. The hair on the back of Mac's neck stood up. Something didn't feel right, and he motioned for them to stop.

Mac felt the other men watching him, waiting for his signal. Three of them would cross the field while the others covered for them. Once those three were safe on the other side, the other four would go.

Chambers, the recon platoon radio operator, nodded toward the clearing, but Mac shook his head. He couldn't explain it, but something told him to wait.

Just then, a rustle in the bushes across from them caught their attention. A young Vietnamese boy no more than sixteen years old stepped into the clearing wielding an AK-47.

Mac held his breath and watched, unsure if the boy was Viet Cong or not, since not all of them wore uniforms. Just as he suspected, several other soldiers no older than the first followed, heading straight at them. Mac now knew they were indeed VC.

Chambers eyed Mac, who remained motionless. If anyone moved, it would give away their position. If they fired, they would attract every Viet Cong soldier within a mile. No, it was better to wait.

Willing the enemy to turn and head west, Mac felt his heart pound in his chest. He didn't want to fire, but if the VCs got much closer, he'd have to.

Brady, the man to Mac's left, shifted his weight. A twig cracked, the noise magnified by the tension in the air. The VCs halted, drawing their weapons as they scanned the bush.

Mac's heart stopped.

Peering directly at their hiding spot as if they could see through the trees, the three young soldiers trained their gun barrels directly at Mac and his men, who remained frozen in their positions.

Mac knew if he and his men opened fire at such close range, the VC soldiers wouldn't know what hit them, but he resisted the signal until the last possible moment. Blowing their cover would defeat their mission and probably cost them their lives. He wasn't ready to make that call.

The men beside him flinched, their muscles taut and ready, their nerves sparking with the instinct to fire. Still they waited.

Just then, someone shouted from across the clearing where several other VC soldiers motioned for the three young men to join them. Mac expelled air from lungs that were ready to burst.

Two of the soldiers immediately retreated, but one narrowed his gaze and studied the bush. Suddenly, he exclaimed something in Vietnamese and raised his AK-47.

Mac's split-second decision to fire was one he'd regret for the rest of his life.

At the signal, Chambers quickly fired and shot the soldier. Just as Mac had feared, a dozen more VC emerged from the trees and pelted them with bullets. Two of Mac's men went down while the rest of them continued firing at the advancing troops.

A bullet whizzed passed Mac's head, but he continued firing. He heard a hollow thud as another one of his men went down.

"Jackson's hit!" Chambers yelled. Mac glanced down to see Jackson's helmet in front of him with a bullet hole in it. Mac kicked it out of the way, reeling from the gruesome sight.

Another man went down—Beckett, the youngest man on their team. From the very day Beckett had joined his team, Mac had felt protective of him, almost like he was a kid brother. Mac was close to all his men, but Beckett was young—too young to be killing people. The boy had already lost a brother in the war. No family deserved to lose two.

Mac grabbed the M-79 grenade launcher lying next to Beckett, whose arm and chest were both bleeding freely.

"Help," Beckett called to him, lifting his bloodied arm toward Mac.

Chambers grabbed the M-79 from Mac and launched a grenade. Mac tore off his shirt and wrapped it tightly around Beckett's arm. "You're going to be okay," he shouted over the din. Grabbing his M-79 again, Mac took aim and pulled the trigger, but nothing happened. He opened the feed cover, flipped the gun over, and hit it on the ground, jarring the shells loose. Debris had caught in the ammo belt. Mac flipped it right side up, slapped the ammo belt back in, slammed the feed cover, and began firing again.

Even though they were getting pummeled, the men in Mac's group who were still standing held off the NVA troops, and one by one, the enemy dropped.

The rat-tat-tat-tat of an enemy machine gun mowed down the foliage in front of them, taking Chambers, who screamed in pain as he writhed on the ground. Mac looked at Chambers, whose shoulder had been hit. Bullet fragments had also shredded the side of his face.

Raging anger filled Mac, and he fired, taking out two of the advancing troops, leaving only four or five standing. "Hang in there, Chambers, we've almost got 'em!" he yelled.

Mac heard a shot and glanced over to see Brody Thorpe fall backward without a whimper.

"I'm out of ammo," Sinclair hollered, throwing his M-60 on the ground and grabbing another one. He immediately began firing, taking out another soldier from the NVA—the North Vietnamese Army.

Then, out of nowhere, Mac felt a hot stinging in his head. A wave of nausea washed over him, and he knew he'd been hit. Still, he continued shooting, wondering why he wasn't feeling any pain. Another bullet whistled past, hitting the tree behind him.

"Lieutenant Mac," Sinclair yelled. "You okay? There's blood—"

"I'm fine," Mac yelled. But he spoke too soon. Right as the words left his mouth, a stick grenade passed through the trees and exploded at his feet. Mac reached down to his right leg and touched grenade fragments, suddenly feeling like he'd just touched a red-hot poker, sizzling his hand. He collapsed back as agonizing pain worse than anything he'd felt in his entire life consumed him.

A North Vietnamese soldier plowed through the trees and stumbled over some of the dead men on the ground. Mac gripped his gun, but it was Sinclair who fired, putting a full magazine through the enemy soldier before he went down.

Mac heard Vietnamese voices coming toward him. The three NVAs charged through the trees and began kicking at the American soldiers on the ground. Opening one eye just a slit, Mac saw the men removing guns, ammunition, watches, and other valuables from the American soldiers. Lying still, Mac prayed the North Vietnamese soldiers would just take what they wanted and leave them for dead.

Mac watched as they searched Beckett, then kicked him hard in the ribs. Beckett's body jackknifed with the blow, then stilled.

Certain the young boy was dead, Mac fought the urge to scream. Then he stopped. One of Beckett's eyelids fluttered, and the boy made eye contact with him.

A prayer of gratitude flashed through Mac's mind, as well as a plea for the rest of his men.

But the NVA soldiers had other plans. After they'd taken what they wanted, they made sure all of the Americans were dead by shooting a few extra rounds into their bodies. Mac's heart sank. All of his men were gone, and most likely he was next. If only he hadn't given the signal to fire, maybe that young Viet Cong soldier would have moved on. Maybe he wouldn't have discovered them hidden in the bushes.

His muscles tensed, waiting for the final bullet that would take his life. Mac's only thoughts were of his buddies. They'd fought together, and now, they would die together.

Yet the bullet didn't come. Mac waited, then saw the NVA soldiers leaving.

Confused, Mac wondered why they hadn't put a bullet through him. Was his injury so bad that they took him for dead?

He watched them leave, and just when he thought it was safe, one of the NVA soldiers unexpectedly turned. Mac closed his eyes, but not before they saw one another. Mac tensed. He was certain that it was over. His moment had come.

But he wasn't that lucky.

The soldier shouted an order to the other two men who were with him. They stopped, turned, and approached Mac with murder in their eyes. Fear claimed him.

Take me, God, he begged. *Death is better than prison.*

Just as the prayer escaped his lips, the men grabbed his arms and legs and jerked him off the ground, causing a horrific pain in his leg.

He panicked. This wasn't right. He wasn't supposed to get captured; his men weren't supposed to get killed. He was supposed to seek out the NVA and radio their location back to the base. Hundreds of American soldiers' lives depended on this information.

NO! Mac wanted to scream. He knew what happened in North Vietnamese prisoner of war camps, and he knew he'd rather die now than spend years rotting away in a camp, inhumanely tortured and stripped of all dignity.

Realizing he wasn't wearing his helmet, he squirmed to find it and received the butt of a rifle in his ribs, several of them cracking with the blow.

Mac cried out in pain, wondering how much more he could bear. Leaving his buddies and helmet behind, God's grace finally fell upon him as he passed out.

* * *

Mac woke up in excruciating pain. Where was he?

Disoriented, he took several shallow breaths to get a grip on the pain and a bearing on his surroundings. The last thing he remembered was being dragged by North Vietnamese soldiers away from his company, who all lay dead amidst the trees, but here he was, in the middle of a field somewhere with the sound of artillery flying all around him.

His mind processed the situation slowly. Maybe the NVA had been attacked or ambushed, and in their effort to combat the enemy, had left him for dead. Either way, he knew he was one lucky soldier. Maybe. He was in the middle of enemy territory. He was as good as dead. He didn't know how serious his other injuries were, but the chance of using his leg was slim. But he wasn't going to lie there to be used for target practice. If he was going to die, he was going to die trying to survive.

He reached to his side and discovered that he still had two or three frag grenades, a smoke grenade, and two or three hundred rounds of ammo, but his M-16 was gone. He felt around his waist and located his canteen and a small mirror.

As his mind cleared, he realized that the first thing he needed to do was get out of the open. His chances of survival were better in the trees.

Crawling army style, he dragged himself slowly, elbow by elbow, through the grass. Any movement could bring artillery and mortar his direction, so he held his breath and proceeded cautiously.

Eyeing a clump of bushes, he crawled over to it, planning to wait until he was concealed before he assessed his wounds and came up with a plan.

Several times he froze as the sound of enemy voices carried on the air. If he were spotted, there certainly wouldn't be any second chances. Yet each time, the voices rose and then faded. Still, he wouldn't breathe easy until he found cover.

With muscles tensed and trembling, he pulled himself the last few feet before snaking his way through a low opening in the branches and finding space to sit.

Sweat poured down his face, neck, and back. The unbearable heat and thick humidity made breathing difficult, yet in the shade, he was able to find some reprieve. He couldn't get a good view of his leg wound, but judging by the blood, pain, and gaping hole, he knew it wasn't good.

Ripping the sleeve off his shirt, he fashioned a bandage to help stop the bleeding and to lend some support to his knee. Hopefully, even if he had to limp the entire way, he would now be able to move on foot.

He waited several hours for the siege of battle to move away from his position, and then, using a dead branch for support, he slowly, painfully, got to his feet.

Wincing as he put weight on his injured leg, he moved a few steps and stopped. The base of the mountain was five to six hundred yards in the distance. He had to cross through a patch of tall elephant grass to get there.

Keeping his head down, he hobbled his way through the grass, noticing that each step actually seemed to become less painful.

After a hundred yards he stopped again. Artillery suddenly sounded from the treetops, and before he dared take another step, the grass in front of him started to move, suddenly parting to reveal a NVA soldier.

With razor-sharp reflexes, Mac threw a frag and a smoke grenade and cut sharp to the left, his heart pounding faster than the bullets flying overhead. He dragged himself as fast as he could, away from the explosion of the smoke grenade behind him.

Without looking back, he headed for the mountains and soon came to a stream. There he waded upstream for a hundred yards to conceal his route, stumbling on the slippery rocks, filling his canteen along the way, and gulping in all the water he could hold. He found a rocky bank where he could exit without leaving a trail, and he hobbled across a valley where he could have a clear view of his back trail. Once there, he took a break, concealed in the brush.

For now he was safe, as he noted that the sound of battle was receding to his rear. But he knew as night closed in that he needed to find a place to hide.

A constant prayer ran through his mind, a plea for guidance, help, wisdom, strength, and protection. Mac knew he couldn't get more isolated than he was right now. He was alone yet not alone, for he was surrounded on all sides by North Vietnamese soldiers who wouldn't think twice about killing him.

But he was on his own. There was no one to help him. No one but God.

He'd been in battle enough to know deep down just how much courage he had. He'd experienced feelings of sheer terror, and of bravery beyond belief. In any given situation, he knew that he would sacrifice his life for any of his men. He'd prepared himself to die, and he was at peace with death.

But that was not how it had happened. Each and every one of his men had been slaughtered right before his eyes. He'd heard their cries, seen them gasp for their last breath. And here he stood, living and breathing. It seemed cruel and unfair.

Not that he wanted to die. But he didn't know how he would ever live with the memory of those last moments with his friends . . . his buddies . . . his brothers.

An ache filled his heart, rending it in two, until the sound of artillery started closing in on the mountain. He scrambled between two large trees and crouched low, scanning the surrounding area for a place to hide.

Locating an area near another tree where thick grass grew, Mac hobbled over and settled in for the night. He shivered against the damp night air, trying as best as he could to keep ants and bugs out of his wounds. A throbbing in his head upset his stomach, and with each drink of water he threw up. In misery he lay there, looking at the stars, thinking of his men. They'd depended on him, and now they were all dead. All because of him. All because of one decision he'd made.

Mac couldn't help but second-guess those last few moments before he'd given the signal to open fire. Would the North Vietnamese soldier have seen them hiding in the bushes?

He would never know, and he was afraid the question would haunt him for the rest of his life. The images of his buddies, bleeding and dying, were indelibly etched into his memory.

The next morning, he woke up and lay there, listening. In the distance, helicopters landed and took off. United States choppers flew over him, and he tried to signal them with his small mirror but had no luck. He heard gunfire between him and the site where his men still lay.

Staying low and hidden as much as possible, he climbed to the top of a hill and found a large log, which he used for cover. Another battle soon ensued, and he found himself caught in the middle. The artillery and mortars continued until dark and on through the night. Mac covered himself with brush and leaves, trying to conceal himself. Between the ants, the cold, and the sound of artillery, he didn't get much sleep that night either, but he knew he was close to the American landing zone, which gave him the hope of rescue.

Daybreak greeted Mac with a shower of artillery that sprayed all around the slope where he hid. When it quieted down, he began moving toward the landing zone, crossing a wide, shallow creek and rocky terrain until he finally approached the perimeter of the landing zone where he knew he would be recognized as an American soldier.

When he broke into the clearing, the landing zone was empty. In shock, Mac realized that the Americans had pulled out and abandoned the site.

An empty despair replaced his earlier hope. He wondered by how many hours—or was it only minutes?—he had missed them. They'd been there throughout the night, and he'd been so sure that they would still be there this morning. But they were gone, and he was still on his own.

With shoulders slumped and a weariness born of a lack of food and sleep, Mac revisited his plan. He hadn't come up with a Plan B, so certain was he that Plan A would work. But it hadn't, and now he was back to the drawing board.

Closing his eyes, he balanced on his left foot to take weight off his injured leg. It had begun to stink, and he knew the wound was infected. He didn't allow himself to dwell on it—there was nothing he could do until he found help—but he feared the damage was severe. At least he could limp. He'd be dead by now had he been unable to walk.

A rustle in the brush behind him sent a bolt of fear through Mac's body. He froze, straining to hear any further sound, praying it was nothing. But the furious beating of his heart and the dread that filled him left no room for hope.

Slowly he turned his shoulder, then his head . . . and looked straight into the barrel of a Vietnamese patrol soldier's gun. Behind that soldier were five others with their sights set on Mac.

He'd almost made it. But the eyes staring back at him had no mercy, no compassion. Just hatred. And he knew that he was just about to discover what purgatory really was.